RED WHITE OR BLUE

RED WHITE OR BLUE

SUE HILLARD

THREE HEART BOOKS

Spearfish, South Dakota

This is a work of historical fiction. Fictitious characters interact with historical legends in sensible, yet fabricated encounters based on thorough historical research and the author's imagination.

Red White or Blue

Library of Congress Cataloging-in-Publication Data is available.

Three Heart Books, PO Box 1013, Spearfish, SD 57783

Cover by Dale Stradinger. Art by Sierra Sky and Dana Sordahl.

ISBN: 978-1-943646-00-5

First paperback edition, 2015

DEDICATIONS

I am deeply touched by each person who took his or her own precious time to be a part of my novel writing adventure: Thank you to Sierra for your lovely art, diligent editing, and teenage insight. You are my daily inspiration. To Steve, for your descriptions of prairie harvests and campfire cooking. To Sherry, for immediately committing to more than any friend should ask of another. To Justin, for reading each and every word, while nicknaming me "Dances without Commas." To Marty, for cheering when the corset burned. To Carrie, for making sure I did not put on a "neckless." To Dana, for your artistic talent and encouragement when I needed it most. To Lornell, for reading all night over the Pacific Ocean. To Bekah, for asking for the sequel. To Jan, for your unfailing encouragement. To Tracy, for your Oglala insight. To Fred, for your networking. To Nancy, for your attention to detail. To Carolyn, for your eagle eyes. To Dale Stradinger, for capturing the vision with your incredible cover. And to Gabriela Fulton, for taking one hundred thousand drops of acid rain and creating a pure, flowing stream.

Gerald Jasmer, Ranger/Interpreter, Little Bighorn Battlefield National Monument, deserves extra thanks, for patiently answering never-ending "minutiae" questions. Without him, this book would propagate unsubstantiated legends. I am especially thankful to Linda Yellow Boy and Beverly Pipe On Head, at the Pine Ridge Indian School, for leading me away from the offensive and toward the Lakota way.

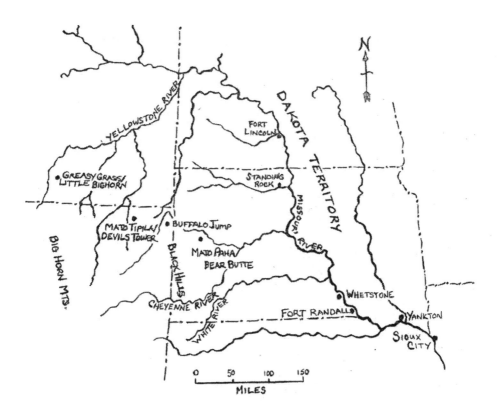

CHAPTER 1

RED

MOON OF RIPE CHOKECHERRIES[1]

JULY 1875

SACRED BLACK HILLS

"ONLY TO THE WHITE MAN WAS NATURE A WILDERNESS. TO US IT WAS TAME, EARTH WAS BOUNTIFUL AND WE WERE SURROUNDED WITH THE BLESSINGS OF THE GREAT MYSTERY." ~Black Elk, Oglala Lakota

I heard the sound of men. White men—wasicu, as we called them in our language. The sun had nearly set as I hunted small game for our dinner. My father, Touch the Clouds, stayed behind to set up our camp for the night. The original focus of tracking rabbit and squirrel shifted to tracking humans, which led me to a ridge, overlooking a creek. As I peered over the ledge, four white men danced in a slow-moving stream as they lifted up small rocks into the air.

"We're rich! We're rich!" they hollered.

Father had taught me bits of their language, but I didn't need it. The men had found gold—gold nuggets from the land that they trespassed upon. My land. The land of my people.

I quickly maneuvered back to camp, where Father waited. Over the last few months, tribe runners had spread rumors of the white man flooding into our land. Nobody stopped him. Father could hardly believe the alarming news and wanted to see the trespassers with his own eyes. So only five days earlier, Father and I left our village on the prairie and rode our horses to our sacred hills.

"Four wasicu," I explained to Father.

"Collect our things. I need to see with my own eyes," Father replied, as he kicked dirt over the small campfire.

My horse, Kola, took the lead as we worked our way to the ridge where I had been an hour before. The sun had set, yet Father and I could see the four white men around a fire. They were eating from tin cans and drinking from glass bottles. I knew the bottles all too well, because the liquid—white man's firewater—had changed the spirit within many Lakota men.

2

Father motioned for me to wait. We leaned against a pine tree and watched, both motionless and speechless, as the men celebrated below and drank beyond their fill.

"Now we go, Ohanzee," my father whispered. "We will take their horses and guns."

We looped around the ridge and tied our horses deep in the forest. On foot, we crept closer to their camp. Close enough to hear their slurred conversation.

"We'll take the bag to Deadwood in the morning. Cash out. Buy some girls. A few card games at the Number 10 Saloon," one said. "Then we'll come back and make a real camp outta this place. Just the four of us." The laughing men slapped each other on the back. I did not understand each word, but made sense of the exchange. They were gold-seeking trespassers who did not care about treaties.

"Go ahead, JoJo, blow it all on sin. We know where to find more," another man said. They shook hands, staggering around. "Partners. Very rich partners!" one of the men repeated over and over again.

Within a stone's throw of the men, I was disappointed to see only one mule tied to a nearby tree. A pack lay beside the worn-out animal. I looked at him, wondering if he would give our presence away, but I saw no intention in his odd eyes, one brown and the other blue. Father gestured to leave the mule alone. I already knew we had no use for him.

We backed away, a safe distance in the trees, becoming shadows in the night. As we peeked between the thick trees, the campfire gave just enough light for us to watch the four drunk men stumble onto their blankets and fall asleep. We waited patiently for the rumble of snores.

Just as we took our first steps toward the camp, two of the men rose from the still-flickering flames with their guns in hand. We froze. Father reached for the bow, slung behind his back. The two men snuck to a pack beside the fire and took the pouch of gold nuggets. Their motions were no longer those of the drunk white men. They left everything else behind and crept to the mule, only steps from where we crouched. Father had taught me well, and we both knew to silently watch and wait. One man untied the mule. The other leaned over, picked up the pack, and hoisted it onto the mule's back. Something clanked.

"Shhhhhhh. You idiot, JoJo!" the prospector whispered, as they led the mule toward us. In the shadows and concealed behind my frozen image, I sensed Father pulling back the arrow in his bow. I could have reached out and touched the prospectors' filthy canvas pants, still wet from their day in the creek. Without moving my head, my eyes darted toward Father. He must have known how I wanted to count my first coup, but his eyes said no. Just to reach out and touch the enemy with a stick or my hand would represent extreme bravery. Father would be the required witness and I would finally have a feather for my hair. Since Father's instinct dampened my impulse, I remained merely a shadow as the white men disappeared into the trees. Their stench remained. I stared into Father's eyes and saw that something had changed within

4

him. I had never seen it before, but I sensed our life would never be the same.

"I have seen enough," Father whispered. "We go home now."

We saw no more trespassers as we rode from our sacred hills to our prairie. When we reached our village, my grandfather, Chief Lone Horn, called Father into his tipi. When they came out, the news shocked me.

"I have chosen you, Ohanzee. You need to do this for our people. Black Robe made me a generous offer. The other Lakota tribes are sending boys your age to study the white-man ways with Black Robe. You will go and do your best," Grandfather said.

"But what will I do there?"

Seeing that Grandfather's voice was weak, Father interjected, "We can't stop this flowing river of white men if we don't understand them. You must learn to speak and write as a wasicu. We have enough warriors. What we need is someone who can protect us in a different way—a very important way."

It was settled. My next course in life was already decided in an unusual way. Typically, the Great One revealed a Lakota boy's future through a dream or vision. Instead, I was forced down this path by Grandfather and Father. This decision did not stem from my heart, but from theirs.[2] I was born a Lakota, a native of the plains. My tribe is the Miniconjou, one of seven Lakota tribes. As early as I can remember, I was taught the values of obedience and sacrifice for the benefit of our people, values that made us strong. So I had no choice. I was heading away from what I knew, taking steps toward white-man ways. My ultimate purpose was set before me: protect my people from white-man deception.

I was apprehensive because I knew little of the man who my people called Black Robe. His full name was Black Robe Lean Chief. My people simply used the name Black Robe for most of the white men who came to tell us about their god, because the men usually wore plain long black robes. Black Robe Lean Chief had personal reasons for inviting the Lakota to live with him at Standing Rock. His goal was for us to learn English and discover the white man's God. I knew he was respected because he moved to our land to carry on the work of Grandfather's friend, Black Robe DeSmet.

Father said we would ride together to Standing Rock, which was not far from our summer camp. Then, he would lead Kola, my horse, back to the camp and give him away to whomever I chose. The night fire was a perfect place to contemplate the recipient of my gift. I watched each person in our band who did not have a horse. The person must be needy, yet kind and levelheaded. Dance with Sun was a bit too irresponsible; she might forget to water Kola every day. Kills Many was an old man in our band without a horse, yet I recalled his occasional violent temper. He would not do. I hoped to keep the gift within our band, but if I had to extend out to the whole tribe, I would.

Then my eyes drifted to Bird Nest, who sat alone in front of her tipi, too far away from the fire to feel the comforting, radiant heat. She was a small, elderly woman with weak legs and a huge hump in her back. Watching her walk sent chills down my spine because the pain of each step seemed excruciating. I wanted to grab her shoulders and straighten her posture, but it was too late. Her story was tragic; one year, her three young children died from a white-man disease; the next year, her husband was killed in a battle. She wandered through the rest of her years as a damaged soul. Bird Nest never remarried and quit taking care of her appearance. Some thought she was a bit crazy, with unkempt hair and her habit of talking to invisible people. I disagreed; she was just different after losing everyone she loved. She did not talk to invisible people but to the Creator. Bird Nest was not affectionate toward humans, probably out of the fear of losing them. Despite this, she was kind to all the animals in our village. She seemed to appreciate routine, chore after chore, day after day. Bird Nest would care for Kola just as well as I did. In turn, my horse would surely give her companionship for the rest of her life, whatever small amount of time may be left.

I walked over to Bird Nest and uncomfortably towered over her. Squatting down at a respectable distance, I dropped my weight to my knees.

"Well, well. My boy. I heard you are leaving us to learn white-man language."

"Yes."

"With their language comes added responsibility."

"I understand."

"Does that worry you?" Bird Nest asked.

"Yes," I repeated, hoping for deeper insight from Bird Nest. I respected her perseverance amid unfortunate hardship.

"I will talk to our Creator when you are gone. I will ask for your fears to go away," she stated in a matter-of-fact way, as if my apprehension had already dissolved.

"Thank you, Bird Nest. I have something to give you. Would you like my horse? He is a smooth ride and very loyal. He will follow you to the creek and warn you of rattlesnakes. I know your legs are weak, and he will carry you from camp to camp."

"I can't accept him," she mumbled.

"Please."

"If I love him, he'll die. Just like my family."

"No. He won't die from your love. He'll be your friend. He'll love you back and appreciate all you do for him. Please take him."

A tear silently dropped from Bird Nest's eye. She looked up at me, in a sort of desperation.

I changed my tactic. "I need your help. I need you to care for him. He is a good horse. You are a good match."

She nodded and it was settled. Kola would go to Bird Nest. Father explained over the next few days that he did not know all of the details of my education. He said that other Lakota tribes were sending students because the opportunity was critical to the survival of the Lakota people. The Oglala tribe, led by Red Cloud, was sending two students.[3] Sitting Bull, chief of the Hunkpapa tribe, was also sending two students, One Bull and Good Bear. I knew One Bull. He was two winters older than I, and as the adopted son of Sitting Bull, I assumed he was destined for leadership. One Bull's and my paths had crossed because Grandfather and Father worked closely with Sitting Bull to keep our Lakota nation strong. Unfortunately, One Bull was mean. When I was a small boy and our tribes gathered together a few times a year, One Bull threw dirt in my eyes when nobody was looking. He also kicked me in the shins and spit in my face. When elders were present, he only appeared aloof. Something dark grew within him.

I did not understand why other tribes were sending two students each, yet Grandfather only assigned me. He said I needed to become independent and did not need a friend as a walking stick to help me along. I thought a friend would make the time more tolerable because deep down, I dreaded leaving my people. I was coming to my seventeenth winter, and the new responsibility I bore toward my tribe was hard to bear.

"What will I do when I am not learning? I will be bored."

Grandfather seemed impatient with me and answered sternly, "Grandson, boredom is the sign of a slow mind. Constantly ask yourself how you can keep growing. The Great One gifted you the legs of a deer. Don't let them wither away. Spend time with One Bull. Your differences are not as great as you envision in your head. One day the two of you may lead side by side. You will not be bored if you keep your hands busy. Ask Black Robe if you can make arrows. He is against war but understands our need to hunt. Be helpful to Black Robe. This is an honor, not a task."

Still, I felt like it was a task.

On the day of my journey to Black Robe, I rose early and found Bird Nest by the creek, patiently waiting for me. The old woman handed me a parfleche, a rawhide-covered bundle, ornately beaded and full of pemmican and gooseberry mush.[4]

"I know it is not much, but it is all I have to give."

"It is beautiful. Thank you," I told her, admiring the intricately beaded pattern that must have taken many seasons to complete.

"Tell me what I need to know," she requested in a thin voice.

Immediately, I knew I had picked the perfect person for Kola, whose name meant "friend." I shared a bit about his disposition, like how he loved to be scratched under his belly. But I left most of Kola's qualities and quirks for Bird Nest to discover on her own. Though I knew giving Kola away was the right thing to do, I was still upset. He was the only possession I deeply valued. My moccasins were a distant second.

CHAPTER 2

WHITE

OCTOBER 1875

NEW YORK

"IT IS AMERICA'S RIGHT TO STRETCH FROM SEA TO SHINING SEA. NOT ONLY DO WE HAVE A RESPONSIBILITY TO OUR CITIZENS TO GAIN VALUABLE NATURAL RESOURCES, WE ALSO HAVE A RESPONSIBILITY TO CIVILIZE THIS BEAUTIFUL LAND."
~Unknown author regarding Manifest Destiny

"The frontier is too dangerous for a refined woman and a fifteen-year-old girl," Dad said.

His frustrated words were deliberately clear and easier to hear than my mother's whispers. My parents had sent me to bed shortly after dinner. I couldn't fall asleep with the hard curlers poking into my ears and head. Plus, I needed to use the privy.

Actually, our house did not have what my mother called "modern conveniences," but, unlike most homes in our New York City neighborhood, the small addition on the back of our house had a white claw-foot bathtub. Most of our neighbors just used a washbasin, a bar of soap, and a wash cloth for a bath. Yes, we had a bathtub which in theory was a luxury. In truth, the water was never quite the right temperature, and it took great effort to draw the bath because we heated the water on the stove. An iron pipe fit into the tub's drain which dropped through a hole in the floor and led to the flower garden. Our privy also had a chamber pot, which I used when the night was too cold or too dark to venture outside to our backyard outhouse. If I used the chamber pot at night, then the next morning, it was my obligation to carry the sloshing pot outside and dump the mess into the outhouse hole.

I stood motionless against the hallway wall. A tense air hovered over my parents' conversation. Mother's voice wavered between a whisper and a piercing plea.

"Do you have to accept? Do you have a choice? Oh, dear me! Dakota Territory? It's full of savages. It's not like you haven't already done your service."

I peered around the corner for a split second. Mother was sitting with her back to me, and Dad was in the seat to her right. They leaned into each other from their padded cherry wood armchairs, polished slick with oil. Dad reached over and gently took Mother's fragile hand. His thick, tan forearm rested on the tabletop. Beside him, Mother wore a perfectly starched yellow silk dress with sleeves of taffeta lace. Femininity bubbled from her

12

fashionably pale skin and her blonde locks, tightly controlled in a sleek bun at the nape of her neck.

"For goodness' sake, Samuel. Didn't you suffer enough at Gettysburg?" Mother asked with a cutting tone.

"I know it was hard on you. It was hard on all of us. Even so, darling, 'orders' are called 'orders' for a reason. I don't have a choice when duty calls," Dad answered gently, rubbing his clean-shaven face. "We are supposed to feel honored by my selection. Too many settlers are being attacked. Positions need to be filled at Fort Randall, and the Indians need to be rounded up and placed on reservations. It could be a lot worse. Fort Randall is supposed to be nice as forts go…right on the Missouri River."

Mother started to weep. "What's so special about Fort Randall? Why not an assignment more civilized? In Washington or something. Maybe President Grant needs a guard. Anywhere but Dakota Territory!"

"President Grant has plenty of guards. Fort Randall is a different story. They've lost quite a few soldiers."

"Killed? By savages?" Mother blurted.

"No, darling. They are deserting. Not sure why—maybe to seek their gold fortunes in the Black Hills now that the army quit arresting them for trespass. Maybe they are just tired of waiting for action at the fort. Men need purpose, and when they wait day after day for a battle, but no battle comes, then some men can't take it anymore. They desert. Fort Randall needs more men to keep peace between Indians and settlers. Darling, I swore to follow orders when I took my commission. I vowed loyalty to the United States. You didn't. You should stay here, if you have any hesitation. Your mother is aging. Just stay, and take care of her and Sara, until I return."

Mother didn't say a word for quite some time, and then I heard her chair squeak as it always did when she leaned to the edge of her pastel brocade–patterned seat. She took a deep breath, yet her voice still cracked. "Well, I gave you vows of loyalty sixteen years ago. We will go with you. I am more afraid of life alone here than a life with you amidst savages. We will go."

I wanted to blurt out questions from my hiding place around the hallway corner. Whenever my parents talked quietly at the cleared dining table, an alarm went off in my head, and I could not resist the temptation to eavesdrop, though I was fully aware of the implied disrespect. Since my parents rarely discussed anything sensitive in my presence, how else could an only child learn what was going on? I weighed the consequences of walking past my parents to use the privy, and I chose to quietly sneak back to bed. I could wait until morning or at least until they finished their discussion and determined my fate.

I couldn't sleep, no matter how hard I tried. Images of Dakota Territory flooded my thoughts. For the last year at Hunter Female High School, I had studied the political turmoil brewing between the settlers who pushed west and the Indians who stood in the way. Our headmaster allowed me to dig deeper into the conflict. My teachers did not go into much detail about settlers' conflicts with the Indians. They were either oblivious to the realities or were trying to shelter the students from horror stories, some of which I pieced together from articles in *The Times*.

My school only tested on the most basic facts, such as:

> Question: What year did Congress create Dakota Territory?
> Answer: 1861.
>
> Question: What is the capital of Dakota Territory?
> Answer: Yankton.
>
> Question: What treaty had a big impact on the boundary lines of Dakota Territory?
> Answer: The 1868 Treaty of Fort Laramie.
>
> Final Question (answer in essay form): What has recently happened in the Black Hills, and how does it affect settlers? Answer: In 1874, General Custer discovered gold in the Black Hills. Before the discovery, Western Dakota Territory was considered worthless and uncivilized with only the Indians willing to live through the extremely cold winters and sweltering summers. Now white settlers flood into the land that the Fort Laramie Treaty granted to the Sioux. Our soldiers are trying to keep them back but greed is persistent.

I was finally getting sleepy and pulled my blanket up under my chin. I wondered if Miss Bee, our housekeeper, had overheard my parents, since her bedroom was on the other side of the kitchen. Miss Bee was twenty-five years old and worked long hours for what she considered reasonable pay. Born into slavery, she gained her freedom after the Civil War. Miss Bee and her sister moved to New York City for a better life. The city was not kind toward freed slaves, especially when they were unmarried young women.

Miss Bee did not offer many details about their life after arriving in the city. She said that they did what they had to do after losing their jobs in a sweatshop. One day, when we were alone in the house, she explained how another ex-slave collapsed on the factory floor from heat stroke. Miss Bee and her sister stopped working and tried to drag the woman from the sweltering factory air. Blocking the door, the manager screamed, "You're all fired!" Then Miss Bee's sister turned and yelled, "You can't fire a dead woman!" The man looked down at the woman's still body with disgust, stepped aside, and then slammed the factory door behind them. Miss Bee's sister took a "bad job" after that incident, and one night she never came back to where they slept in a shantytown at the edge of the Hudson River. Miss Bee said her sister had probably been murdered because she would never "just up and leave like that."

I met Miss Bee on a rainy spring morning when I was eleven or twelve. Dad and I woke up before dawn, for one of our occasional early morning adventures to the market. Pelting rain had slammed against my bedroom window throughout the night but subsided into a light drizzle by the time we left our house. As fate would have it, we took a different route to the market, along a narrow street. Dad and I walked side-by-side, with my arm

16

through his, under a large umbrella, adjusting our strides awkwardly to dodge deep puddles. Water ran off the edge of the umbrella, and if I wasn't tight against Dad's arm, it soaked my neck, sending chills down my spine. Our eyes simultaneously glanced to the opposite side of the street, where Miss Bee crouched in the shadows of a vacant building. She was wedged against a door that barely remained attached to its hinges and returned our gazes with an emotionless blank stare.

"Well, well, what a sight," Dad said. He paused, placed the handle of the umbrella in my hand, and told me to wait. He walked across the street, and, at a respectable distance, he engaged the dark figure in a short conversation. Dad helped her to her feet and picked up her bag. With her left foot twisted stiffly to the side, she followed, limping a few paces behind, until they crossed back over the street and reached me. Dad gestured for her to stand at his side, under the umbrella.

"Miss Bee, I'd like you to meet my daughter, Sara. Sara, this is Miss Bee. She has agreed to be our housekeeper." Miss Bee dropped her eyes and tucked her chin inside her shirt collar. Then Dad said, "Miss Bee, we'll have none of that. Do you understand? You are not a slave, you're hired help, and I want you to act like family."

Miss Bee did not wipe away the single tear that gently ran down her face. She just whispered, "Thank you."

"It's our pleasure," Dad replied.

As if her thanks were inadequate for the dignity within her, Miss Bee continued, "I *will* repay you."

"No need. We all need a little help now and then. Just pass it on someday," Dad answered.

When we stepped inside our house, Miss Bee humbly removed her soggy worn shoes and tucked them in the corner of the foyer. Clumped chunks of wet newspaper dropped from the bottoms of her stockings. I glanced at her shoes, neatly arranged, and saw the marble floor through her soles. Her left shoe was the most worn, with an extra hole through the side, probably damaged from dragging her crippled leg.

Mother must have watched us approach from a window because she dramatically entered the foyer, with her arms crossed in front of her. The three of us, soaked to the bone, stared back at her with uncertainty. Mother gazed down at the wet wads of newspaper on the floor and raised her beady eyes to study Miss Bee.

"Where are the fresh buns?" she asked.

"We found Miss Bee in the rain, and she's quite chilled. She'll stay until she chooses to leave. I'll head out for your buns in a bit," Dad answered.

Since Mother showed no hospitality, Dad and I led Miss Bee to the servant quarters behind the kitchen. We had used this room to stash things that cluttered our home. Mother claimed the items had sentimental value, but in reality, she was a hoarder. I haphazardly cleaned off the single bed and placed all of the knickknacks under the iron bedframe. I tried to fluff up the comforter.

"Will this be okay for you?" I asked.

"I sleep on the floor."

"But we have this extra bed going to waste. It is for you," Dad said.

He told her to settle in and rest since she had probably been up all night—and the night before, and the night before. Dad told me to stay at the house in case Miss Bee woke up while he was at the market. She didn't. While Dad was gone, I overheard Mother complaining to Grandmother that Dad had no right to bring a crippled slave into our home without her permission. I could not tell which irritated her more, the color of Miss Bee's skin or the way she dragged her left leg. Grandmother seemed more open to the thought of extra hands in the kitchen.

When Dad returned a few hours later, he carried Mother's fresh buns, a new pair of shoes, and a shiny ebony cane with a deep purple, detailed handle. He brought the cane into the study, where I was completing a math assignment and I admired the workmanship.

"May I speak with you for a moment?" Mother asked from the doorway.

"Of course," Dad replied.

"No, in private."

Dad glanced back at me as he followed her into their bedroom. The door shut. I continued to sit at the desk in the study and heard the whole conversation through the wall.

"I demand she only stay until tomorrow morning. Look at how you already spoil her. New shoes? A beautiful cane? Honestly, what are you thinking? She's nothing more than a crippled slave!" Mother blurted.

"Now, now. You need to get off your high horse. Miss Bee isn't a slave. Don't forget, we won the war. Sara could use a friend in this house and you could use help. It's the Christian thing to do. Show a touch of empathy, will you? At least muster up a little sympathy. She needs a job—a safe job," Dad reasoned.

Mother was quiet before insisting that I not mingle with Miss Bee outside of our household. "It's just not proper," she repeated over and over. Dad spoke gently with Mother, dampening her anxiety. Dad picked his battles carefully, which must have been why he came home alive after the Civil War. Within a few days, the household battlefield became calm, and a truce was called over the Miss Bee matter. Days turned into months, and months into years. Even though Mother secretly liked the extra help around the house, she relentlessly corrected Miss Bee's manners, psychologically punishing her for being born a slave.

I adored Miss Bee, and she acted like an aunt toward me, or maybe a big sister. I don't know for sure because I never had either. Her big brown eyes peeked out from behind her shiny black hair, and her skin was dark as night. She was as thin as a stick and about my height when we first met. Four or five years later, I had grown another five inches, but Miss Bee had not grown another inch. Well, actually, she had grown quite a few inches but only around her middle. Taste-testing her own cooking throughout the day slowly added pound after pound, until she was quite soft underneath her apron. I thought the extra layer was her safety shield, protecting her from her past.

She had scars, deep scars: five or six across her back and one across her temple. Her clothes covered the wide scars running the width of her back, which I only saw on one occasion, when I accidentally walked in on her while she was changing clothes. Miss Bee never explained the events surrounding her crippled left leg even though it was the most obvious of her external injuries.

Miss Bee's carefree joy covered the pervasive darkness of our home. We humored each other with sideways glances and winks when nobody was looking. When we were alone, the ridiculous formalities disappeared and our secret friendship flourished, filling our space with the unspoken understanding of kindred spirits. I closed my eyes and prayed that Miss Bee would come to Dakota Territory with us.

CHAPTER 3

RED

OCTOBER 1875

THE PLAINS

"WHERE AN INDIAN IS SHUT UP IN ONE PLACE
HIS BODY BECOMES WEAK."
~Sitting Bull, Hunkpapa Lakota

My grandmother, Stands on the Ground, was gloomy on the morning of my departure; I did not understand why, because I would only be gone for two full moons. She handed me a bundle of dried gooseberry branches that she had collected months ago. She also handed me a pouch full of flint, to chip into arrows in my spare time.

"Don't be sad, Grandmother," I told her confidently. "I will learn quickly and be back soon. I will be home before you have a chance to miss me." She turned away and concealed her reaction. Father and I left quickly and rode side by side in silence until the camp was no longer in sight. Then Father started talking, summarizing life lessons that he had thoroughly covered over my childhood. Finally, he broke the horrible news.

"Stay with Black Robe for ten full moons or longer," Father said.

Ten full moons? I felt betrayed. I felt uncertain. I felt out of control of my destiny.

"This is very important. You need a full understanding of white-man language," he insisted.

As the only student from the Miniconjou tribe, I felt all the pressure mounted on my shoulders. Father and I rode in silence for the last few hours of the journey. The tall prairie grass brushed against Kola's chest and split to each side as he pressed forward. The wind whistled through the tops of the grasses, releasing seeds across the plains which would soon be buried under snow. Eventually, we came to a group of buildings, called Fort Berthoud. From the door of a log cabin, a slight white man in a black robe, stepped onto the porch and waved.

"Hello! Welcome! I'm Black Robe," he proclaimed in broken Lakota. A few inches shorter than I, he held out his hand. Father and I shook his overly firm grip, and then he led us inside.

"This is our cabin. This is where we live and learn," Black Robe began. His Lakota was better than our white-man language.

Father and I looked at the dark log structure with no outward expression; but our eyes met, and then we both looked away without needing words. Tipis allowed muted sunlight through the hide for a glowing, warm effect, but this white-man building was dark and musty.

"This is where I sleep and where we study," Black Robe said of the first room. Then he led us to the next room. Frustrated with his Lakota, he reverted back to English: "This is where all the students sleep. Put your things here on the floor."

"Make arrows okay?" I asked, trying out my limited English, as I pointed to my bundle of supplies.

"Yes, I'll trust you until you break my trust. If you break the trust, then I'll break your arrows!" Black Robe chuckled. He seemed good-natured.

Father proclaimed in broken English how he needed to head back to camp. I followed Father to our horses. We momentarily embraced and patted each other's backs. I did not want him to leave, yet he jumped onto his horse. I walked over to Kola and scratched his belly one more time. I reluctantly handed the leather lead to Father, who wasted no time in trotting away. He did not look back.

Emotion crept into my face, so I looked down at my feet, where two pieces of sandstone laid. Sandstone was perfect for stripping bark off branches to make the shafts of arrows. Picking up the rough rocks, I walked to the timber porch and sat down on the edge of the step, wondering when the other students would arrive. They trickled in throughout the day. First, Black Robe greeted them just as he had with me. Then, he suggested I show them inside the cabin. I dreaded the arrival of One Bull, but it turned out uneventful because in front of Black Robe, One Bull was quite cordial. I wondered how he would treat me when we were alone.

In the evening, after dinner, Black Robe encouraged us to gather on the porch. All the students congregated, and Black Robe facilitated English conversation. I gazed at the horizon when Black Robe's words became too difficult and I retrieved the gooseberry branches that Grandmother sent with me. Arrow-making was tedious—a perfect thing for me to do to pass the idle time. I sat down on the porch again, stretched a sturdy branch from my elbow to the tip of my little finger, and marked the spot. I used my knife to cut a shaft to my arm's length, and then I notched the end for the eventual secured point. With the sandstone blocks in one hand, I sanded the shafts by pulling them through the hole at different angles. Once an arrow shaft was smooth, I cut a pattern into the arrow to help it fly true and give it more speed.

After several weeks with Black Robe, I relaxed as I became familiar with the routine. Because One Bull rarely spoke with me, Black Robe sensed the tension between us. He was a perceptive, kind man but did not try to mediate the relationships between students. His people called him Bishop Martin Marty.[5] He seemed happy living with us in the log cabin, even though the roof leaked during thunderstorms. In one room, Black Robe had a bed and table. In the next room, his seven students slept on bunks that pulled down from the walls at bedtime. Black Robe woke before sunrise and spoke prayers that I heard through the wall. Then he celebrated Mass, using the table as an altar, before calling us in for breakfast. Our usual early meal was fresh bread with spices of salt and pepper. Usually, heavy butter was mixed into the loaf. I was not familiar with the yellow mush, but I learned to appreciate it.

I tried to keep an open mind about white-man beliefs, white-man food, and the dark building that we slept in. Nonetheless, some things that Black Robe said just did not make sense. When he watched me eat, usually twice as much as anyone else, he laughed and said I must have a hollow leg. I was certain I did not have a hollow leg, but rather than objecting, I kept my gaze lowered toward my empty plate.

After breakfast, Black Robe taught us our morning lesson, which followed the same chant each morning. I was not sure what the prayer meant. Oddly enough, within a few weeks, the words flowed from my mouth. Black Robe carefully taught us how to spell and speak as the white man. Usually he taught from his Bible. He explained how his people believed in one god, with three manifestations: a Father, Son, and Holy Spirit. My people believed in one god, Wakan Tanka, which means "the Great Mystery." My god also has many different manifestations, with the main four being rock, earth, sky, and sun.

One day Black Robe explained, "I know you grew up believing in your Great Spirit, that he is the mystery of everything around you, and you learned that if you just follow your inner voice, then you're following Wakan Tanka. But you must understand that faith isn't just about the circle of life here on earth. There are more promises for you in heaven when you trust in the Son."

"I do trust in the sun," I responded, thinking how it reliably rose each morning and fell each evening. I thought of how my people respected and honored this glowing mystery with our sacred Sun Dance.

"I trust in the sun," the Oglala student confirmed.

"I do too," said Good Bear, of the Hunkpapa.

"Yes, but I speak of the *Son* of God, not the *sun* in the sky. Here, let me spell the two words for you," Black Robe offered, realizing that the similarity of the words only made his explanation more confusing.

Son. Sun. It seemed irrelevant.

"You see," Black Robe continued, "God is the keeper of your soul. If you believe and follow His word, then you will be rewarded with an afterlife in the presence of God."

I respected Black Robe, though his beliefs were not mine. My people believed that Wakan Tanka had created everything on earth and in the sky. We simply accepted the Great Mystery and did not ask as many questions as the white man. Our eagle seemed to be Black Robe's Holy Spirit, connecting us to higher truths and filling us with discernment. The cycle of life, continuing on and on, is what gave meaning to the earth.

One day, Black Robe pulled me out of my studies and led me onto the porch of our cabin. He said he brought sad news, and then he waited a few seconds, like he was not sure how to tell me. Then he just said it.

"I'm sorry Ohanzee. Your Grandfather has died on your sacred mountain, Mato Paha."

Black Robe placed his hand on my shoulder as the news sank into my core, and I began to shake. I felt the air sucked right out of my body, as I collapsed on the wood-planked porch. He explained how, in the days before Grandfather died, my people were roaming across the plains in search of buffalo. Grandfather was feeling fine, and then one evening, as they camped at the base of Mato Paha, he told Grandmother that he was tired. Grandmother helped him to his buffalo robe, which was spread on the grass inside their tipi, and they fell asleep beside each other. The next morning, when Grandmother woke, his breath was gone. My people carried Grandfather's body to a plateau near the top of the mountain and made a scaffold for his final resting place. I envisioned him, wrapped in his buffalo robe, on a bed made of branches, raised above the ground by four long poles. Black Robe said he did not know any other details. I wasn't sure I wanted to hear anyway.

From that day forward, Black Robe tried to be a closer friend. He seemed to realize my disadvantage of not having another Miniconjou to spend time with. One day, Black Robe was busy translating his prayers into the Lakota language. He asked for my help which made me feel useful and we spent many late nights working on his project. When we weren't translating, we sat on the porch with the other students, and Black Robe told stories about the friendship between Father DeSmet and Grandfather.

"They worked together long before Ohanzee was born," he told us.

"How? How did they work together?" One Bull asked.

Black Robe gently smiled and answered, "Back in the 1840's, Ohanzee's grandfather, Chief Lone Horn, brought a few gold nuggets to Father DeSmet and asked what should be done. Father DeSmet, knowing how a white-man gold rush would create a disaster for your people, told him to bury the gold and never talk about it again. In response, a council of warriors agreed to kill anyone, red or white, who searched for gold in the Black Hills.[6] Their secret pact lasted for years and years."

"Even so, now the secret is out," I mumbled.

"Yes. I'm sorry. It will never be the same for your people," Black Robe answered sadly.

"The Black Hills are sacred."

"I know," Black Robe said quietly.

He told us of Grandfather's requests that the US government grant us land on which we could actually grow successful crops. My grandfather did not want to be dependent on the government rations. I tried to explain to Black Robe how my people became restless when they could not move freely about. I told him that the need to keep moving came from somewhere deep inside. He stared at me, searching, trying to understand.

One evening when all of us sat on the porch, the setting sun began to create many dazzling colors in the sky. Black Robe rushed inside the cabin, reappearing with a colorful box of paints—not dyes made from berries or clay, but vivid colors brighter than any rainbow. Back on the porch beside us, he uncurled a canvas the size of his torso and collected rocks to hold it flat against the porch floor. We gazed at the sunset, and he painted what he saw of the ever-changing hues, from bright orange to deep purple, as the sun said good-bye through a veil of clouds.

I hesitated before finally asking if I could use his paints. He readily agreed, placing the box between us and asking if I would like a canvas. I said no and moved quickly inside to my belongings, out of which I retrieved my arrows. Sitting beside Black Robe on the porch, I picked through the vivid paints. Bright yellow, blue, and red were in larger bottles. Other colors were in smaller bottles, and I wondered if they were more precious.

Glancing at Black Robe's painting, I saw his efforts to duplicate what could not be captured. Still inspired by the Great One's gift, I carefully selected the large bottles of red, blue, and yellow. I squeezed each color onto a scrap piece of wood, and, using a small brush, I began to paint the arrows in my identifiable mark; a line swirled three times around the shaft with wavy lines extending into tiny hearts. I did not have feathers, sinew, or glue, so I could not finish the arrows. Despite that, I could finish the shafts. I felt pride swelling from within, as I set each one aside, propped against the side of the porch to dry.

I only stayed one more month with Black Robe. If not for the brown lacquer clock ticking on Black Robe's wall, then time would have stood still. My presence with the white man was purely physical; my heart was back with my people. I mourned the loss of Grandfather. The sorrow in my heart caused my voice to desert me. I could not focus on what I was sent to do.

The cabin walls suffocated my spirit. The daily white-man routine and schedule became unbearable. I could not stand it any longer. One night I gathered my belongings and tiptoed to the food reserves. I collected bread and a canteen of water, pushing them deep into my parfleche. Before sneaking from the cabin, I wrote a note in my best white-man language and slid it under Black Robe's door. It said,

Black Robe
I sorry no good by.
You wise and kind.
I go home. I pray
to my Sun for you.
Ohanzee

I had faith that Black Robe would understand, and I walked from Fort Berthoud without looking back. At a slow run, I searched for the signs that my people left as they roamed in search of buffalo herds. Scraped rocks or buffalo shoulder blades were placed in prominent locations along their path, painted with our special

Miniconjou red mark to indicate which direction they traveled. With the signs, hunting parties found their way back to the moving camp. After locating a sign, I felt fortunate; my people were only two days from Standing Rock. I slowed to a fast walk because I was not in the same physical condition as when I came to live with the white man. His food and lack of activity had changed my body for the worse.

I spent the night under a lone tree on the immense prairie, staring at the vivid stars and feeling free at last. Distant howling wolves sang a song which echoed against nothing and lulled me to sleep. Meadowlarks woke me at dawn and I continued on the trail, dreading the moment when someone would spot me. At last, a self-serving warrior, Tells the Wind, saw me approaching the camp and rode his horse out to meet me. He asked why I left the school. I did not answer. Instead of offering me a ride, double-bareback to camp, he rode away, shaking his head, and left me to walk alone. He hollered into camp, "Ohanzee is back."

Father met me at the edge of camp, and, without pleasantries, demanded an explanation.

"I just couldn't stay with the wasicu any longer. I yearned for you and Grandmother. I missed the wide skies and open prairie. I missed everything that fills my spirit."

Father said. "It is your choice whether to listen to the Great One or to wander lost and alone. You were selfish, my son. You did what you wanted to do without thinking of our people." He shook his head in disappointment and walked away. I wished that instead he had drawn his bow and shot me between the eyes.

32

CHAPTER 4

WHITE

OCTOBER 1875

NEW YORK

"THE BEST WAY TO PREDICT THE FUTURE IS TO CREATE IT." ~Abraham Lincoln

I opened my eyes and was pleasantly surprised that the morning light peeked through my window. I jumped out of bed, dressed and scurried to the privy. The chilly night air hung in the yard, and when I rushed back into the house, Dad was pacing the kitchen floor with a cup of coffee in his hand.

"You are growing like a weed," he exclaimed, setting his coffee cup on the counter. With his strong hands, he pulled back my slumping shoulders, squaring them into "the correct posture," which seemed much too arrogant for how I felt inside.

"Be proud of your height, Sara. You are lucky to be tall."

I handed back the coffee cup and let my shoulders relax a bit. I knew he was right. Deep down, I liked my height, but Mother saw it as a detriment. Once I overheard her telling Grandmother how I may never find a suitor because young men don't want to marry tall women. I didn't want to care about what she thought, but somehow, I did. Mother's constant criticism tore at my core. To feel safe, I turned to God. I read His word but couldn't hear Him speak. I knew that I was His child, yet I did not know what my future held. Was I only created to marry? Then why did I feel a pull toward nursing—or at least toward helping others? Once Dad said Civil War nurses were the greatest heroes of all. They put their personal lives on hold and willingly took in the horrors of war just to help ease the pain of injured and dying soldiers. The nurses' smooth feminine hands cleaned the wounds of freshly amputated limbs. As the soldiers awaited their fate, their soothing voices offered encouragement. I wanted to be like those women. I wanted to make a difference.

Mother stepped into the kitchen. Her face looked tired. She had been up all night.

"Accompany Miss Bee to the market for fresh buns and fruit," Mother instructed sharply. She handed me four coins that I dropped into my skirt's right seam pocket.

"No, no, Sara. Take the clutch I bought for you. It's much more appropriate. And Sara," she called out as I walked from the kitchen, "don't forget your social skills. Important people are watching you. Act like a young lady."

Mother obviously wanted me out of the house because I was rarely allowed to go to market with Miss Bee, since it was "not proper." I was thrilled to get away with my unspoken best friend. Miss Bee and I stepped onto the porch and shut the solid door behind us. The unusually mild autumn still held a chill within its high humidity, causing me to cross my arms and shiver. Miss Bee, with her worn ebony cane as support, started down the steps and along the edge of Danbury Street. A horse-drawn carriage, with its jingling harness, emerged from the light mist and trotted past. We slowly walked to the market, stepping over steaming piles of horse manure.

I thought back to the day when our paths first crossed, and I was thankful that Dad and I had chosen the different street. Using the most direct route, the market was only two blocks away. Within the first block, I asked Miss Bee whether she knew anything about Dad's orders. She was slightly embarrassed but admitted she had also overhead my parents talking the night before.

"What do you think of it all?" I asked.

"I think I want to come along," she exclaimed.

Half a block from the market, the streets bustled with more energy. We could smell the goods, wonderful and disgusting, depending on the products offered at the booths. The vendors, mostly recent immigrants, stood at the front of their stalls, unwilling to negotiate prices for their goods.

"One dozen buns, please," is all I said, pointing toward the fresh-baked breads lined up on the table like soldiers on a battlefield.

35

The handwritten sign, fluttering in the fall breeze, said, "Hot Buns, 6 Cents a Dozen," a fact that we already knew after years of shopping with the same man. I was not sure of his homeland; perhaps he came from France, because his buns and croissants were flaky and delicious. After he had packaged up the buns, I carefully dropped the exact change into his wrinkled hand.

"I made it a baker's dozen just for your beautiful smile," the old man said.

"Oh, thank you, sir," I replied, avoiding further eye contact. More and more frequently, men of all ages were starting to notice me, which made me uncomfortable. I never knew how to respond.

A completely different ritual awaited at the fruit stand. I had nicknamed the dark-haired Italian immigrant "Crazy Fruit Woman." She had clearly carried her attitude across the Atlantic Ocean. Her homeland was probably glad to see her go. Dad and I learned this the hard way when he brought me to market one day. Each piece of fruit was polished and stacked perfectly on her display table—beautiful, unblemished fruit. Dad reached out to feel a peach for ripeness, and the woman went crazy right before our eyes in front of at least a dozen other market-goers.

"Non spremere il mio frutto! Non spremere il mio frutto!" she bellowed. She definitely had our attention, although we did not understand her language. Like an angel on a mission, a small older Italian man in the crowd interpreted for us, "Don't squeeze her fruit. She is very upset," he said. The latter part needed no explanation. I wanted to scream, "Don't you know who my dad is? Don't you know what he has been through? He fought at

Gettysburg. He has seen things that would make you throw up … throw up all over your perfect fruit!" In truth, I did not actually know much about what Dad experienced in the Civil War. He didn't like to talk about it.

With vast experience from dealing with mother, Dad talked the woman down: "Okay, okay, I'm sorry. It's all okay. It won't happen again." As we walked away, Dad whispered, "I think she needs to go to the crazy house on Hart Island."[7]

Miss Bee and I finished our shopping and started our journey home. Usually when we came back from market, we quietly reviewed the words we had seen during the outing, and I sounded them out for Miss Bee. Although spelling was my weakness, I was good enough to help Miss Bee.

"Okay, remember the sign that said buns? B-U-N-S. Buns."

"B-U-N-S. Buns," she repeated.

As a slave, Miss Bee had never learned to read or write, and I knew I could help. But Mother couldn't know because she would make a big deal out of it, insisting Miss Bee should remain illiterate. I could already hear her, clear as day: "Sara. No. It is not appropriate." So, to avoid Mother's wrath, Miss Bee and I kept the lessons to ourselves.

"Let's go around the block once," I said halfheartedly, wishing the walk could take all day.

"Ahh, your mother is waiting, and the buns will cool."

"Please, Miss Bee. It is for our health. Our emotional health."

Once around the block, I knew asking Miss Bee to go further was futile. She still limped, even with her cane, and moved with difficulty since she carried extra weight. Her curly, shoulder-length locks escaped from her hat, and her smile was magnetic.

"We need to go in, Sara. Can't stay out here forever."

"Wish we could," I said under my breath.

Opening the door, I felt the immediate presence of tension. Dad was nowhere to be seen. He did not usually stick around for breakfast, which I understood, because the meal was more of a ritual than a necessity. I was still full from last night, and the night before, and the night before that. In truth, I could not remember a time when I was deeply hungry. We seemed to eat for the sake of routine, not nourishment.

"Well, I'll cut up fruit and be back in a flash." Miss Bee forced cheerfulness into her words, trying to chip away at the invisible ice in the room.

I sat down at the table where Mother and Grandmother were waiting. Two sets of faded blue eyes stared back at me. My eyes were molasses brown, just like Dad's. Mother's hair was dull blonde and nothing special in the morning without the teasing and curling. Grandmother pulled her thin gray hair into a tiny, tight bun with no stray strands, which perfectly represented her personality. Both women wore makeup powder, even at breakfast. I pondered whom they were trying to impress.

The only sound in the room came from the clicking of the mahogany-and-ivory clock, which hung on sage-green flocked wallpaper. Uncomfortable with the ominous stress, I stood and walked to the fireplace. The white, Italian marble mantel took on a reflective yellow hue after I stoked the flames and added another split log. I readjusted the clock and then the crystal vase atop the mantle. They had been on display since I could remember, and I knew Grandmother treasured them.

"Don't touch those, Sara," Grandmother snapped. I quickly pulled my fidgeting hand away. "They're the last things your Grandfather gave me before he was called up. God bless his soul."

Clanking noises came from the kitchen, and then Miss Bee emerged. I moved back to the table and sat down. Three serving dishes sat between us: buns, covered with a linen towel to retain their warmth; a plate of steaming sliced ham, left over from the night before; and a bowl of fresh-cut fruit, mostly apple slices and orange segments. I first served Grandmother and Mother, carefully setting a little of each item on three small white plates with intricate gold foil swirling around the edges. With my silver knife in my right hand and my fork inverted in the left, I cut though a slice of smoked ham and took my first bite.[8]

Then, as if Mother could not stand it another moment, she dramatically announced, "Well, we have something to tell you, Sara. We are moving to Dakota Territory."

I stopped chewing, sealed my lips and let the piece of ham just sit on top of my tongue. My cheeks almost tightened to a dimpled grin. Instead, I forced my eyebrows to rise, opened my eyes wide, and attempted to appear shocked by the news. Secretly I was thrilled. Grandmother wept, knowing she was losing her daughter to a life of compromises. Mother married Dad knowing that the bad came with the good and she had willingly committed to compromises. To her, the benefits of an upper-class lifestyle were worth the challenges of bearing and raising well-minded children, maintaining her beautiful appearance and proper etiquette in public, keeping a perfectly clean home and entertaining. In my opinion, Mother was an ornament with a not-so-secret agenda: for Dad to rise through the ranks. She wholeheartedly believed that if we played our cards as she directed, she would become a general's wife someday.

"We need to dress and behave in a befitting manner, like a general's family. We need to entertain, like a general's family. And one day we will be a general's family," she said, running her finger along the delicate pattern of her crystal glass, filled with a touch of caramel-tinted brandy.

Entertaining was Mother's means to climb the ladder of elite military society. She overcame her lack of charisma through her skillful ability to maneuver through an elaborate party with precision and grace. No matter the size of the event, she addressed each guest by their proper name. She dressed impeccably, usually in pastel velvet gowns and white elbow-length silk gloves. Her dresses were never revealing, and she accented her conservative image with a small strand of pearls around her neck. Her manicured blonde locks framed a petite powdered face, bringing out the blue in her otherwise unremarkable eyes. She floated around the crowd and said just the right things to each guest.

Miss Bee was quite a chef. We had a substantial kitchen with a large cook stove and wide butcher block counters. When Miss Bee baked, the oven became magical. She taught me to make apple pies, which Dad could not resist. Her smoked hams and beef roasts wafted the mouth-watering aroma of Southern cooking throughout our home. I asked her to teach me her tricks because working in the kitchen was the only aspect of entertaining that satisfied me. Miss Bee celebrated our small accomplishments when something came out just as she had planned. Yet Mother often cast a shadow over us, as she pulled me away from my passion, insisting that the hired help would do a better job without my distraction.

In an attempt to please Mother, I initially tried my best at our dinner parties. First, I stood at the window beside the front door and watched for the guests to arrive. I peeked through the lace-curtained windows, gazing out over the flower boxes, which were filled with ever-optimistic red and white geraniums that always survived the first frost of the season. Because I dreaded the social introductions, I wanted to get them over with as soon as possible. As the guests passed through the heavy wood door and into our foyer, I jumped right into the initial pleasantries.

"How do you do?" I said with a slight curtsy. "It is my pleasure to finally make your acquaintance. I have heard a great deal about you from my father."

They almost always joked, "I hope they were all good things!"

"Of course!" I exclaimed, and everyone laughed to overcome the early-evening tension. Then, as trained, I graciously asked, "May I

41

take your coat?" or "Might you be interested in a duck pâté appetizer and a glass of wine?"

To me, the formalities and small talk were tedious. Almost every guest possessed similar biases because our invitation lists were limited to military officers and their wives. Conversations rolled in a continuous loop throughout the night and routinely focused on the West and Dakota Territory. The conversations humored me, but I kept this attitude to myself. The women asked each other questions, hoping to appear well informed, such as, "Can you believe how the savages killed those poor innocent women and children?" I could only listen to so much of their drama. Then, I tried to eavesdrop on the army officers, but topics were limited to battle techniques used against the Indians which barely held my interest.

Instead of falling deeper into Mother's social agenda, I often feigned illness and escaped to my bedroom. I immediately tore off my dress and corset, and then I sat back on my bed, in bloomers and a robe, reading intently by candlelight. Immersing into the pages of a novel allowed me to venture to wondrous places, where I forgot Mother's disapproving glares and her drills in social etiquette faux pas. My bedroom was a sanctuary, where I had nothing to prove. I knew our guests did not want to hear my academic insight into the Indian Wars; nobody seemed to care about what was important to me. Since as long as I could remember, I had been put through a personal torture; I was forced to be someone I did not care to be. Take my hair, for instance. Apparently, at least according to Mother and Grandmother, all girls must have curly hair. Unless, of course, I had naturally curly hair, and then, I deduced, they would have insisted that I straighten it.

"How am I supposed to sleep on a pile of rocks?" I complained, as Mother and Grandmother wound my hair into stiff rollers each night.

"Oh, dear me, Sara, you're a young lady, and you'd better start acting like one," they retorted. Over and over again.

I was fifteen years old and tired of being told what to do. I was tired of being corrected—corrected by Mother, Grandmother, my teachers, even Dad. They continuously said, "It's for your own good," although a tiny bit of my spirit was crushed with each reprimand. As hard as I tried to please them, my inadequacies were still brought to my attention. I was tired of being told how to look: that I must curl my hair and wear the mandatory corset.

Corsets were one of the worst things in the whole world, and I had been required to wear one for the last few months. I wondered which cruel person had invented them—probably someone who did not want women to breathe; someone who never thought a girl might dream of riding a horse bareback, unencumbered by slats of bone jabbing into her ribcage; someone who thought a girl's time was of no consequence, as she was forced to tediously lace up her corset each and every day. When I complained, Mother and Grandmother told me to focus of something else, such as what type of young man I hoped to catch. Ironically, my mind never wandered in that direction. I was only a bit curious about young men.

Disregarding my lack of comfort in the company of prospective suitors, Mother had already declared to her moderately affluent social circle that I was ready to be courted. I was ready to be proposed to. Like a young filly, forced into a horse auction, I nervously roamed the ring, searching for an escape, and awaited the moment when I was sold to the highest bidder.

CHAPTER 5

RED

MOON OF FALLING LEAVES

OCTOBER 1875

THE PLAINS

"IF YOU TALK TO THE ANIMALS, THEY WILL TALK WITH YOU AND YOU WILL KNOW EACH OTHER ... WHAT YOU DO NOT KNOW, YOU WILL FEAR. WHAT ONE FEARS, ONE DESTROYS."
~Chief Dan George, Tsleil-Waututh Nation, British Columbia, Canada

"Na-wan-kal-hiyu!" the older boys whooped at me, as I kneeled beside a rock for concealment. Na-wan-kal-hiyu? Rise on my own accord? Now? The young warriors blazed past me, bareback on their horses, racing toward their chosen tatanka. The horses were well trained to run close beside the brown buffalo, with each responding only to its rider's leg pressure. We had no use for white-man bridles when both hands were busy with a bow and arrows.

I jumped from behind a rock, shadowed in a small washout. Without thinking of the thundering hooves before me, I ran straight into the cloud of dust our brother creatures had stirred as they raged by. My heart pounded. My legs burned. I chased behind the buffalo herd, which numbered more than two hundred. Inherent dangers loomed among the chaotic beasts; despite our careful planning the day before, the herd's arrival brought great excitement. We could not fail or we would face the grim reality of empty stomachs.

The hunters had formed two lines, one on the right and the other on the left of the herd. When the buffalo panicked, they ran in one direction with bulls in the lead. Our swiftest horses carried our braves, who rushed ahead and turned the bulls back in the other direction, confusing the rest of the herd. Arrows bombarded the buffalo that tried to escape in random directions.

"Run, boy! That bull is for you!" a hunter yelled at me.

I looked to my left and saw an injured bull, already full of arrows. Colossal in stature, he stumbled and snorted. The bearlike, brownish-red hide oozed crimson as he dropped to his knees. I carefully approached from behind. With the churning dust in the air, I heard hooves pounding, animals calling, and my people hollering at each other above the frenzy. As if searching for relief amidst the pain and confusion, my bull turned his huge head toward me and bellowed a fog of musty breath directly into my face.

I stepped back and reached for my quiver.[9] Methodically placing an arrow in my bow, I whispered, "Wopila tatanka" under my labored breath. "Thank you, buffalo. From you, we will live." With a sense of ancient respect, I drew back my bow to my cheek as tight as I dared, for the buffalo tendon string could snap. I aimed at the buffalo's heart. I hesitated. My fingers released the bow string. His snorting did not subside immediately. The most difficult part of any kill was watching when life did not let go easily. This buffalo fought for each breath until he finally released himself to the spirit world. Dry prairie grasses waved good-bye.

The elderly, women, and younger children had packed up our tipis and followed us to the hunting ground. They emerged like mystical ghosts from the dusty cloud on the plains. We had followed our sacred meat source across the great prairie all summer. Now that the winter snows were close, we needed a substantial harvest to sustain us for the winter.

For as long as I can remember, I had taken part in our buffalo hunts. As a small boy, I was only allowed to crouch on distant hilltops to watch the silent, dark speck on the horizon: the herd looked like a brown tick as it moved across the golden prairie. Through hours of patience, still as a rock, I became a warrior in my mind, pushing the herd forward into the ultimate crazed thunder of hoofs.

The buffalo roamed in herds of the thousands then. Now they were one-tenth of that amount. As a small boy, I had watched our hunters, who wore buffalo hides, approach from all directions on horseback, strategically closing in on our hunt. As they let their horses graze, they bent over the horses' necks so that each horse with its rider resembled a humped-back buffalo. The buffalo were near-sighted, and their greatest asset was their sense of smell. Only when the warriors were quite close did an older warrior command that everyone move in, causing the buffalo to stampede. The sound of the pounding hoofs upon the prairie filled every part of my body with excitement.

As I grew, my energy was directed toward productive tasks after the killing stopped. I was assigned to work alongside the women, and I answered the elders' requests.

"Boy, take this liver over to the warriors."

"Boy, take this hide to the drying line."

"Boy, stretch this sinew for thread."

I obeyed as all youngsters did, but I differed in how I ran from one task to the next, because I knew that my quick pace and focus would likely be rewarded with a fresh piece of liver, tongue or kidney. Organ meat was usually reserved for our warriors and male elders so I cherished the opportunity to prove myself worthy of the nourishment.

Father watched my enthusiasm and predicted, "He will be our runner, you wait and see. Then he will grow into a spokesman and protector of our people."

I was fine with being a runner for a year or two, although in my heart, I waited for the day when I could hunt from horseback, rushing in the wind with crazed buffalo around me. I clung to the hope of becoming a protector of our people. Certainly Father meant that I could be a warrior. Or so I assumed.[10]

This hunt was different than any before. First, I was sixteen. I had much to prove to my people because I had let them down by leaving my training with Black Robe. I wanted to show my loyalty and value to the tribe. It would have been easier if I still had a horse, but the hunt started off right anyway. For the first time, my arrow stopped the beating heart of a buffalo. I stared at the bull, who was lying motionless on his side. Blood began to pool beneath the thick brown hide.

Meanwhile, the women put up the tipis again, this time on a nearby ridge overlooking the buffalo harvest. The men had cut and peeled lodge poles years ago. However, camp after camp, the women were responsible for erecting and disassembling each tipi for our circle. Three tall poles, sometimes fifteen or twenty feet long, were set up as the foundation. Then smaller poles filled in the gaps. The tipi was not a true circle, but instead was stretched to form an oval with one end protruding farther than the opposite end; this made the door side steeper than the rear.

After my tatanka kill, Grandmother walked over and handed me skinning and cutting knives.

"Do this on your own," Stands on the Ground said. She was small and frail, but she emanated great dignity. She had taken everything in life much more seriously ever since Grandfather died a few full moons ago. I missed him and smiled at the thought of the Creator picking Grandmother's small frame to give birth to Father, Chief Touch the Clouds. Father took over as chief of the Miniconjou after Grandfather died. Afraid of his strength and reputation, the white man claimed that Father was nearly seven feet tall, but he actually stood six feet five inches. Because of his gentle heart and wise mind, my tribe knew he was a good guide for the times we faced.

"Why finish him on my own?" I asked Grandmother.

"Because you need to know you can."

On my own? Why would I ever need to harvest a buffalo on my own? My people always worked as a team. Six or seven women and children focused on one buffalo at a time. In a few hours, every usable part of the animal was detached from the carcass. Very little went to waste as creativity and necessity took over: Shoulder blades were carved into axe blades. Boiled hoofs were cooked down into a fine glue for feathering arrows. Grandmother made needles from tiny bones. Horns were later sculpted into ladles and spoons. Even my bull's tail would be turned into a switch for flies. The buffalo was a great brother on this earth. He gave us tipis, food, and sleeping robes. Even his droppings made compact and light fuel sources for our fires.

When Grandmother spoke, I listened intently because she was wise and knew the ways of our people. I suddenly regretted that I did not eat more before the hunt, because I was woozy and a little weak. Grandmother walked away.

A buffalo was quite different to butcher than an elk or a deer. Lighter game could be hoisted up on poles, but buffalo bulls weighed up to two thousand pounds and had to be butchered where they fell. First, I pulled the arrows from his hide—six arrows in total. One was mine, and the other five came from two different hunters: Run Along and Black Cub. I knew each hunter's unique design and the colors on his respective arrows. When the butchering was complete, I would return the arrows with the traditional choice cuts of meat to the other two hunters and share the rest with my village.[11]

I set the arrows aside and took my knife in my left hand, cutting through the tough hide from the bottom of the bull's rib cage down the centerline of the his belly. I reached inside his body cavity and moved the intestines to the side until I found his liver. My right hand found the back of it, and I pulled until the tension and weight caused me to pause. Because the liver was large and heavy, I sliced a large piece off from the rest and pulled it from the steamy carcass. Then I put my knife back inside against the attached arteries and severed the rest of the liver free from the carcass. After I released the organ from the belly, I raised the meat

51

above my head in thanks to the Great Provider for this gift of kinship. I brought the liver back down and took the largest bite I could manage. It was sweet and firm between my sharp teeth. The brown beast now soothed my voracious appetite as his blood trickled from the edges of my cracked lips.

The fuzziness in my brain and arms subsided. I reached in and freed the bowels from the cavity with my flint knife. I was especially careful to not puncture the long tubes because the odor would be recognized as far as the village on the ridge. The intestines were difficult to handle because they were heavy and slick; they weighed as much as a ten-year-old boy. As I scooped them out, they oozed over the side of the carcass and down to my feet like a pile of wet, dead rattlesnakes. Three skinny dogs from our village wandered down the hill, scavenging for scraps. The youngest of the three, a large puppy, playfully pulled the guts away, and then all three started playing tug-of-war.

"Get out of here!" I shouted as one of the dog's teeth broke through the bowel and sent a stench through the air. The dogs cowered and crept away.

I needed to gather mental focus and physical strength or this test would never end. I used my knife to slowly peel the shaggy brown hide away from the warm connective flesh. I worked carefully because the hide was extremely valuable. A thick matted coat with a downy layer at the base of the hide slowly dropped to the side, separating itself from the carcass it had shielded for four or five winters. I knew the hide was best suited for a bed cover or winter clothing. If our hunt had been in an earlier season, then the hide would have been tanned for a tipi covering or light-weight clothing. Late winter hunts produced our toughest bull hides, which were sometimes even suitable for body shields to ward off arrows of enemy tribes.

Once the hide was removed, I cut off the buffalo's front and back legs. Then I cut out the takoan, a sinew running the whole length of his back. This section contained a prized meat called tampco. I would offer this cut to one of hunters who initially brought down the bull; this was a small gift of thanks for the large gift before me.

I split the animal along one side of the backbone and cut the long piece into two. Then, with all my effort, I rolled the bull onto its other side and repeated the cut along the backbone with two more pieces. I prepared the quarters just as my people had done over and over again for hundreds of years. First, I saved larger fresh meat cuts for our immediate meals over the next few days. The rest of the flesh would be mixed with berries and dried to make pemmican. I sliced thin strips of meat as long as my leg and as wide as my torso. I would proudly present the meat to Grandmother. She would perfectly space the cuts on a drying rack, set high above the reach of our tribe's dogs. It usually took only three days of prairie winds to dry out the meat, which was cut up into papapuze and pemmican that stayed mold-free all winter.

While working, I had plenty of time to think of how I had been trained for different roles in my village. From a very young age, I was encouraged to run and run. My lungs burned as I made loops around our camp. Then Grandfather and Father taught me survival skills beyond those of any other boy of my age. When I was about eight years old, I began learning other tribal languages even though we already spoke a universal sign language. My family was blessed to be Miniconjou because our tribe had good values and strong family ties. Even as a young boy, I felt destined to be a warrior and then a leader of the Miniconjou. When Father told me to move to Standing Rock for schooling with Black Robe, my hopes of stepping into a warrior position had been dashed. Father insisted that this was an honor, yet deep in my heart, I felt terribly burdened. Now that I had returned to live among my people, my desire to become a warrior burned at my soul.

I took my hatchet and chopped rib bones from the buffalo. Later I would tie them into sled runners, though winter suddenly seemed far away. When I finished cutting away all of the meat, usable bones, and tendons from the second side, I grabbed the bull's legs and rolled him over again. The same process began all over again, as I methodically cut all the way down to the last bits of usable sinew.[12]

On a plateau slightly above the fallen buffalo, tripods of poles rose from the grass. The dust had settled. Bird Nest had collected sticks and prepared a fire, with Kola following close behind. She reached over and hugged him around the neck, like he was the best friend on earth. I missed Kola deeply. Nonetheless, I would never take him from Bird Nest. She was a different woman with him. She had someone to love again, and seemed invigorated by daily life.

Exhaustion overtook me, not from the warm, radiant sun, but from the amount of meat I cut from the carcass, slice by slice. In total, I harvested about the weight of two grown men. As much as I willed someone to offer help, another part of me wanted to prove to my people that I was able to complete what I started. Since I had left Black Robe, I desperately wanted to gain my people's respect.

My stomach growled incessantly. All my people had finished their buffalo harvests, ponies were tethered, and I could smell roasting buffalo ribs over many small campfires. The evening feast was enjoyed without me. Laughter and a sense of prosperity filled the orange sky as the sun disappeared, and dancing images appeared among the flickering flames. I kept working, carefully cutting out the sinews that had joined bone to muscle. Grandmother would use the sinew to replace my old bowstring so as to give my bow greater strength and tension. My arms were tired: I could hardly raise my knife. The western sky faded, and the eastern horizon darkened. Occasionally a village dog barked at my shadow in the moonlight.

Father finally came to my side. "My son, you have done the work of five today. Let the others help you finish. Come eat."

"Grandmother said this is the right thing to do. I need to finish on my own."

"Very well," he answered, not offering assistance. As he walked away, I realized that my future was no longer in my father's hands; he would not interfere with my decision-making. He was releasing me, to determine my path with the Creator.

55

CHAPTER 6

WHITE

DECEMBER 1875

MOVING WEST

"I APPEAL TO YOU AS A SOLDIER TO SPARE ME IN THE HUMILIATION OF SEEING MY REGIMENT MARCH TO MEET THE ENEMY AND I NOT SHARE ITS DANGERS." ~George Armstrong Custer

Conflict and anticipation churned in my mind during the month and a half since I learned of our move west; two negative issues weighed heavily on my heart. First, my parents decided to leave Miss Bee behind to care for Grandmother in New York City. I would make the trip without my best friend. Dad promised to send for both of them as soon as we were fully settled in Dakota Territory. Deep down, I knew Grandmother would never make the trip.

Second, I did not want to leave my school. The classes were quite challenging at Hunter Female High School because each girl was considered gifted. The school was located near the corner of Broadway and East Fourth Street above a saddle store. I walked to school alone, which was the only time in my day when I was unescorted. I usually kept to myself, remaining secluded in my own thoughts. Occasionally I smiled at a nonthreatening person crossing my path, just to see if the gesture was returned.

I studied the usual history, writing, and arithmetic. Plus, when I excelled in a science project, the headmaster allowed me to study anatomy with the students at the adjoining college. Whereas most girls hated school, it was my ticket to freedom. I was initially home-schooled by Mother. Dad watched my passion in science and math develop even though traditionally these were considered "boy studies." Mother and Grandmother were only concerned with etiquette, such as whether I learned to hold my silverware properly. Then, out of the clear blue sky, when I turned twelve, Dad quietly submitted my school application, and I was accepted. Mother said the tuition was a waste of money, but she did not resist because it gave her more time to focus on herself.

When I learned about Dad's assignment to Fort Randall, I asked the headmaster if I could conduct in-depth research into the history of Dakota Territory and the Sioux. He crossed his arms across his thick torso. After a moment, he said sternly, "Yes, Sara; but be careful with your heart. Only you know how much you can take."

I pulled books and newspaper articles from *The Times*; I read all I could get my hands on about the adventure before us. Plains history seemed less exciting than the current Wild West headlines.

The plains had been occupied by many groups of people for thousands of years. As far back as 1650, the Kiowa Indians lived on the plains. They used the land to farm and hunt buffalo. Beginning in the 1770s and 1780s, the Sioux Indians moved west, crossing the Missouri River. By the early 1800s, the Sioux had pushed out the other remaining tribes. They dominated the plains, claiming it as their sacred land. In the last twenty or thirty years, whites began to settle on the wide-open prairie. Recent immigrants and young adults with nothing to their name did not fear hard work and the desire for prosperity lured many west.

The US government made treaties with different groups of Indians, such as the Fort Laramie Treaty of 1851, which gave each tribe a designated area to live in. In the spring of 1858, the Sioux sent their leaders to the United States capital. The Sioux leaders were desperate for the money that our government promised, but the traders who were meant to act as middlemen between the government and the Sioux were not giving out the annuity payments as required in the treaties. Under pressure by the government, the Sioux signed two more treaties, selling more land. In the end, the United States paid next to nothing, and the Sioux Nation lost one million acres that its people had not ever improved into towns; they had only hunted and roamed from place to place. So the leaders of the United States created policies that instructed the Sioux to farm. Because the Sioux had less land, their hunting and fishing resources were limited, and their people were hungry.

In 1861, Dakota Territory was established, which seemed to nullify the 1851 Fort Laramie Treaty. The Indians tried to farm as instructed by the US government, but the great winter of 1862–1863 was one of starvation because their crops had failed. It was all a big mess. And then, ten years later, Custer discovered gold in the Black Hills, which sat in the middle of the treaty land. This discovery made matters much worse. As I voraciously read everything within my grasp, I became increasingly uneasy about the wheels that had been set in motion. We were rolling toward a hornet's nest.

About ten days after receiving his orders, Dad was encouraged by a letter from Fort Randall:

> Dear Major S. Taylor,
>
> It is with great relief to hear of your acceptance of duty to Fort Randall. I will have officer accommodations ready for your family as you will certainly be a blessing to our community. I do my best to make this a family community in the midst of uncertainty with the Indians. Your reputation stands for itself, and I hope you select the finest fifty men you know for this arduous assignment. Fifty men currently assigned to Fort Randall will be added to fill your company upon arrival. Have a safe journey, and we will expect you, on or before December 25, 1875.
>
> Lieutenant General Pinkney Lugenbeel
> First Infantry, United States Army[13]

I sat beside Dad and looked over the letter's precise cursive writing. My stomach growled for no explicable reason. I was completely full from our evening meal: pork and a huge pile of mashed potatoes, a bit of greens, and baked apples with brown sugar on top for dessert. Each day of the week had an assigned menu that never changed from week to week. I thought the routine was boring, but Mother demanded it. Ignoring my stomach, I focused on Dad, who scribbled names on a piece of scrap paper.

"Who is he?" I asked, peering at the list.

"Corporal Anderson."

"Why are you picking him?"

"Because he can trek through the woods without getting lost. His stellar reputation is well founded."

I looked at the next name on the list. "Who is he?"

"Sergeant Zito. I fought with him at Gettysburg."

"Why are you picking him?"

"Because he is a good solid man. He raises morale. He's smart. He will never let me down, no matter what I ask of him. Sara, you ask too many questions. Go to bed."

"But will he say yes?"

"I don't know, Sara. I sure hope so. Now go to bed."

By the next morning, Dad had fifty sealed envelopes personally addressed to the noteworthy men that he fought beside in the

Civil War. He sipped on a cup of coffee and thumbed through the envelopes, pondering which men would join him in the new assignment. Within a few weeks, Dad received thirty acceptance letters. Ten men did not reply, and six declined. The remaining four letters were returned unopened. Dad was out of time, and with frustration, he wrote the War Department, requesting that it assign the remaining twenty men. He specifically asked for men to be assigned based on their proven bravery and not by their rank.

A day before we left, Mother decided that our good-byes to Grandmother and Miss Bee would take place at home, to minimize an embarrassing social scene. Grandmother rode emotional waves, which rose high to a crest of hope for our future and then crashed back down to stoic resignation over our departure; this process was nauseating for me to observe. Mother was sailing on the same rough sea of drama.

That night I snuck into Miss Bee's bedroom. For hours we sat on her bed, cross-legged, whispering in the dark, saying all that needed to be said. We planned to stay connected through private letters. Miss Bee would collect the mail and filter out my letters before delivering the rest to Grandmother. I promised to write as simply as possible.

Our departure morning was tense, and Mother paced the floor, dressed in a fine, light-blue gown and matching wide-brimmed hat, which framed her corn-silk blonde tresses, hanging in columns down her neck. She completed her fashion statement with a pastel-printed velvet cape that seemed ostentatious to me.

While the hired carriage patiently waited in the street, Grandmother held back tears as we stood on the porch.

"Sara. Promise me, child. Curl your hair. Your tresses are hopeless, yet curl them anyway. Wear your corset. Chew your food in a delicate fashion. Lips sealed. Promise me," Grandmother demanded.

I looked at my feet. Since learning of our departure, Grandmother had begun to dye her curly hair with henna, which only accentuated her deep wrinkles. Not surprisingly, she adamantly claimed that her hair had never grayed and was not colored. I did not bother to remind her of the tight gray bun she had carried just weeks before. Her sense of humor was weaker than her vanity.

"Sara. Promise Grandmother," Mother insisted.

"I promise," I answered, in heartless compliance. We hugged stiffly. I turned to Miss Bee and hugged her tight. Miss Bee patted my back to break our embrace as Mother gave us a disapproving glance and headed for the carriage. Miss Bee winked and turned to gently guide my sobbing grandmother into the house.

Dad gracefully hoisted Mother through the carriage door, and I stepped up behind her. He followed us inside and wedged his muscular body between us. The dark-haired driver shut the coach door and jumped back to his seat, where he prompted the horses to move out. Our carriage bumped down the stone pavers. I looked back at our solid gray stone house, hoping for one more glimpse of Miss Bee. She had returned without Grandmother, and she lingered in the doorway, bravely waving until we rounded the corner and rolled out of sight.

We arrived at the railroad station an hour before our train was scheduled to depart.

"Just as I planned," Dad said exuberantly, glancing at his pocket watch before leaping down and offering his hand for guidance. Two men with carts unloaded our trunks, and Dad paid the carriage driver. The ticket counter separated the cashier from the travelers with a beautifully engraved sheet of thick glass. At the bottom of the window was an arched hole, only big enough to slide documents and money back and forth. Dad purchased fifty-three tickets to Yankton, Dakota Territory.

"Track three, girls," he said, turning from the ticket window. A hanging wooden sign with a "3" carved roughly into the plank directed us to the platform. The porters stacked our five huge trunks in a pile and rushed off as soon as Dad handed them a tip, respectfully concealed with a handshake. Wrapping his arms around each of our shoulders, Dad pulled us together for the first time in years—perhaps ever. After a moment or two, Mother squirmed away and rebalanced our tower of luggage. I looked to the opposite end of the platform. Only a few people milled about. Pigeons perched on the ornate roof, and their deposits left stains on the platform where we stood.

Mother nervously dug in her bag.

"What are you looking for?" I asked. She did not answer. Perhaps she was searching for courage.

"If you don't have it by now, darling, then it's too late anyway," Dad said. She continued on.

"Just leave it alone, Mother!" I finally whispered, so Dad would not hear. She glared at me.

As the time grew nearer, the air filled with an excitement similar to that of the busy morning market. Sometimes solo and sometimes in pairs, Dad's assigned men somehow found us among the bustling platform.

"Major Taylor?"

"Yes. And you are?" Dad shook each hand and made introductions between nearby men so they would not linger alone. It was easy to tell which men were part of his hand-selected recruits because the greeting was less formal; a symbolic handshake turned quickly into a robust hug that revealed an intense but unspoken history of respect and gratitude, of bonds forged on Civil War battlefields. And now there was an unknown history, still waiting to be written.

We grew into a small mob, but in our civilian clothing, we drew little attention from others who waited for the train. All of us were immersed in our own individual world, in our own separate pasts, joys, struggles, and dreams. I looked around at the relatives and friends who waited for final good-byes. The children did not seem to comprehend what they were losing, if only for just a few months. For the adults, light conversation did not mask the solemn magnitude of this last moment together. The men promised to write. They promised to send for their families once the West was "tamed" a bit. They promised to come home safe, just as many soldiers had wrongfully promised throughout the ages—a promise easily spoken, yet impossible for some to keep.

The men who were alone stood awkwardly to the side of the group and looked down at their feet, avoiding encroachment on the intimate moments of the others. One man stood out from the rest. He was taller than everyone else, but there was something else about him that caught my attention. Perhaps the oldest in the group, at about forty-five years old, he exuded confidence as he stood patiently with his gaze fixed upon the empty railroad track.

The train's metal-on-metal brakes screeched as it pulled into the station and lurched to a stop. I marveled at its mass and understood why it was called the iron horse. Couples embraced, women wept, children seemed numb, and babies cried. I could hardly wait to get started. The blue-uniformed conductor stood above us, at an open door, and hung on with one hand.

"Aaaall aboooooard!" he bellowed and began admitting passengers.

Our tickets showed that our group was assigned to cars four and five. Dad hollered above the commotion and gave instructions to the men. The unaccompanied soldiers were first to hurry up the train ladder.

"Pick whatever seats you want, girls!" Dad exclaimed.

I squirmed my way through some of the lingering families and climbed up the metal ladder. As I squeezed through the door of the train car, I was knocked to the floor by a heavy canvas bag hurled up to a soldier. When I toppled, I fell against the soldier, who attempted to catch the bag before my body deflected it. He apologized, asked if I was hurt, and pulled me to my feet. A trickle of blood came from an abrasion on my elbow. I told him that I was fine and hid my bleeding arm behind my back. Mother stepped up the ladder and into the car, still clutching her leather convenience bag, apparently worth a pound of gold.

"Dear me, Sara. Could you please act like a young lady? Excuse me, gentlemen, I am terribly embarrassed by my daughter."

Terribly embarrassed? What about asking if I was hurt? Why was it always about Mother?

I turned into the fourth rail car and nearly ran straight into the edge of an unlit potbellied stove. From the car's odor and the smoky film on the windows, I figured the stove burned coal. Wooden benches lined the edge of the car with dented, gilded shelving above. Other benches faced forward like church pews but attached to the scratched wooden floor with thick black bolts. Deeply worn red-velvet seat pads cushioned the benches.

The men flowed into the car and selected their seats, some plopping down gratefully after our lengthy wait on the platform. I quickly selected a window seat next to the black stove. Mother shook her head disapprovingly and told me it would be too hot once the stove was fired up. She pointed to a bench seat facing the front of the train. Once again, the decision was not ever mine to make. I squeezed in, taking the seat against the window.

From my vantage point, a beautiful sea of color swirled on the platform. I felt like I was peering into a kaleidoscope, as the beautiful hats and shimmering dresses danced in the early-winter sun. The women pulled perfectly pressed white hankies from their coat pockets and waved them over their heads, toward their men on the train. The tall man was the last to board. A whistled tune, filled with melancholy, streamed from his lips as he chose an aisle seat a few rows from Mother and me. The train slowly pulled away from the platform. I continued gazing out my window to find the tear-stained faces blurring into a white wave of hankies and broken hearts.

After about half an hour, from the end of our train compartment, a pear-shaped conductor appeared. He was dressed in a blue uniform with buttonholes stretched to their limits, and a billed cap was barely secured on his head. He waddled down the middle aisle of our swaying coach and called out, "Tickets, please."

All eyes turned to Dad, who stood up, retrieved the tickets from his coat pocket, and handed them to the conductor.

"Ahhh. Yankton, huh? Dakota Territory. You'll all be scalped!" the conductor laughed robustly above the clanking train. Nobody smiled. He went on, oblivious to the growing disdain throughout the train car: "If the Injuns don't get'cha, then the mosquitos and grasshoppers will eat'cha alive anyway!"

Dad continued to stand and glared directly at the conductor until the man worked his way through the car and disappeared into the next. When he was out of sight, Dad called out, "Gentlemen, thank you for accepting this assignment. We will trust in our God, our good judgment, our teamwork, and our aim."

The men politely laughed, some more than others, releasing the tension around us. Dad had a lighthearted voice but somehow maintained a commanding presence. He stood with his right hand calmly at his side and his left hand against the back of a bench seat, keeping balanced as the train bumped along the track. His dark brown eyes shimmered in the light that reflected through the train windows. To his silent dismay, Dad's brown hair was receding a bit and prematurely graying. I once asked Dad when he started to turn gray, and he responded, "At Gettysburg, Sara. The first day at Gettysburg." I secretly wished for more details.

Dad went on, gesturing toward Mother and me, sitting on the bench across from where he stood, "For those of you who did not have the opportunity to meet my wife, Mrs. Taylor, and my daughter, Sara, they are accompanying us on this assignment."

I could hear a few men mumble, as if we were additional burdens they had not agreed to carry.

"My wife is quite a seamstress, and you will find Sara's cooking to be a blessing."

I blushed, which I seemed to be doing more and more lately.

After Dad's briefing about what our next few days would entail, he sat down. Most men stared out the window to glimpse my familiar city turning into dirty factories. Then small New Jersey towns appeared between brown orchards and fields. The first leg of our journey, from New York City to Sioux City, Iowa, would take four or five days. Traveling from Sioux City to Yankton, the capital of Dakota Territory, would take another day. Then, from Yankton, we would either take a steamboat or a wagon to Fort Randall.

Mother said she was not feeling well due to the swaying motion of the train. Dad moved her to the end of the coach, where a full empty bench seat awaited—the seat that I had originally selected. She did not complain as Dad stretched out a few blankets on top of the stained seat padding. He laid my mother down, and, like a little girl, she curled her legs up and braced them against the end of the bench seat. Dad wrapped the hanging ends of the blankets up over Mother, and she closed her eyes.

Dad was a man of stability. He took the small things of life in stride. He cared for Mother without complaint. He fought in the Civil War with no lingering resentment. I never saw him wrestle with the complications in his life because he was confident of where he fit into the greater scheme of things. Unlike Mother, he did not focus on climbing the military mountain of ranks and honors. He just wanted to be a good leader—a family leader, a military leader. With this focus came an innate loyalty from his soldiers. When Dad spoke, they listened. When he gave orders, they obeyed.

I turned back to the window with a new sense of independence, because Mother was out of view. Reaching for the white lace hankie in my pocket, I tried to wipe the grime away from the inside of my window, because I didn't want to miss a thing. As I

69

wiped, the window became smeared in soot-filled streaks. The tall man approached with a damp rag in his hand.

"No use soiling your hankie. Here, let's use my boot cleaning rag for the job."

Carefully keeping his distance, he reached across me and wiped the window. A pewter medal slipped from the collar of his shirt, swinging on a silver chain in front of my face. Slightly off-rhythm with the train's rocking against the tracks, the undulating medal's image came into focus just inches from my eyes: an angel with a sword stood victoriously over a dragon that represented all the evil in the world.

"Permit me to introduce myself. My name is Sergeant Thomas Zito. And you, young lady, are Miss Sara," he said with a smile. A faint scent of musk cologne lingered near his clean-shaven face and oiled-back, thinning, dark hair.

"Just Sara, thank you, sir."

"Well, well. Then let's skip the formalities, shall we? I've heard great things about you, Sara. Your dad never stops."

I dropped my head, a bit embarrassed but also in disbelief. I didn't think Dad really noticed much about me.

"What do you think about leaving New York behind?" Sergeant Zito asked.

"I'm not sure. It's hard to leave my studies."

"What class is hardest to leave?"

"Anatomy. Medicine. I might want to be a nurse."

"Why not a doctor? Dakota Territory needs doctors."

"Oh, gosh, nursing is good enough. Mother thinks I should just settle on being a wife."

"Oh, I see." He thought for a moment, holding back a smirk. "Well, choosing to be a wife can be a good thing, Sara. But keep in mind, it needs to be for the right reasons. Whatever you choose in life, well, those choices need to be for the right reasons."

I glanced past Sergeant Zito to Dad, who sat across the aisle, watching us and grinning.

"Now, let's discuss your position as head chef at Fort Randall," Sergeant Zito said.

"Oh, no. I like to bake, but not for the whole regiment," I exclaimed. "Aren't there over three hundred men there?"

"I'm just teasing you, Sara. What's your specialty?"

I thought for a moment, yet nothing came to mind. Maybe baked bread, maybe sugar cookies.

"I'm not sure. I never really thought about it."

"Hmm," Sergeant Zito squinted like he had just tasted something bitter. "Maybe you should think about it." He stood up and wandered off to chat with a group of men who sat a few rows away. I looked over at Dad, who smiled at me. He was right; Sergeant Zito's positive attitude was infectious. I remembered Dad's words describing Sergeant Zito. "He is a good solid man.

He raises morale. He's smart. He will never let me down." I turned back to my smear-free window.

The gentle wooded hills of New Jersey turned into the forested mountain ranges of Pennsylvania. Hour after hour, interesting things continued to roll past my window. In the middle of the day, around one o'clock, the train lost momentum, and well-seasoned travelers anticipated the train's arrival at a station for a long-awaited break. Passengers quickly pulled on coats and grabbed their satchels before stepping to the small wooden platform affixed to the stone station. A line developed quickly, as passengers rudely shouldered into position at the food line, which wrapped from the edge of the train depot to a small wooden shack with smoke pouring from the chimney.

The primitive facilities were located at the other end of the platform. I rushed down the planked landing and waited in line behind ten other women. Because I was upwind from the outhouse, I was able to smell the musty fallen leaves of autumn. Just as it became my turn, the train whistle blew for a departure warning.

Fully committed, I finished my business as quickly as possible, which was a struggle, given my skirt layers. Then I rushed out, slamming the weak-hinged door behind me. I ran back to the train, nearly tripping over a mangy dog, who was begging for a portion of a little boy's sandwich. I climbed into the closest car, fearing the train would pull away without me—a good decision since the train began moving just seconds later. I walked through each car and stepped across to the next with trepidation. The rail track blurred beneath me and I imagined losing my balance and tumbling to a gruesome death. Finally, I reached our car.

"Where have you been, child?" Mother asked in a forced desperate tone, but this was merely a show for the soldiers. Her paper-thin concern was verified when she quickly added, "Did you buy me a sandwich?"

"Mother, I was using the facilities. There was a long line. What were you doing during the break?"

"Resting."

"Well, I guess we'll just wait till tonight to eat."

Just then, Dad came into our car from further back on the train. His arm was wrapped around a brown paper bag. He reached into the bag and handed each of us a sandwich and apple. Dad slipped me an additional small brown paper bag, about the size of my palm, and whispered, "It's for later, Sara."

I unrolled the top and peered inside. Eight lemon drops stared back at me. Each was perfectly formed and coated in a thick layer of sugar.

Mother nosed in, saying, "Not until after your sandwich, young lady. It will ruin your appetite." She turned to Dad, and they frowned at each other. "It's just not healthy," she continued on, draining all joy from the moment.

"Just relax," Dad retorted, "Everything is fine. We are all fine."

Was everything fine? Sometimes I wondered. Depending on the time of day, I viewed my own face reflected semi-transparently in the glass, with the terrain sliding through my image. If the lighting was just right, I saw unfamiliar features, older and a bit more delicate than I had expected; dare I even think I might be pretty? In contrast, though the thought made me feel a bit guilty, I watched Mother's elegance wane as we moved west. As she was no longer able to maintain perfectly applied makeup and coiffed hair, deep wrinkles became apparent in her face. She was not adjusting well; she was always trying to primp in her tiny powder compact mirror.

Train car number three was supposed to be our sleeper car. With bunks stacked three high, each cabin accommodated six sleepers. The bunks had short curtains to pull across for privacy, but the car was especially cold. I chose to lay across a seat near the potbellied stove in car four. Each morning when I awoke and looked out my window, fewer homes, cliffs, and valleys filled the landscape. By the time we rolled into Illinois, the terrain was nearly flat. We changed trains in Chicago and headed for Sioux City. Eating stations became crude shacks in the middle of nowhere, where the train stopped for ten minutes. Most of the shacks were operated by first-generation settlers. The food was tasty, though the selection was limited at best and overpriced at worst. Roasted meat and baked potatoes were the mainstay. After a filling meal, I mistakenly rolled my eyes and yawned in Mother's direction.

"Boredom is a sign of a slow mind. Find something to do. Write a letter to Grandmother," Mother said. She reached into her leather satchel and retrieved a lovely writing pad, pencil, and envelope. "Use the pencil. The pen is too messy on this horrid train." So I wrote, and when Mother dozed, I reached into her bag for another envelope.

The first page on the writing pad was to Grandmother. Concealed underneath, on the next page, was my letter to Miss Bee:

> Dear Miss Bee,
>
> How are you? The trip is good. The soldiers seem nice enough. Mother is on edge. Can you send me a recipe for dessert bread? One of Dad's men, Sergeant Zito, wants to try it. I wish I had taken it more seriously when you were teaching me. I miss you.
>
> Your friend,
>
> Sara

I placed the sealed envelope in my pocket and then started a new letter to Grandmother, which I loaded with impersonal pleasantries.

Sergeant Zito was writing another letter. His penmanship must have been as horrendous as mine because the train jostled us back and forth to the point of making my ribs and neck hurt. Maybe he wrote to a kind woman who overlooked the messy letter as she imagined his deep voice almost whispering his words.

The other men seemed restless. Dad wandered and spoke of western history. Most men paid partial attention, but some listened intently. I followed Dad, intrigued by his slightly varied versions of history.

"It has been going on for years. The Sioux signed the Laramie Treaty in 1851. Things seemed okay for a while, but you can't guess what they'll do now. Just look at the Dakota War of 1862. One day, the Sioux were living as friendly neighbors to the Minnesota settlers. The next day, Chief Little Crow and his people rose up and murdered hundreds of settlers—unarmed men; women, and children."

"There must be a reason," I blurted.

"Oh, there's a reason, all right. They regretted selling their land. They felt trapped. Then their crop failed, and their people nearly starved. They blamed us because we didn't give them an annuity payment of goods and cash like we promised."

"Why not? A deal is a deal, right?" a young soldier asked.

"Well, it's complicated, because Congress didn't appropriate the money. Then the Treasury Department argued about whether to pay the seventy-one thousand dollars in paper currency or in gold. The Indians grew more impatient, drank whiskey, and killed the settlers."

A soldier who had been assigned by the War Department chimed in, "That was then. This is now. The Black Hills are different. We just want to seek our fortunes. Who can blame us?"

I wondered if he would be our first deserter. Dad continued, "It's true, we offered to buy the Black Hills from the Indians because we can't keep the settlers from the gold. They keep sneaking in."

"Well, why not? If there's gold and the savages ain't really using the Black Hills, then what's the harm?" questioned the soldier.

Dad answered, "Well, it's technically breaking our promise. The Sioux held a Grand Council near the Red Cloud Agency in September. The Sioux refused to negotiate with us. They aren't being reasonable. Conflict is in the air."

Mother appeared and tapped Dad's shoulder. "Young ears do not need to be troubled by adult issues," she said condescendingly.

"With all due respect, dear, Sara needs to listen," Dad retorted. "She deserves to know."

I wanted to hug him, but Mother would be furious if I did. Couldn't she see that I had the capacity to process the sometimes gruesome facts of history? I heard Dad's protective message loud and clear. Do not trust the Indians. Never. Never ever.

CHAPTER 7

WHITE

SIOUX CITY DOCTOR

"MY OWN RELIGION HAS BEEN TO DO ALL THE GOOD I COULD TO MY FELLOW MEN, AND AS LITTLE HARM AS POSSIBLE." ~William W. Mayo

The farther west we traveled, the more removed Mother became. I sat with her, looking out the window, with little to say. At first I thought she was bored by the lack of scenery, the wide expanse of country, which had fewer and fewer trees as we progressed. Then I realized it might be more. She seemed more and more worn out, and we weren't even to Fort Randall yet. Mother coughed and coughed, blaming it on the coal stove. Her eyes drooped, and she slept more than ever. I did my best to keep her covered by her blanket, and I kept occupied by writing to Miss Bee and dozing.

"Wake up, Sara. We are here," Dad said, rubbing my shoulder and pulling me from a vivid dream in which Miss Bee and I lived in a tiny cabin somewhere in the middle of nowhere.

"Where's here?"

"Sioux City, Iowa."

I sat up with a sense of vertigo. I looked out the window to regain my balance. The station had a more substantial feel than the others due to its sandstone buildings and crowds of quick-paced women and men with unknown agendas.

"We need to take your mother to a doctor. She is not feeling well," Dad said.

We walked through the streets, and Dad asked people along the way where we could find a physician. Soon we received a detailed response: "Two blocks down, take a left, then you'll see the place on your right. Doctor Harris. He's very busy, maybe out to a homestead with a sick baby. A friend of his is in town visiting with his son. He's a doctor, I think. Maybe he can help."

Dad nodded, thanked the man, and moved ahead with Mother leaning on his arm. I followed a few paces behind. Our feet sounded like competing drums in a marching band, as the boardwalk echoed beneath us.

Above the doctor's office door was an opaque transom window with the words "Doctor R. Harris, Physician" scripted in black, red, and gold. The exterior door was made of thick wood, and a cowbell dangled from a brown leather strap. We squeezed inside the tiny foyer, and Dad knocked on the examining room door. A boy, about my age, popped his head and one shoulder out from behind the cracked door.

"Can I help you?"

"Yes, my wife is not feeling well, and I was wondering if the doctor could take a look."

"Doctor Harris is out on a house call. Don't know when he'll be back. My dad's a doctor, but he's busy sewing up a man whose wagon rolled over on him. Can you wait a moment?"

Dad nodded, and the boy disappeared. We heard the muffled discussion from behind the foyer door. Finally, a man in a bloodstained, white cotton coat appeared.

"How may I help you?" he asked.

Dad introduced us, and the man offered his own name, Doctor Mayo. Dad whispered his request and out of a sense of mercy or indifference—I wasn't sure which—the doctor agreed to examine Mother.

"I apologize, not much space in here, but please, come in. Just finishing up with a poor fellow. I'll take a look at your wife in a moment. I'm visiting Doctor Harris for a couple days. We went to medical school together. A couple fellas brought this man in a bit ago and Doctor Harris is away on a house call."

We followed the doctor into the disinfected room. A cabinet, a tray on wheels, and an examination table were the only pieces of furniture. The boy stood on one side of the table. He smiled politely. We stood against the back wall. Mother hung onto Dad's arm and closed her eyes, as if this would protect her other senses from hearing and smelling the intense situation before us.

"This is my son, William," Doctor Mayo said, gesturing toward the boy. "He's only fifteen, but he helps out in a bind." Doctor Mayo's eyes did not stray from the man on the table, who was draped in a clean white sheet. Below the sheet, a trickle of blood dripped from the edge of the table. "A complicated case we have here."

William almost bowed toward me. Despite the slight grin on his face, he seemed sagacious beyond his years. He wore a blue muslin shirt, cut just below his hip. It had a plain collar and full sleeves. The seam across his upper chest let gathered pleats fall below, allowing a sort of freedom that I only dreamed of.

His dad seemed to sense his son's distraction with me and barked out orders to the boy. William did exactly as he was told.

"William, find the cotton gauze. Pull over the bowl of water. Where's the suture thread?"

The boy quickly dug through the white cabinet to locate what his dad requested.

"This may be too much for a young lady to see," Doctor Mayo warned.

"I'm okay. Please. I'm okay," I answered.

"Well, well. You may have a future nurse on your hands," Doctor Mayo said, aiming the comment at my parents.

"Or a doctor," William chimed in. I took one step closer.

The man's shirt had been cut off and was lying in a heap on the floor. He was conscious, yet in another world. A bottle of laudanum sat on the tray with other surgical instruments. Scrapes and a few deep cuts needed eventual attention. However, Doctor Mayo's focus was on the man's left upper arm bone, which had been snapped in half. The bottom bone protruded from his bruised and bleeding flesh.

"This is called a compound fracture. Of the humerus bone." *It didn't seem very humorous to the poor man*, I thought. I watched as the surgeon pulled on the man's lower arm until the bone disappeared back where it belonged. The man screamed in anguish and then passed out, mentally yielding to the pain that his body was unable to face. Mother followed his example, with added drama as her knees buckled, and she crumbled to the floor. Dad guided her down gracefully, and he sat beside her, resting her head onto his shoulder. I ignored Mother and turned back to the procedure.

"We aren't done quite yet," Doctor Mayo whispered under his breath. "Thank you, Lord, for taking his pain for the moment. Now, William, watch me as I pull again to make sure the ends of the bones are back together. They'll need to stay tight to heal or he'll never use his arm again."

I felt sick to my stomach. Doctor Mayo did what he had described, and once he felt confident the bones were properly set, he pulled a needle off the tray and stitched up the man's wounds. The more I saw the needle threading in and out of oozy flesh, the sicker I became. I fought tunnel vision, but I was not winning the battle. I looked away and took deep breaths. Perhaps if I focused on William. He was busy anticipating his father's needs, yet he still found time to glance at me. William was neither pale nor woozy. He was a very brave fifteen-year-old. I turned back to the surgery but wobbled on my feet.

"William, it looks like the young lady needs some fresh air. I have this covered. Go ahead, take her outside."

William steadied me by holding my forearm with one hand and my shoulder with the other. I leaned heavily on him as we moved outside and sat down on the edge of the boardwalk. I held my head low and the darkness subsided.

"Just keep breathing," William instructed. "What is your name, anyway? I did not catch it."

"Sara. Sara Taylor. I feel so stupid."

"Don't. It just takes a while to get used to."

"How long?"

"It just depends on where you let your mind go."

"What do you mean?"

"Well, this is what I do when I see things that make me feel faint. I tell myself, 'This is not about me. This is not about me. It's about

83

helping this person. My feelings don't matter right now.' It usually works."

"Good to know, but I hope I don't have to test your theory anytime soon."

William smiled. "Where are you heading?"

"Fort Randall."

"Ah. Dakota Territory."

"Will that man make it?" I asked, taking another deep breath.

"Probably, unless infection sets in. Compound fractures are really bad. If you don't get them set fast, it's not good. At least he has a chance, but when he realizes his wife and sons were crushed to death by the wagon, then he may give up his fight anyway."

"Oh, my gosh. I had no idea."

"Yep, really sad. He lost it all. Who knows if he'll fight to survive or just give up?"

I sat up a bit, feeling better from the fresh air. Across the street I saw Sergeant Zito stepping into the general store.

"Let's go to the store," I suggested.

"I'd love to, Sara, but I need to go back in and help Dad. It's hard to work in another doctor's office. Plus, we leave in the morning."

"Where are you going?"

"Back home, to Minnesota."

"Okay. I may see you in a few minutes. But either way, thank you, William Mayo."[14]

"It was my pleasure, Sara Taylor," he replied, and he tipped his head, nodding once with a heart-melting grin.

As I crossed the street, I dodged two perfectly matched palomino horses pulling a black shiny wagon. A handsomely dressed man who was leaving the mercantile held the door open as I entered. His eyes lingered longer than what I felt was appropriate. I slipped inside and found a fascinating assortment of items on shelves and in display cases: fabric, containers full of candy, tools, children's toys, and men's clothing. Over to the left side of the store was a display case full of handguns. Behind the case stood a fat man with light brown, greasy hair, slicked back from his large forehead. A black bowtie held up a starched white shirt, which was mostly concealed by a finely tailored black suit. His jacket's breast pocket was stretched tight, holding three cigars. As he reached into the cabinet, the cigars tried to escape, but he instinctively pushed them back into place. Leaning over the gun case was Sergeant Zito.

"Well, well, a Colt … what a fine gun, but I could have paid five dollars for the same thing in New York."

"Last I checked, you ain't in New York no more. If you're headin' to the territory, best Christmas present you could buy yourself. Eight dollars ain't too pricey. You'll pay twenty when you're being chased by a bunch of crazy injuns."

I walked over to the case and stared at the shiny guns. Sergeant Zito turned to me. His broad shoulders and height only accounted for part of his remarkability. I was constantly pulled to his sense of humor, and his self-reliance permeated the air around him.

"What do you think, Miss Sara; you think I need a seven-shot revolver?"

"How good of a shot are you?" I smirked.

Sergeant Zito chuckled.

"Do you know where to mail this, Sergeant Zito?" I asked, pulling the letter out of my dress pocket. "You seem to always write letters."

"I do. Letters give me hope, Sara," he answered. After a moment of thought, he said, "I'll mail it for you. I'm heading that way now."

I handed him my letter and then wandered around the store. A few moments later, I saw my parents through the store window and I stepped outside.

"What did you find out?" I asked.

"Nothing to worry about, Sara, just a little cold," Mother said; clearly, this was another one of her manipulations of the truth.

Dad gave me his "don't push the issue" look. "Let's go take your medicine," he said, and, holding Mother's arm, he guided her down the boardwalk. I followed behind, realizing how my parents' relationship was full of business and empty of passion. They were not friends. Indeed, they never spoke negatively about the other, but they never laughed together either. It was simply a strained marriage.

We walked back to the train station. Dad's men were propped up against their bags, which lined the sandstone walls. We patiently waited for our next train to Yankton, the capital of Dakota Territory. As we grinded west, occasional tar-paper shacks or sod houses dotted the distant landscape. Usually positioned just below a ridge, the front door of each house faced southwest. Optimistic settlers had planted small trees behind their homes, hoping for future windbreaks. A handsome young man on horseback appeared, riding solo along the plains. I raised my hand and waved. He smiled and waved back. Where was he headed? Where had he been? I surveyed my reflection in the window and wondered what he saw.

Yankton was known as the end of the line, but I knew nothing else of the town. After we pulled into the rail station, I saw only a few pine houses that lined a deeply rutted dirt road. Dad told us to wait on the train while he organized the men. Mother eagerly collected our belongings and told me to look under each seat for stray items. When Dad finally climbed back on board, he explained that our trunks would be left overnight in storage at the station.

"The river isn't frozen, so in the morning, we'll take a steamboat to the fort," Dad said. "Saves us from the bumpy wagon ride."

CHAPTER 8

WHITE

YANKTON, DAKOTA TERRITORY

"PERSEVERANCE IS NOT A LONG RACE; IT IS MANY SHORT RACES ONE AFTER THE OTHER."
~Walter Elliot

"Finally, some fresh air. Okay, girls, let's walk and get rid of our sea legs," Dad said, while shaking his stiff legs on the wooden-planked platform.

"More like train legs," I said. Dad laughed.

"You are a funny young lady, Sara," He said. Mother rolled her eyes at us.

The air was as cold as New York's coldest day of the year, and my hands instinctively dove into my coat pockets. I raised my shoulders to my ears to stop the air from seeping down the back of my neck. Mother clasped Dad's arm when she lost her balance walking along the railroad platform. I felt a little queasy myself, but I was plenty distracted by the town in front of us. We paused at the front of the train station. Only one direction seemed reasonable because we stood at the end of the street.

The river nearly touched the train depot, and I saw smoke curling from a steamboat's tall stacks. We walked up the street, past sheds and a few chalkstone buildings. As Dad led the way, with Mother on his arm, we passed a livery stable entrance. I peeked in at the tired horses, tied in rows and resting from their day's journey. A small boy rushed out of the entrance with a shovel full of steaming manure. He stepped directly in front of me without looking up and rounded the stone building's corner toward the alley. We continued on and crossed another street. Dad nearly lifted Mother up two steps to a wooden boardwalk. Most storefronts had awnings overhead with signs flapping in the sharp wind.

"Well, here we are," Dad said, as he stopped beneath a "Hotel" sign. Mother cupped her hands against her temples and peered through the window in disbelief. A painted sign that was posted next to the door stated in bright red letters, "Door is locked from 2 a.m. to 5 a.m. No excuses. No exceptions."

"Looks more like a barn than a hotel," she commented sarcastically.

"Well, we will be sleeping in a barn, then. It's the only hotel in town," Dad chuckled, trying to ease the stress. He pushed open the large wooden door with a thick glass panel. Our steps crunched against the sawdust-covered lobby floor as we approached the clerk. He stood behind a stained marble countertop which seemed to guard a wall lined with large room keys, each with a specific room number tab attached. Dad asked for two adjoining rooms for one night. The man explained that only one room remained since Dad's soldiers had beat us to the hotel.

Dad shrugged, "Well, one is better than none!"

After a short discussion, the man handed Dad a pen and directed him to sign the register. Then he dropped a worn brass key with an engraved "10" into Dad's hand.

"Up the stairs and to the left," the man said.

Dad reached over and took Mother's elbow, leading her to the stairway. She pulled from Dad's hold and, with an air of protest, grabbed the railing and started to climb. Before she reached the second floor, she wavered and nearly collapsed. Right behind her, as if he had already anticipated the potential problem, Dad dropped the key and our bags in order to balance her weak frame. I picked up behind them, slid past, took a left at the top of the flight, and walked down the hall until I saw "10" on a door. The key slid into the worn lock with ease. Our room was unpainted with rough boards as walls. Two wooden beds were separated by a narrow aisle. At the foot of each bed was a washstand with a ceramic pitcher, washbowl, bar of soap, washcloth, and towel.

Dad pulled back the quilt from one bed and inspected it for bedbugs.

"Looks fine," Dad said, as he settled Mother underneath the sheet. I dampened a washcloth and wiped Mother's face and neck. Then I offered to go downstairs and order a cup of tea to soothe her stomach. Dad handed me a dime. He did not know that Grandmother had slipped five dollars in my skirt pocket on the day we left New York.

Once in the lobby, I inquired about a cup of tea. The man behind the counter said I wasn't in London, and he did not have anything of the sort available, but I could find a strong cup of coffee a few doors down the street. I contemplated leaving the hotel without permission and decided Mother would never know and Dad wouldn't care.

It was nearly dark. Bundled-up men still scurried along the street, purchasing items for their new lives out west. Most seemed rough because of the ragged clothes they were wearing; perhaps they were bound for the Black Hills as gold prospectors. Men outnumbered women at least ten to one. I doubted any woman remained unmarried unless it was her pure choice to go it alone. I followed the boardwalk down a few storefronts until I saw the sign "Mercantile" overhead.

Before stepping inside, I noticed a saloon, with red swinging doors at the entrance, across the street. I sensed someone looking at me; my eyes glanced to the second floor, where a woman peered from the window like a caged animal who had lost all hope. I quickly stepped inside the mercantile and was greeted by a man dressed in a freshly pressed suit. He was apparently living well from store profits. The man stood about my height. His lips were concealed by a slick mustache that turned down on the ends, reaching for his cleft chin. I asked the man about a cup of coffee, and over the man's shoulder, I caught a glimpse of Sergeant Zito at the post office window in the back corner of the mercantile.

"I'm happy to sell you a cup of coffee, but where is your cup?" the man asked.

I had not thought about supplying a container.

"I'd like to buy a canteen for the coffee," I said quickly, with fabricated confidence. "Will you show me to the canteens?"

The man walked me to a shelf, which was home to eight canteens. They seemed identical; each was made of thin steel with an attached cork. I pointed toward one as I used to do at the New York market. The man took it off the shelf, filled it from a steaming coffee pot, and said he would only charge me for the canteen.

"Thank you, I appreciate it," I said.

"Five dollars, please, young lady," he said quietly.

"Excuse me?" I asked. Five dollars seemed greatly overpriced, even with complementary coffee.

"Five dollars. Like it or leave it."

Just then, Sergeant Zito appeared beside me and said, "Excuse me, sir. I couldn't help but overhear your conversation. I believe you just sold me an identical canteen for one dollar. You must have been mistaken when you said five dollars because I'm certain a man of your integrity would not take advantage of a young woman."

The man stared up at Sergeant Zito. Then he gazed back at me.

"Oh, of course, did I say five dollars? I certainly meant one dollar. Sometime I just get my numbers mixed up. My mind isn't quite as sharp as it used to be."

Sergeant Zito gave the man a look of disgust, stood beside me as the transaction was completed, and then walked me back to the hotel. Mother complained as she gulped the lukewarm coffee. She refused to walk to the restaurant that stood just across the street, beside the saloon.

Dad and I stepped out into the frigid air and started down the boardwalk. He looped my hand through his bent arm just as he did with Mother. I held on tight and realized we had not been alone since New York City. I missed our walks to the market; I missed our lighthearted conversations. As we crossed the street, both of us glanced up to the same window from which the woman had peered earlier. A red light shown in the room, but the woman was gone.

Dad opened the restaurant door, and he stepped in behind me. Almost every seat was filled with hungry travelers and local bachelors looking for a good meal. I noticed two tables full of Dad's men. Nobody looked up. With heads held low, they shoveled their meals into their mouths. The men who were finished eating puffed from the ends of thick cigars. We sat ourselves at the last available table, and the waiter approached. Dad ordered himself a coffee and a hot tea "for the young lady." The waiter was the thinnest man that I had ever seen. Perhaps he was ill, because not an ounce of fat padded his body. His face was hollow, with cheekbones projecting outward, against wrinkled skin. The man smiled and disappeared after leaving a sheet of paper with the meal of the day: pan-fried beef, roasted potatoes, greens, and hot coffee.

"What's greens?" I asked.

"I don't know, but it has to be better than the blues!" Dad answered. He laughed and then fell silent, looking down at his coffee cup. I stared at the faded floral wallpaper on the far wall, which was torn in some places, probably from chairbacks hitting it or troubled men picking at it.

"What's going on with Mother? I know something's not right."

"Oh, Sara. Doctor Mayo found nothing. Maybe she's just a bit down. Maybe it's something more. I really don't know what else can be done. Maybe I should have left her in New York."

"Don't say that, Dad. It will be okay. She's bound to pull out of it, isn't she?"

"I hope so," Dad answered. "Maybe she'll settle in fine at Fort Randall. We just need to get her there. If you don't mind, Sara, I'll be up before dawn, to move soldiers and gear to the ferry. Can you handle Mother in the morning, and bring her down to the dock by half past seven or eight at the latest?"

Suddenly I felt like Mother's parent. Who was the child in this family, anyway? I wondered if more and more responsibility would be heaped upon me if Mother didn't snap out of whatever troubled her.

"Of course," I answered.

We ate our meal quickly, partly due to the disgusting smoked-filled room. Still, I could have tolerated the smoke if I hadn't felt the obligation of returning to Mother. The waiter knew all too well how to pack up a dinner for an ailing loved one in a hotel room. Dad paid our bill, and we were on our way.

Late that night, through the single-paned window of our room, I heard a group of men singing a song with the words all mushed together. They banged on the hotel's front door, boisterously demanding entry, while ignoring the posted sign. I sat up in my bed and tried to see through the thick frost caked on inside of the windowpane. With my nightgown sleeve, I scratched a peephole through the frost and peered out, immediately recognizing ten or twelve of Dad's men. None were from his hand-selected cadre. Some were arm in arm, wavering in the light cast from the hotel's lobby window. They knocked persistently at the front door, but the owner did not come.

By the time the drunk men hit their fourth slurred rendition of the "Battle Cry of Freedom," Dad finally whispered, "Go back to bed, Sara. Leave it alone."

"The door is locked. Should I let them in?"

"No, just go back to bed."

"Where have they been?"

"In the saloon. Go back to sleep," Dad whispered.

I couldn't resist one more peek out the window. The men staggered down the street toward the ferry dock. I dropped back on my bed and fell asleep.

The next morning Mother moaned as I urged her from bed. We needed to clean up. I grabbed our towels and soap, toothbrushes, hairbrush, and Mother's makeup. We layered on our undergarments, corsets, skirts, and blouses before sneaking down to the women's bathroom at the end of the hallway. A lady was already waiting for her turn in the water closet.

"Good morning," she politely said as she turned toward us and then looked away. The woman wore the trousers of a man, baggy-legged and made of thick canvas. The bottoms of her heavily frayed pant legs drug on the floor. She wore a soiled blouse with a tattered red cotton scarf knotted around her neck. If not for the faint outline of her breasts, she would have resembled a man. Standing in line to wait for a privy was awkward, and I attempted conversation with the odd woman.

"Are you heading west, ma'am?" I asked.

The woman chuckled. "I *am* the west!" she exclaimed. Her face was weathered, and her clothes carried a layer of body odor. Mother kicked my foot to silence me.

"Are *you* heading west?" the woman asked in return.

"Yep. Heading to Fort Randall," I answered.

"*Yes*, Sara, not *yep*," Mother corrected me. "I will have none of the frontier talk coming from my daughter's lips."

The woman gave me a look that immediately reminded me of Miss Bee. Then she said, "Well, tell the boys hello for me."

"The boys?" I asked.

"The boys, the boys at Fort Randall."

"And what is your name?" I asked.

"Just tell them Calamity. They will know."

I did not fully understand, but I politely smiled and nodded. Then she continued, "You'll need to forget the corsets. You aren't East Coast ladies anymore."

I smiled. Mother frowned.

After cleaning up, I told Mother that we needed to hurry to the ferry dock. She refused to leave the hotel without Dad and insisted on a gentleman escort. After half an hour of trying to persuade her that Dad had asked us to walk the short distance alone, I lost my patience.

"Time is running short, Mother. We need to go or we will miss the ferry."

"Maybe that wouldn't be such a bad thing," Mother said under her breath as she used my arm for support, and we started toward the ferry. I balanced her weight on one side, while I carried the bag over my other shoulder.

As we approached, Dad stood with Sergeant Zito, and the rest of the men were gathered in a nearby cluster. I heard Dad tell

Sergeant Zito, "We need to keep them from the liquor. I was afraid of this, the lack of character; quite disappointing."

"Guess it's better to know now, rather than later," Sergeant Zito commented.

Dad turned sharply toward us and then softened. He apologized for not being available to escort us to the ferry. "I have been busy rounding up my men. Seems some don't want to move on to the fort with us."

A shrill whistle interrupted all dockside conversations as the ferry arrived. Burly men jumped from the steamboat deck and secured the heavy ropes through huge iron cleats. Then a wide boarding plank was placed between the dock and the edge of the ferry. The ferry's name on the side wall of the boat was weatherworn. When I stared long enough, I barely made out *JOSEPHINE* in red block letters. It was late in the season to be moving up the Missouri River by ferry. River travel was always dangerous, but the sandbars, ice chunks, and erratic currents that appeared during the late fall created a risk only a few riverboat pilots were willing to face. Dad walked Mother below the deck and out of the elements. Though the bitterly cold winds stung my face, I stayed above deck as we began to steam upriver.

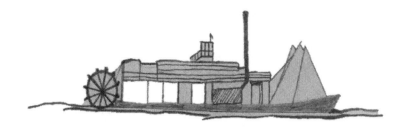

"Well, well, young lady. If you have the courage to lean against the wind, let's see if you have the courage to steer my gal!" called a man from behind the wheel of the ferry.

Let's see if you have the courage to steer my gal? I could hardly believe my ears; I quickly climbed up on the pilot platform and walked toward the man. A cigar hung from his mouth.

"Marsh. Grant Marsh, steamboat pilot of the beautiful *Josephine*. She's a darling, isn't she?" He chewed more than he inhaled on the end of the cigar. Mr. Marsh had a weathered face from years of working in the elements, yet he maintained a distinguished aura with his masculine features. His thick mustache was neat and just covered his upper lip. His nose was defined and straight. When Mr. Marsh smiled, his cheeks were plump and rosy. His full head of grayish-brown hair blew in the wind. His eyes were piercing, in a good sort of way.

"My name is Sara."

"Heading to Indian country, eh?"

I nodded.

"Well, you're getting a fine first look at it from my gal. It's absolutely wonderful out here. It's a thrill. *Josephine* and I work together like a marriage from heaven. Actually, I have another wife too, *Far West*. She's up river right now. Waiting for me."

"How did you learn to do this?"

"Ahhh. That's a long story," he said, rubbing the sides of his face with one hand. He spoke out of one side of his mouth, in a twisted sort of way, which made him hard to understand. "I started young. Younger than you. Great mentors along the way. When I turned sixteen, my chief, Samuel Clemens, took me under his watch. I was his cub pilot. Clemens taught me as much about myself as the river. He taught me to sense every river bend, every sandbar, every depth, every branch and tributary. Tough to memorize because rivers change constantly. Clemens taught me quick judgment. Shame he quit the business. Now he writes. Goes by Mark Twain."

Mr. Marsh spun the huge wheel to the left, avoiding a shallow edge of the river. "Here, Sara. Just hold the wheel steady for a second or two. Then you'll always be able to brag up that you were a riverboat steersman. Not a bad feather in your cap, so to speak," he chuckled. I tentatively held the wheel.

"Ya see, you'll go crazy out here, and things will fall apart fast if you don't make friends with the river. Respect it, and hope it doesn't throw us more than we can handle," Mr. Marsh explained.

A few silent minutes passed before a leadsman dropped a weighted rope over the side of the steamboat to measure the depth of the water. He called out, "Mark 3!" Then he called, "Mark 2!"[15] Marsh quickly took the wheel from my hands and turned from an obstacle that only he could sense.

"Just have to remain confident. I tell myself over and over again, when I face danger, I will not become a coward. I am brave," he said. "It works. What you tell your brain is very important. It's all about freedom. Freedom to make your own decisions. Look at me, I try to be the best at what I love to do: haul troops, supplies, men.

I worked the Mississippi during the Civil War. Then I came out here. Troops and freight up and down the Missouri and even the Yellowstone. Usually fort to fort. It's great work. They don't complain like settlers. Just glad the river ain't frozen solid on us tonight. See how it's just starting on the edges? This may just be the last trip of the season. Different seasons have different things trying to distract me. Mosquitoes and fleas infested the boat this summer. Good thing they froze before this trip. A sweet thing like you don't need no fleas in your pretty hair."

"No sir," I replied, wondering what my future held.

CHAPTER 9

WHITE

FORT RANDALL, DAKOTA TERRITORY

"THE WORLD OWES YOU NOTHING. IT WAS HERE FIRST." ~Mark Twain

The *Josephine* rounded a bend in the river where ice extended further from the riverbanks. Mr. Marsh explained how shallow sections of the Missouri froze first and so he carefully navigated up the middle. Then the pilot spun the wheel to the left, and the ferry pulled up to a landing on the west bank. With the engine still chugging, Mr. Marsh gestured toward shore. I looked at the sprawling cottonwoods before me. He pointed higher up the ridge. About a thousand yards away, an American flag, stiff as a board from the heavy winds, peeked out from the treetops.

"Good luck, darlin'. This fort is a darned safe place considering what else is around here," Mr. Marsh said, patting me on the back. I thanked him and wished him an early merry Christmas. Dad brought Mother from below and said we could take our time and walk to the fort, where he would meet us. Dad stayed back to follow the straggling soldiers, living out his "no soldier left behind" pledge. Mother and I disembarked and followed others who paced up the hillside on a well-worn trail. Once over the first knoll, we saw the fort on the plateau above. I had expected protective walls or a high stockade, but I saw neither. The only obvious strategic protection came from a curve in the river, which gave the hilltop a beautiful view and the barrier of water on two sides. The other two sides were a sea of light brown grass swaying as far as my eyes could see. This would take some getting used to. The vastness surrounding this little cluster of buildings made me feel we were in the middle of nowhere.

"Oh, dear God," Mother whispered as she looked out to the horizon. "Please, God, please. I need more than this."

She struggled to catch her breath as we stood at the end of the parade grounds and stared at our new environment. It was hard to believe that three or four hundred people lived on this plateau. We walked along the edge of a well-established path as a horse-drawn wagon, filled with trunks and boxes, overtook us. The parade grounds were in the middle of the fort, and buildings were situated around the outer edge. I recognized a church, a hospital, and dozens of other unmarked buildings. A low fence defined the perimeter of the fort, and sparsely planted trees and shrubs leaned southeast from taking the brunt of a never-ending gusty wind.

"Good day, ma'am," a soldier politely said as he crossed our path.

"Good day!" I chimed back, when Mother only nodded.

"It's not bad, Mother," I said, trying to raise her spirits. "Look, Mother, two storehouses, a guardhouse, and a hospital."

"I can see for myself, Sara," she replied curtly.

I silently counted five barracks made from timbers. They were about one hundred feet long and twenty feet wide. Father caught up to us with a group of men whom he directed to their barracks.

"Our quarters must be this way, girls."

Dad led us along the road. The aroma of fresh-baked bread wafted through the gusty, cold air, and I automatically turned upwind and identified the kitchen and bakery. Dad took us to a cluster of nice buildings on the southwest side of the parade grounds. The commanding officer's perfectly maintained quarters were simple to pick out. As we approached our assigned quarters, I decided that the houses looked fairly new, with covered front porches and wooden steps to the doors.

"Here we are." Dad said, gesturing toward our new house.

"Is the whole thing for us?"

"No, only half, Sara. See the two front doors? We have one common wall with our neighbors."

"It's still pretty great, don't you think, Mother?"

"Yes, Sara," she answered, only to appease Dad.

Dad opened the left door, and we stepped inside, maneuvering around our five trunks, which had already been dropped off. The main room had a couch and a chair, with a black stove in the corner. The walls and ceiling were covered with wood paneling. A desk sat in the far corner. Stepping past the first room, I saw a small kitchen. A rough table and four chairs sat in the middle of the space. I burst up the squeaky staircase, which led to two tiny bedrooms, each with a window for a view of the parade grounds. Black wrought-iron bed frames with worn mattresses within filled most of the bedroom space. Returning down the stairs, I noticed a large mirror that hung on the wall. It made the room look twice as big.

"This will be fine, Dad. I like it!"

Mother walked over to the mirror and stared into her reflection.

"Do you like it, Mother? What do you think?"

"What do I think? All of a sudden it matters what I think?" She raised her voice higher and higher. I hoped the neighbors weren't home. "I'll tell you what I think. I think I should not have signed up for this. I think this is on the wrong side of civilization," Mother despondently answered.

Dad and I stared at each other. "Well, I need to go introduce myself to General Lugenbeel. Why don't you two settle us in and unpack," Dad said.

I followed him to the door and stepped out, leaving it cracked behind me.

"She'll work it all out, Sara. Don't worry. It's probably just a phase," Dad said before he disappeared down the lane. I stepped back into our new house and looked at Mother, lost in her own private misery.

Mrs. Flanagan, our neighbor, came over while Dad was gone. She was an older, rather round woman, with dyed black hair. She seemed quite charming and approachable. With a heavy Irish accent, she welcomed us to the fort, and we exchanged pleasantries. Her husband, Captain Flanagan, had been assigned to Fort Randall for the last three years. Two and a half years ago, Mrs. Flanagan hopped a train from Pennsylvania and joined him here.

"You'll love it here. You'll just love it here," she kept repeating, filling the silent voids when nothing came from Mother's lips. Mrs. Flanagan's first impression of Mother must have been horrible. I did my best to smooth out the conversation as Mrs. Flanagan's eyes drifted from my eyes to my shoulders and down to my toes. I wondered what she was looking at. *Is it my nasty corset?* I wondered, because Mrs. Flanagan was obviously free from such an encumbrance. She said that we must be tired from our journey as she backed slowly out of our door. I suppose she wished to turn and run.

Falling asleep was nearly impossible on the first night because my bedroom wall was against the Flanagans', and the wall seemed very thin. I couldn't make out what they were saying, but laughter permeated the walls. Their conversation went on and on throughout the night.

It was already the day before Christmas. Mrs. Flanagan knocked on our door and invited us to share Christmas morning with them the next day. Mother refused and said it wasn't appropriate to socialize with strangers on such a sacred day.

"Nonsense," Mrs. Flanagan exclaimed. "We'll have none of your excuses. We'll see you in the morning."

Mother grumbled all day, saying the Flanagans were disrespectful neighbors. I listened again to their late night chatter through the wall. In the morning, Mother refused to get out of bed. Dad and I had a choice to make, and he did the deciding. We left Mother in bed and walked to the other door on our shared porch. Dad knocked on the Flanagans' door, as if we had known them forever.

"Merry Christmas!" they cheered in unison and welcomed us inside. Dad apologized for Mother's absence and said she was under the weather. They did not ask questions and directed us toward their cluttered, worn-out furniture. A small tree, decorated with strings of popped corn and cranberries, stood in the corner of the room. Mrs. Flanagan placed a bowl of cut apples and oranges on their coffee table. She casually served cranberry muffins with thick slices of butter as we sat in makeshift chairs around the table. Captain Flanagan poured steaming coffee for the three adults and placed a hot cocoa in front of me.

Wonderful conversation surrounded the breakfast. They told us how Fort Randall was like a small town, since twenty women and thirty children were making the best of the challenging life. After about an hour of chatting, Mrs. Flanagan whispered, "I believe there are a few presents under the tree for you."

I could hardly believe it because I did not expect a gift from anyone, mostly not the Flanagans. Mother had made it clear over the last few weeks. She said that our move was too hectic, and as a result, there would be no Christmas celebration. She said we'd have a real Christmas next year.

Mrs. Flanagan led me to the tree. Together we sat on the scratched wooden floor, and she reached deep under the lowest branches to pull out a small square box that was tied with a homemade bow of fluffy white yarn. I carefully unwrapped the yarn and lifted the top off the box. Inside was a perfectly formed popcorn ball, almost too perfect to be tasted. I thanked Mrs. Flanagan. She smiled heartily and told me the next present had been delivered the day before by Mrs. Parker, the fort's school teacher. White, waxy butcher paper wrapping was neatly tied with a brown string. A small note attached to the top of the gift read, "Miss Taylor, Welcome to Fort Randall, and Merry Christmas. Your teacher, Mrs. Parker." I quickly opened the box and found two new pencils inside. After this, one box, larger than the rest, still remained under the tree. I thought the box was for Mrs. Flanagan until she handed it to me. Inside I discovered a beautiful blue and turquoise prairie-style skirt and a matching sky blue blouse.

"Oh, my," I exclaimed. "I don't know what to say."

Captain Flanagan chimed in, "Well, when my wife saw you that first day, she figured you needed a new outfit for your new life."

"But where did you find it? Is there a dress shop here?" I asked.

The Flanagans laughed. "No, honey. I had the fabric here, and I sized you up the best I could without ruining the surprise," Mrs. Flanagan said. Her face glowed with joy.

"And then she sewed and sewed for the last two days and nights!" Captain Flanagan laughed. "She even made me stay up late with her, to keep her awake, so she could finish it before Christmas."

The late night conversations that I had heard through my bedroom wall now made perfect sense. But why for me? They hardly knew me.

"You are a special, special girl, Sara. Merry Christmas. I hope it fits," Mrs. Flanagan said.

The second I walked back into our quarters, I went straight up the stairs and to my room with my new dress. My velvet dress and corset dropped to the floor with a thud. I slipped into the new blouse and skirt, which were soft and just roomy enough to fit comfortably over my thin body. Mrs. Flanagan had visually measured me with perfection.

In contrast to our uplifting morning, Mother's mood remained downcast and she stayed in bed all day. I served her tea in the afternoon, and she failed to notice my new outfit. Dad and I wanted fresh air, so we took a walk around the fort, which had been renovated a few years back. The original tiny barracks had been replaced with a few two-story framed barracks that housed the enlisted men. Three more one-story barracks were added to the corners of the parade grounds, and another was located on the north end of the fort. Dad said I was not allowed near the barracks, so I could only wonder what they looked like inside. The hospital, on the north end of the parade grounds, had also been updated. Numerous laundry buildings were scattered throughout the fort. Blockhouses for ice storage were on the southeast and northwest corners, outside the fence line. Northeast of the parade grounds stood two Indian ration storage buildings. A guardhouse and the magazine were very close to the parade grounds. Dad and I stayed away from the chapel, a little embarrassed that we had not attended the Christmas church service.

The next day I woke up early, when Dad let the door slam behind him. I put on my new skirt and blouse. Then I quietly bundled up in my long wool coat and mittens, hoping to leave before Mother woke up. Relief swept through me when our door clicked shut and I was free to explore what I considered the most spectacular building on the fort.

This building was the chapel. Situated just past the north side of the quadrangle, it added great personality and prestige to the fort. The entrance had an inscription: "Christ Church—Erected by First U.S. Inf. 1875." I gazed up at the pointed front door and beyond at a painted angel that looked down upon me from the round window gable above. She was beautiful, a prairie angel. I pushed open the weathered door and stood for quite some time with my mouth wide open. The lingering scent of candle wax enveloped me as my eyes slowly adjusted to the dim light, and the architecture began to reveal itself. Stained glass windows glowed with images that I had yet to analyze.

"It's quite something, isn't it?" said a woman who wa
alone in a pew. She flashed a smile, which I returned.
soldiers sawed the beams from cottonwood trees grow
Missouri River islands."

I looked to the ceiling as I
ran my hands along the
back of a smoothly
sanded pew,
constructed of tight
grain walnut certainly not native to Dakota Territory. The woman
stood up stiffly from her hard seat and turned to me.

"My name is Mrs. Parker. You must be Major Taylor's daughter,"
she said, speaking vivaciously. I cringed at her volume because
Mother had trained me to always speak softly in church.

"Yes, ma'am. My name is Sara," I whispered back.

"Would you like to see the bell tower and spiral staircase?" Mrs.
Parker asked, as loud as before. Without waiting for my reply, she
took hold of my arm and started her tour of the rest of the chapel.
One side of the church had a small library wing. The other side
had a club meeting room.

"The men spared no detail and even imported our organ from the
East Coast," she said proudly.

"How did this all get started? Did the War Department pay for
it?"

.ɔ. By golly, they wouldn't dream of this," she replied in a soft chuckle. "General Lugenbeel, the commander, he came up with the idea. At first, the soldiers donated money and muscle. They placed a huge solid stone foundation under this church. It will never fall. Then they went a few miles downriver and cut yellow chalk rock from a quarry site. They dragged the stone up here to use as walls. But then things did not run too smoothly."

"What do you mean?" I asked.

"Well, the chalk rock was too weak to support the beams. It just crumbled. Then the men had to make walls filled with prairie rock. They were disappointed with the look because they wanted something fancier. By then, the soldiers were pretty decent masons and covered the prairie rock with this beautiful chalk rock. See?" she said, pointing through a window, "the walls are almost four feet thick now."

She went on, "The men kept funds flowing through their paychecks, when they could have been using it for sinful purposes across the river. The whole place cost about twenty thousand dollars, and even local settlers kicked in funds. Magnificent, isn't it?" Mrs. Parker asked.

We wandered and chatted for quite some time before I told her I must return to Mother.

"Very well. We can continue this later."

"How will I find you again?" I asked.

Mrs. Parker smiled, "I'm your school teacher."

"I apologize. I did not make the connection. Thank you, ma'am, for the pencils."

"You're very welcome, Sara. It's my pleasure. See you tomorrow at seven o'clock."

Although I knew I should return to Mother, the horse stable called to me, producing momentary guilt. The squeaky stable doors swung back and forth at the whim of the bitter wind that I was learning was Fort Randall's norm rather than the exception. Horses were contentedly picking at their individual flakes of hay. The musty scent filled my nose as I looked down rows of horse stalls, primarily filled with bays, which were dark brown with black manes and tails. Most had a "US" brand on their left shoulder. Only one man was in the stable, and he was busy with chores. I watched as he moved from horse to horse. He was a private, wearing a frayed, navy forage cap with a black leather visor. The cap's chin strap rested on top of the brim, and it didn't look like it had ever been used. The private looked up and caught my gaze.

"A few stand out beyond the others in strength and beauty, don't they?" I commented, looking across the horses' lined-up rumps.

"Yes, ma'am. A few sure do," the private replied, as he stepped closer. He was not looking at the horses; he was staring straight at me with grayish-green eyes. Sloppy dark brown curls wildly sprung from his cap.

"Oh, my, who is he?" I asked, diverting the awkward attention toward a nearby horse.

"Star. The commander's horse. He's a beauty, isn't he?"

The horse stood a hand higher than the others around him. He was well groomed with a sleek snow-white coat. I looked closely at his forehead and did not see a star.

The private came around the horse that separated us. He leaned against a post, skewing his cap. "You are Major Taylor's daughter?" he asked casually.

"Good guess."

"The boys here have been waiting patiently for your arrival."

"Is that so?" I stated. "I hope they're not disappointed when they learn I'm not interested."

"I'm sure they will be, ma'am. But I'm just curious: what *are* you interested in?"

"School, baking, and horses."

"We heard you were bright and loved to bake, but what does a pretty girl like you know about horses?"

"Not much. But you asked what I was interested in, not where my knowledge lies, Mister … Mister …"

"Jake. Private Jake."

"Nice to meet you, Private Jake. And what are *you* interested in?"

"I don't think I'll answer that question right now," he said with a kind of awkward wink, which nonetheless was very charming.

114

"Fair enough. Then answer this: do you think I could come to the stable? You could teach me all you know about horses."

"I don't see a thing wrong with that idea. We have a lot of tack leather needing oil, and plenty of stalls to clean," he answered professionally, although his gaze did not stray from me.

"I'm not afraid of dirty work, Private Jake. But I'd prefer to get my hands dirty by touching the actual horse rather than the shovel."

"Well, you'll need to take the good with the bad around here. What goes in one end of the horse comes out the other. And it's our job to take care of both ends. That's what the shovels are for!" he said, smiling.

Private Jake. He was quite handsome and jaunty. When he spoke, dimples in the center of both cheeks came and went. He needed no stripes, stars, or medals on his woolen uniform to draw my attention.

That night Mother left my parents' bedroom for the first time in two days. Wrapped in a gray government-issued blanket, she sat in a rocking chair beside the wood stove. Captain Flanagan had given the chair to Dad the day before, claiming they had too much furniture in their quarters and hoped we could use it. Mother rocked back and forth, with the chair creaking each time the rockers hit a weak floor board. Dad sat in a worn chair, and I was settled on the couch. I asked Dad about the horse assignments. He told me they would be made within a few days.

"I sure wish you could have the commander's horse," I said.

Dad laughed. "Sara, his horse is all about show. I want a horse who has heart. A tall horse is not always a better horse."

"Why?"

"Because you stand out when the Indians are shooting arrows at you!" he laughed.

I didn't laugh along, though. Sensitive to my reaction, Dad changed the subject, "I met a lot of nice people today. This will be a fine place for us. And oh, I've just remembered, Sara—school starts tomorrow."

I sat silently, not sure whether I should mention meeting Mrs. Parker.

"The chaplain's job is to save souls and provide schooling for the children and any enlisted men who want to learn to read and write. Well, apparently his passion was in something else," he said with a smirk on his face.

Mother shot a condemning glance at Dad. It amazed me at how she floated between perceptiveness and outright confusion in mere seconds.

"Oh, come now. Sara is no longer a small child," he said, and continued. "Seems like the chaplain took off with a squaw from across the river.[16] In his absence, Major Parker's wife will be your teacher; the army will eventually assign a new chaplain. Mrs. Parker volunteers; she has no official title or stipend, and no prior experience either, but Captain Flanagan says that her heart is in the right place."

I didn't say anything.

"So, you will start in the morning, at the chapel library. Do you know where it is?"

"Yes, Dad. I've already been there."

"Very good. And I expect you to study hard and learn a lot."

"I will, Dad," I answered.

Suddenly Mother blurted, "Where did you get that ugly skirt, Sara? Take it off immediately."

CHAPTER 10

WHITE

DAILY LIFE AT FORT RANDALL

"I WOULD RATHER BE POOR IN A COTTAGE FULL OF BOOKS THAN A KING WITHOUT THE DESIRE TO READ." ~Thomas Babington Macaulay

Starting very early the next morning, I quickly began to learn how everything functioned at Fort Randall on preset schedules; most events were initiated by a bugle call. The bugle ordered all two hundred thirty men through their daily routine, beginning with the 4:55 a.m. call to rise and shine. Every half hour the bugle sounded the next scheduled event: roll call, stable call, water call, mess call, fatigue call, surgeon call, drill mount guard call, mess call, school call, boots and saddle call, assembly call, stable call, water call, target practice call, inspection call, mess call, evening school call, tattoo call, and assembly call. Finally, the last taps played at 9:30 p.m. Lanterns were blown out, and all men were in their bunks by the time the last note sounded on the bugle.[17]

Again, I asked Dad when he would pick out his horse. He said it required shuffling because horses were assigned based on seniority at the fort and the rank of the rider. A day later, while Mother and I were reading in our quarters, Dad called to us from the porch.

"Girls, come out! I have something to show you!"

I jumped up and rushed onto the porch.

"Girls, I'd like you to meet Blue. Blue, these are my lovely girls."

"Oh, gosh, Dad. He's magnificent!" The dapple gray gelding was stunning. He had a streak running from the back of the saddle down the center and over his rump to the base of his tail. The streak looked blue as it glimmered in the sunlight. I put my hand out, and his nostrils inquisitively greeted me. I moved my hand to his forehead and stroked the small white spot centered a few inches above his eyes. I moved to his left shoulder and ran my finger along the "US" brand, which felt like rawhide. I looked up at Dad and smiled.

"He's perfect. He is just perfect," I said, inhaling deeply.

Mother had followed me to the door but just stood at the threshold in silence. She was not adjusting as Dad and I had hoped. Fort life was not terrible and she should have appreciated the predictability, but she was too self-consumed to really notice the fort routine. The men had different assigned jobs to perform each day. Wood was gathered. Men led horse-drawn sleds and carts, loaded down with ice blocks sawed from the river ice from the Missouri. They filled blockhouses with the ice to store for the warmer months. As the weather became more and more miserable, the drills on the parade grounds became shorter and shorter.

On my first day of school, I was out of bed, dressed, and lingering at the bottom of our stairs long before breakfast. Dad asked Mother if she wanted to accompany us to the mess hall. She declined, insisting she needed rest. So Dad and I walked together, arm in arm, and waited in line for our food. Famished, we devoured bacon, oatmeal with molasses, and small piles of pancakes. Dad had hot black coffee, while I washed my food down with a glass of water. We talked about important things, like how the course of a life is determined: whether through choices, circumstances, or fate. I never knew that when he was young, Dad had wanted to navigate the seas. Instead he led a wave of bluecoats into war. When our conversation ran dry, I grabbed our plates and dropped them into a bucket of soapy water at the end of our table. I returned to hug Dad, and then raced to the chapel.

The potbellied wood-burning stove warmed the meeting room, where twenty children started to take their seats around two long wooden conference tables. Mrs. Parker introduced me from her podium. I squeezed in at the end of a table beside a polite-looking girl, about eight or nine years old. The morning passed quickly as Mrs. Parker covered reading, writing, and arithmetic. The lessons were toned down for all levels in the class, and I saw little opportunity to be academically challenged. The small kids were dismissed early, when they became fully distracted and fidgety.

Mrs. Parker took her teaching challenge in stride. Her sole motivation seemed to be the desire to fill her students with a love of learning. She was positive and encouraging. I sopped up the experience like a fresh mop. Mrs. Parker watched me for a few days and then pulled me into the main chapel, where no other students could hear.

"Sara, your spelling leaves a lot to be desired."

"I know. I'm sorry," I answered, quite embarrassed.

"What do you think it is, Sara? You are incredibly gifted in arithmetic, which makes me wonder …"

"Ma'am, arithmetic makes sense," I exclaimed. "It's just like baking. You follow the rules, and use exact measurements for calculated results."

"How do you go about spelling?" she asked.

"I write the word as it sounds in my mind. I know that's not how I should do it, but I don't know any other way," I said, confessing, "To be honest, Mrs. Parker, I hate spelling."

"Well, 'hate' is a strong word. Let's work toward 'dislike,' shall we? But Sara, listen to me," she said, cupping my downcast face in her hands. "Your arithmetic and reading skills are way beyond my teaching ability. I'm afraid that you'll stagnate here if you don't make a plan to challenge yourself."

"I don't know what to say."

"I see that, Sara. I understand. Just make a new plan. Go pick out interesting books in our library. Read them. Learn. Perhaps you'll be the first person at Fort Randall to read every single book in the library. It looks to me like God granted you the gift of knowledge. You need to set goals, and fly like an eagle. Free the twine that binds your wings."

"Twine that binds my wings?" I asked.

"The twine is anyone or anything standing in your way, any doubts in your own mind. Free yourself of those things and soar!"

She hugged me and turned me toward the library wing. The stove was not ignited in the room, and a damp chill sent shivers down my back. Hundreds of books were jammed into the shelves, with no sense to their order. Perhaps I would read the first one on top of the far left shelf and continue right across that shelf before moving across the next shelf down, as if I were reading a page in a book. Then, when I reached the bottom right book on the bookcase, I would move to the next bookcase on the wall.

Over the course of the afternoon, a few soldiers wandered in and out of the library during their free time. After word spread of my goal to read every book in the library, a few soldiers said I could join their reading "club." Mother adamantly prohibited me from taking them up on the offer. She said the soldiers' books would corrupt my mind, and she demanded to preview everything I read. I was not sure if she planned to screen out violence or romance from my reading, but she never asked again and reviewed none of my books. Her mind was somewhere else.

The more Mother faded, the more Mrs. Parker filled the void. Each day, sometimes more than once, Mrs. Parker and I crossed paths across the parade grounds. If nobody else was around, Mrs. Parker offered a single new word. I quickly tried to spell it.

"Beautiful," she blurted.

"Beautiful. B-u-t-i-f-u-l. Beautiful."

"Not quite, honey." Her smile was mixed with sympathy and encouragement.

At my first opportunity, I ducked into the library to look up the word in the worn *Webster's Dictionary*. *What is the point of looking in a dictionary for the spelling of a word when one cannot find the word because the correct spelling is unclear?* I wondered. Using a dictionary was a flawed system, in my opinion. I searched and searched, all around my guessed spelling. Once I found the word that I had butchered in front of Mrs. Parker, I memorized the correct spelling. Then, as inconspicuously as possible, I tracked her down. She was usually helping in the kitchen if she wasn't in the chapel, sitting alone on the same pew, conversing with God. When she stood up stiffly to leave, I approached.

"Beautiful. B-e-a-u-t-i-f-u-l. Beautiful."

"Very good, Sara. You are truly beautiful."

The next day she presented a different word, "tenacious." The next day, "courageous." The next day, "interminable."

"Very good, Sara. You are truly tenacious"," Mrs. Parker said. And the next days she echoed, "Very good, Sara. You are truly courageous" and "Very good, Sara. You are truly interminable."

Mrs. Parker was kindhearted blessing, and she reminded me of Miss Bee. I had become frustrated with Miss Bee's and my limited communication. Mail was incredibly slow and unpredictable when it moved by train, wagon, and ferries from the East Coast to our fort. Mail bags fell off in transit, were burned in post office fires, were stolen, or were just set aside in a warehouse somewhere. At Fort Randall, anyone was lucky to receive a piece of mail, because the last leg of the trip was quite arduous. If the Missouri River was navigable, then the army sent a ferry from Sioux City to Fort Randall once or twice a week. If the river was icebound, though, then the mail traveled on the "Sioux City and Fort Randall Express" stagecoach. The well-used road still took two or three days to travel, and rarely did the stage carry any news from Miss Bee.

Once the mail made it to the fort and into the addressee's hands, there was no guarantee of good news. Hoping for the best, men patiently stood around the postmaster, longing for their names to be called. Mother insisted that I stand at each mail call because she refused to venture out into the cold. Sergeant Zito usually stood beside me, resolved to his fate of walking away empty-handed. For weeks on end, we received no mail. Then, one day, I heard my name. I looked at the face of the envelope as I stepped back toward Sergeant Zito.

"She wrote. Miss Bee wrote," I whispered to him.

"Your friend?" he asked.

"Yes, my best friend."

"Good for you, Sara. Never give up."

I sent at least five letters for each one that Miss Bee sent to me, and I was plagued by discouragement. But Sergeant Zito never received mail, yet kept a positive attitude. Mother's name was called about every ten days. I hurried her unopened letters across the parade grounds while she peered from behind a new thick window curtain that she had sewed together because the existing lace curtains were "too sheer." She silently read Grandmother's letters before passing them on to me. Still self-absorbed, Grandmother wrote only of her daily life back home and how the weather affected her. In each letter, her last paragraph insisted that Mother and I return to New York City because tensions were escalating with the savages. She never said a word about Miss Bee.

My own routine caused days to blend together. Each morning after breakfast with Dad, I attended school and read alone in the library. When I could study no more, I walked back to our quarters and helped Mother with chores. Sometimes she kept me there, like a slave, by creating ridiculous tasks that prevented my escape. Other times she told me to leave her alone and pushed me out of the door. I usually walked to the kitchen and offered to help with meal preparation.

The post kitchen was on the southeast edge of the garrison. The building was only a few years old and was nearly perfect—nearly because someone placed it right beside the barrack privies. We arrived in December, so I had not been subjected to the stench that the others complained of during the summer months.

The head cook, Mrs. Wiesenberger, was a feisty German woman. Four years earlier she had been mail-ordered by her enlisted husband, who was assigned to Fort Randall. She initially took a position as a laundress at the fort, but her true passion was cooking. When the previous head cook died from a bout of dysentery, Mrs. Wiesenberger approached the commander and, in broken English, asked for the position. He asked her to prepare something for him as a test. She melted his culinary heart with a delicious roasted pork and boiled cabbage dinner. An extra side she prepared, creamed peas, was her grandmother's recipe from back in her homeland. Her bread sat steaming, in front of the commander, with a plate of butter waiting beside. The day before Mrs. Wiesenberger had traded with a steamboat pilot: her full box of sweets and smoked jerky for his three bottles of fine wine. Then she carefully paired a glass of wine with each course, and by the end of the night, the fully satiated commander handed her the key to the kitchen. She had been quite protective of her title ever since.

When I first offered to help, Mrs. Wiesenberger hesitated. A few days later she suddenly welcomed me into her kitchen. I think Mrs. Flanagan told her about how Mother sent me out of our quarters when she was in one of her moods. Sometimes Mrs. Wiesenberger actually seemed to need my help; other times she just seemed sympathetic. She taught me how to prepare beef, pork, beans, and bacon "the Mrs. Wiesenberger way."

When the men finished their meals or found a bit of free time, they filled it in various ways, some more positive than others. They played billiards, polished their boots, and cut each other's hair with the thought of minimizing their chances of being

126

scalped by a savage because there would not be enough hair to hang on a tipi as a showpiece. Such was the theory, anyway.

When I was in a quiet mood and wanted to get away, I snuck to the horse stable. Mother objected to this for many reasons. First, I would hear dirty language from the soldiers' mouths. Second, the stable was under construction and filthy. Third, I would never learn to be a lady if I hung around the stinky stable.

In truth, the men rarely swore around me. Their language at times was a bit raucous, yet nothing was directed toward me, and I never felt offended. Seeing that each man knew I was the daughter of Major Taylor, I was clearly off limits for any shenanigans. In my opinion, the stable was a healthy escape, the most glorious-smelling place on earth, where I could be myself among the horses, who represented an odd mix of strength and dependence. They gave and gave to the men, yet needed extensive care.

Private Jake taught me "all he knew" about the loyal animals. I focused mostly on Blue, but when a cavalryman was ill, I took over his horse's care until he was fit for duty. Private Jake and I spent time alone when we led the horses to water. They were never in a hurry, and most approached the trough with caution. Private Jake laughed as we waited; my patience wearing thin as I pressed my cheeks and hands against the horse's coat to stay warm. During the chore, I usually asked questions.

"How did you end up at Fort Randall, Private Jake?"

"Well, I always knew I wanted to serve. Maybe as a priest. But I couldn't really imagine myself alone, forever, without a woman to call my wife. So then I saw a sign at the post office, where I lived in Pennsylvania. It said the government was looking for brave men to serve out West and protect the settlers from the Indians. I thought, 'Hey, I'm brave. I wouldn't mind moving to the Wild West. I'd like to protect the settlers.' Just like that, I enlisted."

"Did your parents approve?"

"It's just my mom. At first she was worried that I'd come home in a pine box, if I came home at all."

"What happened to your Dad?"

"Questions, questions, questions, Sara. Honestly. That's enough for now, okay? I think these horses are done. You know what they say, right? You can lead a horse to water, but you cannot make him drink."

The more I worked with the horses, the more I understood what he meant. Each horse had his own quirks. Blue was no exception. He dove his entire nose into the water trough, past his nostril holes, and then splashed water on me.

Obtaining enough water for daily use presented a strange dichotomy at Fort Randall: water was plentiful in the wide river below, but getting it to the fort was difficult. For military reasons, the fort was built on a plateau, two ridges above the river, which placed us too high for a well. Because the fort needed substantial water, an elaborate process of collection, transportation, and storage was accepted as a cost for increased natural protection.

The water was pumped up the hill in a pipe, which was moved by steam from below. When the water reached our bluff, it settled into a concrete holding tank. Then a water wagon, filled from the tank, distributed the water to the fort. The horses always seemed to appreciate the water most on the days it was freshly dumped into the troughs from the water wagon.

After watering the horses with Private Jake, I worked on Blue. I picked his feet and brushed out his mane and tail. He stood still and seemed to enjoy the attention. When nobody was nearby to tease me about spoiling him, I stood at Blue's side and scratched my short fingernails on the underside of his belly. He bent his neck and turned his muzzle to my shoulder, moving his lips back and forth in bliss and tickling my shoulder in return. I cringed a bit, wondering if he might take a chunk out of me. He never did.

One day, while watering horses, I asked Private Jake when his five-year enlistment commitment was over.

"Well, Sara, it all depends. I have served three years already. You know, quite a few men just walk away and desert when they've had enough. Just doesn't seem right, though. A commitment's a commitment. Two more years of this … it'll go quick. I'm sure of it. I'll save my money, marry the right girl, and I'll be set for life."

Save his money? Be set for life? This seemed a lofty goal at a salary of only thirteen dollars a month. Still, I supposed the money would eventually accumulate.[18] But get married? Really? It seemed like a monumental decision for someone his age. I understood the theory; marriage fills a void, gives a person someone to walk beside and to strive with, together, to share the

129

same hopes and dreams. But what if something went drastically wrong? Or even a little wrong? Like Dad's frustration when Mother rarely left our quarters for any reason other than to eat one meal a day and to visit the privy three times. Dad always tried to coax her to attend a fort dance or to take a walk. When she refused, he was trapped—trapped in marriage.

Dad tried hard, complimenting her when no praise was deserved. "You are such a lovely woman. I just want to show you off a little," he nudged. He encouraged her to meet with the other wives. Mother rejected each idea as soon as Dad raised it. Sometimes Dad invited me to fort events, but I was a mere consolation prize because he was supposed to be taking his wife. As time went by, Dad seemed more and more defeated.

Oddly, Mother thrived on her reputation as the finest seamstress west of the Missouri—or at least at Fort Randall, depending on whom you asked. She stayed up until all hours of the night, sewing on buttons, mending tears, and darning socks. Dad initially had a hard time with Mother's work because he felt it was not "becoming of an officer's wife." He apprehensively agreed to her sewing only under the condition that she not charge the men. As time went by, Dad recognized the joy it created within her. He frequently teased her, asking, "Is that sock holey or righteous?"

I was intrigued by Mother's obsession. She moved our table beside the stove for extra heat and worked away in silence. Her first priority was to mend any government-issued coats because the soldier was without the extra warmth until she returned it. The small items, such as socks, were darned with perfection even though they would be stuffed into boots and never be seen in public. It did not matter to her because she was fully immersed in her passion and filled with purpose.

One day I persuaded Mother to walk around the perimeter of the parade grounds for fresh air. When we walked past the hospital, I asked Mother whether she had been inside.

"Why would you ask me that, Sara? Are you accusing me of something?"

"No, I just thought we could look inside. I think I might want to be a nurse."

"That is ridiculous, Sara. You are not cut out for nursing."

"Let's just see about that," I offered in defiance and stormed up the steps. She hesitated and then followed me inside. There was a small lobby, and beyond it stretched a hallway. All the walls were made out of orangish-red cedar boards. I peeked down the hall and saw six or seven different rooms. The patients rested quietly. A nurse rounded the corner of the hallway and was startled by our presence.

"Oh, excuse me. May I help you?" the nurse uttered, and then recognition crossed her face. "Oh, hello, Mrs. Taylor. I'm sorry, I don't think the stage brought your laudanum in today.[19] Maybe tomorrow."

"Uh, umm," Mother said, flustered. "Sara just wanted to see the hospital. We will be going now." Mother pulled me backward out of the hallway. She let go as I spun around and shut the porch door behind us.

"What was that all about?" I asked.

"You need to mind your own business, Sara, and treat your mother with respect."

Not another word was spoken as we walked back to our quarters. Mother charged through our front door and went straight to her sewing table. I sat on the other side of the room and did mathematics problems.

After an hour of total silence, Mother blurted tersely, "Get over here right now, Sara. You need to learn something useful instead of pretending to memorize facts from your books. Come learn something practical like darning a soldier's sock. I've had enough of your math. It's time to gain practical skills. Wife skills."

I sat beside Mother. Sweat beaded on her forehead, and her hands shook as she taught me.

"This is how you thread the needle. This is how you knot it. This is how you stitch. No, Sara. Not so wide. Take a little more sock in your stitch or it will tear out. No, Sara. Not so narrow."

Could I do nothing right? Could she resist chastising me when I was doing my best? I swallowed deep and obediently listened, trying to mimic her technique while impatiently waiting for Dad to come home. Finally, in a flat monotone voice, Mother told me that it was past my bedtime, and I needed to go to sleep.

CHAPTER 11

RED

TREE-POPPING MOON

JANUARY 1876

BLACK HILLS WINTER CAMP

"YOUR PEOPLE LOOK UP TO MEN BECAUSE THEY ARE RICH ... WELL, I SUPPOSE MY PEOPLE LOOK UP TO ME BECAUSE I AM POOR."
~Sitting Bull[20]

My father, Touch the Clouds, was the new chief of our tribe, the Miniconjou. He was loved by my people for his courage, fortitude, respect, generosity, and wisdom.[21] As we were nomadic people, Father made the final decisions for much of our activities: when we hunted, when we moved, when we raided other tribes' horses. Before the white man came, we had a much easier life. Buffalo were plentiful, and our stomachs were full. When I was a young boy, my people moved frequently to follow the buffalo herds.

Sometimes we stayed in one camp for a few days, sometimes for a few months. Everything we owned was easily dismantled and transported by human, dog, or horse. Then the white man came and killed tens of thousands of buffalo—sometimes for the hides, but usually just for sport. The white man had no qualms about killing our food supply by letting the sacred beast rot in the sun. He pushed us from our hunting grounds and made us fight for our existence.

Each winter, just before the first heavy snowfalls, our village moved to the sacred Black Hills. We settled into a valley, nestled among trees and a creek, to outlast the frigid winter winds. Winter was dedicated to surviving and preparing for better weather. Food had already been preserved. Thick bedding was heaped upon the ground, inside our tipis. The men spent time making bows and arrows. The women made tools and maintained the tipis. The cold weather made it a perfect time of year for Father to sit in front of our fire and pass on our history, since most of my tribe could not read or write. I memorized his stories about the Fort Laramie Treaties of 1851 and 1868, hoping to accurately recite them to my own children someday. His low voice told a story that went something like this:

> The white man, wasicu, came through our land in his wagons. He brought strange customs and disease. We signed treaties to protect our land and slow the flow of white men, but they broke the treaties—again and again and again. Young warriors were tired of broken promises, and they wanted respect.

134

Three years after the treaty, our Brulé people were camped near Fort Laramie as we waited for supplies and food to be delivered according to the treaty. The supplies were delayed, and two thousand of our people waited, starving. A settler was traveling through, and one of his cows lagged behind. So a warrior took the cow, and we ate it. A leader from Fort Laramie, named Grattan, rushed to the scene, and his translator was filled with whiskey. He told our young warriors that they were women and that the soldiers would kill them. My people tried to pay for the cow with many horses. Then one of Grattan's men shot Chief Conquering Bear in the back as he walked away from the meeting. Another trooper shot and wounded another warrior. Our young warriors could take no more. They rose up and killed Grattan and his entire detachment of thirty-two men.

This, my son, is why you have been educated in different dialects and the wasicu language. Even though you left Black Robe early, you are still responsible to our people. Don't let the white man cheat us again. Never sign a treaty unless you understand each word. Do you understand me?

I understood. However, what good was understanding and signing a treaty if the white man broke his promises anyway?

Dust filled the air as the wasicu flooded to our Black Hills. Their arrival caused hatred in our hearts. We were being overrun by those in pursuit of riches. I understood the wasicu ways, and believed they should never be trusted. Never. Never ever.[22]

I stood behind Father and Uncle, as we warmed ourselves by the fire. The days had grown short, and the biting winds had taken on a life of their own. We had greater protection through taking refuge in the Black Hills, yet the cold was part of everything we did. Grandmother made the best soup that I ever tasted. She said it kept our blood warm. Her base was water and dried prairie turnips, called timpsila, which we collected the previous summer. The turnips were mixed with wild onion, fresh rabbit meat or white-tailed deer meat, and buffalo fat. All this was cooked over a slow-burning fire. If we were short of fresh meat, Grandmother added pieces of dried buffalo.

Another night, before a slow-burning fire, Father announced, "The wasicu chief, President Grant, tells us to return to our agencies by January 31 or we will be considered hostile. It is impossible; we cannot travel in this poor weather."

"Do they know the prairie is a death sentence in the winter?" Uncle asked.

"I don't know, but we will not travel until spring," Father said.

"Will this lead to a war?" I asked.

"The wasicu War Department is now taking control. If they are honorable, then they promised to give us freedom to move as we please, as long as the grass shall grow. Do you remember the treaty, son?"

"Yes, Father, the Fort Laramie Treaty of 1868."

"We will wait out the winter and meet in June, as Sitting Bull has asked.[23] We will make a great freedom camp, with all our people, and decide what we should do."

CHAPTER 12

WHITE

CUSTER VISITS FORT RANDALL

"I WOULD BE WILLING, YES GLAD, TO SEE A BATTLE EVERY DAY DURING MY LIFE."
~George Armstrong Custer

"Guess what, girls?" Dad said as he enthusiastically opened the front door.

"What?" I asked. Mother did not look up from her sewing project.

"As of today, at fourteen hundred hours, I'm in charge of the fort![24] The regimental commander of the First Infantry! I'm the replacement for General Lugenbeel!"

"Why?" I asked.

"Well, he is traveling back east for a meeting, and Major Offley has severe dysentery in the hospital. I'm next in command."

"Wow, Dad, I'm proud of you!"

"Let's hope nothing happens in the next week or two. No surprises, right?"

The first day was uneventful. The second day was manageable, with only one medical emergency, when a soldier gashed his leg open with an axe, as he split firewood. But on the third day, things changed. Late in the afternoon I was working on arithmetic at a corner desk in the chapel library when a commotion outside caught my attention. I dropped my book and peered out the window. There, coming down the road, right in front of me, was a group of four horses and their riders. The lead man rode a bay horse that was moving at a fast walking gait, which forced the others to maintain a trot. He was covered in a deep-blue government-issued officer's winter coat. The wool flaps split down the sides of the saddle, and leather boots protruded from the bottom. A red scarf peeked from the collar, and one wild blonde curl, near his face, had freed itself from his heavily frosted winter hat and stiffly bounced to the rhythm of the horse's gait. It was General George Custer — the most famous Indian fighter of all time. At our fort. Unannounced.

I pulled on my coat, slammed my math book into my satchel, slung the satchel over my shoulder, and rushed for the door. I ran toward the stable, following the horse prints in the light snow. I stood around the stable corner and caught my breath before making my entrance. Custer had dismounted and handed his reins to Sergeant Zito, who did not seem the least bit flustered by the visit. Sergeant Zito first saluted General Custer and then reached for the bay's cinch, which he attempted to release. Failing the first time, he put more weight into the strap on his second try.

139

On his third attempt, with a verbalized grunt, of either exertion or disgust, Sergeant Zito finally released the leather strap. The horse let out an audible sigh.[25]

"Shall I leave your horse saddled, or are you spending the night, General?"

"Just passing through, Sergeant. Will be gone in the morning."

"Yes, sir," Sergeant Zito answered, pulling off the saddle and blanket. The cold air caused steam to rise from the horse's sweaty back. Sergeant Zito hesitated at the side of the horse, feeling the horse's underbelly flesh with his finger to determine the extent of cinch's rub damage.

The other men were busy tending to their own horses. They pulled saddles, shook out saddle blankets, and removed bridles with no words exchanged. The men and the horses were completely worn out.

General Custer pulled off his winter coat and handed it to his orderly. Impeccably dressed in a fringed buckskin outfit, Custer's pants hung over knee-high leather jack boots. He swaggered toward the wall of the stable and quickly took off his broad-brimmed, whitish-gray hat. He bent over at the waist and shook his head, freeing the ice chunks that had accumulated during his ride. He threw his head back as he stood up and then used his fingers to comb through his locks of hair and to smooth his wide mustache. General Custer's hair was unlike anything I had ever seen: it was cut straight across at his shoulders, and his large golden ringlets dangled, as if he had worn curlers all day. He quickly repositioned his hat on top of his head and spun back around, to catch me staring.

"Well. Well. What do we have here?" he asked.

Uncomfortable, I curtsied a bit and dropped my eyes with demure modesty. Suddenly something took over inside me, and though my body wanted to collapse from his focused attention, I stood tall, and with deliberateness, I announced, "General Custer? Welcome to Fort Randall!"

"Why, thank you, young lady. And who might you be?"

"Sara. Sara Taylor, sir."

"Well, hello, Miss Sara Taylor," he replied with a steely gaze adjoined to a slight grin that peeked through his frost-covered mustache.

I could not take my eyes off him. The hair, the clothes, and an air of pure attitude. No wonder our fort's Indian scouts called him Yellow Hair and Long Hair. I figured by the faint wrinkle lines on the side of his eyes that he was in his mid-thirties, maybe thirty-five or thirty-six years old, but it was hard to tell. He had a full mustache that covered most of his thin lips when they were closed, which didn't seem to happen very often.

"What does a guy need to do to get someone to polish up these boots?" General Custer asked Sergeant Zito.

"Right away, sir," Private Jake chimed in from behind.

"Not now; tonight. I'll set them outside my quarters. Spit and polished by morning? I can't stand what this territory does to a man's boots!"

General Custer turned to leave. I thought I caught a waft of cinnamon. He paced off with two of his men following behind.

"All this spit and polish for just a lieutenant colonel. I should be paid more than thirteen dollars a month," Jake sighed.

I replied, "He's not a lieutenant colonel. He's a general. And you'd better respect him for that."

"Oh, I respect what he did in the Civil War, all right. But Sara, his rank of general was dropped after the Civil War. He's not an official general anymore. We just call him general, out of respect, but his true rank is lieutenant colonel."

"Once a general, always a general."[26]

"Whatever, Sara. How about this? Let's just run away together," Jake said smiling.

"And where would that get us, Private Jake?" I asked, wondering if his suggestive comments were even serious.

"We could get our own little place and live on love," he said with his hands in his pockets and a smirk on his face.

"Thanks, but no thanks," I replied, suddenly feeling uncomfortably flattered.

"Can't blame a guy for trying," he said, going back to his work.

One soldier lingered in the horse stable, impervious to the cold.

"Can I help you with your horse?" I asked.

"Oh, thank you for the offer. I just like to take good care of him, because he takes good care of me." The soldier was handsome and possibly of Irish descent. He was clearly dedicated to the horse, who was nothing special to look at, so I avoided the topic and diverted my questions.

"What is his name?"

"Comanche. And my name is Keogh. Colonel Miles Keogh, of the Seventh Cavalry."

"Hi. I'm Sara."

"So I heard. Nice to meet you."

I acknowledged his pleasantries with a small smile and nod of my head, and then I asked, "How old is your horse?"

"About fourteen, maybe fifteen. He's getting up there."

"Me too. Is he part mustang?" I asked.

"How did you know?"

"I just studied horse breeds in our library," I explained.

"Well, I think you're right. Comanche looks part mustang and maybe has a little bit of Morgan breed thrown in," Colonel Keogh agreed.

"How did you get him?"

"General Custer's brother, Tom."

When Colonel Keogh saw that I was confused, he explained, "The one with the scar on his cheek. He is the general's brother, Tom Custer. Colonel Tom Custer. Anyway, he was sent to St. Louis to buy fresh horses. Comanche was one of 'em. Tom railroaded them to Fort Leavenworth, Kansas, and then to Hays City, Kansas, where our troops were camped. I picked Comanche up about eight years ago. He was a company horse, but when I saw his eyes, I knew he was meant for me, and I bought him from the army. There was just something about him. Wouldn't you say, Sara? Best money I ever spent, ninety dollars for a heart of gold. He never gives up; it's quite amazing."

I took one step back and looked at Comanche. I couldn't decide if he was a bay, claybank, dunn, or buckskin. One thing I *was* certain of: he had a dark stripe down his back, indicative of a wild mustang. He also had a big, thick neck and large head that showed the Morgan breeding. His legs were short; he didn't standing over fifteen hands high.[27] His only white markings were a small star on his forehead and a ring of white on his rear left foot.

"If you leave the army, will you take him with you?"

"Yep. He's mine. The army actually pays me forty cents a day extra to keep him. Saves them a lot in the long run because I don't keep wearing out their other horses like some men," he said with an edge.

"Was his name Comanche before you bought him?"

"No. He earned the name during a Kansas battle about seven years ago."

"What does it mean?"

"Bravery. With arrows in his rear, Comanche still didn't quit. He gave me all he had, for the entire battle, which spared my life. The debt will last a lifetime, and I'm happy to pay it."

He soothingly talked to the horse as he bent over at the waist and picked up Comanche's front foot. I saw a Catholic patron saint medal dangling from his neck as he inspected each hoof and picked out small stones and packed snow that were caught in the horse's soles.

"You can tell a lot by the way a man tends to his horse. It's only certain men, those of us with deep spirit, who, for whatever reason, cannot trust our hearts to another human; it's those men who feel the strong connection to their horses—a deep bond that's impossible to describe. Wouldn't you say, Sara?"

"Yes, sir," I said quietly, pondering how Sergeant Zito and Private Jake cared for their mounts unlike other soldiers. "What happened to Tom's face?"

"A battle wound from the Civil War. We all have scars, just some are visible, and some aren't."

Private Jake walked into the barn and straight over to us. He was at least three inches taller than me, placing him right at six feet, but still an inch shorter than Colonel Keogh.

"Can I help with the other horses?" Private Jake asked.

"If you don't mind," Colonel Keogh responded. "They need water and feed. I appreciate the help. You can take Dandy, General Custer's ride," he said. "Looks like he could use some serious attention. Dandy is about done, but the general won't let him retire. Too attached," Colonel Keogh said.

"I can see that," Private Jake said a bit sarcastically as we stared at the tired gelding. Private Jake and I went over to Dandy and cleaned dirt from his raw cinch rub. We picked out his hoofs and waited to water all of the horses until they cooled down. I stood at Dandy's left, and Private Jake stood at his right. We comfortably talked over his back, which safely separated our respective spaces.

"Important horses, huh?" I asked.

"They are all important, Sara. Just some stand out as stronger and more beautiful than others."

I blushed, recalling my words from when we first met. Private Jake was the most charming young man I had ever spent time with. He actually listened to what I had to say. He was special; very special. I brushed down General Custer's horse and put salve on his raw belly. By the time I finished, the other horses were happily picking through dry hay. Excusing myself, I walked to our quarters to tell Mother the news. As I approached our front door, Mother peered from behind the front window curtain. She already knew.

"For goodness' sake, Sara. Your hair looks like a mouse built a nest in it. Brush it this instant, before the general sees you."

"Too late, I already met him."

"It's never too late to look like a lady. Do as I say, Sara."

I struggled to untangle my wind-cursed locks of long brown hair, which actually shined like the sea when I took the time to brush them. I quickly weaved a loose braid. Then Mother told me to pass word through the fort that the women should meet at the mess hall. I rushed from building to building, spreading the news. The women reacted in various ways. Most were giddy with excitement, some were just obedient, and a few were clearly inconvenienced. Their reactions reflected their diverse backgrounds, ranging from dedicated wives to mail-order brides. Of all the different women at Fort Randall, I never met one who appeared whole. Each seemed to have a difficult history or a weight on her shoulders.

Twelve of our twenty women gathered around Mother in the mess hall; all were probably wondering if she could step out of her aloof shell.

Mother began, "General Custer is resting in his quarters. As you all know, this visit is totally unexpected. We need a noteworthy dinner, within an hour or two, and Mrs. Wiesenberger needs help." She presented the situation but did not orchestrate a plan. As an afterthought, just before leaving the room, she turned to me, saying, "And you, Sara, make something special."

"Like what?" I asked.

"I don't know. But this is our chance to shine. General Custer is a special man. Make him something special. Now I need to ready myself. I'll be seated at the head table, as you already know," Mother said and rushed out.

The rest of the women stood motionless, as if acclimating to the undefined whirlwind before us. Mrs. Parker's arms were crossed. She reluctantly agreed to help in the kitchen. Mrs. Wiesenberger barked out orders, and we marched without questioning the assignments. The women who were not comfortable in the kitchen set up the mess hall tables. I scurried into the kitchen, and there, standing in front of the butcher block, was Mrs. Parker, staring at a huge slab of fresh beef, wielding a butcher knife, and mumbling to herself. She started aggressively hacking it to pieces.

"Whoa, whoa," Mrs. Wiesenberger barked. "I'm making my special roast beef. Take your hands off it!"

"What's so special about him anyway, by golly?" Mrs. Parker said under her breath. "Why does he get all the attention and the best beef? This was ten cents a pound."

I had never seen even a touch of resentment within Mrs. Parker. I turned away and refocused on my own task of preparing a dessert for the General. I remembered the sweet bread that Miss Bee had taught me to make back home. We baked it in a round pan, and when pulled from the oven, it became a steaming, two-inch tall, heavenly dessert. From all different sections of the kitchen, I collected the flour, butter, baking powder, eggs, brown sugar, and a small packet of dried loganberries that I had hoarded ever since we moved west. I mixed the ingredients, poured them into the pan, and carefully moved it beside the oven, with the plan to slip it in just before the main course was served.

Next, I went over to Mrs. Parker, who had been reassigned to mince onions for the top of the soup.

"Can I help you, Mrs. Parker?" I asked.

"You can help me, all right," she answered. "Just get out of my way."

Flustered, I moved beside Mrs. Wiesenberger, who was seasoning the roast beef. She told me to make the gravy, which I did, by pulling from the oven the previous day's roasting pan, full of beef juice and oils. I added a half cup of milk and three tablespoons of flour, then stirred it all together. Mrs. Wiesenberger watched over my shoulder and then said, "Add a little more flour. Sara, you need it thicker. Now salt and pepper. Let me taste," she added. No matter how much salt and pepper I added, she insisted, "More, Sara. Add more."

About an hour and a half later, I peeked into the mess hall, which was full of anxious, hungry men. When General Custer's group finally arrived, the Fort Randall men respectfully rose from their wooden benches and chairs. The four men from Custer's Seventh Cavalry were something of a legend. Custer himself led the way to the head table, while the others followed, quite subdued by their leader's larger-than-life personality.

An extended table had been set up in the center of the room. A long white tablecloth, pulled from an old cabinet and ironed just minutes before, covered the rustic pine underneath. Dad and Mother stood beside their chairs as General Custer and his men shook hands with them. My parents were quite a sight to see.

Father wore his best officer attire, and mother donned a bright-blue velvet dress with a matching laced blue hat. Personally, I thought it seemed a bit overdone. All of Custer's men, in clean blue uniforms, found their appropriate chairs according to military protocol. Even with the forced formalities, the men still carried personal tin coffee cups, ignoring our fort's carefully placed crockery.

I was nervous and rushed back into the kitchen in order to slide my bread into the oven. Then, just as Mrs. Wiesenberger had planned, all of the kitchen help lined up to carry out the first course: bowls of vegetable bean soup with Mrs. Parker's decimated onion mush globbed on top. We coordinated the soup bowl placement in perfect unison. As we lined up behind the men at the table, I saw that my two bowls were to be placed before Colonel Keogh and Tom Custer. Mrs. Parker happened to serve General Custer. I wondered if she wished to feign an accident and spill the steaming soup onto his lap. A grin momentarily crossed my face. Colonel Keogh recognized me from the stable and smiled.

"Thank you, Sara," he said gently.

"With pleasure," I answered, in my most polite voice. Mother discreetly nodded her head in approval.

Just as Dad was about to say grace, the men dove into their first course.

General Custer sat beside his brother Tom and Dad, who seemed a bit tense with the situation and started with small talk. My eyes wandered to Tom, who was younger and more handsome than his famous brother. The Medal of Honor was attached to his uniform, and the scar on his cheek only enhanced my intrigue.

"What brings you through Fort Randall?" Dad asked.

"Just heading back from a meeting. Sorry for not letting you know ahead of time," General Custer replied vaguely.

"No imposition, General. I just want you treated right. Let me know if I can do anything else to help your men rest a bit."

"Ah, my men are fine. They don't need to rest."

Custer laughed and looked at his men, who offered forced chuckles that lacked sincerity.

As the main course was served, just like the first, the odd social dynamics subsided as the men fully embraced the meal before them: roast beef with my gravy on the side, mashed potatoes, green beans, and fresh-baked bread with butter. I worked my way around the table and refilled empty coffee cups. After about four minutes of silent eating, which seemed like an eternity, General Custer wiped his mustache with a handkerchief.

"Well, well, what a wonderful meal. I appreciate all you've done, ladies," he said and then asked for another helping.

I walked into the kitchen and checked the bread. It was ready, so I pulled it from the oven, sprinkled sugar over the top crust, and slid it back in. A few minutes later, a golden brown-sugared crust enveloped the top of the bread, and bits of loganberries peeked through. It looked delicious. I pulled out the bread and covered the pan with a warm towel, waiting to serve it at the end of the meal.

Back in the mess hall, I lined up against the back wall with some of the women. My arms rested calmly at my sides; Mrs. Parker's were crossed again. When the men were full, they moved their chairs into a semicircle around the potbellied stove. Mother excused herself, and General Custer graciously kissed the top of her hand, thanking her for her hospitality. The women cleared the tables. I refilled the coffee cups again. Then I took my place back on the wall, facing General Custer. He began to tell stories.

General Custer's deep blue eyes were curious. Sometimes they sparkled, like those of a little boy who has just played a trick on his sister. Then, as if between two acts in a play, he paused, and afterward they turned dark and beady with untold secrets. The whistling wind added mystery as it howled against the walls of the mess hall. We were safe inside, toasty warm with radiant heat and burning oration. Truly, Custer was a great storyteller, and everyone listened intently—everyone except his own men, who had obviously heard the same stories over and over again. They pretended to remain engaged, smiling and laughing at the appropriate times, like the supporting cast for his play.

Custer told of his famous 1874 Black Hills gold discovery expedition. I thought of how one expedition changed the course of my life.

"Quite a find I made, discovering gold in those hills," he bragged.

As the night progressed, he became even more loquacious. The spotlight shone only on him. From the depths of the backstage, I built up enough courage to ask, "What is going to happen if the Indians don't go back to their reservations?"

Custer replied, "Not anything for you to worry about, my little darling. Either we'll force them back or we'll kill 'em."

Once I asked the first question, other men followed with their own queries. As the tabletop kerosene lamps burned on and on, General Custer became looser with his words. One of the men standing behind the semicircle of chairs blurted out, "What about Calamity Jane? Do you know her?"

"Oh, do I ever know her!" General Custer humored. "What man in blue with brass buttons doesn't know her?"

"Was she your scout, as she says?"

"As long as she improves the morale of my men, she can call herself anything she wants!"

Most men chuckled. Mrs. Parker snorted and her fingernails left marks in her crossed arms. Calamity Jane. I had not heard of her. The only Calamity I ever met was the woman waiting for the hotel privy. I suddenly realized that perhaps the two were one and the same woman.

General Custer was a not-so-subtle master at directing conversation; he moved here and there, according to his own whims. Somehow he worked in stories, like how far he had come: from being a mere farrier's son to a West Point graduate.

"Maybe I wasn't first in my class, but did you hear how I had everyone obeying orders before we even graduated?" Custer asked, only pausing for a deep breath. "I was in a French class, and asked the professor, 'How do you say "class dismissed" in French?' Well, he told me, and I stood up and left class early. The other cadets followed."

His audience laughed. Then he bragged on and on about killing Indians.

"They hardly put up a fight! We killed almost all of their ponies and took over fifty women and children prisoners." I wondered how many women and children were killed, but I did not have the courage to ask.

"Now, if I defeat the Sioux and Sitting Bull, I'll be famous enough to be president of the United States," Custer said, and then clarified, "Why would I want that job, anyway, when I already have the best job on earth? Nothing can beat my life in the army, chasing down savages. Like my great friend General Phil Sheridan said, 'The only good Indian is a dead Indian.'"[28]

All of a sudden, I realized my dessert had not been served. I scurried to the kitchen, where Mrs. Parker and Mrs. Wiesenberger were drying the washed dishes. They quickly helped to collect clean plates and forks, following me out to the remaining men with the dessert.

As I gently slid a plate in front of General Custer, a waft of cinnamon filled my nostrils. Had someone slipped cinnamon in my bread? I stepped away and nervously watched for his

154

reaction. After a few seconds into his first bite, the edges of General Custer's mouth turned down.

"What's in this bread?"

"I don't know, sir; what is wrong?" his orderly asked.

"This bread is not made according to army protocol. Who made it?"

Nobody spoke. Mrs. Parker and Mrs. Wiesenberger quietly disappeared into the kitchen.

"I did, sir," I said, with hands trembling behind my back.

"Well, well. What a wonderful treat, young lady. This is marvelous. Simply marvelous!"

"Thank you, General Custer," I said lightly between nervous sighs and then cracked a gracious smile. Slipping back into the mess hall, Mrs. Wiesenberger beamed from ear to ear, while Mrs. Parker's nostrils flared.

General Custer put down his fork and asked, "How would you like to travel with my regiment, Sara? What a boost you'd provide to my men. You could help the cook and take part in our adventure. See new scenery. Meet new people. It's all out there waiting for us, Miss Sara. I could even put you on the payroll, as a cook of course."

I froze in disbelief.

"No offense, General Custer, but my daughter is only fifteen, and I would like to keep her with me," Dad insisted.

"I didn't mean to offend you, Major Taylor … but if you change your mind before I leave …"

"I won't," Dad said with a bit more force than anyone expected. "And perhaps you should not mention it again." I caught Private Jake's steely gaze as he stood in the shadows against the other wall, boring a hole through the back of General Custer's head.

"Well, well. Never hurts to ask … Looks like it's getting late; time to turn in, men," General Custer said with a shrewd gaze as he rose to his feet. With his jaw firmly set, he wiped the crumbs from his lap and exited the mess hall. His air of mystery was intriguing, and his comments toward me were sure to start rumors.

After the mess hall cleared, Mrs. Wiesenberger, Mrs. Parker, and I remained to mop the floor. Mrs. Parker scrubbed with the vigor and energy of a young child as she blurted out tales of General Custer's various indiscretions with women. She said his scandalous behavior involved killing an Indian chief, stealing the chief's young daughter, and then fathering her child, now a seven-year-old, blonde-headed boy named Yellow Bird.

"He pretended to hire her as an interpreter. But she didn't yet know a word of English!" Mrs. Parker said emphatically. Only then did I understand her disgust.

The next morning, though I awoke at the crack of dawn, General Custer and his men were already gone.

CHAPTER 13

RED

SORE EYES MOON

FEBRUARY 1876

DAILY LAKOTA LIFE

"ONE DOES NOT SELL THE EARTH UPON WHICH THE PEOPLE WALK." ~Crazy Horse

Our life was not easy. Our world was full of struggle against the forces of nature and, lately, against the white man. Each member of our tribe had unique duties to make our lives easier. The women handled the tipis. When my Grandmother was a girl, her tipi was small, made from only seven buffalo hides and small bendable sticks. The inside was about seven feet from side to side. But then, as we acquired horses, the tipis were no longer moved by our dogs. Because the horses could pull more weight on the travois—the sleds we used to transport our belongings—our tipis became larger. My family tipi was made of strong trees and twenty buffalo hides. It was one of the largest in our camp because Grandfather and Father were good hunters, and Grandmother worked endlessly to prepare the hides. With all different sizes and decorations, the prearranged circle of tipis was quite a sight.

Tipi making was tedious. First the women staked the fresh hides to the ground. They spent the whole day, bent at the waist, scraping away flesh, bit by bit, with a bone scraper. Next the hide was left to dry in the sun for a few days before it was scraped again. The hide was flipped over and restaked, and the same process was done on the other side in order to remove the thick buffalo hair. Then the hide was soaked in water for a few days. Buffalo brain, fat, and liver were rubbed into the wet hide. For a few more days, the hide dried. Finally, the skin was worked back and forth, until it was soft. The whole process took ten days.

My grandmother was an expert at determining the best way to cut hides for the proper tipi shape. She instructed the other women, and they arranged the hides carefully before committing to final trimming and assembling. Women and girls in our tribe had many other jobs. They cooked and dried our meat. They gathered berries and scavenged for wild vegetables and roots. They collected fuel for our fires. From tanned animal hides, they created our clothing and usually decorated each piece. The women also packed up camp when we prepared to move.

Because Father and Grandfather were leaders, my contribution to the tribe was very different. Father taught me to function without food for a few days. I learned to find my way on the treeless prairie, day or night. I ran on foot and often arrived before others who were on horseback. Father taught me to shoot my bow and arrow quickly and accurately. I learned to swim across wide rivers. He taught the other boys and me to use a buffalo robe over a fire to send messages into the air. We covered the fire with the robe and then pulled it away quickly to make the message. Three puffs of smoke meant "danger." And if each tribe passed on the message, it would be relayed hundreds of miles in a day.

Father taught me to sneak through tall prairie grasses. I learned to protect myself by moving with the terrain, just under the vision lines of the white man. Father told me the white man seemed to camp on mounds on the prairie. Although the hilltop seemed safer, it was easy to ambush the white man by arching our arrows into their camp, while we never abandoned our cover.

"My son, you have learned what I have taught. You have not complained. You will be our runner for many seasons to come."

"But I want to be a warrior. I want to protect our people from the wasicu."

Father seemed a bit surprised at my comment, because I was usually silently compliant for the sake of our people. I knew what a legend my Grandfather became after his death. To my people, he was the great Lone Horn, the chief and only Miniconjou who had run down a fleeing buffalo on foot and killed it with his bow and arrow. I had followed in his shadow for my whole life. Now he was gone. I missed his presence, mostly in the dark of the night. It was a change of seasons within my body and the time to speak my heart, which was exciting and frightening, all at the same time.

"But, Father. I can be more than a runner. I almost understand the writing of the white man and the words that come from his mouth. I know how to set up a tipi. I can kill buffalo. I have watched Grandmother treat our ills with herbs. I make my own arrows. I am ready for more. I am ready for war," I pleaded.

Father ignored me and continued, "My son, when has the Creator said you are to be a warrior? He hasn't. The Great One gifted you with strength and invisibility. Use the gifts. Grow in your gifts. Your legs are strong, your head is bright, and your lungs are like a deer. Protect our people in your own way, a wise way. Do you not remember when your name changed from Runs with Heart to Ohanzee?"

"Ohanzee," I thought to myself. It meant "Shadow" in the white-man language.

"You already ran with all your heart. But then the Creator made you invisible to the enemy. Now you can listen to the enemy from the shadows. Someday you will become a great leader. For now, build more bravery, more integrity, and do what you know is right," Father said.

I dropped my head in personal defeat and walked from the fire. Ohanzee. Shadow. I paced to the end of the camp and into the woods for privacy. I sat on a fallen tree that had not been touched by the light snow that had fallen over the night. As I sat and pondered, I kicked my feet back and forth, working my way

160

through the snow. There below me was a cluster of rosehip berries. They were always sweeter if picked after a frost. I bent over, tasted one, and puckered my mouth. I kicked the snow away and collected about ninety berries. They were a gift from the Great Creator and would keep my family healthy for a month.

On one fairly nice winter day, Father pulled me aside.

"Ohanzee. It is time for you to prove yourself. Collect your arrows and dried pemmican. Take your flint knife and medicine bag.[29] Feed our village."

"Alone?"

"Yes, alone."

Grandmother already knew of my assignment and handed me the beaded rawhide bag, which was bulging at the seams. Inside was a pouch of pemmican, dried from my first buffalo kill. It lost nearly half of its weight as it dried in the sun, and then Grandmother pounded the pieces into fine shreds. She mixed bone grease, dried chokecherries, rosehips, and pin cherries with the meat. Once mixed into a paste, she squeezed it into clean buffalo bladders and intestines for storage. As the long winters wore on, pemmican was prized. If prepared carefully, it lasted three years without molding, and one small portion provided the nutrition of a full meal.

I set out alone, committing to only two possible outcomes: I would either die or return with a deer. I walked for nearly a full day, until I found a deer trail running through a spring fed creek that was still flowing despite the cold. With no game in sight, I placed myself windward of the trail, my back to a tree and my bow easily within reach. I waited and waited. The sun quickly dropped from the sky.

At dusk, just as the winter sun was setting through the trees, a small white-tailed deer came down the trail. It paused, scenting the air, possibly sensing my presence. The deer was a young buck, perhaps a two-year-old. I waited for the deer's attention to be diverted, which finally happened when he dropped his head for a drink. Slowly I reached for my bow and set the arrow. The deer looked up again, and I froze. When the buck's desire for water overcame his inherent sense of fear, he dropped his head for a final drink. My arrow was ready. I aimed quickly for his heart and lungs. A shot just behind his shoulder would bring him down. I released the bow string, and the arrow scored a direct hit. The deer lunged forward with two bounds, across the creek, and then he dropped at the water's edge on the other side. I walked over and saw that my arrow had almost traveled completely through his body. I stood a slight distance away, until the life faded from his eyes. Out of respect, I waited a few moments for death to set in and for his soul to prepare for the sky beyond. "I take you only to feed my people. Thank you, beautiful animal," I told the figure, which was still after his nervous system finally gave up.

I opened the lower cavity of the deer with my knife. The scent of wild game wafted through the still air. I cleaned out his intestines, careful to not puncture the lining. The heart and liver were removed whole, left in pristine condition. I prepared to carry the buck home, just as each fifteen or sixteen year old boy had done for decades as a right-of-manhood initiation. Usually the boy came back to camp about two days later with a buck or doe hanging down his back, legs draped around his shoulders. Only a few never returned, which was quite sad for the entire village.

In the dark, I finished cleaning the buck, and just as I was wiping my knife clean on the grass, I heard leaves rustle. I froze; only my eyes darted toward the sound. Another buck, this one larger, was approaching the spring. Without thinking, I slowly reached for my bow and another arrow. This one did not sense my presence as the first had. Perhaps the wind and darkness offered no clues. He nonchalantly walked to the stream, dropped his head, and began to drink. The back of my neck twinged with excitement as I drew my bow and took my shot. Things quickly turned for the worse. My shot was not as accurate as the first. Surprised and rushed, I shot the second buck in the center of his torso, behind his heart, where no vital organs were damaged. The buck jumped from the creek, with the arrow in his side, and ran for cover in the trees.

I rose to my feet and physically paused, though my mind raced on as the situation sank in. What a mistake it was to have acted on excitement and not have thought through the consequences. I could not take the shot back, and I dropped my parfleche and arrows. I plunged through the creek and scurried up the hillside in pursuit of the injured buck. My legs burned as I gasped for each breath of air. Occasionally I caught a glimpse of the buck's white tail maneuvering through the tall cover. To let him flee, with the arrow through his torso, was a disgrace. To track him until he yielded from exhaustion was my only option.

After thirty minutes, I finally began to gain ground. The buck bedded down just a few yards from me. Within two body lengths of him, I stared at his heaving ribcage. The back of the arrow protruded from his side and wavered with each labored breath. I reached for my bow and arrow, only to be reminded of their absence. I pulled my knife out of my hip pouch and calmly talked with the buck. In the next instant, I grabbed his short antlers with one hand and sliced his neck with the other. Blood gushed out to the rhythm of his heartbeat, and then all subsided and his neck went limp.

With only a sliver of moon to see by, I needed to make a decision. I had placed myself in quite a predicament. Darkness. Two dead carcasses, one weighing around 125 pounds and the other around 140 pounds. Walking without extra weight, I was one day from my village. If I wasted one carcass and returned with the other, none of my people would know the difference. I would pass the test. Yet I would know, and the Great Creator would know, how I took the life of an animal and did not utilize his meat, instead leaving it there to rot; this would make me no better than the white man. If I carried both carcasses back, it would take twice as long to reach camp—probably four days instead of two. Father would worry, but he would be greatly satisfied once I came into camp. I would know, and the Great Creator would know, how I did the right thing. My decision was made.

In near darkness, I cleaned the intestines and lungs from the second buck. Then I spent the next four hours dragging him back to the first buck by the creek. I collapsed at the edge of the water and drank until I was bloated. I left grandmother's pemmican in

164

the parfleche and nourished myself with a raw piece of deer meat. When I regained my strength, I tied the back legs of the first buck together with sinew and hoisted the looped legs over my head, like a cape. I stepped a few paces to sense the load. It seemed manageable. Then I grabbed the back legs of the second buck and pulled them behind me, like a horse pulling a travois.

I only made one hour of progress toward my winter village before I fell to my knees in pure exhaustion. I leaned against my kills, and their dissipating body heat surrounded me. I pulled the parfleche under my head to use as a pillow. The night lasted forever, and the heat from the carcasses waned to nothing. The next day I tried a new technique as I worked my way back to camp. I carried only one deer for one hundred yards. Then I would drop it and walk back for the other; this made twice the walking but half the weight, which my body seemed to appreciate. By the end of the second day, my back ached, and I argued with my arms, which protested that they could endure no more. On the third day, as I approached my village, something inside me changed. A new energy, from deep within my core, renewed my spirit. As word came to the camp, my people watched me approach, and I slung the lighter buck on my back, while dragging the other. Father was greatly satisfied.

A few days later Father told me to prepare to leave the village. That night we had a small ceremony around the fire, for the future success of our mission.

"Soon we will travel to Greasy Grass to meet with our brothers. Sitting Bull has called the gathering to discuss our changing times.

But for now we will go look for the enemy who takes our buffalo and breaks our treaties."

"Father, will we fight?"

"It is not my goal, but we must be ready. We want to see the wasicu for ourselves, and just watch," he said. As an afterthought, he smirked and added, "Maybe you will find a horse for yourself, my son ..."

I was not certain what he meant by "find a horse." Even so, I was excited at the prospect. The next day Grandmother placed a pack, filled with pemmican and a buffalo bladder for water, on my back. "You may need to be the runner, Grandson. You may need to run for your life. For our lives. Do as your father says." I nervously smiled. She never spoke actual words of love, but her actions screamed her feelings: the endless hours she spent crouched in thickets, picking plums and chokecherries; meticulously pounding out the pemmican; and putting up our tipi, time and time again.

As we left the village, I walked behind the horses. We were not in a hurry, and it gave me time to think of our summer meeting at Greasy Grass and what I hoped to learn from Sitting Bull. He was a great warrior and a symbol of our old sacred life before the arrival of the white man.

CHAPTER 14

WHITE

MARCH 1876

ORDERS

"BY FAITH ABRAHAM OBEYED WHEN HE WAS
CALLED TO GO OUT TO A PLACE THAT HE WAS
TO RECEIVE AS AN INHERITANCE. HE WENT
OUT, NOT KNOWING WHERE HE WAS GOING."
~Hebrews 11:8

Long-standing Fort Randall soldiers said the winter of '75 to '76 was horrible—the worst that they had ever seen. Dad said General Sheridan wrote to Washington, DC, and informed the government leaders that the army was compelled to suspend operations on account of the severe winter weather. At an officer meeting, Dad learned that the same consideration was not offered to the Indians, and if they were not on their reservations, then they were considered hostile. He told me that a month earlier, on February 1, 1876, Secretary of the Interior Zachary Chandler had notified

Secretary of War Alonzo Taft that the compliance deadline had expired. The matter was then turned over to military authorities.

So it was war, as the winter wind continued to blow. Dad seemed content at Fort Randall, and his men caused few problems with little opportunity to purchase liquor. Dad worked outside quite a bit, and the cold wind wore him down. His congested cough was exacerbated by the frigid air. One evening in early March, Dad came to us with news. He did not make small talk, as he went straight to the stove and rubbed his hands above it.

"Girls, I just received orders from the secretary of war to reestablish a deserted fort."

"What? Where? Why?" Mother gasped.

"It is not far from here. Just twenty miles upstream on a little creek off the Missouri. The Whetstone Agency. It was set up in 1868."

"Why isn't anyone there now?" I asked.

"We thought the Sioux would settle in the area. For a while, tribal members lived nearby and took their rations and government annuities from Whetstone. But then Spotted Tail and Red Cloud moved away. The army converted it into a holding facility for supplies heading to Spotted Tail and Red Cloud's people. It's been closed down for three or four years now."[30]

"Just tell me one thing. What's the use? What's the use to any of this, anyway?" Mother asked.

"General Lugenbeel told me to reestablish the fort because he sees unrest on the horizon. We will become the supply support system for the upcoming campaigns. Just think, I will be in charge."

"In charge of the whole fort? It will be yours? You'll be a general!" I exclaimed.

"No, I'm afraid there's not much to it. The place isn't like Fort Randall. We'll have to rework it."

"Is it safe?" Mother asked.

"It should be, once it's set up. It already has a stockade, a few buildings, a stable, and a jail."

"Can we come with you? There should be plenty of cleaning, and organizing, and cooking, and—can we come with you, Dad?"

"If you want to try it, I'm okay with the idea. It's not far and you can change your mind and come back. You never know, it could be easy, and we may never see one Indian. Or it might be tough— the most difficult thing we've ever faced. If you want to try it, then come. Just know, you girls can come back, if need be."

"Let's try it, Mother! We can start our own fort. Fort Taylor!" I encouraged her, grabbing hold of her arm.

Dad smiled at my enthusiasm. "I'll hand-pick my twenty best men. It'll take three days to get there; maybe two, if we push it. We'll take just enough food and ammunition to get us by until we send for backup. The fort has been deserted for years, so there should be long dry grass for the horses; we'll take extra grain just in case. Shouldn't take more than a month before we are set up."

Mother was behaving strangely. She stared at the far wall, with no apparent focus.

"Mother? Mother?"

She did not answer.

"Mother? Are you okay?"

Nothing.

I walked alone, across the grounds of Fort Randall. The wind chilled me to the core, but it did not feel dangerous because wood-burning stoves were just steps away. I walked to the cozy chapel library, wondering if I could borrow a few books for the journey. I wandered down each row of shelved books, looking for the perfect title. If I could only take one book, which one would it be? I turned to a middle aisle of books that seemed full of undiscovered treasures. If only I had more time. I ran my fingers down the book spines, mesmerized by the embossed textures and gold shimmers accenting each title. Some books were tattered, and the threads of the binding stuck out a bit. Others were smooth as silk and clearly new additions to the library. I randomly slid different books out of the tight shelves for closer inspection. All of a sudden, from the other side of the shelf, a hand burst through a space between the books and forcefully grabbed my wrist.

I instantaneously pulled back and blurted an uncontrolled, ear-piercing squeal.

Private Jake popped his head into the gap, where his hand had just seized me.

"Jake! You rat!" I hollered, nearly punching him in the face out of reflex. Instead, my hand stopped short, and my fingers were suddenly caught in his soft, wind-tossed locks. With trembling hands, I awkwardly released him.

He burst out laughing and fell back against the wall. His laughter went on and on from the other side of the bookcase. He gasped, "Did I scare you?" Then he went immediately back to uncontrolled laughing. I couldn't help but giggle.

Once we settled down, Jake gestured for me to sit beside him on the floor. I stepped around the bookcase and stood in front of him. He looked up at me for a moment, without saying a word, and then, as sincere as ever, he said, "I heard the news and had to come find you."

"Why?" I asked.

"Because. Sara. Please. You really shouldn't go. Please stay here. Stay and take care of your mother. I want you to wait, until you know it's safe."

"It's safe. The Indians aren't even in the area. They're still in the Black Hills for the winter."

"Some aren't, Sara. We don't know how many are out there. Just stay safe here."

"Why?" I whispered, looking around to confirm that the library was empty.

Jake dropped his voice, to a low, deep whisper. "Because I'm crazy about you. The first time I saw you, I knew. You took my breath away. It'll kill me if something happens to you."

"Jake. You are crazy! I'm not looking for a husband. I need to go. Dad needs us with him. We always stick together as a family."

Jake continued, ignoring what I said, "I stare at you, Sara. I watch you with your dad's horse. I watch you tend to your mother. I see the sparkle in your eyes, as we cross paths throughout the day."

"You're imagining things, Jake. I need to go. It's as simple as that."

"I'm sorry, Sara. I could agree with you, but if I did, then we'd both be wrong. I'm not imagining anything." Jake silently rose to his feet and walked with determination from the chapel library.

A few days later, when I could no longer see Fort Randall on the southern horizon, my stomach churned with the finality of my decision. I had not said good-bye to Private Jake. He was never in the stable when I tended to Blue, and our paths did not cross. It was probably better that way because I needed to forget all about him and move on. I felt a sense of finality and loss.

We were on our own: a party of twenty soldiers, twenty-four horses, Dad, Mother, and me. Twenty-three of the horses carried one rider and two packs, one for the rider and one for general supplies. One extra pack horse carried ammunition and fifty pounds of hay. Each soldier had one hundred rounds of personal ammunition, his issued rifle, two weeks of rations, a wool blanket, shirts, socks, underwear, pants, wool gloves, a hat, and a jacket.

Our group was also given four Lee's breech-loading rifles to test in the field.

I didn't ask anyone if I could take a book from the library. I just did it, discreetly stashing it in my pack with my other personal belongings. I felt a huge sense of guilt and regretted my rationalization; I would ask for forgiveness if I was caught instead of initially asking for permission. On our day of departure, I was able to layer almost all of my clothing over my thin frame, allowing for extra space in my pack, where I stuffed the book and a small bag of oat treats for Blue. I was hardly recognizable, with my bulging body and my face covered with a wool scarf. There was no room for vanity on this journey. Each horse carried a load of one hundred pounds, split between two packs, which were covered with waterproof rubber blankets.

About an hour away from Fort Randall, just as the energy and excitement of the journey waned, a soldier rode up beside me. His face was covered with a bandana, to ease the burn of freezing flesh.

"Some ride, huh?" he mumbled through the wind.

"Yes," I said quietly.

"Think we'll get scalped?" he asked, coughing a bit and then clearing his throat.

I spun around to stare at the soldier, "Jake!"

"At your service, my fine lady," he answered.

"What are you doing here?"

"I asked your dad to pick me, as one of his finest men. He knows that I take great care of our horses, and when I told him how I could track, he said he'd give me a try. Now, if I could get his daughter to give me a try."

I did not say a word, only grinning safely behind my scarf.

We rode on. The horses, weighed down with our supplies, still seemed thrilled to be out of the fort. Dad and Blue led the way, as Blue never allowed another horse to overtake him. Spirits were high, and a few of the soldiers even bantered with Dad.

"Did they take away your rank of major when they took away seventy-nine of your men?"

Dad laughed with them. "They'll be right behind us, as soon as we call for them."

"Are you sure? Maybe they just want to get rid of us."

We covered about fifteen miles of ground, crossing windswept highlands where little snow stuck. We stayed along the western ridge, where the snaking Missouri slithered below. The river had taken on a new, reserved personality and was frozen solid. We came to an area that was sheltered by thriving timber against the riverbank. Dad told us to set up camp.

As the sky darkened, I collected firewood while staying within sight of our camp. I felt chills running down my spine; I was certain that something, or someone, in the woods was watching me. I made eight trips back and forth, while some of the men tethered the horses and others set up tents. Sergeant Zito arranged my collected wood into two separate areas and started fires. With two burning, all of us could keep relatively warm because our white canvas tents were placed tightly around each heat source. The tents buffered much of the unrelenting wind, but they did little to protect our privacy. As the only two females in the party, Mother and I slept in the clothes that we had put on at the fort, prior to our journey.

The next morning calm but deathly cold temperatures permeated our clothes. We hustled around camp to stay warm, all working together to gather ourselves for the day ahead. This was a day I would never forget, because I spotted my first true Indian. Three warriors stood as still as statues, on a ridge, quite some distance away. I was a bit unnerved and wondered if dozens more hid behind the ridge, out of our view. But nothing happened — at least not then.

As we began to move up the path, keeping the river to our right, the wind picked up again. I watched the snow churning around us and could not determine whether it fell from the sky or just vertically pelted us, over and over again, as it swirled on the trail. The horses were subdued, and most of us dismounted and led them along to save their energy. Walking kept my toes moving and took away the sting of the bitter cold. We moved from dawn until dusk, and Dad thought we covered ten miles.

Sometime in the middle of the second night, the tides of fate rolled out of our favor. During night watch, Private Jake heard a noise coming from the tethered horses. As he inspected the line, he saw that four were missing.[31] He called alarm, and everyone woke from an already light sleep. The men helped secure Private Jake's prisoner and listened to the condensed version of the crisis. They hoisted saddles onto our remaining horses. Dad led the way on Blue, calling out orders and warnings, as they tracked down the thieves. A pitch-black sky did little to guide them on their way.

CHAPTER 15

RED

MOON WHEN DUCKS COME BACK

MARCH 1876

CAPTURED

"SHALL WE SUBMIT OR SHALL WE SAY TO THEM, FIRST KILL ME BEFORE YOU TAKE POSSESSION OF MY LAND." ~Sitting Bull

We left most of our people at our winter camp, deep in the Black Hills. Four warriors traveled with Father and me. We went south from our winter shelter because Father said he wanted to see how many white men were actually invading our sacred hills. We found white-man villages spotting our land like hail from a summer storm. Some of the villages had thousands of people, which reminded me of our large summer gatherings.

We stayed camouflaged in the trees, and the white men never saw us. Father was discouraged and said we should continue to the great river, to see if the white man's river fort was also infested with the white-man locust. We turned east onto the prairie, passing the desolate Badlands. After many nights under the stars, we approached Fort Randall from the north.

Father looked over a ridge and reported, "Twenty wasicu soldiers, their horses, and two fat wasicu women. We will follow them and see where they settle." Father continued, "I think they have a few too many horses for their own good."

The other men chuckled, as the group passed below us without even looking up. At dark, the group set up camp, near a thick grove of trees, beside the river. We hid deep in the trees and watched a white girl, not yet a full woman, collect wood for their fires. She was not fat, but only covered in layers of clothing. She seemed tall for a girl and her fine facial features were fascinating.

"We are here for their horses, not their women," Father said quietly, after he saw I could not take my eyes off the young woman.

We did not take their horses that night. Father said we would follow them for another day and learn their habits. We studied their horses and discussed which one I should take and call my own. I had my eye on a beautiful gray who seemed to be the white chief's horse. He led the way all day long and seemed to have a strong spirit; the horse, which was powerful yet not too tall, seemed perfect for me.

We followed for another day and strategized our raid as the white people settled into their new camp. We waited until the soldiers fell asleep. Then Father told me to sneak in and collect a horse from the end of the line. I snuck through the trees while the other warriors stayed within my sight, still keeping their distance. One soldier was on guard, and he walked the circumference of the camp, around and around, without ever deviating from his routine. I crept to a spot behind a tree, close to the line of horses. As soon as the soldier finished checking the horses, I snuck up, cut the rope from the first horse's tie-down, and quickly led him into the dark woods. About twenty feet in, one of our warriors, whose cheek still carried a fresh scar from his last raid, took the rope. I crept back and repeated the process.

The second horse walked willingly away from the others, as did the third and fourth. I ducked below a branch and saw that the soldier had completed most of his loop. The next horse was the gray. I don't know if greed or poor judgment blinded me, but I didn't listen to a cautious voice from my soul; instead, I rushed back and cut the gray's rope. He resisted, pulling his head back and snorting. I put my hand against his nostrils to familiarize him with my scent. He resisted. A bit unnerved, I looked back for the soldier, who was certainly approaching. I could not see him, so I tugged once again at the horse's lead, and he obeyed. Not five steps from the horse line, I felt a cold rifle muzzle against my head.

The soldier told me to turn slowly and head toward the fire. I pretended to not understand his words, and he gestured me toward the fire. I lost one moccasin when it snagged on a tree root,

179

but I did not stop to pick it up, because I thought that the soldier might kill me. He jammed the gun into my ribcage as I walked in front of him. The soldier screamed at the top of his lungs and woke their camp.

The soldier reported the news, as I stood there, frozen, with my hands up. The young white woman was on her feet and staring right at me. Two soldiers pushed me to the ground, sat on me, took my knife, and tied my hands behind my back.

"They stole four horses. Just found this savage sneaking off with Blue."

The soldiers jumped on their horses, and the white chief led his men away from camp and into the woods. After a long while, they returned, empty-handed. I wondered where Father was. The gray, which should have been mine, was covered in sweat and heaved air through his flared nostrils.

"Well, well," the white chief said, staring at me, tied up by the fire. "Nice work, Private Jake. At least we have something to negotiate with now."

"What do you mean, Dad?" the white girl asked. She was the daughter of the white chief.

"It's pretty simple, Sara. We'll keep the savage as a hostage. He may come in handy to get our horses back—and our ammo, our grain, our hay. And they stole our four new breech-loading rifles."

The white girl went by the name of Sara. From the white chief's words, I also learned that while I led horses away, Father and the other warriors raided their supplies.

"It will be okay. The fort should have plenty of grass within the walls," the white chief assured the girl. I knew the grass was extremely poor near Whitestone, as the soil was red and the grass as gray as the clouds overhead. The soldiers rebound my hands and tied a rope around my neck. I wondered if by day's end I would be dangling from a tree, silently swaying with the wind. Then they tied the end of the rope to the back of a horse's saddle. Sara looked down at my feet and saw I was missing one moccasin. When she looked at me, I gestured toward the woods, tipping the top of my head and directing my eyes to where the moccasin rested. I watched carefully as she walked to the picket line where the remaining horses stood. She looked on the ground.

The woman called to her, "Sara. What on earth are you doing?"

"Nothing, Mother; just looking around."

"Get back to the fires; it is not safe out here."

The woman was Sara's mother. I was not sure what I would do without my moccasin. The ground was cold, and my foot would freeze if they led me along on their journey. If they hung me, it wouldn't matter anyway.

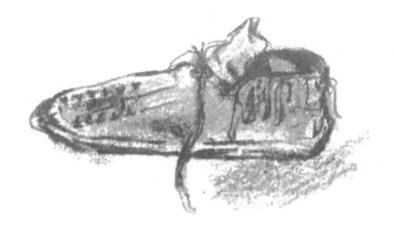

I watched Sara return to the center of camp. When nobody was looking, she quietly dropped my moccasin at my feet, and I slipped it on, unsure of what motivated the girl to do such a thing.

About half an hour later, the sun began to rise. Now without enough horses, the wasicu were forced to make new arrangements. Sara's mother was set up on a new horse, but Sara and a tall, strong soldier walked at the back of the group, with two other soldiers, who walked backward as much as they faced forward, searching the trees behind us with long guns pointed at their enemy ghosts. I walked along, tied to the last horse in the line; I was not afraid because my people would rescue me.

CHAPTER 16

WHITE

WHETSTONE AGENCY

"THE BEST THING ABOUT THE FUTURE IS THAT IT COMES ONE DAY AT A TIME."
~Abraham Lincoln

When Private Jake hollered, the camp became tumultuous. I went from a restless sleeper to a sweating, flush-faced fighter. Private Jake, with his prisoner, appeared from the tree shadows. A savage. He was tall enough to be a man, but he had a lean build, similar to someone my age. His skin was smooth and copper-colored. Sleek black hair extended past his shoulders. He wore buckskin pants and a beaded buckskin shirt. In the firelight, I noticed the prominence of his chiseled cheeks and nose. With eyes cast down, I only caught a glimpse of his eyes, which were darker than black coffee. He appeared neither afraid nor aggressive, and one foot was bare.

Without a moccasin, his foot would freeze. Perhaps it already had. The savage motioned toward the trees, and I reasoned that he lost it during his struggle with Private Jake. Mother yelled at me just after I caught one shimmering glimpse of the moccasin, stuck at the base of a thicket. Without breaking stride, I reached down and grabbed it. I placed it under the outer layer of my coat and with my forearm, pinched it in place against my body. Mother did not watch as I walked past the bound savage. He stood with his head as low as physically possible. I released the moccasin and it dropped next to his bare foot.

The Indian seemed resigned to his incarceration. When daylight broke, as the horses walked out of camp, he never fought back or cried out. Hours into our journey he slipped on the icy trail and fell to his knees. The noose dug into his flesh as he was pulled along, struggling for a foothold. A four-inch gash was torn in his pants when they got snagged on a rock, before he finally regained his footing. The resulting abrasion in his skin oozed as he walked, and it stained the buckskin surrounding the tear. The savage did not make a sound as he continued on. Then I saw blood rolling down the rope around his neck and dripping onto the snow.

I watched for quite some time and finally couldn't stand it any longer. I quickened my pace and caught up to him. As we walked along, I asked, "Doesn't that hurt your neck?"

No response. He remained aloof. I did not blame him.

"Sara, quit talking to that worthless savage thief," Mother uttered from the back of her horse.

I looked over at Sergeant Zito, who saw the Indian's condition and glanced back at me with a confusing expression—of pity,

184

with anger mixed in. He halted the rider, loosened the rope around the Indian's neck, and looked underneath the ligature. Sergeant Zito made an awkward face and retied the rope around the Indian's waist, against his buckskin pants.

Dad pushed us hard all day. He was uneasy about the possibility of lingering Indians and wanted us behind the fort walls before dark. Our progress was slow as we dipped down into frozen creek bottoms and then back up onto flatland, which stretched like a tabletop, until the next creek broke the monotony of the landscape. We often lost sight of breaks in the Missouri River as they meandered across the prairie floor.

A sudden calmness came over the prairie, and the sky turned dark. Pockets of even more frigid air descended upon us. Dad rolled his eyes and said it felt like a blizzard coming on. Luckily we were close to our destination. The sunlight disappeared, and only dim light came from the horizon as we approached the deserted fort. Whetstone Creek meandered back and forth and had very high bluffs on each side, making it difficult to navigate. But there it was, our new fort.

"We made it, Dad. We did it!" I called ahead.

"Just barely," he replied.

"This is no Fort Randall," Mother blurted from beneath her stiff scarf.

She was right. Whetstone sat on a low bluff, overlooking a small stream with leafless cottonwood trees scattered near the creek bottom. I could not see the familiar Missouri River because a hill to the north obstructed the view. The fort was tiny and dilapidated. I waited to hear objections from Mother, but none came. She just kept her head down, tucked inside her scarf. Whetstone was fortified with stockade walls, which were still intact yet desperately needed repair. Dad opened the flimsy gate, and we went inside.

He seemed a bit discouraged or overwhelmed as we surveyed each building and saw the long-term work in front of us. The entire fort consisted of five buildings: a one-room log building that was scarcely larger than a storage shed, two larger buildings, the stable, and the jail. A pathetic parade ground—much smaller than that of Fort Randall—was covered with six inches of snow.

I ignored the obstacles set before us and instead focused on the short term; we had made it to shelter, and it was warmer and safer than sleeping in canvas tents near the creek. Dad said the three of us would sleep in the shed, which I immediately named the "cabin" because it sounded more substantial. The other men split up in the two larger buildings. The front half of one was reserved for a kitchen and gathering area. The multipurpose building was split down the center, with two blankets hanging from the ceiling, which enabled the men to sleep with a hint of privacy. Wood-burning stoves were in the middle of each building, and after dinner, the men tore down the blankets and tried to reflect the radiant heat back to where they slept; this was not ideal, but it was our only reasonable alternative until real barracks were built.

Dad and three other men led the Indian into the jail after checking the window bars and door. The key was still in the lock, as if

186

someone had consciously left it there, years ago, and under unknown circumstances. The jail was tiny: perhaps twelve feet long by twelve feet wide, with a wooden door secured by heavy wrought-iron latches. Rusty metal bars, running up and down about six inches apart, blocked the window from escape. Dad shoved the Indian inside and dropped a blanket on the floor. The Indian stood, emotionless, and did not pick up the blanket. Blood still dripped from his neck.

"I'll get him fixed up with water in a bit," Dad said.

"I have him covered," said Sergeant Zito. "You tend to the troops and your family."

We returned to the barracks, where Dad noticed leaky sections of the roofs that allowed snow to seep down onto the rotting plank floors. He suggested that the soldiers pitch tents inside the existing buildings, for added warmth and protection from the snow.

I went back to our cabin and set up our tent. Mother lay down under the canvas and fell fast asleep. With a lit kerosene lamp, I curled up beside her, ignoring the wind and distant coyote calls. I studied my only book, *A Sketch of the Early History of Practical Anatomy*, published in 1874. As I turned the pages, I learned of the greatest anatomist of all time. My eyes widened as I read the name of none other than Leonardo da Vinci, who dissected human bodies and then drew them in red chalk; these sketches were housed in the British royal collection at Windsor. I had picked the best book in the Fort Randall library.

The next morning I scurried around the cabin and cleaned up what I could. Field mice had deserted the nothingness long ago but had left scat trails thick enough to show how they lingered long after the last soldiers abandoned Whetstone. The cabin was surely not a house, but it protected us from bitter winds. I was prepared to call it home.

Mother and I bundled up and kicked through snow to reach the barrack, where we set up a kitchen and prepared our first meal for the men. They had already collected firewood and started to secure the fort, even though the new snow slowed their progress. All things considered, we were managing fine. As each day came and went, an additional four or six inches of snow piled up on everything around us. Some days the drifts made the stockade walls and buildings resemble solid ice ghosts. Then the next snowfall would accumulate on top of the existing ice. Dad mumbled that the storm was our curse, and he sat by the stove and wrote out a message:

> General Lugenbeel:
>
> We have made it to Whetstone with a few
> significant setbacks. Four horses and a large
> portion of supplies were stolen by savages on our
> second night from Fort Randall. We had no
> casualties and seized one Indian prisoner, more
> than just a boy, but not yet a full-sized warrior. We
> made it to the fort with all men and the remaining
> twenty horses, which are still in decent health,
> given the lack of grain, as it was also stolen. The

men are working hard to secure the fort, which is in very poor condition. I request more men, horses, ammunition, horse feed, and food rations. We are short in all areas. The Indians keep a respectable distance from our fort walls; however, the situation remains tenuous. Upon sending this courier, we are currently at myself, nineteen soldiers, a woman, a girl, nineteen horses, and one prisoner.

Very respectfully,
Major Taylor

Then Dad left our cabin. A few minutes later he returned with Private Jake, who followed Dad's example by stomping snow off of his boots before coming through the door. I looked around, knowing already that there was nowhere to sit other than the floor. So I stood. Private Jake smiled at me. I wished that I had combed my hair.

"Private, I need to discuss something with you," Dad started. I held my breath, wondering if our earlier hints of affection were going to be addressed. "You are one of my best scouts. You are young and strong and I need your service." I sighed with relief. Dad did not know.

"Yes, sir," he proudly responded, with gleaming eyes and shoulders set square.

"In the morning, carry this message to General Lugenbeel at Fort Randall. It's important. Then you can rest there or guide the reinforcements back here."

"I'd very much like to return, sir."

"Well, see how it goes. We are depending on you. Do your best, Private. Take Blue. He's the best horse of the lot. I'll ride your horse until you come back."

Jake stared at Dad in disbelief since taking a superior's mount was completely against protocol.

"Thank you, sir, but I could do no such thing. I'll be fine on mine."

I finally spoke up, "Private Jake, if you have space, will you kindly return my book to the chapel library?"

"Oh, one slipped into your bag, huh? It would be my greatest pleasure," he said, and I noticed an uncertain and suspicious look on Dad's face. Private Jake quickly left the cabin.

The next morning I shadowed Jake, waiting for a moment when we could be alone together. Finally, while tacking his horse, he pulled me aside.

"Please, take Blue. He'll help you get back to Fort Randall," I begged.

"You need him here, Sara. I just know it, deep in my soul." He lifted my hand to his lips and lightly kissed the back of it. He glanced up into my teary eyes and smiled lightly. "Wait here, Sara. I'll be back. I promise."

Another soldier walked in, not aware of any indiscretion. We both stood tall, and Private Jake talked at full volume: "Just put your book in my saddlebag, and what did you say you wanted in exchange?"

Formally, I replied, "Anything medical. It's up to you." His dimples appeared with his steadfast grin.

"Very well. New books will be here in five or six days. Please, show patience, if it is longer." And with that, Private Jake winked his uncomfortable wink and was gone. I was not certain that he would return. He may have doubted it himself, yet he still had the courage to face his assignment straight on. Traveling in groups was dangerous; traveling alone was worse. Yet danger was on the surface of all that we did. It did not take much imagination to feel surrounded by a tribe of revenge-filled warriors.

Dad was unnerved by the boldness of the horse thieves. With only a handful of infantrymen to guard the fort, Dad did not allow search parties for food. Occasionally a stray rabbit slipped under the stockade wall, and fortunately for us, we had a tiny taste of protein. The horses did not fare as well. The fort sat on unproductive ground with very rocky and poor red soil. As a result, even years after being abandoned, plus with the thick bed of snow, there was little grass available for the horses.

Day after day went by, and Dad kept promising, "It's just a waiting game. They should be back soon with rations; any day now." But backup never came. The winter storm put us on the defensive, with our bodies already frozen within a bubble of isolation. Morale slipped. I passed the time by climbing the ladder to the top of the guard post and looking out at the white prairie. Sometimes I thought I saw figures in the snow.

One morning I woke later than usual, completely chilled to the core. Mother was already at the makeshift kitchen, preparing another bleak breakfast. I slipped out of our cabin. By only the light of dawn, I barely made out two figures through the blowing snow. I approached and saw Sergeant Zito. The other figure was a dead antelope, hanging from a rope, attached to the flagpole.

"What in the world, Sergeant Zito?"

"Today our stomachs will be full! Did you pray for a miracle last night, Sara? Because this darned antelope came running straight through the fort wall last night, while I was on watch. He asked to be put out of his misery," Sergeant Zito chuckled. "This wind and snow can even make animals go crazy!"

I knew the antelope had not breached the wall. Sergeant Zito knew that I knew. He clearly had broken fort regulations. With only a sliver of a moon, he snuck out in the cover of darkness and risked his life for a meal. Perhaps we were worse off than I previously thought.

Each raging gust caught the antelope's suspended body, which swayed back and forth. Sergeant Zito cut out the edible parts. I pretended it was surgery, assisting Doctor Sergeant Zito, with his steady hand and deliberate directives.

"Take this liver and backstrap to your mom," he instructed.

I obeyed and when I returned to Sergeant Zito, he was whistling in harmony with the howling wind. I positioned myself away from the long, gutted opening of the antelope's belly and blurred my vision by slightly crossing my eyes, trying to minimize the gore. I wished to see only white—the antelope's perfectly white rear end, the white snow drifting at our feet. But my eyes were pulled to the blood dripping into slimy pools of yellow and red. As the outer edges froze, they turned the snow a snuff-colored brown. I started getting queasy and turned my head away, hardly tolerating the sight. How would I ever grow up to be a nurse if I couldn't stand the sight of blood? I tried to focus on something else that was equally disturbing: the antelope's sad brown eyes staring into mine. I grew braver each time I returned from dropping off chunks of meat to Mother. I took deep breaths and looked into the antelope's eyes again. The brown had grown fainter as the raging snow collected on his eyelids.

When all the edible parts had been cut from the carcass, I ran back to our kitchen to help Mother. She had done nothing to prepare the meat and stood staring at the blood, which drained from the pieces of muscle and dripped off the edge of the table.

"Mother? What's wrong?" I asked.

"Nothing, Sara. Here, help me clean up this bloody mess," she said, snapping out of her daze. I complied and then seasoned the meat with salt and pepper. I sliced it and laid it in pans over the fire, fueled with wood from the ravine. Our supply of wood, stacked in the corner, was shrinking quickly because we could not safely collect more.

"This is the best ODM I have ever tasted," Sergeant Zito claimed, and then started whistling at his plate. "Don't you agree, Sara?"

"ODM?"

"One-dish meal! Never thought it would taste so good, did you?"

He was right. The antelope, tough and without side dishes, still gave us a sense of comfort and a renewed will to persevere. We laughed at Sergeant Zito's explanation of how the antelope appeared in our fort. Nobody bothered to look for the breach in the wall, not even Dad. After our meal, I heard Sergeant Zito and Dad converse in a near whisper.

"The horses are in terrible condition. Worse than us," Sergeant Zito reminded Dad.

"I know, I know. They have pawed through the snow for a few weeks now. I know there is nothing left."

"Extra men aren't coming, not soon enough anyway."

"Let's give them a few more days before we make a run for it," Dad told Sergeant Zito.

The next day a soldier on the lookout announced that a band of Indians was approaching the stockade. The news created a feeling of terror across my chest.

Dad took quick and decisive action. He ordered one of the soldiers to the ammunitions pile, to collect and dispense our last ammunition. After about ten minutes, the soldier came back in desperation, stating that the ammunition packed back at Fort Randall had been the wrong caliber for the rifles. Dad hesitated and said, "Then we will have to make due with what we have."

Dad ordered all of his men to go to their issues and return with every round of ammunition in their possession, to be collected and equally distributed. Sergeant Zito was first to unload his ammunition pack and turn it over. Dad counted out three revolver rounds and handed them back to Sergeant Zito.

"I need you to stay here, with my wife and Sara. Quickly, come with me. We must talk in private."

CHAPTER 17

RED

BIRTH OF CALVES MOON

APRIL 1876

JAIL CELL

"WHEN YOU ARE IN DOUBT, BE STILL, AND
WAIT. WHEN DOUBT NO LONGER EXISTS FOR
YOU, THEN GO FORWARD WITH COURAGE."
~Ponca Chief White Eagle

My jail cell was only twice the length of my body and just as wide.
The room was the size of a small tipi. Despite that, I felt
claustrophobic. The only window faced toward the horse stable.
In the cold, I was thankful for the limited space, but my bones
ached from the constant chill.

Late at night when most of the soldiers were asleep, I heard Father
calling to me; calling to me as a coyote calls into the night. My
people communicated this way because it went unnoticed by the

white men—at least by most. But I had watched the tall soldier they called Zito for days, and I knew he was different. He was aware. He was wise. He slept in a building next to my jail cell. He would hear me if I returned the animal call. Then he might kill me. So I remained silent.

I envisioned my people anticipating the perfect moment to strike the fort and rescue me. I imagined them standing on a butte, watching and waiting. They would take a pinch of medicine from their pouches, offer it to the four winds, the sky, and the earth. Then Father would place a bit of the medicine in the nostrils of the horses, to make them strong for battle. Next, a pinch of medicine would be dusted over each warrior for protection. They would sneak up on the fort and bravely rescue me. I patiently waited, and waited, and waited. One night, two nights, three nights, four nights; Father's coyote call searched for me. The fifth night all was silent, except for one lone coyote, howling at the moon. I was alone. They had given up. They thought I was dead.

My Creator had set a new course, but I lacked the vision to see where he was directing me. I created a plan on my own: to watch my captors and figure out a way to flee from this madness. No energy would be wasted on useless grieving or pondering why I was left behind. I needed every bit of inner strength to survive and escape. As the days and nights wore on, my prison became a cold burden, chewing at the edges of my sanity. I only had one blanket for warmth, and I pulled myself into a drawn-up knot, to trap my core body heat.

I was acquainted with hardships on the prairie, surviving sixteen cold winters. Yet I could not stop shaking, even when Zito slipped me chunks of cooked antelope through the window. If I stared at the stone walls much longer without keeping my mind active, I could go crazy, just like Sara's mother. The woman peered at me a few times, and I saw it in her eyes; she undoubtedly slipped into madness. I decided to keep busy by learning all I could about my captors. I would find their weaknesses. The chief's name was Major Taylor. Zito was second-in-command. Major Taylor's wife was just called "mother." Of all the people at the fort, Sara was the most worth watching. She was a much-needed distraction from my predicament. Plus, her eyes did not lie.

I stared at Sara with a sense of intrigue because she was different than the girls in my tribe. She did not drop her gaze when our eyes met, and she visually locked onto me, which had the effect of throwing cold river water on my face. I was filled with awe when I looked into her clear eyes. Her face was not perfect. Even so, she was surreal to me, with her ruby-red, wind-burned cheeks. Her brown hair was messy. It shimmered only when the sunlight caught it just right, reflecting the sun's warmth, and I dreamed of touching it. Her skirt blew in the wind, and I could see her brown leather shoes and dark stockings underneath.

Sara did not look at me through the bars as though I were only a prisoner. I gazed back, wondering where she came from and who she really was. Each time when I was on the verge of losing my sense of reality, my Creator brought Sara to my window. My pulse quickened. Completely unaware of how her gaze worked upon me, she gazed at my torn buckskin pants. She was curious about the small bag hanging from my hip and watched as I pulled out herbal salve and rubbed it on my neck. The wound was not incredibly deep, but it would heal faster if I tended to it.

Sara studied my beaded moccasins. They were my treasure and carried Grandmother's spirit. Her worn hands had delicately threaded the beads through the buffalo leather. I remembered sitting beside her as she worked, telling her that I didn't need fancy moccasins. Grandmother didn't look up, but she gestured for me to come closer as she whispered, "Special moccasins for a special Lakota."

"What do you mean, Grandmother?"

"You have the training, you will have the wasicu language, and most of all, you have the heart. You will speak for our people someday. You will make a difference. You won't just live, my grandson. You will make a difference."

I wondered how Grandmother fared now that Grandfather had been called by the Creator. Did she believe I was dead also? Did she still quill the most handsome moccasins of all Miniconjou? I prayed to the Great Spirit that her heart would be calm and patient, somehow sensing that I would return. Since our Creator communicates through visions, I prayed she would receive the message.

Familiar cries came from above. I peered from the bars of my window to catch a glimpse of sandhill cranes migrating north in a long, organized formation. The weather was breaking. The cranes brought the promise of spring to the white-covered plains.

Sometimes I felt like a snared animal staring at its trapper—out of control, facing my fate. My stomach growled, complaining about how long it had been since my last true meal. I resented how the soldiers called me "savage." Why not "warrior" or even "red man"? I didn't call them "land-stealing murderers." But in the darkest moments of my confinement, I admit, I thought these things about the wasicu. My soul was in a dark place, and I begged for sleep, even restless sleep, because praying for a dream or vision had resulted in nothing.

One night, the Great Mystery filled me with fortitude and endurance. With my mind now strengthened, I was suddenly warm and knew I would survive on the little bits of food thrown between my window bars. Before my capture, I strove to become a great scout. Perhaps I was in confinement for a greater reason, a greater purpose. Perhaps the Creator merely wanted me to listen and obey.

I didn't say a word in English. As each day passed, I wished to communicate, but I learned more by remaining silent; like the day when Major Taylor and Zito had a quick conversation beside my window. Major Taylor said that while he was away, Zito was responsible for Sara and her mother. He ordered Zito to use their three remaining bullets to kill Sara, her mother, and himself if my people broke through the stockade wall. Major Taylor said that it was better for them to meet their maker than to suffer at the hands of savages. Zito promised to carry out his wishes. They shook hands and went about their business.

CHAPTER 18

WHITE

APRIL 1876

SPRING BLIZZARD

"WE WALK BY FAITH, NOT BY SIGHT."
~2 Corinthians 5:7

I followed Dad into the stable, and he started to saddle Blue.

"What are you going to do, Dad?"

"We're going to push back the savages and go for help. Stay here, with your mother and Sergeant Zito," Dad said, pausing to let this sink in. "Now listen to me, Sara. You are a wonderful, strong girl. You are a survivor and I love you. You need to take care of your mother … the best you can. But listen to me, Sara. Your best may not be enough," he grabbed my face between his callused hands. "Your mother ran out of her medicine."

I started to tear up. His words frightened me. Dad continued to gently hold my face.

"Now look at me, Sara. You cannot give someone else the will to survive. It must come from within. Do you understand?"

I nodded my head and said, "Please come back, Dad. I need you. Please come back."

"Don't you worry, sweet thing. We'll be back together before you know it."

Dad crouched down and dug through his tack box. I stood behind him as he decided what to take and what to leave behind. As he grabbed an extra blanket from the bottom of the box, it snagged on a key hanging from the edge of the lid. He mumbled, "Won't be needing that anytime soon," and threw it back in the box with the grooming supplies.

"What's it for?" I asked.

"The savage's cell door."

He slammed the lid shut and touched the revolver on his hip out of habit. His rifle was slung across his saddle. Blue pawed at the dirt until Dad scolded him. Before climbing on Blue, Dad hugged me with a deep, everlasting embrace.

"You are my special, special girl. I love you."

"I love you too," I said. There was nothing else to say.

Dad rode away from the stable to meet up with the eighteen mounted soldiers who were waiting by the gate. He spun around and hollered back at me, "Hey, Sara! You forgot to say good-bye to Blue!"

"Oh, sorry! Good-bye, Blue! I love you! Hurry back!"

Dad waved again, and Blue took the lead as the other men followed. Sergeant Zito stood at the gate and secured the latch behind them. With his rifle in hand, he walked toward the guard tower. The lookout was two-tiered. The lower stand had a decent view over the wall and provided some protection from the brutal wind. Upon arrival at the new fort, Dad's first project had been to construct a higher vantage point than the existing tower. The men constructed the tiny platform about seven feet higher than the original, which actually made a roof over the original lookout. I don't know if Dad planned it that way or if it was just luck.

A near whiteout made Sergeant Zito's sentry position useless. It was April, yet spring could not gain a foothold on winter. Day turned to night, with an additional six inches of snow blanketing the earth.

"You are too cold, Sara. I can watch on my own. Just go spend time with your mother," Sergeant Zito shouted against the wind.

I plowed through the snow and jumped the snowdrifts in my way. When I opened the door to our cabin, Mother was sitting in her makeshift chair. Her upper body swayed back and forth, like she was in a rocking chair. She stared at the bare, rough-hewn tabletop.

"Mother? Are you okay?"

She glanced at me, said nothing, and turned back to the table.

"Mother, listen to me. Remember that night at the table back home? Remember? Well, I remember it quite well. You told Dad that you were not afraid of the frontier. You said we'd be fine, and we'd stay together as a family. Do you remember?"

Nothing.

"Well, look what you've done. You've deserted your family. You are off in some ugly world, all by yourself. You're my mother. Remember? Start acting like it. Come on, snap out of it."

Mother quit rocking. She stared directly into my eyes for a moment, and then her focus passed right through me. In despair, I wrapped her in another blanket and tried to sleep. When I woke, I looked over at Mother, wearily slumped in her chair. I thought of Sergeant Zito waiting for Dad. I boiled our last bit of drinking water and made a small cup of coffee. Then I quietly left the cabin, trudging to the lookout.

"It's all okay, no news is good news. They are probably on their way to Fort Randall," Sergeant Zito shouted down from his night guard position. I carefully climbed up the ladder and stood beside him. His eyes were dark and tired. He shook underneath his heavy coat. Sergeant Zito wrapped his hands around the tin cup with a US stamp on it. Concern covered his face; he did not need to put it into words. We waited and waited. Finally, we heard something different over the wind's song against the stockade wall. The faint sound was a horse's whinny. They had returned!

"Sergeant Zito, it's them! It's them!" I hollered.

Sergeant Zito and I looked out onto the barren whiteness. Nothing. Then Sergeant Zito bent over the wall to look directly below us, on the other side. "Open the gate, Sara, it's Blue."

Blue and Dad, I thought, as I unbolted the barricade. Of course, it's Blue and Dad. I forced the gate, pushing snow away as it opened. Only Blue stood before me, on wobbly legs, ready to collapse. I grabbed the dragging reins, which were frozen stiff, and I coaxed him to the stable area. A thick coat of ice over his eyes nearly rendered him blind. Chunks of ice filled his nostrils. Sergeant Zito pulled the saddle off quickly, and we noted a knife gash on his shoulder.

"Start rubbing him down," Sergeant Zito instructed, as he dropped the saddle on the ground.

"With what?"

"Just your hands—rub fast, build up heat, warm him up, quick, or he's a goner."

I rubbed Blue's neck. Sergeant Zito removed the damaged bridle and examined Blue's shoulder wound. The horse stood there, frozen in place, not needing restraint.

"Oh, my gosh," I gasped, when I moved to the far side of Blue. An arrow pierced his hip. He was a bag of ribs, and I watched the end of the arrow move back and forth, with each breath sucked in and out. Sergeant Zito yanked out the arrow, and Blue did not even flinch.

"Now, Sara, you need to fix up these wounds, do you hear me?"

"Where's Dad? Where are the others? What has happened?"

"I don't know, Sara. I'll find out. I'll find out."

I collapsed in tears.

"There is no time for crying right now, Sara. You have to help Blue. Remember what your Dad told you? You are a survivor. Right? Now get to cleaning Blue's wounds," Sergeant Zito said sternly.

From Dad's tack box, I pulled out gauze and a bottle of antiseptic, trying to recall what Private Jake showed me about doctoring horses. Did he say to keep the treatment superficial or to dig deep into the wound? Did he say to cover it or leave it in the fresh air? My hands shook, partly from the cold and partly from the sight of the blood dripping to the frozen ground.

"It's not about me, it's not about me," I silently told myself. I walked over to Blue's low-hanging head and looked into his eyes. What had Blue seen? What had he gone through? I longed for him to speak details of the murky defeat in his eyes.

I am not sure how much time passed, but the morning light had not come. Blue's wounds were clean and the ice was off his body when Sergeant Zito returned and threw his issued blanket over the back of Blue.

"I have a plan. I am going for help," Sergeant Zito said. He placed his revolver in my hand. "If I don't come back, and if the Indians attack and come into the fort, you need to barricade yourself in your cabin, with your mom. If they are determined to get to you,

you need to be the brave girl that you are. You need to kill your mother and then turn the gun on yourself. Do you understand? I promised your dad."

"Yes."

"I'll sneak out and follow their tracks. Maybe they're on their way to Fort Randall and Blue just fell into the wrong hands. I'll find out. Take care of your mother, and I'll be back soon."

When Sergeant Zito squeezed out of the gate, he waited until I latched it from within. In the dark, I walked back to our cabin and checked on Mother, which was a waste of effort because she did not even notice me. I talked to her calmly and said Dad would be back soon. Then I ran to the stable. With the dressings on Blue's wounds, he had not lost much additional blood. The subzero temperatures made infection unlikely. There was hope.

As I went back to the lookout, I stopped, squinting into the dark jail cell. The savage was curled up, in the corner, with three blankets over him. He was slowly accumulating things in his cell, and I knew they weren't gifts from Mother. I ran back to the lookout tower and waited. Every hour or so I repeated my rounds: Mother, Blue, savage, tower; Mother, Blue, savage, tower. After a few hours, I scanned the vast prairie from the tower and thought I saw a figure in the snow—perhaps many figures in the snow. Then I lost sight of everything when the blowing whiteouts flowed into what seemed like infinite proportions. The faintest hint of light seemed to cast a new shadow of grayness over the land.

I heard a noise below—a savage scaling the wall? I ignored my promise to Sergeant Zito about using the bullets to end our suffering. I suddenly wanted revenge and decided to fight. I held the revolver in both shaking hands and reached over the wall. The figure was directly against the wall, inching along. I aimed the sights, looking for something to focus on but not seeing a definite target. Three bullets. That is all I had. How would I use them? A few seconds passed, which seemed like hours. Then I heard a melodic whistle piercing the unceasing wind.

"Sara! Open the gate!"

I rushed down the ladder, skipping every other rung and slipping on the last icy step. Falling to my knees, I continued to hold the revolver above the piled snow. I staggered to my feet and stumbled to the gate, unlatching it with one smooth click. Sergeant Zito slid in and quickly locked it behind us. I dropped my gun in the snow and hugged him until it hurt. Then I looked up into his face. After only a few hours, he looked a decade older. The creases told a horrible tale without him speaking one word. I knew it was bad. Really bad.

"They are all gone, honey."

"Gone where?" I asked in disbelief.

"Gone, forever gone. Dead, honey. They were attacked by Indians. Blue is the only survivor. All the men, some of the horses."

"How do you know? Did you see them?"

He dropped his head, and tears streamed down his frostbitten cheeks. "Yes, I saw them."

"Did you see Dad? Are you sure?"

Lines of grief were etched across his forehead, and he wept. I could not believe it. It must be a bad dream.

"Better left unseen," Sergeant Zito mumbled, as if he read my mind.

"What if some are still alive? What if Dad is just hurt? Take me now. I can help him."

"No, Sara. You need to believe me. They are all gone. I promise you." Sergeant Zito's uncontrolled sorrow lasted about five minutes.

I was in shock; finally, I managed, "We need to bury them."

"Sara, it's too dangerous. The Indians are out there, somewhere. We have to let it be. There are just the three of us now. We have to readjust our thinking."

Let it be? That's it? Just let it be?

When Sergeant Zito and I delivered the news to Mother, all she said was "Dear me." She looked away from my needy eyes and called for pen and paper, as if the deep-seated instinct of an army officer's wife had suddenly taken over her psyche. Had she pondered this situation in the past and was now acting it out? I mutely obeyed, retrieving paper and pencil.

"This is formal, Sara. Bring the ink. It is socially required."

I walked to our pile of belongings and retrieved the ink bottle. She placed the paper on our table and positioned her hand and pen. When she dipped it into the ink, the tip came out clean, since the ink was nearly frozen; its consistency was thicker than that of coagulated blood.

"Oh, this dreadful place," she cried out.

I handed her a pencil. In shaking script, she wrote,

> General Lugenbeel of the First Infantry:
>
> Major Taylor is dead. Corporal Anderson is dead.
> All of the privates are dead. All but Sergeant Zito,
> Mrs. Taylor, and Sara Taylor were attacked by
> savages. They watch and wait. We are next. We are
> out of food and ammunition. Send reinforcement.
> Please hurry.
>
> > Currently in hell,
> >
> > Mrs. Taylor, my girl, Sergeant Zito,
> > one horse, and one savage prisoner

210

Her hands trembled as she signed the bottom and handed it to Sergeant Zito. "Deliver this to Fort Randall right away," she barked.

"Yes, ma'am," he replied, glancing at me with dark shadows under his bloodshot eyes. We walked out of the cabin.

Mother never seemed to realize that her letter was undelivered. She never spoke of Dad again. She did not console or embrace me as I cried myself to sleep. She had never cared for me in that way, and now she became even more detached. She was a damaged woman; something was not right in her head. My heart physically hurt in the most vivid way, yet she was blind to it—or perhaps she saw it and did not care. I needed consoling, and I went to the horse stable to be with Blue. I buried my face against his neck.

"He's a great horse, isn't he?" Sergeant Zito said, moving toward us. We had little left to do since the men and other horses were gone. Just the sight of Sergeant Zito trying to be a pillar of strength brought tears to my eyes. I pulled my own emotions back inside. If he could do it, so could I. Then he touched my shoulder to console me, and I collapsed into his arms.

"I feel empty, just a shell, with all the blood drained out," I whimpered.

"It will be all right someday," he assured me as I sobbed. "I've been there before, Sara. I've been in the deepest, darkest place you can imagine. And then deeper and darker."

"When?"

We both dropped to the stable floor and sat shoulder to shoulder.

"It's a long story. Still painful. My wife and I had a lovely daughter, like you in many ways. She was everything to us. Then the fever tore her away. We couldn't do a thing. The doctors said to wait and pray. We lost her, and my wife never spoke again, not since the day that I covered our girl's grave with the last shovel of dirt."

"What was her name?"

"Charlotte. Oh, my beautiful Charlotte. She had your vivid brown eyes. Sometimes when I look at you, it feels like I'm looking right at her again. Her entire life, I did all I could to protect her. She was such a gift of joy," he sighed, and his voice quaked, "Most of all, she had a kind heart, just like you."

"Where is your wife now?"

"At an insane asylum. On an island, Hart Island, in the waters just east of New York City."

I knew stories about Hart Island but spared him the horrible tales. Sergeant Zito stretched out his stiff knees before he went on. "It's a place for all sorts of crazy-minded women. I did my best to care for her, but she became worse and worse as the months passed. She just stared at the wall, and nothing was left inside of her. No fight. I told her over and over again, 'Rose, you have a reason to live. The reason is me.' But she wouldn't listen. She just stepped off the cliff and didn't claw her way back up."

"Are your letters to her?"

"Of course. The soldiers teased me and thought I was courting someone. They were wrong. Rose has always been my one and only. When I accepted this assignment and dropped her off at Hart Island, she was allowed one change of clothes and no valuables. I slipped a small rock, the shape of a heart, into her skirt pocket. It was all I could think of. Maybe the letters and the rock will nudge her back to sanity."

"What do the doctors say? Will she get better?"

"They don't really know. I can only hope that the nurses read my letters, but who knows what it will take, because she loved Charlotte beyond anything I've ever seen. She put every ounce of her being into that girl."

I listened until he was through. Then we sat in silence. Finally, I said, "Well, let me finish up with Blue, and we can go eat something."

"There is nothing left, Sara."

"Then what do we do?"

"I'll sneak down to the cottonwoods and collect more sticks and water. The stockpile is gone. We can go for quite some time without food, but we need water," he said. My stomach growled.

"I'd rather be cold than take the risk of you leaving the stockade again."

"Well, we'll see," Sergeant Zito contemplated, winding and unwinding the chain of his patron saint medal from around his finger.

The snow continued to pile up against the man-made structures within our fort walls. This was not like back east, where snow gently accumulated in level blankets along a field; in Dakota Territory, prairie waves crested at eight feet in some places. With each passing moment, our situation became more and more desperate.

A few days later, I realized that we were prisoners within our stockade walls. I woke up in bed starving, shivering, and irritated at the howling wind. For a few minutes, I pulled the five layers of blankets over my head to see if my breath would become a visible steam. It didn't. I peeked over at the floor, in front of the door, expecting the familiar morning snow that drifted under the threshold. Because there was no snow on the floor, I hoped the storm had passed and the worst was over. I rolled out of bed and quietly put on all of my layers of clothes. Mother remained still. I eased the door of our cabin open only to face a huge, crusted snow bank—higher than my waist—that had piled up against the door overnight. I crawled on all fours, up across the top of the crust; then I turned back around and wedged the door shut. The soul-stabbing wind was at my back and pushed me effortlessly toward the stable.

I came around the corner of the jail to find Sergeant Zito sliding another blanket through the window bars. Dad's dead soldiers obviously didn't need their blankets; why not share them with someone who still could benefit? Now the prisoner had three under him, to insulate his body from the frozen ground. He had an extra two on top.

214

"I know you fed him," I said, staring into Sergeant Zito's worn out eyes. "Or he'd be dead by now. You couldn't just let him starve. His people killed Dad."

"This young man did not kill your dad. His food came out of my rations, not yours. But anyway, it doesn't matter anymore because we're out of food." He told it like it was—no more sugar coating. We walked to my cabin to deal with Mother. Sergeant Zito started with the update.

"They aren't coming, ma'am, at least not any time soon. We need to head to Fort Randall before we're too weak to travel," he told Mother.

"They will come," she answered.

"No. They may not know we're in distress. No more waiting. If we don't move before the storm ends, then the Indians will certainly come back for us. If we wait for help, we might starve to death. We're out of food. No more mirages, ma'am. It's not safe to collect wood. There's no ammo, either. We'll make a run for Fort Randall right before dawn. Can't risk being spotted by Indians," Sergeant Zito said.

I thought about Sergeant Zito's words, "They may not know we're in distress." If Fort Randall didn't know our precarious situation, then Private Jake never made it there with Dad's message. I always believed in my heart that Private Jake had delivered the message and was just waiting for the storm to pass, but now I had doubts.

This one was different than all other journeys. We had no real choices to make—no wagons to stuff full of needless possessions, no food to carry; just layers of clothes to insulate us.

Mother paced our dirt floor all night. Periodically she paused, gazing through the darkness at a new crack between the boards, which needed strips of gunny sacks wedged in to help keep out the blowing snow. I woke up about six times and tried to coax her back to bed.

"Mother, you need your rest. This is going to be a tough trip. You need to rest. Lay down."

"Sara, tell your father to take me away from this God-forsaken place."

"Okay, Mom, I will tell him. Now lay down and rest." I pulled a blanket from my bed and wrapped it around her. She continued pacing; backlit by the last remaining coals from our stove, she now looked like an Indian woman, stepping to the cadence of the gusting wind.

"Where are you going?" Mother panicked, as I rose from bed for the last time.

"I'm going to go get Blue."

"Don't you dare go look at the savage. Leave him to freeze to death, just like they've done to us."

"Oh, Mother. We won't freeze to death. It'll all be okay," I told her, hoping that she did not hear the doubt in my voice.

I traversed the drifts to the stable. The wind had picked up since the night before; it cut my face like a knife. I pulled my coat collar high up on my cheeks. The deep stabbing sensation quickly turned into a sharp sting and then subsided into a burn by the time I turned into the stable. Blue was in the corner of his stall and whinnied as I approached. His bucket was half-filled with water that was already freezing on the surface.

"Good morning, Blue. How are you? Are you ready?" His hoof repetitively scuffed the frozen ground; his ribs protruded from his sides. I wondered if he would be a help or a hindrance on the journey before us. The sparse grass was gone. Blue was starving to death. *I* was starving to death. We were all starving to death. Instead of saving the little energy I had, I walked to the area where our other horses used to stand. Bits of grass that had not been edible a month ago now became a treat for Blue. I picked up single stems, and he vigorously snatched them out of my hand. I decided to lead Blue to Fort Randall with a halter and rope because a cold bit would tear at his mouth. Mother would travel on his back, in Dad's saddle, since she was too frail and confused to walk.

I left Blue tied in his stall and headed back to check on Mother. As I walked past the jail, I was drawn to the Indian's window; he was curled up in the corner. "Don't you dare go look at the savage" rang through my mind. "Leave him to freeze to death, just as they've done to us." I spun around and walked back to the stable; dug through Dad's tack box; and threw out a curry comb, a canteen, a dusty pocket knife, and a hoof pick. The key was gone. I grabbed Dad's canteen and ran over to Blue's water bucket.

217

Pushing past the frozen top layer, the canteen guzzled up the slushy water below. Through the screaming wind, I faintly heard whistling as Sergeant Zito approached. I quickly capped the canteen and ran back to the tack box. I threw everything back inside except the knife, which I placed in my coat. The lid of the box slammed shut. Sergeant Zito rounded the corner of the stable and staggered a bit in the wind. He was physically spent.

"Oh, Sara ... Good morning. What are you doing?"

"Just came to get Blue ready," I said and concealed the canteen under my coat. "I'll go get Mother now. What's the temperature?"

"From the look of Blue's water bucket and my stiff cheeks, around ten below zero," Sergeant Zito answered. After a quick look at my face, he frowned, pulled his hands from his gloves, and pressed his palms against my cheeks. "You have a little frostbite going on. We'll have to be careful today because the windchill is bad. We'll just do our best; think warm thoughts."

He placed his hands back into his gloves and smiled a weary smile. It was still dark as I slinked from the stable. My heart pounded in my ears as I peeked in the jail window and called in a loud whisper, "Hey! Indian! It's water! Drink it before it freezes." The canteen barely fit between the bars, and it clanked when it hit the frozen floor. No sign of life came from the curled-up bundle.

Each day I had worn a descent path between the stable and our cabin. But as I walked back to prepare Mother for the journey, I noticed the wind had already erased my early morning tracks. I reestablished my path once again.

Mother sat beside our stove, wrapped in a blanket. The last remaining fuel loyally burned, but it was only enough to cast the faintest touch of heat into the air.

"What are you doing, Mother? You need to get ready for our trip."

She refused to leave the fire.

"Mother, let's get going."

Nothing.

"Mother, this is the day! We're going home!"

"Home?" She asked with a glimmer of light from within her blackness.

"Yes, home! We're going back to the right side of civilization."

"New York? All three of us? Your dad's been reassigned?"

"Yes, Mother. Back to New York. Dad's been promoted."

"To general?"

"Yes, Mother. To general. It's finally happened, just as you planned. Now we need to get going and layer our clothes for the trip."

Mother marched straight to her belongings in the corner of the room. She fingered her way down through the layers of perfectly folded, dirty clothes.

"Oh, what will I wear for my trip home?"

I reached around her and pulled out four layers of her warmest clothes. Mother grabbed my arm and stopped me.

"Sara. Back away. I am not a child. This is my choice."

She insisted on pulling on her corset and started to lace it up.

"Help me," she said. Her stiff, cold fingers struggled with the laces.

"No, Mother, we have to go. Take it off. The rescue party sent word, Mother. They need us to hurry and meet them halfway," I said convincingly. I did not feel a bit guilty for lying.

"We will not meet them without our corsets on. It's not proper."

I pitied Mother as she struggled with losing control—whether it was control over orders from Washington, or erratic train schedules, or blizzards, or hunger, or Indians. By attempting to remain "proper," she simply appeared ridiculous. I reluctantly helped tie the corset laces over her emaciated, skeletal frame. Then I handed Mother each layer of clothing, one piece at a time.

"Now put yours on," Mother said.

I refused. Enough was enough. She started to cry as I held her arm and pulled her toward the door. Mother dropped to the floor and refused to go further. I tried to drag her, but it was no use. I was too hungry, cold, and exhausted.

"Mother. Get up. I can't carry you. The men will be waiting. We don't want to be late."

Finally, she pathetically crawled toward the door. I saw Dad's Bible peeking out from under a small pile of his folded clothes. Beside it lay my corset. I picked up Dad's Bible, which was worn around the edges from his late night, candle-lit talks with God. I stuffed it securely in my coat pocket. Then I grabbed my corset, walked to the fire, opened the stove door, and threw it in.

Sergeant Zito was waiting outside with Blue. He placed Mother on Dad's saddle. I then wrapped extra blankets around her body and tucked them into each other. Mother stopped crying. Her legs were terribly exposed, with only a few layers to protect her from the piercing wind, though she would have it no other way. Before we left the cabin, I persuaded her to let me wrap her shoes with old rags for insulation. She only agreed when I told her that we would take the wraps off just before meeting the rescue party.

Sergeant Zito flipped the twisted iron latch and pushed. Snow had drifted against the other side.

"Nothing is easy, is it?" I called to him through my cloth-covered face.

"Nothing worthwhile is ever easy, Sara," he replied, reaching his leg around the partially open gate and kicking the snow away. He worked the door back and forth until there was enough space for Blue to squeeze through. Then he came back to us, breathing heavily, and said, "Okay. Let's get going. We have a lot of ground to cover."

Sergeant Zito broke a trail as he trudged through snowdrifts, which ranged in height from ankle-deep to waist-deep. I followed, leading Blue, with Mother— now wrapped in all of the remaining blankets from our cabin—slumped on his back.

"Keep moving, Sara. Idleness and sleep are not the answer to the cold," Sergeant Zito reminded me. We were reduced to mere worn-out prey trying to find our way.

Sergeant Zito was confident in his route and frequently pulled his small compass from his pocket to check our heading. He knew that 170 degrees would lead us straight to Fort Randall as long as we persevered against the subzero temperatures. We stayed above a frozen creek's tree line, where the snowdrifts had little to cling to. As we moved, without cover or protection, the whiteout made it impossible for me to determine our progress. Did anyone else know our dire situation? What Indians waited to attack? Where was the love of God? When would the blizzard lift?

We walked for two hours in a total whiteout. Finally, Blue gave up and fell to his knees. Mother dramatically fell from his side and collapsed on the snow beside him. Sergeant Zito walked back and pulled her to her feet. She refused to bear an ounce of her own weight as we encouraged her to take another step. At last, Sergeant Zito carefully let her drop to the snow.

"We will leave Blue and keep walking," Sergeant Zito commanded. Mother did not respond. She was mentally gone. Again, Sergeant Zito lifted her up around the waist and held her tight against him. Mother flopped over like a rag doll. He yelled at her and shook her shoulders, but she did not respond.

"Go on," Mother blurted, startling us with her first words of the journey. "I will stay with Blue and wait for help. Help is coming. I sent the message. They will be here soon," Mother continued, clearly in a delirium. I rewrapped and secured the blankets around her and felt her clothes, which were frozen stiff around her bony, trembling shoulders.

"Mother!" I screamed. "They are not coming. We are going to freeze to death if you don't keep moving ahead."

She did not respond. The wind continued to blow. I began to cry. "Mother! You have to fight! We can do this!"

"No, I will wait here with Blue. I can't go on, Sara. Just go."

I went to Blue and rubbed his neck. What could I say to a horse who gave his all, and yet it wasn't enough? I regretted even the thought of leaving them behind. Sergeant Zito uncinched the saddle from Blue's back and propped it up for Mother to lean against. I slid the horse blanket underneath her. Mother seemed far more delicate than I had previously admitted to myself. She closed her eyes and drifted off.

But I couldn't do it. I couldn't just leave.

Suddenly Mother's eyes shot open. "*Sara! I order you … Go!*"

Sergeant Zito reached for my hand and led me away. I did not look back. I wept, as each step was another step into nothingness. We were weak. I could no longer feel my feet, and I stumbled frequently. Sergeant Zito continued in front of me and retraced his steps when I fell behind. Dozens of times he pulled me from drifts where I had lost my footing. We made little progress over the next hour. Finally, we dropped to our knees in total exhaustion.

"We are in trouble, aren't we?" I asked.

"Just a little, but it will all be okay." Sergeant Zito crawled a few feet, on his hands and knees, and then rolled onto his side. He wedged his body against a drift that had accumulated behind a large rock. "Well, let's see where our heading is," he said, once again pulling his compass from his pocket. Sergeant Zito held the compass flat in his stout, shaking hand and slowly turned it, searching for a true north reading. He stopped turning it and shook the whole compass, like a dog scratching an itch. Then he set it flat on his palm and tried to read the arrow again. "Ah, forget the stupid thing. Who needs it anyway?" he stated casually.

"What happened? What's wrong?"

"There's a moisture bubble inside. Makes the needle stick. Must be a weak casing, cracked in the cold. Don't need the stupid thing, anyway."

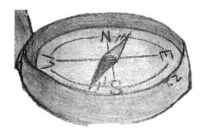
I wondered how long we had been going in the wrong direction. Without moving from his position, Sergeant Zito flung the compass side-armed, into the whiteout.

"We'll be fine, Sara. I just need to rest a bit," he said, even less determined than before. As he lay on his side, Sergeant Zito told me to press my back against his belly so that he could shield me from the bitter wind while we took a break. I started to feel a little warmer against his body mass.

"It's destiny, Sara. We'll find our way. You'll find your way. I'll find mine," Sergeant Zito whispered. Then he began to whistle in harmony with the wailing wind. Somewhere in the night, I became drowsy and seemed to float away to a comfortable place. I no longer shook. I don't know how long I was there, but by the faintest morning light, when all was too still, I turned around and stared into Sergeant Zito's frozen face, and I knew he was gone. I was alone.

The snow blanketed everything, even the sounds around me. I was freezing to death. With every breath, I stepped closer to where I would spend eternity. I was not afraid, but I was not at peace either. Tired and colder than ever before in my life, I remembered Sergeant Zito's words to keep moving. But he was gone. I wondered if his wife, back east, would even miss his letters.

"I love you, Sergeant Thomas Zito," I whispered, wondering if he was still with me in some way. I screamed out in complete anguish, an agony that only God could hear. Then I curled up again, within his frozen shell, totally devoid of hope. Someday, when the storm faded and help arrived too late, someone would find us, but would not understand anything about our unique, enduring friendship.

The wind bit my face. I pulled at my frozen coat collar, looking down to realize that I was wearing Sergeant Zito's winter issue jacket. He had taken off his protection and placed it on me in the night, enabling me to live while knowing he would die—the ultimate sacrifice. I curled tightly against his massive body and wept. My shallow breaths rose and fell as I faded in and out of consciousness. The snow drifted over Sergeant Zito's back. Tears froze my eyelashes shut. There was nothing left to see anyway. I let go. The wind lured me into a death song, which was much easier than a fight.

The wailing wind and whiteout cleared as I somehow rose above myself and moved toward a beautiful orange-and-yellow painted sky. The pain and cold were gone. A sense of peace filled all voids within me. Dad waited, and then gave me a huge hug. I was safe at last.

"You cannot come," Dad gently said. "You need to go back."

"No," I adamantly resisted.

His tone changed; a softness rounded the ends of each spoken word. "Rise, Sara. Get up, girl. Get up, girl. Rise."

Dad had never spoken to me in that way before. Why did he say "rise" when I was already on my feet? And why did he call me "girl"? He never called me "girl." I tried to force my frozen eyes open. Through the blur, I saw a dark-skinned finger gently clearing the snow from my face.

"Get up, Sara girl, we must go."

I left my dance with death only to hear soft words cast toward me from the smoke of a winter breath. I squinted in the bright snow. It was the Indian from the fort. Our prisoner. He had escaped.

226

"Go ahead," I mumbled, "Just kill me. Scalp me. Do whatever. I don't care," I moaned, fully defeated and showered with pain.

"We go," he said gently. He grasped my arm and leg, sliding me out of the protection of Sergeant Zito's frozen corpse. The Indian reached behind his back and retrieved Dad's canteen. He took off the cap and tipped it into my mouth.

"My mother. We have to help my mother," I mumbled and tried to stand up. I barely moved. From behind, the Indian grabbed me, wrapping his arms underneath my armpits and lifting me to my feet. "We go," he repeated. I collapsed as soon as he let go. He gave me another drink of water. I turned back and stared one last time at Sergeant Zito. "We go," the Indian said again, lifting me. I wobbled but stayed on my feet, and he led me away.

"We are going the wrong direction," I told him.

"No, you turned the wrong way in the storm. You walked in circles. Follow me or die."

My skirt caused me to stumble with nearly every step. But walking warmed my core, and as I came to my senses, I became aware of the excruciating windchill. The Indian continued to urge me forward, and soon we rounded a turn on the trail, revealing an emaciated snow-encrusted horse with his head held low, dutifully guarding a large mound of drifted snow.

"It's Blue," I told the Indian, who stayed back as I staggered toward the drift. I wiped away the snow to find a tight blonde bun of hair, confirming the inevitable. I carefully pulled back more snow, already knowing what I would find, yet still hoping I was wrong. Mother's eyes were slightly open and fixed forward—no more emotion, no more fear; just a frozen gaze, somehow demanding that I move on. "Oh, Mother," I wept. One final time she did not embrace me. She couldn't.

CHAPTER 19

RED

SPRING BLIZZARD

"REMEMBER, GOD IS COLOR-BLIND. HE DOES
NOT SEE THE COLOR OF THE PEOPLE NOR HEAR
THE LANGUAGE OF THE NATION. HE
RECOGNIZES ALL PEOPLE BY LOOKING TO
THEIR HEART TO SEE THE PERSON'S
SINCERITY AND HONESTY."
~Grover Horned Antelope, Oglala Lakota

I was completely wrapped in my self-made cocoon when I heard a clanking noise across the room. Without food and water, the bitter cold weakened me quickly. I had not seen Sara or Zito at the window for at least a day. I floated in and out of a frigid fog. Suddenly, in the darkness of the night, out of nowhere, I felt at peace. The Creator had spared me.

As I came to my senses, with a new determination to live, I uncovered my head. Within arm's reach rested a canteen and a key. I sat up and fumbled with the top, took a gulp of water, and pondered my fortune. With the gift came an obligation. The Great Creator placed people together for a reason. My surroundings spontaneously transformed from a prison of confinement to a shelter from the storm. When I finally reached through the bars and turned the key in the lock, I knew what I had to do. The door released, and I was free.

I wrapped three blankets around my body. Mentally I was confident that the blizzard would not lure me to my death. I was not as certain about Sara, her mother, and Zito. The wind might drive the breath from the girl's lungs and any remaining sanity from her mother's head. It seemed the woman lacked whatever fortitude Sara might possess.

I was almost a day behind them and needed to follow their tracks quickly to make up lost ground. I vigorously swung my arms, rubbed my feet and face, and made a plan. I left the fort and walked only an hour before stumbling upon a snow-covered body and the nearly dead horse. Faint tracks continued on. Wasted away, the horse was of little use to me; I left him to decide his own fate. The mound of snow beside the horse nearly camouflaged the still body beneath. I did not push away the snow to see who had yielded first. Whoever it was had already taken a final breath and passed to the other side.

I followed the tracks as they wandered more and more off course. They rarely continued in a given direction and looped back upon themselves in one section. It looked like a hopeless ending for all three of them. Daylight approached, and the whiteout eased. The tracks finally stopped at a large stone, where body-sized snowdrifts prepared me for the worst. I squatted down and noticed the smallest crack in the snow's crust, which opened and shut with the thin breath of someone below. I pushed the snow aside, revealing Sara, who lay curled up before me. Her eyes were frozen shut, and her breath was faint. She looked close to her death walk. I brushed away the snow from the figure behind her. It was Zito. His gray, still face told me that he had already crossed over.

I stood up and tucked my wet hands high under my arms for warmth. I wiped snow from Zito's corpse and pulled the stiff leather gloves from his wide hands. Sara's breath was faint as I picked ice from her lashes and frozen tears from her cheeks. She was nearly gone and I said, "Rise, Sara. Get up, girl. Get up, girl. Rise."

She seemed to respond a bit, so I picked her up and put Zito's gloves on her hands. We backtracked toward her mother. I tried to make a wide path by shuffling my feet along in the snow. Despite that, Sara continued to catch her skirt on drifts. She saw her mother's frozen face but did not wail in sorrow. The horse was looking better in the daylight, and I decided to try to keep him with us. My plan, decided in my jail cell, was to walk toward the setting sun, hoping to catch up to my people.

During the spring and early summer, my village typically moved weekly. I looked for my people's signs, confident that Father would guide me back to them. When I saw none, I blamed the snowstorm. We walked at a slow pace, but Sara still fell behind. I looped around to urge her forward. Her gait was stiff and weak;

she had to keep moving or she would freeze. The horse wobbled while obediently following in our tracks. He could not bear the weight of Sara, but he was not a significant burden either. The horse stomped through the crusty snow cover to reach frozen grass and ate the bark from any trees we came upon. When he was thirsty, he ate snow.

Sara grew weaker and eventually could not go on. I lifted her onto the horse's back, knowing it might be the end of him. He grunted from the added weight but carried her dutifully. I whispered a quiet prayer for his strength and led them carefully over the icy tundra.

I found myself repeatedly looking into Sara's deep eyes. Although this was inappropriate in my culture, I did not resist because when I looked closely, I saw her feelings as they changed within her. I saw sincerity and pain. Her eyes even warned me when she wandered into sorrow, or perhaps despair. I wondered if her mother's emotional weakness had been passed down to Sara.

"Sara, you are too tired. Lock the sorrow in your heart for now. Look ahead; we can't look behind. Focus ahead. Do you understand?" I asked.

She only responded with a squinty stare. I wanted access to her inner thoughts but a more immediate issue demanded focus. My people were moving toward Greasy Grass for the summer gathering. Father told me how our entire people would meet there to decide our fate with the white man. I had made the journey to Greasy Grass many times, but never on my own. If I missed the gathering during the moon of the Greasy Grass, I would not be reunited with my family, and it would be difficult to find them.

Sara was my source of the dilemma. She was a hindrance because she slowed my journey, not on purpose but because she was a white girl. Her skirt flowed in front and behind her as she stepped in my tracks. Even though I pushed the snow aside, her skirt kept hanging up on the snowdrifts. Sometimes she collected and gathered the extra fabric in front of her with her shaking hands, and suddenly I was able to see the previously hidden legs inside, stumbling along and moving in and out of my view.

Sara did not have my stamina, and I was tempted to leave her behind with the horse. Yet, at the thought, I felt sick and could not accept her probable fate. Zito had saved me, when I was their prisoner. He brought me food, water, and blankets. Somehow, in the last few days at Whetstone, Zito and I had signed an unwritten treaty with our eyes, a treaty between a free man and a captive man. The agreement was to do the right thing and protect Sara. She could not survive alone on the prairie—not without learning new skills. I knew it. Zito knew it. I had given Sergeant Zito my silent word; the white man broke treaties, but not Zito. He gave his life for Sara. I would not break my promise to him.

If we were to reach Greasy Grass, our pace had to change. I looked at Sara's skirt and then separated strings of buffalo cord from my thick belt. I squatted, facing Sara, grabbed the bottom of her skirt with both hands and ripped the fabric upward. She gasped. Two long lean legs stared back at me. I spun Sara around and did the same in the back. I layered the front piece of her skirt over the piece covering the back of each leg, and then I wrapped the buffalo cord around the cloth, which encased her calves and thighs, transforming her skirt into a pair of pants. Her narrow waist held it all together at the top. She had to stop frequently to push pieces of fabric back into place, but at least her legs were free.

The blowing snow waned. I found decent protection in stands of trees, in deep ravines, and in a dugout cave. When we were heavily protected, I stopped early in the day and let Sara rest until late the next morning. Each night I pulled Zito's gloves from Sara's hands and studied her long fingers, which were as red as chokecherries. I taught her to squeeze her hands into fists for better circulation. She did.

I clamored up the banks of frozen creeks and dug through the snow into the dirt, where plant bulbs might be buried. Only once did I find a group of seven breadroot bulbs: timpsila. Two were the size of duck eggs; the others were shriveled and barely worth the effort to dig up. Although my people would have normally dried the root and then ground it into flour, I ate it raw and forced Sara to do the same.

"Ugh! What is this?"

"It's a breadroot. I think the wasicu call it a prairie turnip."

"What are wasicu? Are you trying to poison me?"

"Wasicu is you. Someone who isn't one of my people. It is not poison. It will keep us alive."

We were at the edge of starvation, but Sara seemed oblivious to our bleak state. At some point, even my own stomach went into denial and stopped alerting me of imminent disaster. When I laid on my back, I could feel and count every single rib. My hip bones protruded like a skeleton, even through my layers of clothes. I glanced over at Sara, and the moonlight revealed an equally desperate physical condition. I needed to find a way to feed us.

"You need to pray to your Father in the sky, Sara. If you believe in prayer, you need to pray now," I said and began out loud: "Oh, Great Mystery. You are king of the grasses and the animals. Reveal a way to feed us. We are weak and cannot continue much longer." Then I curled up in one of my blankets and fell asleep.

The next morning a warm, dry wind descended upon us—a snow-eater wind. I knew my Creator had blessed us. I had seen it years before: first, a harsh winter storm, and second, a warm strong breeze that raised the temperature forty or fifty degrees in just a few hours. A peace came over my desperate heart, and the wind soothed my frostbitten face. Sara stretched her stiff arms and legs out from underneath her blankets and groaned.

I stood up and walked through the snow, which was quickly turning the prairie into a spongy tundra. The softer ground would help Sara's painful feet. I walked away from where she rested and looked at the melting drifts. A brown stick-like image caught my attention. No trees were in the area. I stepped closer and saw another gift: a frozen grouse, killed by the freak storm.

Sara crawled to her knees and came to me as I pulled the thin grouse from the bank. A few bites of meat could be salvaged.

I began to quietly thank the grouse for his ultimate sacrifice.

"Are you actually talking to a dead bird?" Sara asked sarcastically.

"It's a grouse," I answered.

"Why are you talking to it? It's dead."

"I am thanking it and my Creator who sent us the meal."

"Your Creator? It was mine!" Sara answered. She finally became aware of the warm wind against her face, and it brightened her eyes. Perhaps a smile even crossed her face, but just for a moment. Sara pulled off her coat and slung it over her forearm. Something shiny fell to the ground. She quickly reached for it and turned her back, to put it in her pocket again.

"Give me your coat."

"Why?"

"What's in your pocket?" I asked.

"Nothing," she lied.

I forcefully pulled Sara's coat from her arm and reached into the inner pocket. I pulled out a knife and a Bible. I returned the Bible to her pocket and opened the short blade of the knife. Testing the sharpness on the edge of my finger, I was stunned when blood emerged and trickled off, melting garnet-colored holes in the snow at my feet.

"It's mine, give it back."

236

"No."

"It's my dad's. Give it back."

"No."

Then she wept. I just stood and watched her.

"Please, I beg you, I don't have much left from my dad."

I put the knife in my pocket, not trusting Sara because she had already lied to me. Sara dropped to her knees, and I rummaged through each pocket of her clothing. All of the rest were empty, except an inner pocket on her big outer coat. A pendant lay tangled in its chain at the bottom of her pocket. I untangled the chain and squinted at a rough image of a winged warrior, with a spear, standing over a snake-like creature. As I dropped it back inside the same pocket, I felt a sealed envelope, conformed to the shape of Sara's ribcage and slightly wet around the edges. She was surprised at my discovery and cried after looking at the address. I stuffed it back in the coat pocket and sat Sara on the coat to shield her from the damp ground. With Sara's knife, I cut through the frozen breast of the grouse. I could only dig out two pieces of breast meat, both about the size of my thumb.

"Here. Suck on this and chew it as it thaws."

With the other piece, I did as I had directed Sara, while I collected our blankets and prepared Blue for the day. Sara sat motionless on top of the coat. Her face was turned upward toward the elusive sun. She reached underneath herself and pulled the envelope from her coat pocket. I watched over her shoulder, as she stared, emotionless, at the neatly written words on the envelope: "To: Mrs. Rose Zito, Women's Lunatic Asylum, Hart Island, New York."

Sara asked for the knife, and carefully cut down one end of the envelope, blowing the edges open. A one-page, neatly folded letter waited inside. She took a deep breath, and read:

My Dearest Rosie,

How I long to see your beautiful face. I have loved you since the first day I set eyes on you. Are you resting and feeling better? I am not sure if you received my last letter, because I sent it with a soldier courier during a blizzard, and I am not sure of his fate. The blizzard has closed in, and we need to head back to Fort Randall. My thoughts are always on you and how you will fare if I do not make it. I will fight for my life, like never before, because I have a girl to save. Her name is Sara. She reminds me of our beautiful Charlotte. Please understand, Rose, I can't wait any longer. I need to try to save her. 2 Chronicles 15:7 tells us to "be strong and do not lose courage, for there is reward for your work." I beg you, Rose. Don't waste your life on the pain behind you. Don't lose courage. Step out and be who the great Lord intended you to be. Please remember, I love you deeply and completely. I long for the day when I can hold you again, whenever and wherever that may be.

Your husband,

Tom

Sara's voice cracked with his last words. She wept until her eyelids swelled. I retrieved the knife. We took extra time that morning. Once she was standing, Sara began to move delicately forward, like she was walking across the coals of a fire.

"What's wrong with your feet?"

"Nothing," she lied.

"What's wrong with your legs?"

"Nothing."

I was surprised by her perseverance as she limped from camp. All of a sudden, pent-up questions tumbled from Sara's mouth.

"What is your name?"

"Ohanzee."

"How do you know English?"

"My father sent me to Black Robe, a white-man priest, to learn your ways. I am a protector of our ways."

"Why didn't you talk to me when you were in jail?" she asked. I cracked a smile and did not answer.

"Am I your prisoner?"

"Now I have something to negotiate with," I answered.

"How dare you!"

"I am only using the words of your father."

"So how did you escape from jail?"

"Zito. He slipped the key through the bars."

Just then, the warm wind took on an added scent. I raised my nose. It was something dead—perhaps an animal. Maybe an old buffalo had wandered off to die. The aroma was clearly rancid, and I cautiously walked closer.

"Stay here," I instructed Sara, as I stepped over a quickly melting snowbank and down into a gully. There, on the ground, was a warrior, as dead as a bullet could make him. He was badly decomposed, scattered by coyotes who feasted on the easy meal. I could not tell what tribe called him their protector. I walked up and crouched near his skull, which had a large, splintered hole in the forehead. Looking straight down through the first hole, I could see a small, symmetrical round hole through the back of his skull. He had been shot in the back of his head. His last moments were not spent fighting but instead, running away. I grimaced, and prayed for his soul to become brave.

Then I collected his belongings for our use. Everything a brave normally traveled with was still on or near his body: his bow and quiver full of arrows, flint and iron-filled stones, his parfleche, a buffalo bladder filled with water, and a medicine pouch. Wedged under his hip bone was something shiny. I delicately rolled the bone away, revealing a pristine Bowie knife. Double-edged at the tip, the knife fit perfectly in my hand. I moved all of the belongings a short distance from the scattered bones because giving the corpse space somehow seemed respectful.

I turned around to find Sara and the horse staring at the remains. The horse's ears were tipped back, nearly touching his mane. His nostrils flared as he snorted at the sight before him. I walked to Sara's side and tried to gently lead her away, afraid for her mental state. She pulled from my grip and stepped closer to the body.

"Come, Sara, let's go."

"Please, do you mind?" she said and pointed at the body.

"Do I mind what?" I asked.

Sara sat back down on a sun-warmed rock and pulled off her tight leather shoes. The heels were worn away, and the leather soles were soaked. She then pulled off her stockings, revealing puss-filled, rotting toes. Frostbite had consumed her feet, and yet she had disregarded her pain. I dropped to my knees in front of her.

I thought she might die but tempered my alarm and said, "Oh Sara, these are not good feet," taking them in my hands. She offered a faint smile. I remembered Grandmother putting buffalo oils and sage on Father's raw, blistered flesh when he returned from a hunt with badly frostbitten feet. Sara's were worse. She was in serious trouble but seemed oblivious to it. I pulled a tightly bound bundle of sage leaves from the medicine pouch. With no buffalo oils, I opted to wrap each toe carefully with the leaves and tucked the ends in place. I pulled the moccasins from the bones of the fallen man's feet. The moccasins were slightly larger than mine. Sara's feet were tiny. I took off my moccasins and handed them to her.

"Hohan," I said, "Wear them." Sara said she couldn't wear my moccasins. I ignored her mumbled reasoning and placed them on her feet, securing them loosely over her wound dressings. Her inward breath was a painful gasp of air, but she did not cry out as I anticipated. Sara then pointed at the warrior again.

"I need his pants," she said.

I inspected the warrior's moccasins. They were darker than mine and clearly converted from the smoked top of an old tipi. The beadwork was not remarkable. Even so, the seams were meticulous; someone had taken great care in their construction. I slid them on my feet and stepped gently toward the scattered skeleton. I gently pulled the pants from the warrior's leg bones and shook out the shells of the scavenger bugs. Few were alive due to the frigid weather that had passed just a few days ago. Once again I looked inside the pants, which were in excellent condition given the circumstances. I brought them to Sara, and we both stared at each other.

"I can do it. I have to. Go ahead, turn your back," she said quietly.

I turned away, but all my other senses were very keen. I had seen little exposed skin of a white woman, because they always seemed covered from head to toe. Even at Black Robe's school, the visiting women wore silly hats. Sara was the first white girl that I had ever studied; first from behind the bars of my jail cell, and then as we walked through the storm. She was the first white woman I ever touched, on the day I pulled ice from her eyelashes. Now, with my eyes cast away, I envisioned every part of her. I heard the horse paw at the ground and nibble the first green blades of grass. Then I heard Sara take off my moccasins, drop her skirt, step into the pants, and place my moccasins back on her feet.

"Okay," she said, "You can turn back around."

I was relieved that the temptation was over. I spun around slowly, stirred by the figure now standing before me; the top half was a beautiful white girl, the bottom half was the dead warrior.

CHAPTER 20

WHITE

TRAVERSING THE PRAIRIE

"THE COLD PIERCING WIND WILL BID DEFIANCE
TO OUR PROGRESS, YET WE WILL PENETRATE
OUR WAY WITH FIRM STEP AND BOLD HEART."
~Corporal Lambert A. Martin

I stayed near the warrior's body and let Blue graze, feeling
relieved that the chinook was melting the snow around me.
Where drifts sat earlier in the day, water now pooled, unable to
soak into the already saturated turf. Armed with the dead man's
bow and arrows, Ohanzee set out to track small game. I stared at
the body before me, while brushing back a stray wisp of my hair
that had lodged at the edge of my dry lips. It was surreal. I looked
at the bones, scattered about, and I was haunted by deeper
questions. Who really decided who lived and who perished? Was
my dad right when he said that our own individual choice
determined whether we fight to survive or yield to death? I had
no answers. The only certainty was gut-wrenching pain when I let

my mind wander to the loss of Mother, Dad, and Sergeant Zito. I missed Mother the least, which filled me with guilt. Instead of burning energy in analysis, I tried to keep my mind busy elsewhere. I wandered off to collect firewood, assuming Ohanzee would be successful with his new weapons and we would soon have meat for the fire.

I made eight trips back and forth from a tiny grove of fallen scrub oak trees. Each armful yielded only five or six small branches, balanced upon one another, as they poked and scratched my arms. Ohanzee returned with a grin on his face and a dead prairie chicken hanging beside his hip. He saw my collected pile of branches, took out a rope, and wrapped it all into one loose bundle—his people's way, an easier way.

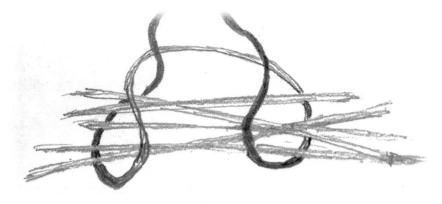

We moved away from the warrior's body but stayed in the same ravine. Ohanzee struck the flint against the iron pyrite to start a fire.

"We are lucky to have wood tonight, but there are other things to burn if you are on a treeless part of the prairie," he said.

"Like what?" I asked.

"Think about it. What else is fuel?" Ohanzee asked. He was trying to make me think like a survivor.

"My blanket," I answered sarcastically.

"Perhaps, but what about buffalo chips?"

"The dung?"

"Yes. It lights fast and burns long; maybe not the best flavor if the droppings are fresh. Just pick the old ones," Ohanzee smiled and I noticed his perfectly straight white teeth.

"Wohan," he said, handing me the bird.

"Wear them?" I asked.

"No, not hohan. Wohan! Wohan means 'cook them'!" Ohanzee laughed, a bold laugh, and then he accidentally dropped the grouse into the tiny fire, extinguishing the flames.

"Ha!" I giggled. It felt good to break the tension. Ohanzee was completely tickled and started the second fire without complaint. Then he taught me how to clean the bird. We stuck a wet stick through the length of its torso and held it over the fire. I was more thankful for this meal than any other in my life. "Thank you, Lord, for nourishing our bodies," I whispered after taking the first few bites.

Ohanzee went through the dead warrior's parfleche. He pulled out a small, waterproof bag and opened it.

"What is it?" I asked.

"Just wait."

He squeezed a chunky liquid, like jam, over my cooked meat and told me to try it.

"It's gooseberry mush. Don't ask me how to make it. I leave that to Grandmother."

The sweet, earthy flavor caused me to think back to Miss Bee and her lovely jams. Though I stood beside her on several occasions while she canned, I never seemed to get the consistency quite right when I tried alone. It came out too runny.

"That's okay, Sara," Miss Bee said. "We can always use more syrup!" Truth was, we had enough syrup to last a lifetime.

I looked over at Ohanzee. He was still chewing the meat from the grouse's thigh.

"We need to bury your warrior. It's the right thing to do," I said.

"What makes it right?"

"Well, he should be put in a box, a casket. It protects his body. And he should be buried six feet deep. We should put a marker at the end where his head rests."

"He is not a white man, and your way does not make sense. If we had trees and buffalo robes, it could be different. But he is already becoming part of the earth. We will leave him alone, and show him respect. Plus, we don't want to waste more time, because we need to keep moving. Tomorrow is another day, Sara."

I wondered if he was right, because my pain was moving from my toes, up my legs, and into my hips. My body was in a battle and I did not tell Ohanzee about my worsening symptoms. He probably knew from rewrapping my feet each morning. When we came to springs and creeks, Ohanzee insisted that I soak my feet and rub off the dead flesh. Each evening he sought a flat camping spot, along the bend of a creek. We let Blue graze nearby and he stayed close on his own will.

Finally, one day as Ohanzee treated my feet, he said that I would die if he did not cut off three of my rotting toes. He explained how they were not healing and would cause infection in my whole body. I knew the medical term: gangrene. I nodded in affirmation, because I had been hiding a high fever for days. At night, I had even been hallucinating.

Ohanzee pulled Dad's knife out of his pants and sterilized the blade over our campfire. Then he approached me and quickly tied thin sinew around the base of each bad toe. Before I could question his abilities, his steady hands swiftly cut through the rotting flesh of the three smallest toes on my right foot. I squeezed my eyes shut and screamed out, and the fire within me quickly turned into a black calm. When I woke, Ohanzee was sitting at my side, stroking the side of my face with his rough fingertips. I looked up at him in desperation.

"Make it go away," I cried to him. "Please, make the pain go away."

"I can't fix it, Sara. But I'm here. I'm here."

I just wanted the day to end, and the pain to diminish. Ohanzee remained at my side. The day turned to night, and I slept restlessly. Yet when I awoke, Ohanzee said I needed to circulate the dirty blood in my system by moving around. Blue's wounds were nearly healed, and he was slowly gaining muscle mass and strength. Ohanzee said Blue could handle my weight for a while and carefully lifted me onto his back. Blue never faltered, but it was nearly as painful to ride as to walk along. My feet throbbed when they dangled at his sides. I tried pulling my knees up against my chest and braced my feet on Blue's neck. It was not secure, yet Blue never spooked along the way.

The chinook winds melted the snow more quickly than it had initially accumulated. The sky seemed friendlier. Dewdrops hung on the edges of last year's dry prairie grass. From atop Blue's back, I could see trails that had been trampled in the grasses, randomly crossing back and forth—not human trails, but great animal trails, trodden deep in certain areas and scant in others; trails around large rocks and down the sides of ravines. Within a few days, glittering spider webs appeared between the blades of fresh green grass and extended across the trail. Blue's knees destroyed the fine webs as he obediently marched on. Ohanzee did nothing to conceal our path, as he assumed nobody would bother searching for me.

When I slid from Blue and limped along behind Ohanzee, I stepped gingerly to avoid jamming my wounded stubs into protruding rocks. Ohanzee's initial expectation for our daily progress was vigorous, but after lopping off my toes, he seemed compassionate enough to back off on his demands. I still did my best to keep up and placed my feet in the exact prints where Ohanzee trod. Despite my uneven gait, I was pleased with how quickly I adjusted my balance without my three toes. I had things

249

to be thankful for: my fever subsided, I quit hallucinating, I was alive, I still had Blue, and Ohanzee wasn't so bad.

"Just think, Ohanzee. I bet a white girl has never ever stepped exactly where I step, here on the prairie."

"Perhaps. But I am certain of one thing, Sara," he said. I waited for his next words, which seemed to take forever to surface. "Never before, never ever on this soil, has a seven-toed white girl stepped."

We both laughed at the thought, which was the first time I sensed something inside me telling me things would work out. I felt that we would both make it back to our respective peoples.

"Tell me about your buffalo. Why do you love them?"

"They behave, just as my people behave. They protect their cows and young calves, by standing guard at the outside edge of the herd. They stand facing the wind in blizzards and don't suffocate like your cattle. They are brave and face the storm head on. When traveling in storms, they take turns upwind, rotating to share the burden. It is the way of our people, not of yours."

Ohanzee sat down and pulled off his moccasins.

"What are you doing?"

"I am feeling the ground. It helps me think more clearly. The great Lakota medicine man Sitting Bull walks barefoot every day. The soil, the dew on the grasses, the vibrations of the earth—it is our ritual for comfort with the earth."

"It's just the ground, right? Dirt, grass, rocks."

250

"Oh, Sara. You don't understand. The white man knows of the physical world, but our people know of the spirit world. It is all connected: man, earth, sky, sun, moon, animals, and plants. All created by the Great Spirit, Wakan Tanka. We must be in balance with the seasons and the rhythms of life."

"Are you superior to the white man?" I asked bluntly.

"Yes," he answered.

"How dare you."

"Don't you think you are better than me?" he asked in return.

I rolled my eyes. "Am I free to go? Can I leave, alone, in any direction I wish?"

"Yes," Ohanzee answered.

"If you teach me to live on the prairie, what do I have to do to pay you back?"

"Nothing you don't want to do," he replied.

"But I'll be indebted to you."

"You don't have to pay me back. Just help someone else, someday."

"But that's not how it works," I said.

"That's not how it works for *you*. Okay, Sara. If it makes you feel better, teach me to understand your written word."

"I only have Dad's Bible," I answered.

"I just need to learn, Sara. The Bible is fine."

"Why do you need to learn?"

"Because I broke a promise. I need to do the right thing now."

"What promise did you break?" I asked.

"I don't want to talk about it," Ohanzee stubbornly insisted.

"Fine, then," I retorted, feeling a bit dejected. "So what *do* you want to talk about?"

"About what a hollow leg means," Ohanzee answered.

"What?"

"Black Robe told me I had a hollow leg. What does that mean?"

I laughed out loud and then regretted it, hoping I didn't hurt his feelings. "It means that you ate a lot. You ate so much food that you must have a hollow leg for a place to store it all. It's a joke, Ohanzee. A joke."

"A white man's joke; not very funny," Ohanzee replied under his breath, and he walked ahead.

In silence, I followed behind. I saw the vastness of the prairie. Spring brought forth the sweet smell of buffalo grass. The melody of small birds rejoiced over the warm breeze. After dark, I heard a shrieking noise that broke the peace of the black night.

"What is that?"

"Ungnagicala. Your people call it a screech owl."

I lay back and listened to the call. The bird was perfectly named: its screech pierced my ears.

"Why do they do it?"

"To scare mice. If a mouse is still, the owl will not see it. If the mouse panics and runs, then the owl will swoop down for the kill. It is all about remaining calm and not panicking."

Ohanzee then made the same call back at the owl.

"How do you know how to do that?"

"We grow up learning the sounds of nature as a way to communicate with our people."

"What other sounds can you make?"

"Coyotes. We communicate through coyote calls."

I thought back to the nights at the fort, when coyote lyrics covered the star-filled sky, like an eerie symphony.

"Did your people call for you when you were our prisoner?"

"Of course," he answered.

"So why did they go away?"

"I did not return the call. They thought I was dead."

"Why didn't you answer?" I asked.

"Zito would have heard me."

"But you lost your people."

"I will find them again. They will be at Greasy Grass," Ohanzee said with certainty.

Another owl called out in the night: screech, then I counted to myself, one, two, three, four. Screech, one, two, three, four, five, six, seven, eight, nine. Screech. I listened for at least an hour to the nocturnal chant. The owl never called out before less than a four-second gap, and after more than a nine-second gap. I drifted to sleep.

Our food supply grew as we continued west. Jackrabbits and cottontail rabbits were our daily staples. Ohanzee was an amazing hunter, and I rarely feared where our next meal would come from. We saw occasional antelope, but my eyes still longed to spot a buffalo. Ohanzee spotted marsh hawks and short-eared owls in places where I would never even have picked them out of the landscape. As we traveled west, prairie grasses, buffalo grass, bluestem, and wheat grass turned a bit shorter and thinner. The spring waters brought goldenrod, asters, and sunflowers, which reminded me of Miss Bee's colorful flower garden back home.

One morning we were awakened by the sound of something beating on the ridge above our camp.

"Inila! Quietly, Sara, follow me," Ohanzee whispered.

We crawled up the dirt embankment and peeked our heads over the edge to the prairie floor. The grasses were fresh and shimmered in more shades of green than I ever dreamed of. There, not twenty feet away, was a male sharp-tailed grouse, with his orange chest dramatically puffed out of proportion with the rest of his body. He pounded his wings against the ground, trying to impress a prospective mate.

"Wow, they really have to work at it, don't they," I exclaimed.

"Everything good is worth fighting for, Sara."

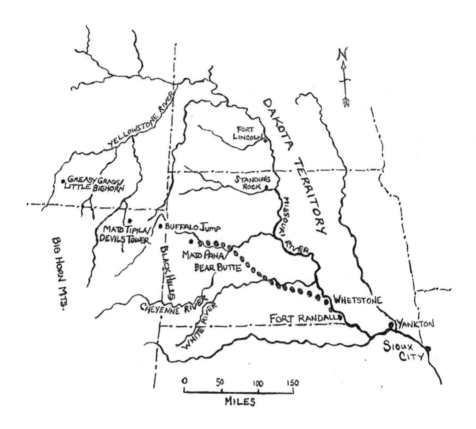

CHAPTER 21

RED

MATO PAHA (BEAR BUTTE)

"GOD MADE ME AN INDIAN."
~Sitting Bull, Hunkpapa Lakota

Sara was slowing us down more than I had expected. Her feet were barely healing, even though I bathed them and draped them in wild sage every day. We needed to travel at least fifteen miles a day. The journey was much delayed even though she rotated between riding Blue and stumbling along. I encouraged her to ride Blue as much as possible, but she complained that her invisible toes caught fire if she did not keep moving her legs. All day long she went back and forth, trying to find the perfect balance, hoping to become friends with her pain.

"Sara, how are your feet?" I asked.

"Fine."

I turned around and walked backward, just in front of Sara, watching her gait.

"Can I teach you how to walk, because your feet need a chance to heal?"

"Please."

"Your feet turn outward, and your body passes between your steps on the inside of your feet."

"So?"

"Walk like a red man, with your toes straight ahead. Your body will follow, and your feet will be happy. Your legs will be stronger. You wear special moccasins. Walk softly, not hard on your heels like a white man."

"How do you know all these things?" Sara asked.

"It is passed down in stories, by our elders. We learn naturally."

"Well, I learn things by reading books, and there was nothing in the library about walking softly," Sara said, humoring only herself.

She did as I said, concentrating on her new smooth gait. By the end of the day, she seemed a bit more comfortable. Though Sara slept soundly at night and ate well every day, her pain still sucked the energy from her. The horse continued to gain strength by grazing on prairie clover and wild alfalfa. As we walked along, I tried to distract Sara's pain-filled mind by teaching her to scavenge wild onions and rosehips.

I hunted at the end of each day, before the sun departed. I was limited to small animals, like turkey and duck, because the horse was not healthy enough to carry Sara plus the meat of an antelope on his back. I could not justify a large kill if we did not harvest the whole animal and pack the meat with us. I felt pressured and obligated to successfully hunt every day. We only needed to reach Greasy Grass without starving, because once I was united with my people, hunting would become a simple group activity, where everyone worked together and nobody went hungry.

"Will you do me a favor, Ohanzee?"

"Perhaps," I answered.

"Will you call my horse by his name?"

"I do. He's a horse, isn't he?"

"But he has a different name. His name is Blue."

"I thought blue was a color," I said, trying to joke with her. "He isn't blue, he's gray," I tried again.

"I know. But it's his name. Just call him that, okay?" Sara asked, now annoyed.

"Okay," I answered, giving up on white-man humor.

I suddenly became overwhelmed by a name issue that had burned at me for quite some time.

"Sara, if I call your horse Blue, then you need to stop calling me a savage. My name is Ohanzee. I am Teton, Lakota, and Miniconjou. I am not Sioux."

Sara said nothing, appearing confused, but humbly nodded her head.

"I need to rest, Ohanzee. I really do," Sara pleaded. "Can't we stop and rest?"

"No, we need to keep going," I said. I knew just the thing to lift Sara's spirits and keep her moving toward the far western horizon, where a welcoming sight grew from the prairie floor. Nearly exhausted, Sara did not seem to notice the twelve-hundred-foot-high mountain, which grew more prominent as the hours rolled on; or perhaps she saw it and did not care.

"Let me tell you a Kiowa legend that my grandfather shared as we hunted for berries near here."

"Is it true? I only want truth," Sara said sharply.

"Just listen, and then you can decide. Once the Kiowa people lived on the prairie, before my Lakota people pushed them from this land. A Kiowa boy was playing in a valley with his seven sisters. He was looking for adventure and asked the Creator to change him into a bear because he wanted to scare his sisters. The Creator granted the wish, and the bear appeared before the girls. They were indeed frightened and ran away, which angered the bear, because he just wanted to play. The anger caused the bear to grow. The larger the bear grew, the more fearful the children became, and they called out the Creator to protect them."

"This isn't true, Ohanzee," Sara exclaimed.

"Just listen," I said. "A giant tree stump appeared, and the children climbed on top as it grew up above the valley where they had played. The bear clawed at the sides of the stump as he tried to climb up to reach the children."

"Ohanzee, this isn't true."

"I will take you there, and you will see. It is many days toward the setting sun: Mato Tipila. Your people call it Devil's Tower."[32]

"Does the mountain still have the claw marks? What happened? Did the bear eat the children?"

"The mountain has claw marks, but please let me finish. The girls cried out for help, again and again. The Creator sent a giant eagle to carry the children away from the bear. The eagle flew across the prairie toward the rising sun, and the bear chased them. Finally, the bear collapsed, in exhaustion, onto the prairie floor. He fell asleep and never woke again. He became our sacred mountain, Mato Paha. You call it Bear Butte."

"So what happened to the eagle and the girls?"

"The eagle continued on and carried the seven sisters into the heavens, where they are now seen as the stars of the Pleiades."

"So what is your lesson?"

"To only ask the Creator for something that results in good, not bad," I answered.

"I think it means your Creator will protect us," Sara said.

I smiled, gesturing toward the bear-shaped mountain. "We will climb the sacred sleeping bear."

I tied Blue's front feet with a rope, loosely enough to let him wander and graze but without allowing him enough freedom to run off. He immediately dropped his head into the fresh clover as I led Sara up the side of the mountain. When she slipped on loose rock, I reached for her hand. She hesitated and then clasped mine. I balanced her through difficult sections and then reluctantly let go, wishing the entire path required assistance.

"What makes this place special to you?" Sara asked, slightly out of breath.

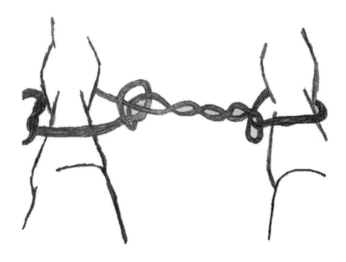

"It is where we are very close to God. He talks to us here. He has a special gift for us when we reach the top."

We continued quietly because Sara was out of breath. I took an easier route, away from the normal trail, since Sara's feet seemed to bother her. We were weaving up the steep mountain, through the trees, when we came upon a death scaffold: a buffalo robe wrapped around a familiar body, my grandfather's body. He was suspended about six feet high on a wooden-poled scaffold. The winter had caused little deterioration to the sacred ground. The buffalo grass, beneath the scaffold, was especially green and vibrant, with yellow butterflies fluttering in the breeze. We stood before the circle of life—the passage from death to life again.

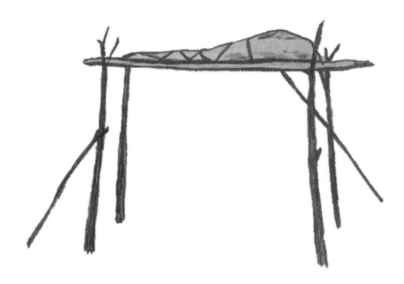

"I saw photos of death scaffolds when I studied in New York; thought it looked crazy. Why do you put your dead in the air?"

Sara asked, after looking through the treetops at the prairie floor below.

"To keep the wolves and coyotes from them. It honors their bodies and still lets them return to dust. The dust nourishes the grass. The buffalo eat the grass. We are blessed by eating the buffalo."

"There you go again," Sara said impatiently. "Don't you see, when I look out at the vastness of the prairie, I feel insignificant. Small. Like it doesn't really matter whether I live or die."

"We don't worry about those things, Sara. We just live to make our Creator proud and fulfill the chains of the circle."

I am not certain why I did not share with Sara the details of who lay on the scaffolding that we stood beside. Perhaps I did not want to burden her. More likely I wanted it to be my own secret— one last sacred experience with Grandfather; an experience that a white girl would not understand, or did not deserve to share. I felt compelled to pay my respect, and I sang a prayer to the Creator for the shell of a body that was slowly becoming one with the earth. I looked to the sky, where a golden eagle soared high above, and I fought back a tear.[33]

"Let's go," I urged and pulled her up the last bit of hillside, before the final plateau. The top opened before us to all things below. I led Sara straight to a gap between two large rocks that I knew from previous encounters with the mountain. A cold water spring bubbled up through the sleeping bear. We dropped to our knees and drank.

"Here is His gift to us," I explained. When our thirst was quenched, I stepped with Sara over the last crest. The entire prairie of grass spread as far as we could see.

"Have you nothing to say?" I teased. "Sara ran out of words?"

"It's breathtaking."

"It is. But I come here for more than the beauty. For years and years, it has been an important meeting place and also a purpose-seeking journey. We gather here at the beginning or end of summer. We trade news and goods when we aren't seeking insight from the Great One. Before I was on this earth, in your year of 1855, White Whiskers— you call him General William Harney— and thirteen hundred white soldiers attacked a peaceful Brulé village of Little Thunder. They smoked my people out and killed hundreds, including many women and children. Sara, White Whiskers pretended to be our friend, and then he massacred us. A few of my people were taken as prisoners."

"How do you know this is true?"

"My cousin, Crazy Horse, was one of the prisoners."

"I don't want to talk about this. Let's just go," she suggested.

"No, I need to be heard," I answered.

We looked out at the expanse of prairie. A color palate of every shade of green spread before us. The Black Hills, to the south, were the deepest emerald green on earth, nearly black, except for the slightest sparkle from the sun. The prairie was a more vivacious green, with streaks of lighter and darker hues, depending on the location of creeks laying before us.

"After White Whiskers killed our people, the Lakota, Dakota, Cheyenne, and Arapaho nations gathered at Bear Butte after the 1857 hunts. We were twelve thousand strong, and all of us together discussed our course of action. We did not know that a few days earlier a white man had found gold in our hills. The white man, named Warren, said my people must be defeated for your people to get rich. But this mountain will always remain sacred, no matter what you steal from us," I told Sara. She did not seem to listen.

"Ahh. So how does your Creator talk to your people?" Sara asked, totally off point. She seemed at ease as she gazed out over the prairie meeting the hills. Did she see the welcoming tranquility? I could only hope. The hills were safe and gentle compared to the harshness of the prairie. Even a white girl should be able to feel it.

"Through visions and prayer. My father's cousin, Crazy Horse, had a very important vision here, about five years ago. From atop this mountain, Crazy Horse had a vision of a town with white men. The vision was full of commotion. Our people lived in shacks and white-man clothes, drunk on whiskey. Then huge battles caused death. Some of my people came back to prayer and happiness, to our ceremonies and sacred songs. More and more of my people rejected your whiskey. A sacred tree began to grow. Beyond the tree was darkness, and a hole that people were trying to climb out of. Some in the hole had lost hope and could not see the light. The tree had people of all races dancing in joy underneath the branches, and they formed a circle around the tree. When Crazy Horse came out of his vision, he was very sad at the pain facing his people. He climbed down the mountain and told his father, Worm, about the vision. His father directed the Lakota to unite against your people and your ways, even though we might lose."

"Why do you even bother to fight if you are going to lose?" Sara pulled a wild purple flower from the narrow crack between two pieces of rock. I reached over, taking the flower from her fingers and placing it in her messy hair. She was beautiful—truly beautiful.

"Because our courage will be told down through the years and then our people will never fear the white man. One day your people will come to the Lakota, seek our wisdom, see the circle of earth and sky, and unite all men under the one Great Spirit."

"Oh, there is one Great Spirit, all right. But you have it wrong. One true God created this world, but he already sent his son, Jesus, who saves those who believe and have faith."

"But your faith is full of shortfalls. You pray shallow prayers. Don't you see? Wakan Tanka is everywhere. It is everything. Someday you will ask our people for guidance."

"Only the Holy Spirit guides us, according to God's will. Not Crazy Horse's will," Sara replied, looking at me with feverish eyes as she contemplated my suggestion of her hypocrisy.

I fixed my posture, standing tall in my buckskin leathers and said, "Crazy Horse's vision will come true. This mountain does not lie. Mato Paha helps us understand."

"Understand what?" Sara asked.

"Understand things, like knowing that your people are stealing our land, our way of life."

"We paid you for it!"

"Not the Black Hills," I said.

"Well, we *will* pay you for it!" Sara retorted.

"We will never sell it."

"But it's not like it has been yours forever. It was not always your land, Ohanzee. First, the Arikara pushed out the Kiowa. Then your people pushed out the Kiowa and Arikara. You have only claimed this area for the last eighty years. The Kiowa were here since 1650. You pushed them out, and you stole their buffalo hunting grounds. Did you pay them for the land? No. Just as you said, many miles back, the white man does not own the earth and the sky. Well, neither does the red man."

I did not say a word. I thought of how we were still pushing the Crow and Arikara from their lands as we moved farther and farther west, desperately searching for buffalo. I thought of how often we raided Arikara villages: almost five hundred times in a three-year period. My people were a superior force on the plains, and so we were entitled to whatever we chose to fight for.

Sara continued with a shaking voice, "And now you claim the Black Hills are your sacred land. Really? Wasn't it the sacred land of the Kiowa before you ran them off? Have you ever heard of Manifest Destiny? We are simply utilizing open land, just like you. It's all about perspective, isn't it, Ohanzee?"

When no words came to me, I stormed off, leaving Sara on top of the mountain. Or at least she thought I did. In actuality, I felt responsible for her and cut back up through the trees, secretly watching and wondering what choices she would make. Sara waited a while and then took one more long drink from the spring. I hid, just out of sight, and then silently flanked her all the way down the mountain. Larks and sparrows flirted with the treetops above. Sara descended carefully, as if her feet slammed into the front of my moccasins. Chipmunks fearlessly crossed the trail in front of her. When she reached the bottom, I remained hidden.

Sara had a few choices before her. Would she continue west, hoping to cross the path of the white man or find a military installation? Or would she return to the east and try to find her way back to Fort Randall? Could she make it alone with the skills I had taught her? I mentally released her and waited to see her path. I tried to convince myself how much easier my journey would be without her if she chose to head back east. For some strange reason, I did not want her to go.

She worked her way around the base of the mountain until she found Blue. She untied his leg rope and sat on the ground while he continued to graze. Sara tried to braid her hair while she called out my name a few times. Then she sat in silence. Finally, when I could hardly take any more waiting, she stood up stiffly, climbed on Blue, and continued west.

CHAPTER 22

WHITE

BAD DAY

"WHAT DOES NOT KILL ME MAKES ME STRONGER." ~Friedrich Nietzsche

I was stunned by the powerful colors of the sky as Blue paced toward the falling sun. The warm rays of early summer kept us thoroughly comfortable as the hues faded into deep blues and oranges, leaving a beautiful, dust-filled sunset. We covered quite a bit of ground, always certain Ohanzee would be just ahead; perhaps he would set up camp while waiting for Blue and me. I planned to apologize as soon as we reunited. The land rolled, with ravine after ravine to navigate. Yellow clover patches shimmered like the lemon drops that Dad bought for me on our journey west. I deeply missed him.

I continued on as the low light cast shadows across my trail. Grass rustled nearby, and my heart skipped a beat. I felt a sudden sense of danger, and my throat tightened. Before I could reason through what had made the noise, a white-tailed deer burst from the grasses in front of me, quickly catching my scent and diverting its path toward safety. Another hour passed as I searched the western horizon for any sign of Ohanzee's campfire smoke. There was nothing but the dim purple emptiness of prairie as the sun finally set. I came upon a substantial creek with clear water. I did not know which way to follow the bank in search of a safe crossing. I knew Ohanzee would be heading into the sun. I needed to catch up with him. Looking to the left and then the right, I second-guessed choosing both directions. Then I lost courage and wondered if I should even continue onward. I was free to turn around and head back east, to what I knew. Something deep inside told me to continue the course into the unknown.

"Well, Blue. It's just you and me," I said, rubbing his neck. "Where shall we cross?"

With no apparent head turn or tail swish from Blue, I arbitrarily directed him left and followed the creek to about three hundred feet downstream, where a shallow area made for an easy crossing. I slid off Blue and removed my moccasins. Raising them over my head, I stepped carefully across the sandy bottom. Blue followed two steps behind me, sinking his nose deeply into the water, half drinking and half playing.

It was quite dark, and I became nervous at the thought of setting up camp alone. I considered whether I should save time by not washing my feet. The wounds seemed a little better, but Ohanzee still insisted that I soak the amputated stubs whenever a clean water source appeared. My moccasins were already off, and my feet were muddy. I reluctantly decided to take a few minutes to wash away the mud, and then I would be on my way again.

Blue dropped his head to graze and worked his way upward on the five-foot bank above me. I knew he would not wander far. The rushing creek conquered the day's mundane prairie song as I studied the eroded creek bank, whose exposed prairie grass roots extended two feet deep from the soil's surface above. I turned to the creek and stepped upstream about ten feet to reach undisturbed water, where a tree had fallen and then become caught against the creek bank. With each step, a cloudy path meandered with the current. I sat on a dry section of the partially submerged trunk and reached over to drink from my cupped palms. When the current ran clear and my feet were clean, I pulled them from the cool water. A fly went straight for my wounds, and frustration overcame me; no matter how careful I was, my foot was still a host for flies in search of rotting meat.

My heart leaped again, this time at a loud "crack" that rose above the creek's melody. It came from the bank above. Was it Blue? Or a broken tree limb snapped by the wind? I dropped my injured foot back into the creek for a few more minutes and then lightly tiptoed out of the water and back against the bank, trying to minimize the amount of mud left on my feet. I sat down, put my moccasins on, and felt the familiar sense of danger through my veins. Then everything went black.

I regained my sense of hearing first. I found myself in the middle of a nightmare. My head and neck painfully beat to the rhythm of my racing heart. Men were laughing. Something had my ankles and was dragging me along, in the dirt. My head bounced along the ground because I was too woozy to support it. Then I lost consciousness again. When I came back to my senses, I was

273

sprawled out on the hard ground. My hip was against a sharp rock, yet I willed myself to remain still. The top of my head throbbed. I kept my eyes tight, but the campfire flickered its light against my eyelids.

"What'll we do with 'er?" a man's voice asked.

"What do you mean, JoJo? I know what we'll do with 'er," a gruff man responded. Both men burst into a sinister laugh.

"Then what?"

"Then whatever we want. We can kill 'er and take 'er horse, or we can keep 'er for a while."

"Maybe she can cook."

"She can surely keep us happy."

They laughed again. I opened my eyes to just tiny slits, peeking out through my lashes at the reality before me. My captors were two white men: tall, skinny, and dirty. They wore canvas pants with suspenders and filthy, unbuttoned white shirts. They passed a bottle back and forth, not interested in much else other than hocking up the nastiest spit in the territory. Clearly they were prospectors heading to the Black Hills. One mule was tied to a tree, still wearing his pack. Blue was tied beside him. We were in the middle of the ravine, the creek was beside us, and we were surrounded by tall grasses and scrub oak trees, all thriving on the water source.

"You didn't have to drop such a big rock on her head."

"Least I got 'er," he slurred, as he reached into the bag beside him and pulled out a pouch.

"Well, I'd like to have a little fight in 'er, ya know?"

"She'll be fine in no time. Deserves every bit of what we give 'er; traveling alone out here, wearing injun pants and moccasins. She's beautiful and crazy!" They laughed again. One of the men dropped tobacco along a half-creased cigarette paper; he then rolled it, licking the edge, reshaping it, and tapping it on his dirty thigh.

"Well, if the mule drops dead, she can carry our gold."

"Too heavy, she wouldn't last." He lit the cigarette that was wedged between his lips, took a huge puff off the end, and then dangled it between his first and second fingers. The end of the cigarette continued to glow, and he occasionally blew the ash off the burning tip.

Gold. They were not going *toward* the Black Hills, they were coming *from* the Black Hills.

Screech! A few moments later, screech again! I heard the familiar sound of a screech owl and pondered his viewpoint, from the treetops overhead. Screech! One, two, three, four, screech! One, two, three, screech! One, two, screech! One, two, three, four, five, six, seven, eight, nine, ten, eleven, twelve, thirteen, fourteen … screech! This was not the right cadence for an owl. I knew that much. Ohanzee! He was nearby and telling me to remain still. I feigned unconsciousness, yet was as alert as a mouse in the grasses—not panicking, just waiting.

CHAPTER 23

RED

BAD MEN

"COURAGE, ABOVE ALL THINGS, IS THE FIRST QUALITY OF A WARRIOR." ~Carl von Clausewitz

When I saw Sara heading for the Beautiful River, I assumed she would set up camp for the night. I took my time and lingered behind. Then the situation turned bad—really bad. I desperately wanted Sara to understand my screech owl call. I was trying to remind her that she needed to remain as still as a mouse. The fight was not hers. She needed to protect her heart and wait. I feared that she would not fully understand her vulnerability as a woman. The odds were against her if she tried to fight.

I crouched in the darkness, concealed by tall, swaying grass, as the white men talked of their plans for Sara. I fought to control a boiling rage and heard myself swallow. How arrogant that they would come to my land, uninvited, and overpower a girl who was becoming more and more important to me. How dare they bring their ugly ways of disrespect. How ignorant of them to not consider the price they might pay. Did they not know how I had nothing to lose? Did they think I would let them take my buffalo, and then my land, and finally Sara?

I tried to control my anger, so that I could form a solid plan against the men. I quickly reasoned through different options. If I tried to stab each man with my Bowie knife, I would surely not succeed unless I was very quick, and the men were either asleep or very drunk. This first reckless thought subsided as I realized that I would place Sara and myself in grave danger if I failed. Sara's life was in my hands. If they killed me, then Sara could be imprisoned for the rest of her life, however long or short it may be. I felt heavy with responsibility—there was so much to lose, and so much to live for.

I stalked the stalkers, crossing the creek, downwind from the men and the crumpled pile of a young woman. As I crept closer, I held my breath, slowly placing my toes down first, followed by my heels. After a few steps, I stopped, filled my lungs, and listened. Then I repeated the process, holding my breath and walking carefully. When I was very close, I slowly dropped to my knees and crawled a bit closer. Peeking above the waist-high grasses, I waited patiently for the right moment.

One of the drunk men stood up, stumbled, and said, "I think it's time to wake 'er up." The other man laughed. I reached for my quiver, while noting the direction of the wind and its influence on the flight of my arrow. The man walked over to Sara and started kicking her in the side. She remained still. I silently placed an arrow in my bow. Then he grabbed her ankles and used his body weight to drag her away from the fire and toward a dark area under a tree, where his bedroll was spread. "Awake or not, girl, I'll take you," he grunted.

I drew back my bow, hesitated, and then released my arrow. He snorted, dropped Sara's ankles, sucked in a huge gasp of air, and crumbled next to her feet. I did not watch his death struggle. Instead, I let the moonlit prairie grasses wave good-bye as he gave in to his fate.

I peered back at the other man, who continued to sit at the fire, with his bottle of liquor numbing his pathetic existence; he was completely unaware of who was taking whom. Relief showered over me when Sara crept in my direction. We hid behind the cover of tall grass, and I pulled a strand of hair from the corner of her mouth. I gently touched the skin of her cheek and stared into her eyes, confirming her sanity. From the first day I met her, I had questioned her fortitude, but now I knew. She had courage and a strong mind. We looped around the campsite and reached Blue, who was tied beside the mule.

The second man had leaned back against a fallen cottonwood and had his bare feet propped up near the fire. He was mumbling to himself about what he would do to Sara once it was his turn. I untied Blue, and Sara went to the mule. I gestured "no" because he would slow us down. She defiantly grabbed the pack from the mule's back and slipped through the grass on our westward heading. By lightly rubbing his shoulder, I thanked the mule for not alerting the prospector to our presence. "Animals understand evil," I thought, as I noticed a white stream of fur running down his chest, like the marking on some of my village dogs. I stared at his face and found one brown eye and one blue eye. I had seen this mule before. Hesitating, I reassessed whether we could use him in our travels. After deciding against it, I quickly led Blue from the ravine and reunited with Sara. She tried to put the pack on Blue, but her arms crumpled and she gasped in pain. I grabbed the bag and lifted it over his back.

"Sara, this is too heavy," I whispered.

"Do as I wish. Please," she said, grabbing her neck out of pain.

"If you take the pack, then I count coup," I negotiated.

"What's that?" Sara asked.

"Take Blue up to the top of the draw and then turn back to watch," I said, handing her my bow and quiver of arrows.

I waited a few moments for Sara to cover the distance, and then I walked silently toward the remaining man at the fire. His back was toward me. I could smell him—that same mixture of dirty body odor and whiskey. I approached and tried to calm my pounding heart, afraid he may hear it beating through my skin. The man's odor became awful, and I breathed from my mouth.

When I was one stride from him, I reached out. I had not decided ahead of time where to touch the man. It didn't really matter. I extended my arm a bit more and lightly touched him on the shoulder. Exhilarated, like a cougar in the woods, I bolted for safety, into the trees. He jumped out of reflex, screamed, and fumbled for his gun. I ran in the opposite direction of Sara and

Blue, to minimize the chance of her involvement. Overly focused on my escape, I nearly tripped over the dead prospector at the base of the tree where he had dropped. The other man shot his gun toward me, yet blindly, into the darkness. He howled profanities as I cut a serpentine trail through the tall grasses. Once at a safe distance, I watched the man, who was too terrified to leave the fire. He bellowed for his friend, in panicked distress. Not worried about being heard, I swiftly looped around the camp to meet up with Sara.

As we continued west, the man's panicked voice mixed with the prairie wind. It became impossible to tell which was which. Under the cover of darkness, we did our best to stay in lowlands and draws. We walked in silence for quite a while, long past when we needed to do so; we were not yet ready for words. Sara seemed to be in shock. I thought about my kill and counted coup. We had just experienced the same situation together, and yet in such different ways.

"Why on earth did you do that?" Sara asked.

"Do what?" I asked.

"Touch him. What good was that?"

"I counted coup. I was brave."

"Actually, you were stupid. What a bad decision," she said, fists clenched on her hips.

"You should be proud of me. What unarmed white man would approach and touch his enemy?"

"Not one, unless he was crazy. You took a gamble, Ohanzee. A stupid gamble. Why did you do such a thing?"

"Now I have more worth."

"What worth?"

"Respect, a coup feather, and possibly a horse."

"Not worth it, Ohanzee. What if you had been killed?"

"Then I would have died brave. Either way, I win."[34]

"And if you die, it's at my expense. I lose."

"You think too far ahead, Sara," I said.

"You don't think at all, Ohanzee. How far out do you really plan? Or do you just go day by day and not worry about if you live or die? Do you not aspire to anything? Like where you want to be in ten years?"

"Where I want to be in *ten years*? No wonder you don't see what I see, as we walk along. You are too busy looking over the horizon, where only the Great One can see. My people only plan for enough food to get us through the winter. The Great One watches over everything else. Ten years is far away, Sara. I probably won't live for another ten years anyway," I said.

"Well, I think you are wrong, Ohanzee. I think you need a plan," Sara answered.

We walked in a wavering fashion because I was focused on tracking small game for a meal. A few hours away from our encounter with the prospectors, we had enough space to stop when we found water and a protected camp for the night. I shot a rabbit and left it whole, dangling it from Blue's pack like a warrior hangs a scalp. Blue was lagging, and I was too tired to look for good protection. I accepted a fully exposed camp on the open prairie.

Sara pulled the packs from Blue's back and winced. While I organized my blankets, she dug through the pack and returned, carrying a tin cup and a cast iron fry pan.

"Oh, great. You wore out Blue tonight, all because you wanted a pan to cook with? Tell me this. Which of us is making bad decisions?"

Sara ignored my comment, responding, "You said you need to learn to read, so let's read." She pulled her dad's Bible out of her pocket, set it on her lap, and let it fall open.

"Why do you always do that?"

"Because maybe, just maybe, God will direct me to something pertinent—to words meant just for us."

"Ah. It's a white girl's vision," I said.

"First Samuel 24, verse 4. 'The men said, "This is the day the Lord spoke of when he said to you, 'I will give your enemy into your hands for you to deal with as you wish.'" Then David crept up unnoticed and cut off a corner of Saul's robe.'"

Sara stopped reading and stared wide-eyed at the page.

"Well, well," I commented, "looks like even Samuel counted coup."

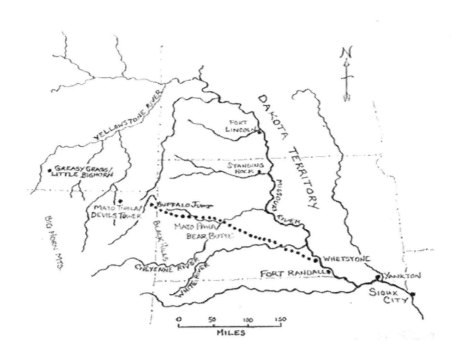

CHAPTER 24

WHITE

THE MIDDLE OF NOWHERE

"THE TRUE SECRET OF HAPPINESS LIES IN TAKING A GENUINE INTEREST IN ALL THE DETAILS OF DAILY LIFE." ~William Morris

Before pulling anything out of it, I shoved my hand toward the bottom of the prospector's pack. Ever since being hit over the head with the rock, my hands had been tingling, like they were going numb. Deep in the bag, I felt a long rope, and then my fingers rubbed against canvas—two canvas bags. I needed room to maneuver my hand, and I pulled out a skillet and cup, setting them aside. I quickly submerged my hands back into the grungy pack and flipped open the top of one canvas bag. Inside were small deerskin pouches, tied at the tops, with heavy string. I palmed one of the weighty pouches, filled with small stones of different sizes. I did not have to see the color of the contents to verify the fortune. We had struck it rich.

I dropped my head against Blue's side, took in a deep, soothing breath, and silently thanked the Lord for allowing something good to come out of such a dark, demoralizing incident. Then I returned to the fire and read the Bible to Ohanzee. It seemed to be the right thing to do, but my headache worsened as I tried to focus on the blurry words. I touched the top of my skull, where a large goose egg–sized bump was tight with fluid. When I turned my head, I felt like my neck burst into flames, but since complaining would not help, I kept it private. Luckily, Ohanzee fell asleep after a few verses in Samuel, when he was vindicated after Saul counted coup.

I walked around the perimeter of the camp and collected dry buffalo chips and prairie grass. The stars were brighter than ever—a thousand times brighter than from my porch in New York City, where they barely peeked through into the manmade commotion. It struck me how some stars were tightly grouped into different constellations, as if they needed company. Others were rogue stars that did not fit in anywhere.

I started a fire, but it smoldered and went out. The day's stress had drained me, but I was still determined to make a meal for Ohanzee. I started it again, with greater success, before wandering down a little draw and discovering a stand of lambsquarters. I pulled up two handfuls of the plant, knowing it would wilt into nearly nothing. The grit on it would overpower the flavor unless it was rinsed in a creek. I stashed it in my pocket for the next day's meal.

I skinned the rabbit and harvested the breast meat and the thighs. Even though Ohanzee usually cleaned our game, I was fairly proficient myself just from observing. Blood and animal innards did not bother me anymore. I gathered more buffalo chips and doubled the size of the fire. Peeling a layer of fat from next to the rabbit's skin, I greased the skillet and sautéed thin slices of rabbit meat.

Ohanzee was stretched out on his blanket, sleeping in front of the fire, which cast shadows across his face. As I gazed over his exhausted frame, I saw how handsome he was.

"Here, Ohanzee. A piece of meat," I said proudly, nudging his shoulder. He barely stirred at first, but then his eyes opened.

"You take it," he replied, staring into the flames.

"You need to eat," I insisted.

"No, thanks."

"I need you to eat, Ohanzee. I made this for you."

We eventually compromised and shared the rabbit, each devouring our own smoke-flavored portion. We had nothing left to drink because we had not filled our canteen and buffalo bladder at the river after the prospector incident. Blue was restless, but we could do nothing for him. We stared at the fire, and Ohanzee seemed ready to nod off again.

"Ohanzee. I'm sorry."

"Sorry?"

"For what happened on the mountain and for our arguments. I wasn't very understanding. I didn't respect your beliefs."

"My heart has been heavy since I left your side. I'm sorry about those men."

"Thank you for saving me. I'll never ever disrespect you again," I said.

"Never *ever*?" Ohanzee asked, smiling.

"Never *ever*."

I realized that as we traveled together a special relationship was developing between our two strong, independent personas. I placed my blanket about five feet from his, sat down, and watched our campfire smoke obscure the sky. Ohanzee slid his blanket a little closer to me. I wasn't sure if he moved to get away from the drifting smoke, or if he just wanted to be nearer to me. Either way, I was pleased. I pondered his broad shoulders, his bravery, and his self-discipline. He never seemed rattled by our difficult circumstances. I wanted to face each future challenge as it materialized and not lie awake at night worrying about things that may never happen.

Even more intriguing was Ohanzee's ability to know what I was thinking. Somehow he conveyed to my heart the feeling that I was not alone in my thoughts; he was right beside me. The more I understood Ohanzee, the more I liked him. But to fall in love would be inexcusable. It would be inappropriate and wrong. We came from two very different lives. He was who he was. I resisted his strong and charming peculiarities because I needed to reunite with my people, and he with his. It would be overly complicated to do anything else, and any romantic connection could only end in heartbreak.

"Goodnight, Ohanzee," I whispered as the rasp of crickets turned to stillness.

A whispering morning breeze brought the prairie back to life. We continued on to the melody of full prairie opera, with blowing wind and calling birds. Grasshoppers mimicked the sound of rattlesnakes, which seemed like a cruel joke directed straight at me. When a covey of spiked grouse made me jump, I recognized my overreaction. I was startling at almost everything, still paranoid because of the events of the day before. Blue and I progressed slower than usual due to his added load, and we fell far behind Ohanzee.

We finally caught up when he paused, overlooking a bluff. Ohanzee motioned for me to look over the edge. A large hole lay before us, and I felt a bit of vertigo while peering about forty feet below, where bleached buffalo bones were scattered about.

"What is this?" I asked.

"It's one of our buffalo jumps. My people used it for many generations. It was a trap. We made the shape of a 'v' toward a buffalo trail. We squatted down and made a sort of loose fence, with each person in sight of the next. As the herd approached, our buffalo caller coaxed the herd into the trap."

"How?"

"He wore the hide of a buffalo calf. He joined the herd as one of their own, tricking them by mimicking their actions; like dropping his head to graze. Then, he ran in circles, to get the attention of the bulls. He cried like an injured calf, and then ran toward the cliff. The bulls chased him and the rest of the herd followed. At just the right time, we jumped up, whooping and hollering until they stampeded off the cliff's edge, to their death below. Some of our people stood below and killed the injured ones who bellowed and roared. Eventually, it calmed down, as they were speared and beaten to death with clubs."[35]

"What happened to the buffalo caller?"

"He jumped to the side at the last second which was very dangerous. Once my people collected enough horses, we hunted on bareback and quit using the buffalo jump."

"*Collected* enough horses? You mean *stole* enough horses!" I said, immediately regretting my sarcasm. I quickly changed the subject. "Look, Ohanzee—a stream."

Blue seemed to smell the water, and as we walked, his pace quickened until a cool stream surrounded his submerged nose and relieved his thirst. We were rarely dehydrated or starving because Ohanzee almost always found daily water and killed small game for dinner. In this way, our evening routine became comforting. I collected fallen branches or buffalo chips from the prairie while Ohanzee cleaned the game. When I returned, he started a small fire. I learned to scavenge for greens during the day. Sometimes we had wild asparagus, or lambsquarters, to simmer over the fire with wild herb water or fat from the day's kill. Whether we ate rabbit or grouse, we were always satisfied. Ohanzee either skewered the carcass to roast the meat on the upwind side of the fire, or he buried the meat under a bed of coals. Then, once I had acquired the fry pan, I preferred sautéing thin slices of the meat with our greens.

One night, after a nearly perfect dinner, the yellow moon shone bright against the creek bottom where we camped.

Ohanzee looked up from our campfire and said, "I don't know if you will ever understand. You keep thinking of the ground we walk on as a human nation. You want more things. You take gold rocks from the earth to buy more things."

"But the Bible says humans are in charge."

"And this is the problem. Don't you see how Mother Earth sustains us on this journey? We are not in control. We are just lucky enough to be chosen, moment by moment, to exist, as a small piece of this world. My Creator permeates every bit of me. You just move through your day, and pray when you are in trouble."

Ohanzee's words knocked me across the head. He was right. I was usually distracted from the present, planning my actions without consulting God.

"I see your point. You may be right, Ohanzee. You may be right."

CHAPTER 25

RED

UNWELCOME VISITORS

"PART OF THE HAPPINESS OF LIFE CONSISTS NOT IN FIGHTING BATTLES, BUT IN AVOIDING THEM." ~Norman Vincent Peale

I awoke to a coyote call—actually, two calls from different sources. Our fire still smoldered, giving us away. I jumped to my feet, stumbling on the blanket that I had been wrapped in moments before. I kicked dirt into the fire in the slim chance they had not seen the smoke yet; it continued to trickle out of the dirt mound. I squatted near Sara for a moment and listened to the human calls from the ridge above our camp. They were not the calls of my tribe.

"Sara, wake up," I whispered. She rolled over.

"Sara, wake up," I whispered louder.

She sat straight up and stared at me.

"What is it?"

"Shhh."

"Ohanzee, what is it?"

We listened at the piercing sound of distant coyotes.

I grabbed Sara's hand and pulled her to her feet. We walked, crouched over, to the tree where Blue was tied.

"Stay here; don't leave," I told her.

I grabbed my bow and slung the quiver of arrows over my shoulder. After creeping out of our camping ravine, I worked my way around the ridge, toward the calls, which abruptly stopped. I froze and crouched down again, as still as a rock, waiting for further clues. My thighs burned. In a bold move, I returned my best coyote call. Within moments, two warriors on nearly matching paint horses appeared. I recognized them: One Bull and Good Bear, the Hunkpapa students from Black Robe's school.

"Well, if it isn't the Miniconjou boy," One Bull said. "The one who ran away."

"I didn't run away."

"You weren't smart enough to finish your English school with us," Good Bear teased, "not enough courage to stay for your tribe."

"You are not speaking the truth," I rebutted defensively. "I learned what there was to learn from Black Robe, and I could not stay in the wasicu cabin another day. It suffocated me."

"Why did you betray your tribe? Just because the walls suffocated you? You are selfish. We finished the school. We have value. But what about you?"

I did not want to tell them about falling into a darkness when Grandfather died. I did not want to admit how disappointed my family was when I returned early. Worse yet, in the hope of redemption, I had failed again by becoming a prisoner of the white man. What a disgrace I was; my tribe presumed me dead. So much for my name Ohanzee. The white man had caught the shadow.

"Why are you here?" I said, changing the subject.

"On our way to Greasy Grass. Many tribes are gathering, you know. But we need a few hours of sleep. We will share your camp."

I nodded in compliance, but my head raced. Swinging down from their horses, the Hunkpapas followed me, down the hill, to our campsite. I had no choice and called Sara from her cover. She cautiously emerged.

"Ohanzee has a woman!" one exclaimed.

"She's a wasicu!" the other added.

"Is she your wife?" they teased.

"No. I am returning her to her people."

Sara stood behind me, in a submissive posture, minimizing eye contact.

"Leave her, and come with us. We need to hurry. If you leave her, the wasicu soldiers will probably find her before she dies. They are milling about, all around us. Have you seen them?"

"No."

"Well, they are near. Yellow Hair's army will soon come from Fort Lincoln. Maybe you don't notice, because you are too busy staring at your wasicu wife," One Bull teased.

"She is not my wife."

"Then leave her and come with us to give the news to our people."

"I cannot leave her. She won't survive."

"Whose fault is that? Not ours. Surely you have taught her to shoot a bow."

"No."

"Why not?" One Bull asked.

"She's a wasicu," I answered.

"I can see that," One Bull answered. "So if she dies, what is it to our people anyway? She is not worth anything more than her scalp."

A rage brewed in my soul, but I remained composed. My journey with Sara appeared strange to them, yet I knew it was the right thing to do.

"It's all a matter of perspective, I suppose," I answered.

The Hunkpapas smirked and said I was crazy to risk retaliation from white soldiers.

"You know, the wasicu soldiers will figure that the girl is your slave, that you kidnapped her. They will kill you—hang you like a horse thief, or shoot you like a buffalo."

"It is the chance I take."

I placed myself between Sara and the others. The two warriors took their packs from their horses' backs and started to go through their things. They individually pulled each of their belongings out, trying to impress Sara, who sat in silence, concealing all emotion. First, a bladder food bag, full of pemmican. Then, their bone breast plates and hair wraps. Finally, neatly beaded leggings, and makeup kits filled with paint and porcupine tail brushes.

As they squatted by the fire, I noted their full quivers, hanging at their hips. Sara turned and looked back at their horses. I wondered if she saw the bags hanging off the saddle horns. Each contained a headdress, wrapped carefully to protect the feathers.

Sara prepared her bed and securely wrapped herself in her blanket. I waited for her rhythmic breath of surrender. Then I reclined beside her, as a buffalo bull protects his cow. It began to rain, and the storm joined me under my blanket, but I did not move from Sara's side. At dawn, One Bull and Good Bear gathered their belongings and quietly left our camp. I pretended to sleep, but we knew better. The sun appeared as a dusty orange mural on the eastern horizon—the Creator's first gift of the day.

Sara woke a few hours later, not stirring while I packed up camp. Still exhausted, she rode Blue. I walked at their side as his feet kicked up an eye-burning dust. The grasses were becoming thinner and more brittle than the soft spring grasses that flourished behind us. Sara had minimal awareness of the animal world around us.

To pass the hours of the day, I pointed out hawks and birds in the sky, teaching her the Lakota words for robin, lark, sparrow, blackbird, hawk, turkey buzzard, and falcon. White-tailed deer were abundant, as were squirrel, raccoon, chipmunk, and porcupine. On the darkest nights, we were sometimes treated to the distant call of a screech owl. The Great One had kept away rattlesnakes and bear, although I continued to remain alert.

Sometimes I forgot that Sara was a wasicu. But then she started asking never-ending questions, and I was quickly reminded of our differences.

"If those men were from your family, why did they desert you?" she bluntly asked.

"They aren't from my family, they are Hunkpapa."

"Hunkpapa. What does that mean?"

"Head of the Circle."

"What are you?"

"I told you. I am Miniconjou."

"You don't get along with each other? Do you do anything together?"

"Sometimes we hunt together, but mostly we hunt on our own and just unite each summer at Greasy Grass for our council. Thousands of our people go. The leaders discuss hunting grounds and the white man. The rest of us celebrate life and renew friendships. Some of us look for a wife or husband from another tribe."

"What does 'Miniconjou' mean?"

"Those Who Plant by the Stream."

"Do you really plant by the stream?"

"No, your people stole our land."

She gave me a frustrated look and held her tongue. I grinned and walked away.

Finally, toward the end of the day, I saw that we were closing in on Mato Tipila.

"Remember the story that I told you? About the Kiowa boy playing with his seven sisters?" I asked.

"Of course."

"Well, there it is: Mato Tipila, or Devil's Tower, as you call it. See it?" I asked, pointing toward the sacred place.

"I think so," Sara said, straining her eyes.

"It's the tree stump from our legend. Remember?"

Blue kept a steady pace without my urging, and as the miles rolled on, the mountain grew larger. Sara and I seemed to talk less and say more. By the time we reached the mountain, Blue was lathered and showed signs of fatigue. The summer heat was increasing each day, and Blue suffered the effects.

"Sara, we should lighten Blue's load. We will be stuck with a lame horse if we don't let him rest."

She mumbled a few things that I did not quite hear, and then she pulled the two bags of gold out of his pack and strapped them to her own back, with the prospector's rope.

"I'll carry it myself. Now leave me alone."

"Sara, you are not strong enough to carry those rocks. They don't matter. Leave them on the trail."

"Over my dead body."

"Maybe you should pray to your white God. Maybe he will lighten your load," I said to Sara, hoping she would recognize how silly she was.

"Well, maybe I will," she replied. "I prayed for food, and He gave us the grouse and led us to the warrior's body."

"Your white Creator didn't give us the grouse or the body," I corrected her. "I called to *my* Creator, and it is *my* God who provided those things. He is the Creator of all things around us."

"So is *my* God!" Sara shook her head in annoyance but kept walking. Her feet were almost healed now that she walked with her toes straight ahead, as I taught her.

As we approached Mato Tipila, the mountain's mystical beauty was overwhelming. It took little imagination to visualize the bear clawing for the children on top. I gazed up at the sky of Mother

Earth. She handed us only a new moon, with little light for guidance.

"Let's climb to the top," I challenged Sara.

"And where would that get us, Ohanzee?" she asked.

"Who cares? We will see it when we get there. We could camp on the top."

"You are teasing, right?"

I laughed. "Yes, Sara. It's a joke. But I could climb to the top, if I wanted."

"You'd never make it," Sara said bluntly, not realizing the fire she kindled. I wanted to prove her wrong.

"Watch me," I retorted, jumping up on the first level of a rock ledge, where two pieces of granite united to form a toehold. "Come on, Sara. Just try it, the rock is stable. Use your hands."

Sara dropped her packs of yellow rocks and jumped up on the first ledge, stubbing the tip of her moccasin on a rock. She winced and did not continue. I saw a huge column of dust in the distance, just one shade lighter than the darkness surrounding us. I wanted the better view that the next-highest ledge would provide.

"What are you looking for?" Sara asked.

"Just wait here, I'll be right back." As I climbed, I became distracted, pondering how Sara and I had already traveled for two full moons. We would find my people before the next full moon. I was not overly concerned about our next few days, when we would enter Crow territory, because they feared my people. For years, we simply invaded their land. But in contrast, the Arikara fought against us much harder as we pushed them west. We had violently battled hundreds of times in the last few years, fighting for the only remaining buffalo hunting grounds. I wanted to avoid contact with the Arikara because Sara would be a prize.

I stretched upward from a toehold, trying to see if the dust column came from wasicu, my people, or a herd of buffalo. Suddenly, my foot slipped off the edge of the rock, which my full weight had entrusted. I grasped for anything. My fingertips only touched air. It felt like forever; I fell in slow motion. All breath was taken from me as I hit the dry ground. Bright lights of pain shot inside my head, inside my legs, and across my back. Coyotes began to howl—cries of agonizing pain. My world went black.

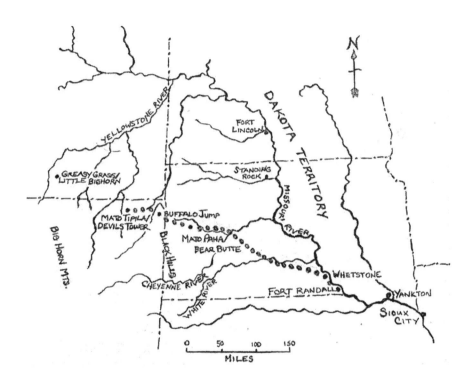

CHAPTER 26

WHITE

DEVIL'S TOWER (MATO TIPILA)

"WHEN YOU GET INTO A DANGEROUS PLACE, DON'T TURN COWARD." ~Mark Twain

"Ohanzee!" I screamed, peering over the ledge. "Ohanzee!" There was no response.

"Help! Someone help!" I screamed out, over the vast, silent prairie, realizing the desperate foolishness of my call. I wasted time staring into the darkness, as it only stared back at me. Quickly I climbed down the rock, fumbling for fingerholds, which I could not sense because my hands were numb. Although it did not take long to reach the bottom, Ohanzee was already surrounded by a pool of warm blood. "Oh, my gosh, Ohanzee. Ohanzee?" He was face down, his form crumpled and lifeless. "Ohanzee!" I cried.

An animalistic sound came from his lips—not really a cry, but not a groan either. I stood over him, took a deep breath, and tried to grasp reality. No obvious injuries appeared on his back. I carefully

302

rolled him over. Ohanzee gasped in pain, taking in fast, shallow breaths. One of his thigh bones was protruding out of the front of his pants. I gagged, unable to control the reflex. "It's not about me, it's not about me. Don't stare at the blood, it's not about me. It's about helping Ohanzee," I thought.

I ran to where Blue was tied and started pulling things from the packs, not sure of what I was searching for—a miracle, perhaps, but no miracle occurred. I needed a plan, and I needed it quickly, before Ohanzee went into shock and died.

"Make it go away, Sara. Make it go away," he groaned.

"I will, Ohanzee. I will. But you need to take deep breaths. You need to stay with me." At first, he seemed to listen, but after a few deep breaths, he turned his head to the side and vomited on the dusty ground.

I put my arms under his shoulders and moved his torso one foot from the mess. I spent the next half hour vacillating between staring at his leg and digging through our packs. If I put a tourniquet above his fracture, then he would certainly lose his leg. If I covered him with a blanket and rode for help, then Ohanzee would die of shock or infection, or would be torn apart by a bear. If I made a travois and drug him to Greasy Grass, infection would probably set in, unless I pulled on Ohanzee's leg and reset the broken bones. I realized that this last option was the right thing to do. I had seen Doctor Mayo do it; now I had to try it myself.

I carefully grabbed his heel and pulled. Ohanzee cried out. The splintered bone remained exposed. I pulled again, this time harder. The bone seemed to shrink toward the hole but did not go back inside. I nearly vomited. His taut thigh muscle prevented me from easily reconnecting the snapped bones. I mustered all of my strength, sat at his feet, and braced myself against Ohanzee's stable leg. This time when I pulled on the fracture, I did it with all my might, leaving nothing in reserve. The jagged bone disappeared inside his flesh. Blood gushed from the open hole. Ohanzee gritted his teeth and passed out.

I grabbed the prospector's pack and flipped it upside down, emptying everything onto the dry ground. A rolled-up piece of canvas, about the size of my hand, was carefully tied with a filthy brown cord. Embroidered in blue thread on the edge of the canvas were the initials J.G. I untied the cord, noticing the bloody dirt on my hands; my mind flashed back to the long, filthy nails of the prospector who dragged me away from his fire. Secured deeper in the rolled canvas were tiny scissors, a needle, and a piece of thread, looped in a figure eight pattern. It was a mending kit, probably given to the prospector by his sister or mother; no other woman in her right mind would give a proper sendoff to such a disheveled monstrosity of a man unless, perhaps, she was relieved that he was leaving.

I pulled Dad's knife from Ohanzee's bloody pants. Then I walked the forest floor and quickly selected straight pine branches to brace his leg. When I returned, small, iridescent, blackish-green beetles had already discovered the pooling blood and crawled up his leg, searching for the source. I flicked them off, wondering where they came from in the first place.

My hands shook so much that I could not thread the needle. I steadied myself against a pine tree; I then managed to thread the needle and knot the end of the thread before I returned to stand below Ohanzee's feet. His legs appeared straight. I pushed on both sides of his broken thigh, with equal pressure, just to be sure that the bones of both legs were in line.

I used the corner of a blanket to put pressure on the wound, soaking up blood in the process. When I released the cloth, Ohanzee's blood gushed out again. I took the needle and thread in my hand, pulled the wound together with the other, and began to stitch, just as Mother had taught me to darn a sock. The stitches were very loose because the flesh swelled before my eyes. Just then, when I tugged, the thread snapped. I needed a better plan.

The parfleche had a rolled up piece of sinew, but without a way to thread it into the needle, the sinew was useless. I stood, perplexed, staring at Ohanzee's wound, which was about five inches long and gaped two inches across. I would leave it open and somehow keep it protected. I wrapped strips of blanket around his stick-braced leg, knotting the strips as tightly as I could muster. He continued to lay as still as a dead man.

As I worked through the quandary before me, a travois sketch from one of my texts came to mind. If I could rig one quickly, then I would not have to leave Ohanzee behind. Blue could drag him to Greasy Grass. Five hours later, a rough pine travois rested beside Ohanzee. The prospectors' rope became valuable as I tied the travois to Blue's makeshift harness.

I collected our belongings, some of which had rolled below our sloping site where Ohanzee laid. I drug the travois against Ohanzee's side and tried to lift his shoulders. It was no use. I sat beside him and waited, wondering if he would ever wake up again. Finally, he groaned.

"Ohanzee. You need to help me with your weight. We need to lift you onto the travois. Can you do that?"

Ohanzee was delirious, saying, "Omakiya. Omakiya. Help me, Sara. Help me." Then he started asking, "Why is the buffalo blowing hot air on my leg? Tell him to stop. My toes are burning."

"There's no buffalo, Ohanzee."

"Sara, tell the buffalo to stop licking my face. It's wet." He was right. His face was dripping in sweat; he was full of shock and fever. Ohanzee fell in and out of consciousness. He mumbled dreamlike details of encounters with his grandfather. They feasted together, but then his grandfather was told to return for important work.

I was exhausted and alone. I lay beside Ohanzee and prayed for strength, asking God to stand beside me as I grew weak. He gave me His word. "Those who wait upon the Lord shall renew their strength. They shall mount up with wings as eagles. They shall run and not be weary. They shall walk and not faint" (Isaiah 40:31). *Oh Lord,* I prayed. *Help me walk and not be faint. Help me persevere.* I rolled over toward Ohanzee and realized that he may die, right there beside me, just as Sergeant Zito had. Ohanzee's breath grew faint. I wiped the perspiration from his face.

I needed to rest for just a few minutes, so I closed my eyes. I woke up hours later. I was famished. Ohanzee was unconscious. He looked nearly dead, and the stench of excrement overwhelmed me; he had lost control of his bladder and bowels. I knew right then that Ohanzee would probably die if I did not try something, anything.

I wandered down into a ravine. Miraculously, a small spring flowed, and I dropped to my hands and knees, drinking from the trickle of clean water. I went back up the hill to Ohanzee and grabbed his buffalo bladder and Dad's canteen. Then I dug through my bag and pulled out the blue and turquoise skirt that Mrs. Flanagan had made for me at Fort Randall. I cut off a long piece of the soft fabric and ran back to the spring. I filled the containers, wet the fabric, and rushed back up the hill. As I carefully cleaned up Ohanzee's mess, I hoped he would not wake up in the process. I threw the stinky piece of skirt under a bush and then poured water into his half-open mouth. He gagged, coughed, and opened his eyes.

"How do you feel?"

No response.

"I have to get you out of here. You need your people. I'm weak, Ohanzee. We need food. You need help."

His eyes remained open; still, no words gathered on his tongue.

"I have to move you onto the travois. I need your help."

Ohanzee tried, but his arms were useless. I had no options left but to risk accidentally separating his fractured bones again. With a deep breath, I pried him up on one side. While balancing his body with my shoulder, I pulled with all my might and wedged the travois underneath him. Then I let him down. His body was halfway on the travois, and I pulled and pushed from the other side until he was firmly centered for travel. He did not cry out once, though his face contorted in excruciating pain. I tied the travois to Blue, who stood like a statue. When everything was as secure as possible, I walked to Blue's head and urged him to move out. Very carefully we worked our way down the slope.

Before reaching the prairie floor, I realized the bags of gold were still at the base of Devil's Tower. I tied Blue to a pine tree and ran back up the hill. The gold was exactly where I had dropped it before Ohanzee's fall. I swung the bags over my shoulder and returned to Ohanzee, where I secured them under his head.

"How am I supposed to talk with my Creator, with a bag of rocks under my head?" he asked wearily. His words reminded me of my torturous curlers and the sleep I lost for the sake of others who preferred curly hair. How frivolous this had been. How vain Mother was, forcing me to be someone I wasn't. The hours and hours I spent trying to please her only distracted me from discovering who I truly wanted to be. Anger welled inside and energized me in an unexpected way.

We plodded along and came out of a long grove of trees, where a stench wafted through the air. I halted Blue, and he immediately dropped his head to graze. Without hobbling him, I walked toward the smell. About twenty feet from the trail lay a fly-infested buffalo carcass.

"Now what do I do?" I whimpered, though nobody heard. In defeat, I collapsed and sobbed beside the rotting buffalo. A few minutes later, I opened my eyes and gasped as the ground crawled around me. Ants, beetles and flying insects were finding their next meal. Jumping back to my feet, I slapped bugs off my pants and blouse. They stung and bit me from underneath my clothes and inside my moccasins. I stripped down, dancing before the buffalo, until my flesh was finally my own. Completely naked, the hot breeze chilled my exposed skin, and a realization spoke from within me. I was done: done with being a victim of circumstance, done with living as Mother had expected me to, done with second-guessing everything that I did.

I picked the remaining bugs off the insides of my pants, blouse, and moccasins. Hesitating and cherishing the breeze against my skin, I finally put my clothes back on and carefully approached the carcass with Dad's knife in hand. The blade was only three inches long, so I worked my way through a layer of fly-infested fat; then, as I sliced deeper, I cut out a small chunk of fresher red meat.

I walked back to the travois.

"Wake up!" I snapped assertively, slapping Ohanzee's sweaty face. "You need to eat, Ohanzee. Eat!" I demanded of Ohanzee, holding a small bite to his lips. I forced a tiny piece of raw meat into his mouth. He gagged as I stuffed the bite deep into his

309

mouth. My rough hands forced his jaw open and shut. He started to chew on his own.

I returned to the bloated buffalo. My stomach only tolerated a few bites of the raw, warm meat before I cut away chunks of the deepest meat and rolled them up in a piece of my skirt, storing them in Blue's bag. We had enough meat to sustain us for four or five days.

Perhaps if I packed Ohanzee's wound with his medicine bag herbs, then he would heal. I reached for the small bag attached to his leg.

"Don't, please, I need to die with my medicine bag."

I ignored him and opened the top, only to find it stuffed with grass. "What is wrong with you? This is only grass."

"It's my strength, Sara. My protector in battle. And it will be my guardian spirit in death."

"You are going crazy. Ohanzee! What do I need? Flowers? Herbs? What will stop your infection?"

"The Creator has set the course. I don't worry. I don't fear."

"Ohanzee! Stop it! What plant will help your leg? What stops infections?"

"The purple coneflower."

"What does it look like?"

"It's purple," he murmured, with the edges of his lips turned up.

I searched for the flower but returned empty-handed.

"Sara, help me up. We'll walk to my people."

"Ohanzee. You cannot fade out on me. Listen. I need your help. I cut off the buffalo's tail for a fly switch. Remember how you told me about swatting flies?"

Nothing.

I jammed the buffalo tail into Ohanzee's limp hand.

"Now, Ohanzee; my job is to get you to your people. Your job is to keep flies off your leg. Do you understand?"

Surprisingly, he began to swat his blood-soaked pants.

I am not sure if Blue sensed the urgency of our situation, or if he was annoyed at the whipping noise behind him, but he picked up the pace, and walked faster than I had seen him move over the last two months. Dirt puffed out of the edges of my moccasins as I stepped along the trail. My nostrils burned from the dust. Yet we walked on without rest.

Day after day, Blue faithfully stumbled on. Occasionally, he dropped his head, to sneak stems of dust-covered grass. I rested while he nibbled, knowing full well that these snacks would not sustain him much longer. By evening, white billowy clouds transformed into black giants in the far-away sky, lighting up the horizon but bringing no rain as we weaved west along game trails. The continuous dragging sound of the travois sent shivers down my back. Talking out loud helped mask the scratching noise, so I spoke with Blue about our future. What if I actually

311

delivered Ohanzee to his people? Would they steal Blue? Torture and kill me? Or would his people welcome me to stay with them of my own free will? Would I return to white civilization? Or would I wander the prairie, alone with Blue, until I discovered who I was deep within my soul? Would I face my future with red, white, or Blue?

A sharp snap brought me back to the present. Ohanzee slid sideways behind Blue due to a broken travois pole. Blue calmly stopped and waited. Any other horse would have spooked and sent the entire contents of the travois, man and all, scattered across the prairie like a tornado. I quickly untied the travois, and Blue dropped his head to graze.

Repairs took a few hours because I had to find a replacement for the snapped left pole. The travois was not as secure as before, but it would have to do. We had one hour to test the new drag before a chilly night stopped our journey. I built a fire and wondered why the prairie had such erratic weather. The day had been blistering hot, with grasshoppers continuously jumping up and clinging to my legs. Ohanzee continued hallucinating; he was being called somewhere, but his strong constitution held on to life. Just as Ohanzee quit moaning and quieted for the night, my eyelids grew heavy. Blue gave a small, unalarmed whinny. I looked up, and through the firelight, I saw a shadow disappear into the trees. I was not afraid.

I quit counting the days and nights, but it must have been over a week before we came to a ridge and stared down upon a valley. Tipis extended for at least three miles, and I could not see the end of the Indian camp from north to south. Columns of white smoke rose from what seemed to be thousands of small cooking fires, independently rising and then joining all others in a cloud of static smoke that hovered above the camp. Numerous eroded hillsides flowed together, as their dirt-covered gullies all led to a river that was maybe eighty feet wide. The water was as blue as the sky.

Ohanzee lifted his head from the travois. "You did it, Sara. You did it. Greasy Grass. Should be seven tribes of our nation. Look for my Miniconjou camp circle." He put his head back down and closed his eyes.

"How can I tell them apart?"

Ohanzee mumbled on, "Go across a small stream. Keep heading south. My tribe's place stays the same within the circle. It's our custom, each time we come together. Just ask."

"Ask who? Who do I ask?"

"The Akicita."

"Who's the Akicita?"

"You'll see," Ohanzee said, never opening his eyes.

As I led Blue toward the village, warriors appeared out of nowhere. We were surrounded. Akicita—the police society.[36]

One of the men, dressed only in a leather breechcloth and moccasins, jumped off his horse and grabbed me. I could do nothing but cringe; I was entangled by his hands, which rubbed up and down my body.

"Enough," Ohanzee mumbled from the travois.

"Hahn! Mila!" the man hollered out to the others. He pulled Dad's knife from my pants. I knew it was gone forever. Another warrior jumped from his horse and yanked the reins from my hand. He was dressed in a similar breechcloth, with his thighs and calves exposed. The breechcloth was secured at his waist with a quill-decorated belt. The second Akicita led Blue. I followed behind and noticed the thinly beaded stream of silver strung on leather and attached to his shiny black hair.

"Ohanzee is Miniconjou. Please, take us there. The Miniconjou," I pleaded from behind. They did not respond. "Miniconjou. Do you understand? Miniconjou."

"Miniconjou?" one asked, finally understanding.

"Please."

The men seemed to relax a bit as they led me down into the valley. They carefully crossed difficult sections of the terrain. The river had at most a depth of three or four feet, with a quicksand feel to the bottom. The current was strong, and Ohanzee was miserable as we crossed, groaning with each sharp motion. On the bank of the creek, Indian children caught grasshoppers in the long prairie grasses and delivered them to older children. They stopped and stared. Then they returned to attaching each grasshopper to a bone hook, which was tied to a narrow line of buffalo sinew and secured to a stick fishing pole. One boy crouched near the water's edge, flicking small stones into the stream. His hair was unmistakably blonde. Other children played games with sticks beside him.[37]

Cottonwoods edged the creek. As I followed the men, I looked around at the camps before me. Fresh-killed game hung from trees. Horses grazed. The people milled about in the tranquil evening breeze. What a beautiful place they had selected: ample water, grass, and wood for fires, as well as plentiful fishing and hunting. It was a sort of paradise, offering valuable reunions between the people of the great prairie.

The men led us to a large tipi, decorated with rows of quilled pendants along the side of the door. The buffalo skins were painted with animals and beautiful designs. From the top, a scalp streamer fluttered in the breeze. One Akicita tapped on the east-facing door and entered after a call came from inside. A few moments later, a distinguished chief appeared, adorned in clean buckskin clothing and a sharp headdress. He looked at me with intrigue and then at the travois. For quite some time he gazed down at Ohanzee, and then cracked a smile of recognition.

"Ohanzee, son of Touch the Clouds." He walked back to the door of his tipi and called inside. Three men stepped out and whooped when they saw Ohanzee. He turned to the Akicita and released them. I humbly stood before the four men.

"I am Chief Lame Deer. This is High Backbone, Fast Bull, and Hump. Who are you?"

"Sara. Sara Taylor."

"We heard many moons ago how Ohanzee was missing. We thought he had been called to the Creator. How is it that you bring him to us?"

I started to explain the last four months of my life and how my path crossed with Ohanzee. As quickly as I began, I stopped.

"Sir, Ohanzee has a broken leg and needs attention in the worst way. Can you call for a medicine man?"

"He is coming. We are setting up a tipi now. Go on with your story."

I looked over at three women who were quickly raising a tipi, and I wondered how such efficiency was achieved with almost no words. Turning back to the leaders, I continued. The men listened intently to my story and then spoke in their language. Chief Lame Deer assured me that the medicine man had a special gift of healing broken bones.

Two men drug the travois to the new tipi, though Ohanzee was not cognizant of the move. I followed behind. The inside of the tipi was translucent and magical as the evening light filtered in. Buffalo rugs cushioned the floor, and the women motioned for me to sit down. Once the men settled Ohanzee onto extra layers of floor covering, the medicine man and Fast Bull removed his buckskin leggings, stripping him down to his breechcloth. A slender cord remained tied around his waist. Ohanzee mumbled how his thigh was on fire, and then he passed out.

"This Miniconjou is clearly full of fortitude," Fast Bull said from the door of our tipi. He left for a few minutes and returned with a woman. "This is Monahsetah. She will help you."

I nodded. She nodded.

"What is your name?" she asked.

"Sara. Are you Lakota?"

"No. Cheyenne."

"What does your name mean?" I asked.

"It means 'spring grass.'"

"How do you know English?"

"Difficult story." She changed the subject quickly, "The medicine man prays for purification first."

He looked at Ohanzee's swollen leg and walked to the bottom of his body. Monahsetah glanced at Ohanzee's wound and gasped when she realized his grave condition. Thin streaks of gray infection ran up Ohanzee's thigh. The medicine man measured the length of Ohanzee's legs with a stick and made a few contemplative grunts as he decided his course of action.

"I did all I could," I told Monahsetah.

"You did more than expected," she whispered.

Monahsetah was kind and demure; I could tell from the moment I saw her. If she had been a student at my school in New York City, we would have been best friends. She said she was twenty-five years old, but she looked only twenty. Her brown skin was blemish-free, and her eyes were deep and despondent. Her long, black hair was well kept in two thin braids that extended to the middle of her ribcage. She wore a plain caramel-colored deerskin dress with little embellishment other than a beaded hemline. Her moccasins were gorgeously beaded in fine pink and yellow roses.

"Will they cut off Ohanzee's leg?"

"Oh no. Never. It is better to die than to cut off an arm or leg. The body must be whole when it crosses over."

Then Monahsetah interpreted the medicine man's flowing monotone words. "He wants to know how you put Ohanzee's bone back inside his leg."

I explained how I reset the leg bone, similar to what I saw done on an arm by Doctor Mayo. Monahsetah relayed the information. The medicine man squeezed Ohanzee's swollen leg muscle. He nodded with understanding. Then he studied the damaged flesh, oozing infection. He said something to Monahsetah, and she disappeared, returning a few minutes later with a bowl of creek water. The medicine man cleaned Ohanzee's wound with a soaked rag. He dabbed until the rag was slick with fluids, and then he rinsed it in the bowl. He chanted as he repeated the process over and over again. Then he applied powdered sage and crushed purple coneflower to the surface of Ohanzee's rotting flesh. As a final dressing cover, he set fresh sage leaves across the wound. He immobilized the whole leg using rawhide-wrapped buffalo thigh bones as splints on both sides of Ohanzee's tightly wrapped thigh. He placed a light buffalo hide over both legs and began to speak.

"The Creator said you put the bones together correctly," Monahsetah interpreted.

"Now what?" I asked quietly, not sure if I actually wanted to hear the answer.

"Now we wait. The infection is bad. Very bad."

The medicine man initially seemed annoyed with me in the tipi. Monahsetah told me to keep my eyes cast down and stay to the left side of the tipi. I obeyed, and his tolerance increased. I watched intently for hours as he chanted over Ohanzee's body. I prayed to my Lord for Ohanzee's healing.

Monahsetah came and went from our tipi, tapping on the door each time she entered. After quite some time, she gestured for me to follow her outside. Monahsetah shyly walked me past tipis, to the outer rim of the village. She pointed to an area where the grasses were trampled and slit trenches were dug along a cluster of cottonwoods for privacy. The trenches were about six inches deep and narrow enough to straddle.

"This is the area to relieve yourself," she said calmly. "I will bring you here when you need to go. Cover it when you finish."

I nodded my head, mentally comparing the small trenches to chamber pots and outhouse holes; the trenches drew no flies, caused no smell, and allowed the waste to decompose more quickly.

We walked back toward our tipi, where a fire smoldered. Monahsetah took a thick branch and stirred down through the coals, a layer of dirt, and a final layer of leaves. At the bottom of the small pit was perfectly cooked fish, probably from the children's success in the river. Monahsetah lifted the fish from the fire and carried it to our tipi. I ate the flakey fish after Ohanzee refused the bites that I placed at his lips. Monahsetah shook her head in frustration, left the tipi, and returned with roasted buffalo meat and fresh green herbs. He still refused. Monahsetah sat with both legs off to the side, and we quietly ate the fish and buffalo, staring at our semiconscious patient.

"It is his choice whether to eat or not. It is not your battle, Sara. Are you nervous here? Twelve thousand or more of us, one of you," Monahsetah said.

"Just a little. How did you know to meet?"

"Everyone spread the word. Mostly through our runners. It is mostly Lakota—all seven tribes. Arapaho and Cheyenne came when Sitting Bull said it was important. Some say twenty thousand are here. I think there are about two thousand warriors," Monahsetah explained.[38]

"Unmarried warriors looking for a wife?" I asked, wiping sweat from under my hair, stuck on the back of my neck. "Maybe you should take a walk around the village?"

She grinned but did not leave. "It is hot. I can raise the sides of the tipi for ventilation, but then you will have no privacy. All my people are curious and will look in."

320

"It's okay, either way."

"Let's leave them down for now. Privacy is important. More important than comfort," Monahsetah said. "We live closely, and gossip breaks us down. It makes life difficult for some of us."

I pulled myself to my knees and looked into Ohanzee's face. His skin had a slight gray cast, which I hoped was caused just by the opaque tipi walls. His neck had a prominent scar from the day that he had been dragged behind our cavalry horse. Monahsetah gazed at the tipi skin just as Mother once stared at the wall of our barrack. A few ants were scaling the buffalo hide.

"Can I brush your hair?" Monahsetah asked carefully.

She didn't insult me; I knew my hair was a disaster. For months, since leaving the fort, I had used my fingers as a comb and pulled my messy locks into a loose bun or tried to weave them into braids. To create a bun, I used small sticks snapped from branches, pushed straight through the clump of gathered hair to hold it at the nape of my neck. To make braids, I tied off the ends of my hair with green stems of grass. No matter what I did, my scalp constantly itched from mites and fleas.

"Please," I answered. As Monahsetah carefully brushed, she caught snags which brought tears to my eyes. It had been weeks since the prospector dropped the rock on my head, but my neck pain was nearly intolerable.

"Do you wish to wash it?" she whispered. I nodded. She promptly left and returned a few minutes later.

"Han maske," she said, entering the tipi. She carried a large wooden bowl, full of stream water. "Han maske," Monahsetah repeated: "Hello, lady friend." She bent my head over and dropped my hair into the water, pulling in the wild strands. Then she took an oily wash and scrubbed my scalp, massaging the oil into the locks. We waited, and then she rinsed out my hair with fresh water.

"What is the oil?" I asked, merely to break the silence.

"Buffalo brains. They help kill the little bugs. Suffocates them. Makes your hair shiny."

I shouldn't have asked. She rinsed it again and combed it smooth.

"Sorry I don't have cinnamon oil for you," she said softly.

"What do you mean?" I asked.

"Cinnamon oil in your hair, just like General Custer. Is it not the wasicu way?"

I recalled the cinnamon scent coming from General Custer when I first met him in the stable and when I served him the dessert at Fort Randall. The greatest Indian fighter of all time put cinnamon oil in his hair?

Monahsetah asked, "Do you want your hair like a wasicu or like my people?"

"Your way."

Monahsetah carefully parted my hair down the centerline of my head and braided each side. When she finished, the braids were perfectly even and rested on my collarbones.[39] The new style felt liberating; the small chunks were out of my face, my scalp no longer itched, and a bun of hair was not pressing against the nape of my sore, sweaty neck.

"Oh, Sara," Ohanzee said, peering at me in a delirium. "If I clean myself up and walk, I will wait a very long time in front your tipi for a chance that you'll join me under my robe."[40]

Monahsetah giggled and dropped her eyes. He was definitely suffering from fever.

"I will even give a few horses for you," he added.

"You don't have any horses," I whispered. Monahsetah giggled again. We sat in silence for a few moments and then Ohanzee's words tickled us again.

My foot throbbed. I asked Monahsetah if it was acceptable to take off my moccasins. She nodded. The fresh air seemed positive, and I wiggled and stretched my remaining toes. Monahsetah looked over, and when she spoke, I expected her to ask about my foot. Instead she asked about my life at the fort. I reminisced about Dad, Mother, Sergeant Zito, and Private Jake. I told her about the food and the beautiful horses.

"Do you know Yellow Hair?"

"Yellow Hair?"

"Yellow Hair. Long Hair. George Custer."

"Yes."

"And his brother? Tom Custer?"

"Yes. I met both of them," I explained, telling her how they came through Fort Randall and spent a night, before returning to their post.

"How was he? What was he like?"

I repeated some of his self-proclaimed accolades, but skipped the "Any good Indian is a dead Indian" story. She continued asking pointed questions about the Custer brothers.

"Why do you ask so many questions?"

"Because they killed my father as we flew a white flag from our tipi. They killed twenty-six women and children, and thirteen men, including my father."

"When?"

"At the Battle of Washita, when I was seventeen years old."

I thought back to General Custer's night at Fort Randall and how he claimed that they had killed over one hundred warriors. Conveniently, he failed to mention the white flag or twenty-six massacred women and children.

"I'm very sorry, Monahsetah. Then what happened?"

"I was taken captive by the Seventh Cavalry." She was interrupted when someone thumped on the side of our tipi. Monahsetah called him in. It was One Bull.

"Hau kola," he said cautiously. And then he turned to Monahsetah and me, and continued, "Hau haNkasi."[41]

Ohanzee barely cracked open his bloodshot eyes. Monahsetah whispered, "Han sic'esi" and backed out of the tipi.

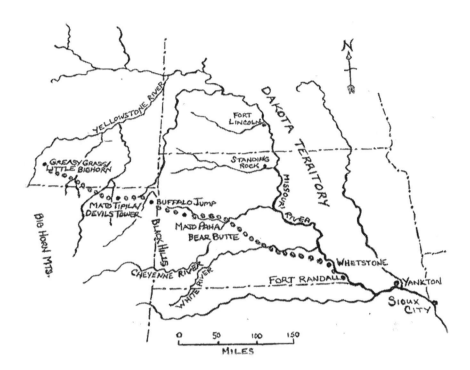

CHAPTER 27

RED

SATURDAY NIGHT, JUNE 24, 1876

GREASY GRASS

(LITTLE BIGHORN RIVER)

"THERE ARE NOT ENOUGH INDIANS IN THE WORLD TO DEFEAT THE SEVENTH CAVALRY."
~George Armstrong Custer

I barely remembered my fall. I recalled losing my footing, and then I only remembered pain—intense pain. Somehow Sara managed to reset my leg and tend to my needs while I faded in and out of consciousness. With each beat of my heart, pounding pain filling my confused mind. I did not have much sense of reality as shock and infection took over. My pleading eyes begged for help, for relief from the pain, for Sara to be brave and think clearly. Yet I did not have the strength to speak.

Despite her exhaustion, Sara made good decisions. She was always at my side, moving me, feeding me, and raising water to my lips. If Sara hadn't remained calm, I would be scattered across the prairie, nourishing the buffalo grass. If she had left me alone and gone to search for help, I would have been a feast for bears or coyotes. I was greatly relieved when the Akicita surrounded us because then I was safe. Then, amid the flush of relief, I realized what Sara risked for me. If I could have, I would have risen from the travois and strangled the Akicita for the way he unnecessarily touched Sara. She was not a threat. He was selfish and disrespectful, which elicited murderous thoughts from a hallucinating man.

I remember One Bull visiting our tent. He pretended to be unaffected by my condition, but I saw him gag from nausea as he viewed my bloody thigh oozing through the blanket.

"Ohanzee. You are brave. I may be Hunkpapa, and you Miniconjou, but I consider you my brother," One Bull told me.

I had nothing to say.

"I did not mean to question your integrity out at the camp with Sara."

One Bull glanced down at Sara's bare feet and studied her amputated stubs. He pondered silently for quite some time.

"We tracked you since Mato Paha."

"How did you know?" I whispered hoarsely.

"We climbed the mountain. I was born there. Your grandfather died there. But you were a few days ahead of us. I saw your moccasin tracks, and the wasicu's tracks of only seven toes. I stood where you stood, at your Grandfather's body. I know I am not Miniconjou, but I respected Chief Lone Horn, and Ohanzee, I respect you."

I nodded, yet had no energy to speak.

"Ohanzee. You need to know something. Your father and grandmother are not here."

"Dead?"

"No, they are fine. Your cousin Crazy Horse gave me the news. When they lost you in the horse raid, your father returned to the Cheyenne River Agency to care for your grandmother. He is not here at Greasy Grass. He doesn't know that you are alive. I promise to take you home—one way or another."

It was deflating to travel across the vast prairie with Sara only to find that I was still weeks away from Father and Grandmother. I could hardly believe that a Hunkpapa, one who had taunted me for years, claimed he would take me home. One Bull said a few more things and then left. Monahsetah came in and announced that the cavalry was heading toward our camp.

"Are your people afraid?" Sara asked.

Monahsetah answered, "No. Not afraid. They would be crazy to attack us. We are too large in numbers. They don't dare face us in battle. They lost against us just last week.[42] They would be insane

328

to attack this many warriors, who fight best when protecting their families." Then Monahsetah looked at us with a startled revelation written on her face.

"Weeks ago, on the Rosebud," she said, "Great Chief Sitting Bull was in a sun dance."

I had witnessed many sun dances. Sitting Bull's breast muscles were pierced, and cord was strung though to secure him to the pole of suffering.

Monahsetah continued, "Long after others had torn their attachments away, Sitting Bull refused to end his suffering, seeking a vision. After two days without food or water, he collapsed. Some winyan brought him food and water, and they forced it in his mouth. When he came back to us, he told of what he saw."

"What is 'winyan,' and what was the vision?" Sara asked.

"Winyan are Lakota women. Sitting Bull saw soldiers falling like grasshoppers, into our camp." Monahsetah stared off for a moment and then looked at Sara. "Your people are coming to kill us, but our warriors will kill them instead. Sitting Bull saw it, and it will come true."

In the darkest part of the night, the camp stood still, while I chewed on a piece of buffalo hide. I cried out to Wakan Tanka, to take away my suffering. My leg was on fire, and I did not know how much more I could take. Sara opened the flap for fresh air.

"Ohanzee, someone is on the ridge above us, looking down at our camp."

I had no energy to act on or ponder what she said.

CHAPTER 28

RED

JUNE 25, 1876

BATTLE OF GREASY GRASS

(BATTLE OF LITTLE BIGHORN)

"WHEN A WHITE ARMY BATTLES INDIANS AND WINS, IT IS CALLED A GREAT VICTORY, BUT IF THEY LOSE IT IS CALLED A MASSACRE."
~Chiksika, Shawnee

Sunday, June 25, 1876, was a hot day, and my fever seemed to compete with the rising temperatures. Early in the morning my fever was low. With my leg fully immobilized and no longer bouncing on the travois, my pain had diminished to the point where I did not want to die. Still, I had an aversion to facing reality. The cycle of pain was still overwhelming, and sometimes I turned my head to the side and vomited from the agony.

Sara and Monahsetah took turns tending to my hygiene, wiping vomit from the side of my face and dumping containers of excrement. I was too sick to feel embarrassed. Sara cleaned my skin so I would not get sores where my flesh contacted the bedding. When Sara rested, she quietly sat beside me. Then, as only Sara could do, she broke the silence with more questions.

"Monahsetah said you would rather die than have your leg cut off."

"Yes," I answered.

"Why?"

"It's complicated. It is better to go to the Creator in a whole body."

"Why didn't you let me die instead of cutting off my toes?" she asked.

"Because you are a white girl. Your Creator doesn't care."

"Did you do it to disgrace me? Like mutilating a body on a battlefield?"

"Of course not."

I could tell Sara doubted me. More tiring questions followed.

"What about your grandfather on Bear Butte?"

"What about him?"

"Why didn't you tell me it was him?"

"You wouldn't understand."

"You didn't even try me. Ohanzee, listen. Maybe I would be able to understand. I understand more than you think."

"Like what?"

"I understand you were humiliated before your tribe when you left Black Robe early. I understand you were trying to save face when you tried to steal our horses."

"We did steal your horses."

She held her tongue and paused before continuing on, "I understand you were deserted by your people."

"They didn't desert me. They thought I was dead."

"You have a weight on you, Ohanzee. You are dwelling in your past. I don't know exactly what it is. But you don't have to prove yourself to me. We both know what you did for me. You saved me. Do you remember when you told me to look forward and not backward? You also need to focus on the future now. Look ahead or you'll die from the struggle inside your heart and not from your broken leg."

I did not dare tell Sara of another struggle within my heart: my longing to embrace her. She kept my lifeblood flowing in more ways than she knew. I was afraid to lose her, yet I wanted the best for her. I struggled with my thoughts.

Just then One Bull opened the door without tapping first. He said troops had marched in the area and might start a fight. Sara looked out of our tipi door and said my people were gathering in small groups. I heard some people say that we should move our camp to a better strategic battle location since we had not come to this spot beside the creek with the intention of fighting. Instead, as the first tribes arrived, they picked out nice shady spots, near the water and good grazing. After the first group put up their tipis, another group arrived and placed theirs in their designated area, relative to the people already there.

If there was ever a day I wanted to be a warrior, this was the day. Yet I could do nothing except lay in the tipi and listen. Monahsetah said a new village rumor was spreading about a boy named Deeds; the cavalry had just murdered him as he searched for stray ponies. Since our large village had no single leader, I knew what would follow. Some warriors dashed to quickly collect their ponies, but most felt secure in our numbers and waited, unalarmed.

What happened next is a bit convoluted because, as the day warmed up, so did I. Fever overtook me, and I only remember bits of what my people said as they came and went from our tipi. I knew soldiers moved toward our camp but never thought they would attack once they saw our numbers. But scouts and soldiers surprised us and attacked our village from the southeast. They killed six fleeing women and four of our children. I could hear the screaming and chaos as women grabbed nearby children and raced to relative safety at the west end of the village. All belongings were left behind. Old people tried to escape, limping along. Lost, confused children turned in circles in the dust, crying for their families.

"Sara, get low! Bullets. The battle is now," I mumbled to Sara, who listened and lay on the ground beside me. Just then we heard the first bullets pierce our tipi skin.

"It will be bad, Ohanzee. The cavalry will outgun you."

"Maybe, but our braves are fiercest when they protect their families. They mostly have arrows, but some have big surprises."[43]

Monahsetah crawled on her hands and knees into our tipi, and told us the news: "Sitting Bull just instructed his nephew One Bull to leave his gun and carry Sitting Bull's rawhide shield to go out to talk peace with the soldiers."

"Did he do it?" I asked.

"He tried. Good Bear went with him. They rode side by side and made it to just thirty feet from the troops when the soldiers began firing. One Bull killed a few soldiers, but Good Bear was shot in both legs, and his horse ran away. One Bull dragged him to safety."[44]

Monahsetah crawled to the door and peered out. She said a whole group of soldiers was within two hundred feet of our tipis. Young warriors were mounting their horses and charging bravely into the line of fire. The cavalry retreated across the river, and about thirty-five soldiers were killed before taking a defensive position in the tree line on the other side.[45] Warriors slaughtered soldiers who tried to run off, counting coup on some before killing them. Our women motivated our men by screaming the tremolo.

"Why do they make that whooping war call? Is it to scare the soldiers?" Sara asked.

"It excites the warriors and makes them feel brave. Does it scare the wasicu?" Monahsetah asked.

"I don't know how it couldn't. Where is Sitting Bull?" Sara asked.

"He jumped onto his horse bareback and rode off to his mother's lodge," Monahsetah answered.

I envisioned Sitting Bull's black stallion, whose presence was nearly as grand as that of Sitting Bull himself. The horse would not spook at the battle around him. They would reach his elderly mother's tipi and lead her to safety.

The battle raged around us, and all I could do was remind Sara to keep her head low. Bullets tore holes through our tipi leather and sometimes sheered our timber support poles, knocking chunks of wood onto our heads. Sara and Monahsetah took turns crawling to the tipi door to survey the scene outside.

More soldiers were spotted on another hill, moving down Medicine Tail Coulee to attack the village by way of the ford. A group of warriors rushed downstream to face them.[46] The soldiers halted mid-charge, halfway across the river, where the leading soldier, in full buckskin leather, was shot off a sorrel horse with four white socks. His body was carried on the back of another horse as they retreated. The soldiers regrouped and rode along the ridges, searching for a way to attack.

Sara looked out our tipi and saw warriors riding horses in all directions, kicking up the dry soil. Sara said she could not see anything beyond fifty feet because a solid cloud of dust obstructed her view of the battle. Warriors continued to come and go, some in fine buckskin leggings, some with bone breastplates against their torsos.

I heard the warriors cheering, "Hoka hay!"

"There is no organization out there. No command. What does that mean—hoka hay?" Sara inquired.

"Today is a good day to die," Monahsetah replied.

I heard warriors hollering "Hiyupo," which means, "Come on." Monahsetah said she saw an Indian horse go down. The warrior calmly took the leather from around his neck and walked away bravely amidst the battle around him.

When Sara looked out again, many white men lay dead. Then she saw Crazy Horse calmly walk past our tent; his face was fully painted, with a blue lightning streak extending from the top of his forehead, past the left side of his nose, to the tip of his chin. Quite formidable, he wore only a breechcloth and moccasins. Wrapped around his taunt bicep was a quilled armband.[47]

"Why does he have red spots painted on his body?" Sara asked.

"His dream told him how to be painted for war. The spots represent hail," Monahsetah answered.

Monahsetah heard Sitting Bull command his warriors to let the retreating soldiers flee; he hoped they would go tell the rest of the white men about the fight. The young warriors did not listen and continued to taunt the stranded soldiers.[48] After running off the group of soldiers, the warriors cried out, "Crazy Horse is coming!" Riding nearly naked on a buckskin and white paint horse, with a single hawk feather tied in his hair, Crazy Horse inspired a new counterassault. The warriors were excited because they knew the effect of Crazy Horse's vision on Bear Butte; no white man could harm him. He rode beside fleeing soldiers, daring them to shoot him.[47]

Monahsetah snuck out of the tent as the cavalry fire diminished. She was gone for quite some time. I saw a large puppy crawl under the side of our tipi and cower under Sara's blanket. She seemed to find comfort in stroking his shaking body. I did not have the heart to tell her that he would probably be someone's next meal.

Monahsetah returned to report how elders, women, and children had gathered on the benches west of the village to safely view the battle. She said warriors stripped the bodies of thirty-two soldiers and scouts, taking the leather from dead horses' bridles but leaving the iron bits. Saddles were looted for older men in the tribes. Other warriors set grass fires throughout the valley. Later Monahsetah told us that ten warriors had been killed. Sitting Bull said they should end the battle because it was a victory.

The camp was nearly deserted, and Sara sat in the tipi with me, only daring to whisper. When Sara grew impatient, she peeked out the tipi door. She did not see Monahsetah, but she said dogs wandered about, waiting for their owners to return. The warriors were still scattered on the hillsides and continued to whoop challenges to the soldiers in the trees. Sara saw women starting to wander back from the western lookout, and they caught the uninjured cavalry horses that had spooked from the fighting.

Monahsetah returned hours later to announce that over two hundred troopers lay dead or dying. The fortunate soldiers were killed instantly; I heard cries as the injured faced their grisly last moments at the hands of my people.[49] Monahsetah said the women marched uphill, singing victory songs. They stripped the uniforms from the dead soldiers. They dismembered many men, scattering heads and arms along the field, in the belief that limbless men could not come back from the spirit world to fight again. As a final coup de grace, some warriors fired the soldiers' issued pistols, at point-blank range, into their skulls.

That night dust and gun smoke still filled the air and hung heavy over the camp. Sitting Bull held an informal council. Monahsetah snuck deep into the shadows of the meeting, still within earshot. When she came back to our tipi, she said that Sitting Bull was very disappointed and somber. Earlier in the day, he had spread the word that the white men's bodies should not be mutilated and looted, but only the Hunkpapa obeyed the wise man. He said that because our people took the white men's possessions, they would covet those things forever and be at the white man's mercy. Sitting Bull said it must be remembered that the troops had compelled the warriors to fight. His vision had been fulfilled, but he warned that the victory was temporary because more soldiers would come.

CHAPTER 29

WHITE

MONDAY, JUNE 26, 1876

RED WHITE OR BLUE

"I AM NO BIRD; AND NO NET ENSNARES ME:
I AM A FREE HUMAN BEING WITH AN
INDEPENDENT WILL."
~Jane Eyre, by Charlotte Brontë

I slept little that night. A group of women came to our tipi and told us we would be moving a short distance, to a nearby location. I waited with Ohanzee, who was devastated to hear that his Miniconjou friend High Horse had been killed fighting on the commanding ridge. Late that evening Eagle Elk, another Miniconjou friend, went back on a cavalry horse to where he had left his dead friend during the heat of battle. Eagle Elk stayed with the corpse of High Horse for hours, mourning amidst the scavengers and mutilators. Then he slung his friend's body over the horse's back and slowly led his horse and friend to the

Miniconjou circle. He delivered the body to High Horse's father. Eagle Elk refused food and went away to weep alone.

The village was taken down and then reassembled, as a mirror image of the first camp, farther from the soldiers who were still entrenched on the hilltop. The village women were busy setting up tipis and making preparations for the rigid ritual of Lakota burials. Monahsetah explained that we were moving our camp to different ground because bad luck hovered where a village had been attacked.

The custom of dealing with dead warriors was quite formal. First, tipis were selected, and the family that had lived inside each was told to move into a different tipi, usually that of another family member. Then scaffold burial beds were placed inside the vacated tipis. The thick air hovered over the eerie scene of the women washing the warriors' corpses in the creek. Once clean, the corpses were moved back to their burial tipis by horseback. The relatives dressed the bodies in the dead warriors' finest war clothes, which became their burial clothes. When the village moved on, the mourning families would leave all of their possessions behind, along with their dead warrior, symbolizing their total loss.

In the new camp, I lay in the darkness beside Ohanzee, unable to sleep. As the night wore on, the smell of dust and gunpowder turned to a fragrant smell of wood smoke. Wailing continued all night, as dead warriors' relatives grieved and chopped off their own hair, sliced their heads and legs with knives, and even cut off their own fingers to express deep sorrow. From the sound of men

341

staggering past our tipi, I think they were drinking whiskey from the soldiers' canteens. Finally, at dawn, I fell asleep.

I woke up to renewed fighting. The warriors continued to pressure the soldiers who were left in a circle on the wooded ridge. I felt terrible for the wounded soldiers because I knew they were surrounded and had no access to water.[50] Sitting Bull went to the menacing warriors and told them to stop shooting. He told them to leave the soldiers alone because the warriors would have larger armies to fight later, especially if the warriors killed the trapped soldiers. The warriors finally obeyed Sitting Bull and returned to the village.

I stood at the tipi door and looked through the settling dust and smoke. Hundreds of Indians—women, warriors, and children—roamed about, looting the bodies of the fallen cavalry. Grieving women, who had lost loved ones, mutilated the soldiers' bodies, cutting off private parts and limbs.[51] As two women began to mutilate one body at the top of the ridge, they were stopped by another woman. It looked like Monahsetah, but through the smoke, I could not be certain.

Later in the day, Monahsetah came to our tipi.

"Han maske," I said, as she entered.

"Han maske," she answered. "The Custer brothers are dead."

"General Custer?" I asked, in disbelief.

"Yes. And Tom."

"Are you sure?"

"Yes. They are on the ridge. Something inside me said to search. I walked up the hill and found George. His hair was clipped short and was thinning on top. One shot went through his chest and one right here," she said, pointing to her left temple. "There was another arrow," she paused, almost as if she regretted the words.

"Another arrow where?" I asked.

"Where no man would ever want one."

My eyes widened. "I can hardly believe your words," I said, under my breath.

She wept but continued. "It was too late for Tom, but I told them not to mutilate George, since the brothers are our family. Instead, the women jammed an awl through George's ears, so he will hear better and not break treaties in his afterlife."

Tears filled Monahsetah's eyes. I stood in shock beside her as she pulled out a knife and sliced off her long braids at the base of her neck. She began to wail, like a lone coyote on a summer prairie night. Sitting Bull rode past our tipi, somber and grand. He crossed the blood-soaked battlefield without emotion.

How could this have happened? I thought about the Custers' visit to Fort Randall—George Custer's restless spirit; how he appreciated my dessert; how he bragged about killing Indians; his red tie bandana, fringed buckskin shirt, and high jack boots; how he said he might be elected president of the United States; how he wanted me to accompany them on their adventure. He was a larger-than-life man, out to singlehandedly punish the Indians. He had done it before. How had he failed this time?

343

Ohanzee called me to his side. He tried to clear his throat. I lifted a buffalo bladder full of river water to his parched lips, and he took one sip before managing, "I have heavy thoughts you need to hear. I know you are afraid, but I beg you, Sara, do not run away from fear. Never ever. Promise me. One day, you will feel complete. Remember when I told you to lock up your feelings inside your heart?"

"Yes."

"Well, soon you will let them out. You will look back and understand. You will become whole and strong."

I did not fully understand, though I believed. A huge part of me wanted to stay with Ohanzee.

After quite some time, when he had regained some energy, Ohanzee continued, "I feel called by the Great One, perhaps soon. But I will still be a part of the prairie. Sara, hear my words with your heart. Perhaps you will sense me as you go on. Perhaps you will feel me with you."

"I don't want to leave you, Ohanzee. You'll make it, I know you will. Remember? Your people are survivors. You can't give up. You are a fighter."

"You'll be okay. More soldiers are coming, and you must wait, and go with them," he said.

"You can't tell me what to do."

"This is true," Ohanzee sighed, already exhausted from speaking.

344

In the afternoon, Sitting Bull announced a southern departure toward the Bighorn Mountains. Women worked together and took down their tipis. They stacked them as usual, on their sturdy travois. Word of soldiers having been spotted to the north flowed through camp. They were headed toward us.

I began to pack up my few belongings in the tipi. The medicine man rewrapped Ohanzee's leg. I closed my eyes for a moment, exhausted by the last few weeks. The light nearly blinded me as the door to the tipi was silently opened. Silhouetted in the light stood Sitting Bull. He motioned for the medicine man to leave the tent. The great leader glanced at Ohanzee, whose eyes were closed, and whose face was flushed from fever.

"Sara, we talk," Sitting Bull said and sat down, facing me with crossed legs. I immediately complied, in awe of his presence. My knees shook as I failed to remain composed.

Sitting Bull's face was worn and creased from years of enduring nature. "You are a brave girl. You risked greatly to return our Ohanzee. You stayed with him as the battle came to us. I saw you look out of the tipi the night before battle. I stood on the ridge, looking at the camp. I prayed to Wakan Tanka and asked for us to be saved and protected. The Great One has done this. Now your work is also done."

"I can stay with you and take care of Ohanzee."

"No. You cannot come. You place our people in great risk. You must wait here, in a funeral tipi. We leave two behind. You stay in one for safety."

"But I don't want to leave Ohanzee."

"Did you take him as your husband?"

"No."

"Then listen, Sara. If you come with us, you will place our winyan and children in danger. The soldiers will seek revenge. They will kill us and take you. Even without you, there will be no nights in the coming moons when an attack might not come upon us."

I sat silently and let the words sink in. "But what about Ohanzee?"

"Only our Creator knows Ohanzee's fate. He is very weak and may be called to return to the soil. It is not for me to decide. It is for Ohanzee and the Great One to discuss. You must know that even our strongest men usually die from this kind of broken bone. You put it back in his leg, and the bones found each other. You are our skinny white medicine girl, but you cannot stay with my people. You must wait for your soldiers."

I began to cry. Sitting Bull rose with a slight grunt of stiffness and then walked silently out of the tipi. I never saw him again.

A few minutes later three women peeked inside. I was crying over Ohanzee, who seemed to have awoken from a delirious state. The women dropped the door back down and whispered from behind the door. If only I knew their language.

"Sara. You must listen to Sitting Bull. He is wise," Ohanzee said. His weak voice was barely audible, and I bent my head near his, placing us closer than ever before. "Wait in the funeral lodge.

Please. The other soldiers are near. Wait until they look inside. You will be safe and back with your people."

I continued to weep.

"What, Sara?"

"What about you? Who will take care of you? What if you get worse?" I asked.

"You have done well, Sara. You brought me to my people. I am not afraid to die."

"But it's up to you, Ohanzee. You decide to fight or not."

"Life is a circle, Sara. My circle started the day I was born. It is complete when I die. It's the way it is. I am not afraid."

Monahsetah entered the tent and touched my shoulder, motioning for me to come with her. I turned back to Ohanzee.

"But you can't be done yet. Your circle can't be complete. Please, you must have a reason to live … please, you must have a reason," I pleaded.

"I do" is all he said before closing his eyes. I kissed him on his sweaty forehead and turned away; Monahsetah's dark eyes gazed upon us with an eerie expression of empathy. I wept as Monahsetah somberly and gently guided me to a funeral tipi. I turned around and saw three men carrying Ohanzee out of our tipi. He was secured to a new, sturdy travois. The men were careful in their motions, so Ohanzee did not stir or cry out. Five women were already dismantling our tipi for their journey, whose destination was unknown to me. I turned back to the funeral tipi and followed Monahsetah into a dark shadow that was victorious over the smoky glow of sunlight that was still trying to illuminate the tipi walls.

Two scaffold burial beds stood side by side. Monahsetah pulled me to the far wall of the tipi, where a buffalo hide had been set up on the ground for my comfort. An additional blanket was at the foot of the buffalo hide. She gestured for me to sit down and pointed to a small area beside the hide, where food and water had been placed.

"You should be fine. The other soldiers will be here soon."

I nodded. Monahsetah lingered, repositioning my bedding and food.

"Monahsetah, will you help me with something?" I asked.

"Yes," she answered, reaching for a braid which was no longer there. Instead, she ran her fingers along her collarbone.

"I was attacked by two white men on our way here," I said, surprised that my voice wavered. "Ohanzee killed one white man, and he counted coup on the other. Can you make sure Ohanzee is rewarded with the feather?" I requested, as my voice cracked with emotion.

"Did you see him do it? There must be a witness."

"I give you my word. I saw him complete both acts," I confirmed.

"Then he shall be recognized. I give you *my* word."

"Thank you," I sighed.

Suddenly, light shone forth from the doorway. The young blond boy with golden-brown skin stood before us.

"Mother, it's time for us to go."

"Yes, Yellow Bird," she answered, glancing back at me.[52] She smiled faintly and backed out the door, with her son reaching for her hand.

As my eyes adjusted to the dim light, the silhouettes of two motionless warriors emerged; each lay on a scaffolding of four crossed posts. They wore intricately beaded shirts and leggings. Their moccasins had beaded soles. Each man's face was painted bright red, with different symbols painted on top. The corpses were perfectly clean and smelled of herbs, not of death. Feathers adorned their combed and greased hair. A piece of buffalo suet was in each man's mouth, a symbol of the food that would sustain each body as it traveled to the spirit world. Their bodies were embraced by their own buffalo robes, with tools of war and cherished possessions at their sides. Hanging from each scaffold were rawhide strings of two white scalps. The hair was long and red.

Within half an hour, the camp was fully dismantled around me, and all grew silent. I did not need to look out of the death tipi. Ohanzee and his people were gone. I sat and contemplated the stillness of death and how it did not bother me to be trapped inside a tipi with two corpses. A sense of tranquility overcame me as I realized that I was not trapped but free: I now had confidence that nothing could shake me after what I had faced over the last nine months. Absorbed with introspection and the reality of being completely alone, I barely heard the rustling sound outside. Without fear, I sat motionless and listened for quite some time. Was it a dying man left behind? An animal? I crawled on all fours to the door and carefully peeked out. There stood Blue, tied to a tree beside the tipi. He faintly whinnied. I went to him and hugged his neck, taking in his scent and breathing out the oppressiveness that emanated from the deaths around me.

On the ground, propped against the tree, was a large pack. Leaning against the pack was Ohanzee's bow and his deerskin quiver with seven arrows. I set them aside and dragged the pack away from Blue's feet, curious about the hidden contents: pemmican packs to last about a month, a ball of buffalo cord, water bladders full of creek water, fire-making tools, my cast iron pan, a cavalry holster, and a belt with a Colt seven-shot revolver and a bag of attached ammunition.

Much to my surprise, at the bottom of the pack were the two bags of gold that I had not seen since I placed them under Ohanzee's head on the travois. I lifted the bags out of the pack and guessed they weighed about thirty pounds apiece. I was not sure of the value of gold. Still, I knew I was a wealthy young woman—if I could hang on to it.[53] I tipped the pack to shake it out. Along with menacing red ants, a small bundle of wrapped hide dropped to my feet. I untied the sinew and carefully unwrapped the leather, like a treasured Christmas present; Dad's pocket knife and Sergeant Zito's Saint Michael medal gleamed at me. I studied them; secured the knife into a holster pouch; and slid the chain over my head, tucking the cool medal under my blouse.[54] I refused to shed a tear as it warmed against my heart.

I led Blue to the creek, and he drank wholeheartedly. I heard a noise and looked up, only to see a wounded horse standing with his head hung low in the distance. I took Blue back to the tree and tied him up. Then I walked back to where I saw the wounded horse. He had vanished.[55]

The next day,[56] when a soldier opened the funeral tipi, only the two bodies remained inside; no white man would ever know I had been there. I was already nine miles east of the battlefield. Blue and I traveled along the lowlands, and so we were invisible to any soldiers in the area. We were merely a single shadow as we journeyed east across the prairie, leaving behind the stench of death and the eerie smoke-filled air that still hung over the battlefield. I doubted that I would ever see something so disturbing again, though one thing I had learned in the last month was how unpredictable life could be.

I was not certain I made the right choice by leaving the funeral tipi. Clearly, my life was forever altered in unforeseen ways. Part of my decision was based on my sense of being lost in a culture that had never embraced me. Crossing paths with Ohanzee and spending those months together had only been chance events. And as Sitting Bull said, I was not welcome to continue with the Indians. Yet I did not fit into the life of the military either, because my heart was now divided. I was riding away from a life of indifference, a life of constant compromise—the life Mother chose. I would find my way, with Blue. We were two survivors on the vast prairie.

As we solemnly paced along, I thought I heard something
following behind us, but each time I glanced back, I saw nothing.
Blue occasionally looked to his left, where Ohanzee used to walk,
leading us mile after mile. Was Ohanzee beside us in spirit? My
rational thoughts concluded that no, this was not possible, though
the mere contemplation offered a sense of comfort.

I missed him already. I missed the savage horse thief. I missed the
young man, seeking his way just as I, with his own strengths and
weaknesses, virtues and sins. Would I ever make sense of the
great risks that we took for each other? Would I ever feel content
with what we had shared and not ache for more? A shadow
crossed over Blue's neck. High above, a soaring golden eagle
danced with the swirling winds of the prairie.

The End.

NOTES

[1] The Lakota moon calendar consisted of thirteen annual moons, each lasting twenty-eight days. The calendar did not identify individual days. The calendar began in the spring, and every three years an additional moon was added to bring the lunar calendar into alignment with the solar calendar. Some tribes had distinctive moons, but generally the spring moons were called: Moon When Ducks Come Back, Moon of Making Fat, and Moon When Leaves Are Green. The summer moons were called: Moon of June Berries, Moon When the Chokecherries Are Ripe, and Moon of the Harvest. The fall moons were: Moon When Leaves Turn Brown, Moon When the Wind Shakes off Leaves, and Moon of the Rutting Deer. Finally , the winter moons were: Moon When the Deer Shed Their Horns, Hard Moon, Moon When Trees Crack from the Cold (after the effect of subzero temperatures on the sap within the trees), and Moon of Sore Eyes (due to snow blindness).

[2] A Lakota's vision or dream determined his future actions and path in life. When one's life role was revealed through a vision or dream, then the other members of the village did not interfere or question the validity of the experience. Lakota parents had hopes for their children but did not normally force them into specific roles. Instead, each person was to listen to his own inner voice.

[3] Red Cloud was not from a prominent family but built his status through his own bravery in war and his negotiation skills with the United States. The United States yielded to Red Cloud on many

stipulations during the negotiations of the Fort Laramie Treaty of 1868.

[4] The parfleche (pronounced: par flesh) is untanned buffalo rawhide, usually used to make bags. The hide was first soaked in a water and lye solution to remove the buffalo hair and then was stretched to dry. The hide was used to make shields, drums, and backpack-type bags. Parfleches were usually decorated with beadwork and had a flap over the opening to protect belongings inside. The beadwork pattern was unique to each family, similar to medieval knights using a coat of arms to protect and identify themselves. With unique family designs, parfleches were easily identified within the village as their carriers traveled from place to place.

[5] Bishop Martin Marty was born in 1834 in Switzerland. His father was a shoemaker. He received a formal education and was ordained as a Catholic priest in 1856. Marty was ordered in 1860 to Indiana, where he restored a faltering abbey. Then, in 1875, without approval, he personally changed a prayer, causing a Benedictine uproar. He relinquished his abbotship after being asked to serve as a priest in the Dakota Territory. Marty had wanted to be a missionary since learning of Father DeSmet years earlier. Bishop Marty moved to Dakota Territory in 1876, but for the purposes of this book, his teaching of Ohanzee took place in 1875. In reality, he settled on the Standing Rock Reservation about one month after the Battle of the Little Bighorn in August 1876. He quickly gained favor with the Lakota and became a sort of apostle to them. The Lakota did call Bishop Marty by the nickname Black Robe Lean Chief.

Sitting Bull completely trusted Bishop Marty, and in the spring of 1877, Bishop Marty traveled to Canada at the request of the US government. Marty was sympathetic to the Lakotas' plight, but after eight weeks with Sitting Bull and his warriors, he finally gave up in trying to persuade them to return to the United States. While in Canada, Bishop Marty sent letters to the US government in an attempt to clear up misconceptions regarding Sitting Bull's intentions.

Upon Bishop Marty's return to Standing Rock, he built a school for Lakota children. He opened a second school at Fort Yates in 1878. Bishop Marty took it upon himself to write a Lakota language dictionary, and he translated many Catholic writings for the Lakota. Four years later, in 1881, Sitting Bull and his followers eventually returned to the United States. They surrendered, and Sitting Bull was baptized by Bishop Marty in 1883. Two thousand Lakota were converted to the Catholic faith at the time. Bishop Marty died in Saint Cloud, Minnesota, in 1896.

[6] Pierre-Jean DeSmet was born in Belgium in 1801, and he became a dedicated Jesuit missionary throughout the West. He was highly sensitive to the issues of the Indians, and many tribes embraced his faith. The Flathead Nation of Iroquois Indians was convinced of his truths and requested "black robes" (that is, priests) to baptize their children and heal their sick and dying. Attempts were made to reach the Iroquois, but these attempts failed because the Lakota prevented passage across their territory. On the fourth attempt, in July 1840, Father DeSmet offered his first Holy Mass in current-day Wyoming. He was trusted by many tribes and was accepted into their villages. Father DeSmet was known as the

"Friend of Sitting Bull" because he persuaded the chief to negotiate with the United States during the 1868 Fort Laramie Treaty. He performed Catholic baptisms for approximately twelve hundred Indians. Father DeSmet died in 1873 in St. Louis, Missouri. DeSmet, South Dakota, was named after Father DeSmet, and the town later became famous as the childhood home of Laura Ingalls Wilder.

[7] Hart Island is a small island east of the Manhattan borough of New York City and at the western edge of Long Island Sound. The island was used by the Union as a Civil War prison camp, and it later became a lunatic asylum for women, a tuberculosis sanatorium, and a boys' reformatory. It continues to be used as a potter's field, where destitute and unidentified bodies are buried in mass graves.

[8] European style, also known as continental style, involves the positioning of silverware while dining. In this style, diners place the inverted fork in their left hand and the knife in their right. After cutting meat, diners place the bite-sized piece directly into their mouth with their left hand. If the food is soft, such as potatoes or rice, then the right hand guides the knife blade to place the food on the back side of the fork, with the tines pointing down.

[9] The quiver was a leather sheath that held arrows, and was usually hung from the side of a Lakota's torso by a strap, similar to a purse. The quiver was typically made of durable deerskin or buffalo hide to resist arrow piercing because the arrows were placed tip side down. For easy access, most quivers were open at

the top. The speed and accuracy of the Lakota archer determined his success as a hunter and warrior. Proficient warriors could shoot one arrow every three or four seconds, at a range of six hundred feet. Quivers were often decorated with beadwork or paint. They were also adorned with fringe or feathers. The quiver straps were decorated with quillwork, which was a process in which the Lakota softened and dyed porcupine quills and then weaved them onto leather items.

[10] Lakota infrastructure separated tribal members by age. A Lakota's childhood development determined their role as adults. Wisdom, experience, and maturity were highly valued and elders were greatly respected.

[11] The Lakota did not hoard their food from other villagers. The hunter who killed the buffalo was entitled to choice pieces of meat, including the tongue and organs. The hide also remained with the hunter who killed the animal. The rest of the animal was used for the sustenance of the entire village, which was an effective charity to those who were young, old, and injured.

The method of food disbursement is an example of how the Lakota practiced communal living ideals. In contrast, the white men perceived themselves as more civilized and embraced private ownership to the opposite extreme. This social condition led to a completely different way of life as the white men worked to survive on the plains. Whereas the Lakota worked together and lived together, a system that rewarded each member of the tribe, the white settlers were incredibly isolated and relied on their own works for social significance and survival. American settlers were focused not only on surviving but on making more money, buying more land, building a better home, and becoming more powerful.

[12] Buffalo were very adapted to the harsh climate of the plains. They were hardier than the settlers' beef cattle. Buffalo tolerated the frigid cold with relative ease. During blizzards, buffalo turn toward the blowing wind to keep their lungs open for oxygen flow. To this day, beef cattle turn their heads away from the wind, which allows ice to build up in their noses. In extreme blizzards, this causes the suffocation of entire herds of cattle.

As late as the 1840s, over thirty million buffalo roamed the prairie, shaking the ground with their thundering hooves. The Lakota rode hardy ponies and lived in tipis, which allowed them to follow the natural movement of the buffalo. Lakota life and survival were intertwined with the vitality of the buffalo, which was their sacred animal. Standing at six feet tall at the shoulder, a two-thousand-pound buffalo sustained an entire family from late fall to early spring.

The buffalo meat, rich in protein, also sustained the plains inhabitants throughout the year. They dried it in the fall and ate it throughout the winter. They used the horns for soup ladles and tanned hides with mashed buffalo brains. The Indians stretched tendons for bowstrings and washed out the intestines to form pouches for water and other liquids. Boiled hoofs made a sticky glue, used to hold many things together. Sinew, a dried cord formed from the tendons, was used to sew clothes. Buffalo chips were diapers for their babies and a source of fuel for fires. Horns were transformed into headdresses. Skins were tanned and decorated for winter robes and tipi covers. The small pieces of leather were utilized in moccasins and bags. Buffalo rawhide was formed into saddles. Bone marrow was considered a diner's delicacy. Buffalo teeth were used on clothing and in jewelry as ornaments. Buffalo brains were mashed into hides as a conditioner. Finally, any leftovers went to their dogs and puppies, which the Lakota eventually ate, usually in a stew.

[13] A fully staffed company consisted of seventy men, usually with one captain, one first lieutenant, one second lieutenant, four sergeants, four corporals, two buglers, one blacksmith, and fifty or more privates.

The famous Seventh Cavalry typically had twelve companies of seventy men assigned to each at full strength. Approximately nine hundred men would have composed a complete Seventh Cavalry. The average company, however, only averaged forty to forty-five men.

General Custer assigned cavalry mounts to each company according to horse color. The E Company rode gray horses. The other companies rode bays, sorrels, and other colors.

[14] Doctor William Worrall Mayo was born in 1819. In 1859, he set up his first medical practice and was known as the "little doctor" because he was only 5'4" tall. His son, William James Mayo, was born in 1861. Doctor Mayo applied to be a Civil War surgeon, but he was rejected. In 1862, after thirty-eight Indians were executed for a fight near New Ulm, Minnesota, Doctor Mayo stole Stands on Cloud's corpse, dissected the remains, and displayed them in

Le Sueur, Minnesota. The family settled in Rochester, Minnesota, in 1863. William James and his brother Charles Horace followed in their father's footsteps by also becoming doctors. William James Mayo joined his father's medical practice in 1883, when a tornado caused great injuries throughout Rochester. Charles Horace Mayo joined his father and brother's practice in 1888. As their practice expanded, they added additional physicians and focused on a team approach to medical care, which was unique in those years. Eventually, the Mayo Clinic was created and is still well known today throughout the world as a premier medical treatment center.

[15] Steamboat steersmen needed confidence to avoid disaster along the river. The leadsmen dropped weights, which were attached to ropes, over the side of the steamboat. When the weights dragged on the bottom of the river, the amount of rope was measured for an accurate reading of river depth. Different terms were called out to the steersman to notify him of the depth of the river. A call of "Deep 4" meant four feet deep. A call of "Mark" was one fathom, which equaled six feet. A call of "Twain" was defined as two fathoms, and so a call of "Mark Twain" described two fathoms, or twelve feet.

[16] The term "squaw" is considered extremely derogatory and offensive to the Lakota. It was created by the white man in the 1600s to refer to any Indian woman or girl.

[17] At assembly, the men stood in formation in front of their barracks, and roll call was conducted. Stable call and water call were for the cavalrymen, who went to the stable to feed, water,

and groom their horses. Fatigue call was for soldiers assigned to a work party, which usually included the jobs of fort repair, construction, cleanup, snow shoveling, summer gardening, cutting firewood, hauling water from the river, cutting river ice blocks, and storing ice blocks in the winter. Surgeon call directed sick soldiers to report to the hospital dispensary for an examination. If they were deemed sick, they received "quinine and pills" and were given the day off. The midday meal was termed "dinner." Usually the largest meal of the day, dinner routinely consisted of corned beef, roast beef, or stew. Potatoes and vegetables were usually offered, and coffee was always available. The evening meal, called supper, was not usually as large as dinner, unless distinguished guests visited the fort. Sometimes supper consisted only of leftovers or fresh bread and coffee. As most of the men were illiterate, the fort offered school in the evening to help soldiers learn to read and write. Tattoo call was an announcement to the enlisted men that it was time to prepare for bed.

[18] Private wages were thirteen dollars a month. In contrast, Major wages were one hundred and fifty dollars a month.

[19] Laudanum was a highly addictive opiate narcotic, used in the late 1800s as a home remedy and as a prescription for the relief of various pains and diarrhea. Laudanum was inexpensive in comparison to a bottle of wine or gin because it was considered a medication and was not taxed. The drug was prevalent among all social classes. For example, Mary Todd Lincoln, the wife of President Abraham Lincoln, was addicted to laudanum.

[20] Interview with Sitting Bull, *New York Herald*, November 16, 1877.

[21] The Lakota strove for basic virtues of good character: Bravery and fortitude were qualities that both men and women focused on. In addition, men were encouraged to be generous and wise, while women strove to be trustworthy and bear children.

Courage. For most Lakota, this virtue was the easiest to attain, as one acknowledged having fear but then maintained control over it, mastering emotion for the sake of bravery. One needed to have courage in battles and in protecting family members. Children were taught to be brave from a very early age and were taught to face danger without running away. In warfare, counting coup was one of the bravest acts of all, because a warrior put his life on the line by reaching out and touching his enemy with his coup stick or hand. Counting coup was much braver than just shooting the enemy from a distance.

Fortitude. An important element in Lakota character, fortitude implied bravery in the midst of physical pain and the ability to restrain oneself in a stressful situation. The white man often misinterpreted fortitude as indifference. In personal relationships, the Lakota lacked outward emotion, which was an expression of self-control. When two Indian friends met after a long separation, they spoke few words in their greeting and clasped each other by only momentarily placing their hands over each other's shoulders. They did not look each other in the eyes because such an act was much too embarrassing even for close friends. When greeting each other, the Lakota displayed no outward excitement and certainly no giddiness, because such actions would show lack of fortitude. Lovers were never affectionate in public, and private affection was not bragged about.

The antithesis of fortitude was fear. Without fear, the Lakota survived as invincible for many generations, placing other tribes in subordination through intimidation and a sense of arrogance and omnipresence during battle.

Generosity. Generosity was expected because all resources were to be shared among the village. The expectation was for young hunters to provide food, shelter, and clothing to their entire village, in this way supporting elders, children, and the injured. The Lakota were honored if they did not accumulate property for their own disgraceful use. If one was blessed in property, it only remained a blessing if that person gave most of the items away. Horses and food were gifted to the less fortunate on a frequent basis. Custom dictated how the recipient would then give something in return, even if he or she could only afford a small token of their appreciation. To be considered "stingy" was a horrible insult to the Lakota. Though generosity was not technically a virtue for women, they still valued generosity and beaded beautiful items of clothing or moccasins for the elderly, orphans, and injured.

Wisdom. Wisdom from the elders, as they gave advice to their villages, was highly valued. Wisdom was not tied to education or intellectual superiority. Instead, wisdom was intertwined with the other values, including the concept of giving away material possessions. Wisdom fostered a deeper

363

understanding of and insight into the supernatural. Proper intervention in disputes between others, solid war and hunting party tactics, and providing inspiration to others were indicators of wise tribal members.

Disrespect, ignorance, stupidity, and dishonesty were the contrasting behaviors to wisdom. If a person tried to maintain healthy relationships, striving toward the supernatural and a strong connection to the universe, then that person was highly regarded. If a man helped others and his words came from God, then he received the rare title of "Wicasa."

Truthfulness. Truthfulness was important for both men and women, but was critical for the tight community of women. If a woman was untruthful, her words were forever disregarded. Unity was essential for the tribe's survival, and gossip was devastating to their cohesiveness. Lakota women were constantly in the presence of the other women and the children of the community, while the men were able to remove themselves for hunting and war. As a result, given their confined living conditions, women were more prone to gossip.

Childbearing (for women). A woman who had many children pleased Wakan Tanka. Embracing motherhood and rearing a respectable family were the ultimate achievement of Lakota women.

[22] The 1868 treaty was violated as white settlers and gold seekers flooded into the Black Hills; its legality seemed undermined by the chance for prosperity. Lakota runners were sent to all the tribes, to request an assembly at the Red Cloud Agency on

September 1, 1875. Red Cloud delegated Spotted Tail to visit the Black Hills and find out what the white man had discovered. The US government was confident that it could buy Black Hills mining rights and avoid violating the 1868 treaty. The United States held a conference to negotiate the sale of the Black Hills, but its leaders considered the Indians' demands extravagant. The conference ended on September 29, 1875.

As a result of the failed negotiations, all military restrictions on the gold rush were removed. The Lakota were on shaky ground, but they did not cower. They moved with the buffalo to Powder River. On December 6, 1875, the commissioner of Indian affairs instructed his agents to order Indians to return to their agencies before January 31, 1876, or else be regarded as hostile. Compliance was nearly impossible because the villages had taken shelter in the Black Hills. Severe winter conditions across the frozen prairie made this forced travel a death sentence due to the lack of adequate food and shelter. By March 1876, eleven thousand white men already lived in the town of Custer, in the southern Black Hills.

[23] Sitting Bull (Tatanka Yotanka) became iconic to the white man, and he represented a more complex personality than was typical for the Lakota. To his own people, Sitting Bull was well respected as a leader, strategist, philosopher, religious adviser, healer, and family man. He vowed to fight for his people's way of life and resisted the change forced upon his people by the United States and white settlement. He fought until he realized the hopelessness of the cause.

[24] Military time operates on a twenty-four-hour clock. The first twelve hours follow the traditional American twelve-hour clock. Then, from one o'clock in the afternoon to midnight, the hours continue on sequentially. For example, one o'clock in the afternoon is thirteen hundred hours (1300) in military time, and seven o'clock in the evening is nineteen hundred hours (1900). Military time eliminates the need for a.m., p.m., and the colon between hour and minutes.

[25] George Armstrong Custer had two personal horses, Victory (a sorrel with four white socks) and Dandy (a bay). Dandy was Custer's older mount, and they had been together since shortly after the Civil War, when he purchased Dandy from the United States during the Wichita Campaign in Kansas during the 1868–1869 winter. Custer chose Dandy because of his high spirit. Though the horse did not have perfect conformation, he was an incredibly loyal horse. He was never tethered at night, yet he always remained close to Custer's tent when traveling on campaigns. Dandy was hardy and survived frigid winters by digging through snow to reach grass and chewing the bark off of cottonwood trees. Dandy was aging by 1876, and Custer relied more and more on Victory as his more energetic battle horse.

[26] During the Civil War, the Volunteer Army was established to combat the Confederate Army. The United States needed high-ranking commissioned officers to lead the US Volunteer Army, and as a result, hundreds of men were promoted to high rank by brevet. ("Brevet" means a type of military commission that gives the person a higher rank without the corresponding pay.) In 1863, George Custer received the brevet rank of brigadier general.

Custer was nicknamed "boy general" because he was the youngest man in US history to wear stars on his shoulders. At the end of the Civil War, Custer was a major general of the US Volunteer Army. In peacetime, his rank dropped back to lieutenant colonel, as did the ranks of other men who received wartime brevet ranks. In 1866, Custer accepted an appointment as lieutenant colonel in the Seventh US Cavalry. In 1876, George Custer's official rank was lieutenant colonel, and he was officially addressed as Colonel Custer. However, the courtesy of the times was to address a man according to his highest rank achieved during his service in the Civil War, even though it was a brevet rank. With this in mind, out of pure respect, Custer was addressed as General Custer.

Similarly, Miles Keogh received a brevet rank of lieutenant colonel during the Civil War. Of Irish decent, Keogh was recruited to serve in the US Volunteer Army as a cavalry officer. He rose to the brevet rank of lieutenant colonel before dropping back to a captain after the Civil War. Out of respect, he was addressed as Colonel Keogh.

[27] The height of a horse is measured in "hands," each equaling four inches. A horse is measured from the ground to the top of his withers (shoulder). The number of whole hands is followed by a period, and then any remaining inches follow the period. For example, if a horse was five feet one inch high at the withers, he would be considered "15.1 hands."

[28] "The only good Indian is a dead Indian" was actually a modified quote of General Philip Sheridan. In January 1869,

Comanche chief Tosawi surrendered his tribe to General Sheridan. He said in broken English, "Tosawi good Indian." It is documented that General Sheridan actually replied, "The only good Indians I ever saw were dead."

[29] Medicine bags were filled with a variety of different herbs picked from the plains and the Black Hills. Some of the most used herbs were purple coneflower (to treat inflammation, snakebites, and colds), blue flag (to treat earaches), mint (to treat colic), horsemint (to treat abdominal pain), sweet cicely (to treat wounds), and wild licorice (to treat intestinal distress and toothaches).

[30] The post at Whetstone Indian Agency was officially used from 1870 to 1872. Located just east of the town of Bonesteel, this federal stockade consisted of two blockhouses on the Missouri River and was designed as a subpost to Fort Randall. The Whetstone Agency site was permanently covered by the Missouri River due to the construction of the Fort Randall Dam, which was built from 1946 to 1956, under the authorization of the Flood Control Act of 1944. Upriver from the dam, the natural riverbanks were overcome with backed-up water, which widened the river and covered the remains of the Whetstone Indian Agency.

[31] Spaniards introduced the horse to the Lakota in the middle of the eighteenth century. Historically monumental, the Lakota culture adapted quickly and prospered with the new resource. Horses nearly ensured successful buffalo hunts. They carried riders and supplies, which provided a quick means for attack and escape. As a result, the horse was greatly valued by the Lakota.

The role of Lakota men was even altered by the plains horses, because the Lakota no longer struggled to meet the food requirements of their people. Until the buffalo were decimated by the white man moving west, the Lakota were rarely hungry. Herds were plentiful, firearms were available, and horses were a valuable tool. With food needs covered, the Lakota became focused on war, and a result, became more aggressive.

[32] Devil's Tower, known as Mato Tipila in Lakota, is a monolith land feature that rises over twelve hundred feet above the prairie floor in northeast Wyoming. Many different legends relate to the mountain, possibly due to the unusual "claw mark" vertical indentations around the entire rock formation. The site is sacred to the Lakota and was the location for numerous sun dances.

[33] Miniconjou Chief Lone Horn was also known as One Horn. He was born in 1790 and signed the Treaty of Fort Laramie in 1868. It is believed that Chief Lone Horn's nephew was Crazy Horse. Lone Horn died of old age near Bear Butte in 1875, shortly before the Sioux Wars of 1876. In 1876, the Miniconjou split into two factions: Chief Lone Horn's son, Touch the Clouds, became the leader of his own tribe of Miniconjou; Chief Lone Horn's adopted son, Spotted Elk, became chief of the other faction, and he was killed at the Wounded Knee Massacre in 1890. Spotted Elk was also known as Big Foot.

[34] Counting coup was the foundation of Plains Indian warfare. The white man fought to kill, while the red man valued courage more than killing. As a result, an Indian warrior was not rewarded for killing unless he touched his enemy while the enemy was still

alive. The strike could be from his hand, lance, war club, bow, quirt, gun barrel, or coup stick. A coup stick was a piece of wood, usually decorated with duck feathers. The idea behind counting coup was to dash in and touch the enemy, an act that showed more courage than shooting the enemy with an arrow or a gun from a distance. French Canadian trappers named the custom "coup" because it means "blow" in French.

After a battle, Lakota warriors gathered and told their version of their role in the battle. Once details were agreed upon, the first warrior to count coup painted his face black with a mixture of buffalo blood and ash to represent victory. The warrior who counted second coup could unbraid his hair. If the enemy was killed after coup was counted on him, the warrior wore an eagle feather in his hair. If the enemy did not die but was subject to the coup, then the warrior wore his feather horizontally, with the same honor as if he had made the kill.

[35] The Vore Buffalo Jump is an archeological site located between Spearfish, South Dakota, and Sundance, Wyoming, just off Interstate 90. The site was discovered while constructing the interstate in the early 1970s. A forty-foot-deep sinkhole provided the perfect drop for the Lakota to stampede buffalo over the cliff and to their deaths. The preserved site is the final burial ground for the butchered remnants of up to twenty thousand buffalo. Vore Buffalo Jump is open to visitors during summer hours and continues to be excavated.

[36] To be invited into the Akicita, a young man needed to first prove himself by facing a battle in any capacity. He would have a

better chance of membership if he killed an enemy, came from a prominent family, or had a vision quest. If a man was unfaithful to his wife or committed murder, he lost membership in the Akicita society. Further, if a man had accumulated great wealth due to stinginess and unshared blessings, then he was eliminated from Akicita consideration. Once assigned to the group each spring by their individual tribe, the Akicita watched over the camp and preserved order. When the camp moved, the men policed the move in order to keep stress low and ethics high. They made sure buffalo hunt rules were adhered to. They punished civil wrongdoers but left punishment for criminal wrongdoing in the hands of the family of the guilty.

37 In the Lakota community, warfare was instilled in its members from a very early age. Children played war games and learned warfare strategy. The Lakota were permeated by a sense of superiority that reinforced their domination of the prairie. By the time a Lakota boy was twelve or thirteen years old, he may have participated in a war party as a water boy, while being carefully chaperoned by elderly members of the party. Nonetheless, just being present at a battle was considered an important step toward the progression of becoming a warrior.

38 Initial battlefield analysis estimated that up to two thousand tipis had been in the area. It has since been determined that on the night of June 25, 1876, the village moved adjacent to their previous camp. With this information, it is currently estimated that approximately one thousand tipis spotted the valley. With the typical seven or eight inhabitants in each tipi, the estimated

number of warriors at the camp is between fifteen hundred and two thousand warriors.

[39] The two options of Lakota braid styles identified whether the female had reached puberty or was still a child. Braids of young girls were weaved on each side of a center part. They were secured together with a pendant in the center of the girl's back. Once a girl reached puberty, the braids were also on each side of a center part, but they were worn loosely in the front.

[40] Courting was highly regulated by Lakota culture. It was socially inappropriate for males and females to pursue each other in private circumstances. Chance encounters during the day were overlooked, but the female's family watched closely to preserve her moral fortitude. If she had a brother, he was to protect her for the sake of the entire family.

When the female was ready to marry, an interested young man showed his interest by approaching her tipi in the evening darkness. If she came out, he opened his blanket to her, and they could talk under his blanket. This created a safe environment for the young woman because people were coming and going from the village. She had the control to either embrace the suitor or cut the visit short in hopes of moving on to another young man.

Since it was difficult to get to know a future spouse, other than from chance encounters during the day or courting beneath the blanket, both individuals received most of their information about the other person from other members of the tribe.

The blanket carried symbolism as the most decorated item in any young man's wardrobe. Blankets were painted and embroidered with porcupine quills. Young unmarried men often wore robes with quilling tribes across the bottom and four large medallions.

Lakota custom prohibited marrying within one's own band. As a result, many courtships took place at Greasy Grass in the summer and in winter encampments in the Black Hills. The young men regarded courtship as a challenge and did everything they could imagine to increase their odds of success. They wore their nicest clothing, groomed their hair, and plucked their beards in hopes of being more attractive.

[41] "Hau kola" (pronounced how kola) was a warm greeting, usually said by a male to a male friend. It literally means "Hello, male friend." Another more serious dimension of "kola" was a pact between two Lakota to be a team and inseparable friends for life. Everything became earned and shared together. "Han maske" (han mashke) means "Hello, female friend" and is spoken from female to a female friend. Traditional Lakota etiquette required a male to say hello to a female first, by saying, "Hau haNkasi" (ha[ng]kashi), and then she could respond by saying, "Han sicesi" (han sich'eshi).

[42] One week earlier, on June 17, 1876, some of the same warriors, including Crazy Horse, defeated General George Crook in the Battle of the Rosebud (Battle Where the Girl Saved Her Brother). Crook had twice the men of Custer's force, and fought against half of the warriors collected at Greasy Grass. Reports of General

Crook's casualty numbers were greatly varied, with approximately twenty deaths and thirty wounded. About the same number of warriors were lost, but the Lakota remained on the battlefield as General Crook retreated. Custer was not aware of Crook's battle as he entered his last day on earth. It is unclear whether the knowledge of the battle would have altered Custer's aggressive action on June 25.

On the morning of the Battle of the Little Bighorn, Custer's Indian scouts warned Custer about the size of the tribal gathering. They could tell from the trails left by arriving tribes that the future was grim if Custer did not wait for reinforcement. It is unclear why Custer continued to push on without waiting for additional troops. Some believe he was afraid the Indian conference would scatter, making a victory unlikely. Other historians give Custer the benefit of the doubt and note how he was working with limited information. While at Fort Lincoln, he may have relied on information that overstated how many peaceful warriors were staying on their respective reservations. If Custer did not know how many warriors were in the valley, or exactly where the village was located, it would be reasonable for him to split his troops and attack from numerous sides, to minimize the chance of escape.

Some historians believe Custer was pushing for a battle victory because his hopes were set on the presidency of the United States. It has been reported that Custer told his scouts, including Bloody Knife, that he would become the Great White Father in Washington if they won any battles during the campaign. Custer brought an Associated Press newspaper writer, Mark Kellogg, on

374

the campaign to expedite battlefront news back to white civilization. If he did desire the presidency, Custer may have felt pressure to rush into battle, in the hope that he could become a quick sensation in time for the Democratic convention beginning June 27, 1876.

[43] According to archeological evidence at the battlefield, about fifty percent of the warriors are thought to have carried forty-five different types of firearms, including muzzle loaders, cap and ball, and repeating rifles made by Winchester and Henry. The remaining warriors were armed with traditional bow and arrows, which proved quite effective since the natural trajectory of an arrow allowed it to arc into the enemy while the warrior remained behind cover.

[44] Good Bear was shot in both legs, and one was broken, with bones grinding against each other. He tried to crawl away from danger. One Bull looked back from his fleeing horse and saw the predicament. He returned to his friend and wrapped a rawhide thong around Good Bear's torso and dragged him out of the line of fire. Then One Bull pulled Good Bear onto his horse, and One Bull, on foot, led his horse into the village. Good Bear recovered from his injuries and later moved to Standing Rock.

[45] This was Reno's group of men, who believed George Custer would back them up with an attack from the opposite side of the village. Custer's help never materialized, which left Reno in a precarious situation, where he struggled to save his remaining men.

[46] This describes General Custer's push from the east toward the village. Some Lakota witnesses suggested that General Custer charged down the ravine, stopped in the center of the river, and was shot. They claimed that Custer's troops pulled him onto a horse and retreated back up the hillside. Other historians dispute the story and believe that George Custer and his men reached the river but backtracked up to a higher vantage point.

General Custer's final mount was a Kentucky Thoroughbred sorrel with four white socks. His name was Victory. "Vic" was favored by General Custer for his quick walk and maneuverability in battle. Like many of the cavalry horses, Victory was probably caught by native warriors. A few people reported that Victory was found dead, near Custer's remains, yet the accounts are disputed. Other reports claimed a warrior named Walks under the Ground acquired him.

[47] Crazy Horse was nearly six feet tall and lean. His light brown hair, light complexion, high nose, and narrow face were not typical features of the Lakota. He was a quiet man until he was in battle. Crazy Horse had the childhood nickname of Curly. He never wore a war bonnet, but only a single red-tailed hawk feather worn in his loose hair. In preparing for battle, he painted hailstones on his body, drew a lightning bolt across his face, and ate dried eagle heart and brain along with wild aster seeds. He passed a sacred stone over his horse's body, believing that this would make him and the horse invisible to their enemy. He was known by his people as a great warrior and leader in battle. The Oglala, Brulé (pronounced brew-lay), and Cheyenne were led by Crazy Horse.

48 Retaliation and defense were well-respected warfare motives. As a self-righteous sense of supremacy pervaded unorganized young warriors, conquest and possessions became a focus. They often planned their war parties in secret, since the elders were more inclined toward peace. Elders knew warfare was necessary to gain hunting grounds, but they did not approve of war for the purpose of plundering. As a result, the young warriors' war parties often snuck away from their villages in the middle of the night to eliminate conflict as they sought wealth and prestige.

49 There were numerous accounts of Tom Custer's Company C performing mass suicides when they realized the final moments were upon them.

50 Twenty-two soldiers volunteered to obtain water from the creek using kettles and canteens. They faced intense fire, and the sharpshooter assigned to cover the others was shot in the leg. Even though the sharpshooter's leg was amputated, all twenty-two men survived and received medals of honor for their courageous act, which hydrated many severely injured soldiers.

51 Scalping and mutilations have been a violent part of history for centuries. Historically, white European settlers carried out much of the scalping that occurred in America, as they received bounties for the scalps. For example, in 1723, the state of Massachusetts paid one hundred pounds of sterling silver for each male Indian scalp and forty pounds for the scalp of an Indian woman or child. The Civil War Confederate soldier Bloody Bill Anderson was known for scalping Union soldiers, and he decorated his saddles with the "trophies."

The Lakota had a tradition during and after battles. When a loved one was killed, the family expressed grief through the mutilation of their enemy. At the Battle of the Little Bighorn, most soldiers were mutilated. Reno's men were more mutilated than Custer's men, perhaps because they fell closer to the village and young boys shot arrows into their corpses. Hands and feet were cut off with hatchets and sheaths, mostly by passionately distraught women who wept at the loss of their related warriors.

Worth pondering is the fact that in previous Indian War battles, horrendous mutilations were performed by US troops on Indian men, women, and children. For example, white soldiers cut the genitals from the Cheyenne women at the Sand Creek Massacre in 1864. Newspapers and public opinion quickly labeled Indians as "savages" for scalping and mutilating their enemy, yet US soldiers were behaving in the same manner but were not assigned the same label. It can be argued that the white man's mutilations were even more barbaric since no cultural significance was tied to the white soldiers' behavior.

To the Lakota, mutilations were not an act of cruelty but an act of expression for the warriors, an act that fueled their aggressive behavior and ultimately made them better warriors. The Lakota did not scalp merely to retaliate or to display the trophy. The Lakota believed that human hair held a spiritual essence. From the Lakota perspective, taking the scalp of an enemy meant the enemy lost all control over his life, because his living spirit or "soul" lived within the scalp.

52 Great speculation will always remain on whether either Tom Custer or George Custer fathered Monahsetah's son, Yellow Bird. While at West Point, George Custer was treated for a sexually transmitted disease, and he was possibly unable to bear children. Nonetheless, George Custer was clearly enamored with the Cheyenne woman, as he described Monahsetah as "an exceedingly comely squaw, possessing a bright, cheery face, a countenance beaming with intelligence, and a disposition more inclined to be merry than one usually finds among the Indians. She was probably rather under than over twenty years of age. Added to bright, laughing eyes, a set of pearly teeth, and a rich complexion, her well-shaped head was crowned with a luxuriant growth of the most beautiful silken tresses, rivalling in color the blackness of the raven and extending, when allowed to fall loosely over her shoulders, to below her waist." (Custer, *My Life on the Plains* [Lincoln: University of Nebraska Press, 1952], 415).

If George Custer was sterile, then Tom Custer may have been the father of Yellow Bird. Tom Custer was never married, but he fathered a child in Ohio prior to the 1876 campaign.

Monahsetah was pregnant when she was seized by the Seventh Cavalry, and she gave birth approximately two months later. In the following year, she gave birth to Yellow Bird.

53 In 1876, the value of gold was approximately twenty-two dollars per troy ounce. Approximately fourteen troy ounces equaled a pound. If Sara had sixty pounds of gold, it was worth approximately eighteen thousand dollars in 1876. In 2015,

adjusted for inflation, the amount would be worth approximately four hundred thousand dollars.

[54] Patron saint medals were frequently worn by the military. Some wore a particular medal because they were named after that saint. Others wore the medal with the feeling that it would give them added protection. Still others wore the medal as a devotion to their faith. In the Catholic faith, followers believe that saints intercede to God on their behalf.

In this story, Sergeant Zito wore a Saint Michael medal around his neck. Michael was considered a protector and leader of God's army against evil. He is an archangel in Judaism, Christianity, and Islam. In the Bible's book of Daniel, Michael is referred to as a great prince who protects the children of Israel. In the book of Revelation, Michael leads God's army and defeats Satan's forces.

[55] The injured horse was Comanche, Colonel Miles Keogh's horse. When the soldiers assessed the battle scene, they heard a faint whinny from a ravine and discovered Comanche. They gave him water and urged him to his feet. Comanche was shot and unable to walk. The soldiers tended to his wounds and transported him to the steamer *Far West*, which was waiting at the present location of Hardin, Montana. The steamboat pilot, Grant Marsh, transported the horse and wounded soldiers back to Fort Abraham Lincoln at a record-breaking pace. Comanche was nursed back to health, was never ridden again, and lived out his life in the Seventh Cavalry. For ceremonies, he wore a saddle with military boots turned backward in the stirrups and was draped in

black. Comanche died at Fort Riley, Kansas, in 1891. He was mounted and exhibited at the 1893 Columbian Exposition in Chicago. He is now exhibited in the Natural Science Building at the campus of the University of Kansas.

[56] On June 27, 1876, the Seventh Infantry and the Second Cavalry moved upstream along the Little Bighorn River and arrived in the valley below the battlefield, which was scattered with the corpses of General Custer, his men and horses, and bodies of warriors in funeral tipis.

GLOSSARY

Accentuate: to emphasize or single out as important.

Akicita (ah-kee-chee-tah): warrior, member of the village police.

Aloof: cool and distant. Conspicuously uninvolved, typically because of distaste.

Arbitrarily: based on a random choice or personal whim.

Arduous (AR-joo-us): difficult and tiring.

Arikara (uh-RIK-er-uh): a member of a group of Indians, of Pawnee origin, who inhabit the northern plains.

Aspire: have an ambitious plan or a lofty goal.

Barracks: soldier living quarters.

Bear Butte: a geological feature in western South Dakota, also known as Mato Paha.

Boisterous: full of rough and exuberant spirits.

Bowie knife: a fixed-blade fighting knife, popularized by Jim Bowie in the 1830s. These knives were highly prized and were traded among the Lakota.

Brevet: an unofficial, high-rank title bestowed during a time of war upon someone who did not receive corresponding pay of the higher rank. During peacetime, the brevet rank was removed and the prewar rank was reassumed.

Buffalo chips: buffalo dung, usually left in piles on the prairie.

Bustling: moving in an energetic manner; full of activity.

Camouflage: an outward appearance that hides the true nature of something; a disguise.

Campaign: a series of military actions to complete a goal.

Canteen: a metal container to hold liquids, similar to a water bottle.

Cavalry: soldiers who ride horses.

Civilian: someone not in the military.

Company or troop: a group of soldiers.

Condescendingly: showing superiority, snobbishly.

Coup: a sudden blow.

Coup de grace: a death blow to end the suffering of the severely wounded.

Covey: a group of grouse.

Curtly: concisely; abruptly.

Demure (di-MYUR): reserved, modest, quiet, and polite.

Desert/Desertion: the act of leaving duty without permission.

Despondent: having low spirits due to the loss of hope or courage.

Devil's Tower (Mato Tipila): a sacred Lakota site where sun dances were frequently performed. This unique geological feature is in northeast Wyoming.

Dilapidated: in a state of disrepair.

Disheveled: untidy.

Emanate: give out or emit.

Empathy: the ability to identify with another person's situation.

Enlist: to join the army voluntarily.

Enlisted man: a soldier in the army.

Enthusiastic: having or showing great excitement and interest.

Exude: display strongly and openly.

Farrier: one who shoes horses and trims their hooves.

Fatigue: work duty.

Faux pas: an embarrassing act in a social situation.

Flourish: grow vigorously.

Formidable: extremely impressive in strength or excellence.

Gangrene: the death and decomposition of specific bodily tissue, resulting from poor circulation or bacterial infection.

Garrison or post: another name for a fort.

Guardhouse: where guards work; a fort's jail.

Han maske (han mashke): "hello" spoken by a female to a female friend.

Han sic'esi (han sich'eshi): "hello" spoken by a female to a male.

Hau (ha): hello.

Hau kola (ha khola): "hello" spoken by a male to a male friend.

Hau haNkasi (ha[ng]kasha): "hello" spoken by a male to a female.

Hypocrisy: insincerity, by pretending to have beliefs that one doesn't really have.

Infantry: soldiers marching on foot.

Innate: inherent, intuitive, unlearned, natural.

Inspection: checking the status of soldiers by a list of protocol.

Interminable: endless.

Introspection: the contemplation of one's thoughts, desires, and conduct.

Irrelevant: not connected to something else, not important to a particular subject at hand.

Jaunty: having a cheerful, lively, and self-confident air.

Lambsquarters: a fast-growing, weedy annual plant that has a flavor similar to chard. It is nutritionally dense, with high levels of protein, vitamin A, and vitamin C.

Livery stable: a stable where horses were kept. Horse owners paid livery stable owners a daily, weekly, or monthly fee for their services.

Loquacious: full of excessive talk; wordy.

Magazine: place where ammunition is stored.

Maneuver: a military training exercise; a move requiring skill and care.

Maske: term used by a female to refer to a special woman friend.

Mato Paha: see Bear Butte.

Mato Tipila: see Devil's Tower.

Melancholy: a feeling of sadness.

Mess hall: place where soldiers ate.

Monahsetah: a woman's name, pronounced Moan-ah-see-tah.

Monstrosity: something deviating from the normal; something excessively bad or frightening in size, force, or complexity.

Nocturnal: active during the night.

Oblivious: not aware of, or not concerned about, what is happening.

Omakiya: "help me."

Ominous: threatening

Opaque: cloudy; blocked.

Ostentatious: designed to impress or attract notice.

Papapuze: Dried jerky meat.

Parfleche: an Indian bag, typically made of rawhide and decorated with beadwork, similar to a backpack.

Pervasive: prevalent, spreading broadly in an unwelcome manner.

Precarious: not securely held or in position; dangerously likely to fall or collapse.

Privy/Outhouse: toilet in a separate shed with a hole beneath the seat to collect waste.

Quandary: a state of uncertainty or perplexity that requires a choice between equally unfavorable options.

Quarters: assigned place to live.

Ration: certain amount of food given to each soldier.

Receding: pulling back or moving away.

Recruit: a new soldier.

Regiment: a large military unit made up of troops or companies of soldiers.

Relentlessly: harshly; unforgivingly; persistently.

Reminisced: looked back on.

Sagacious: showing keen mental discernment and good judgement; clever; intelligent; knowledgeable.

Scandalous: causing general public outrage by a perceived offense against morality or law; dishonorable.

Shenanigans: actions done with mischief; silly or high-spirited behavior; pranks.

Sentry: the soldier on guard duty.

Sign or signpost: a marker placed in a prominent position by a village whose members wanted someone to know which way they moved. Painted symbols identified the tribe and the message. Signposts were made of sticks or buffalo shoulder blades.

Suet (SOO-et): a hard white fat on the kidneys and loins of buffalo.

Sympathy: pity for someone's misfortune.

Takoan: a sinew running along a buffalo's backbone, from the shoulder to the base of the tail.

Tampco: deliciously tender meat along the takoan. It is referred to as "backstrap" in English and is cut into the most delicious and special steaks.

Taps: bugle call, sounded at night, ordering lights out. Taps is also performed at some military funerals.

Tatanka: buffalo

Tattoo: Bugle call to tell soldiers to go to their barracks and prepare for bed.

Tenacious (tuh-NAY-shuhs): persistent; determined; untiring; insistent.

Tersely: sharply.

Timpsila: prairie turnips.

Tranquility: an untroubled state, free from disturbances.

Tremolo: a high falsetto yell that was used in Indian culture. The women's tremolo was simply a high-pitch sound made by the tongue rolling against the roof of the mouths. The men used a different whooping technique: bouncing their fingers over their mouths to make their scream tremor.

Tumultuous: showing a state of commotion, noise, and confusion.

Undermine: erode; wear away; damage or weaken.

Vindicate: clear of blame; prove to be right.

Voracious: showing a tendency to eat very large amounts of food; having a wolf-like appetite.

Wakan Tanka: the Great Spirit, the Great Mystery, the Creator, Woniya.

Wasicu (was-i-chu): non-Indian. Today, the word may carry a negative connotation, suggesting greed. When the word was originally used, its meaning was positive.

Winyan: Lakota woman.

Wopila (wu-pi-la): thanks. The term was used to give thanks for everything; it could be a broad statement of thanks within a community.

TIMELINE

Pre-1800: The Great Sioux Nation, consisting of Dakota, Nakota, and Lakota speakers, unified and called themselves Oceti Sakowin, meaning "Seven Council Fires." They numbered about seven thousand people. For many generations, natives fought amongst themselves for all things provided by the Great One. The Chippewa drove the Sioux from the northern lakes and forests, into the woods, and then down to the prairie. The Sioux Nation was vast, extending north from the Platte River. The western boundary was the Bighorn Mountains, and the eastern boundary was the Missouri River. There were seven Lakota-speaking tribes of the Teton Sioux Nation: the Miniconjou (Plant beside the Stream), Hunkpapa (End Village), Oglala (They Scatter Their Own), Sichangu (Brulé), Sihasapa (Black Foot), Itazipcho (San Arcs), and Oohenonpa (Two Kettles). Around 1750, horses were first obtained by the Oglala, and they would transform the daily routine of the Lakota. Approximately sixty million buffalo roamed the plains.

1804: The Lewis and Clark expedition met the Lakota.

1818: Smallpox outbreak within the Lakota.

1834: Bear Butte and Devil's Tower (Mato Tipila) represented the spiritual center for the Oglala Lakota. Trading posts were placed near the Laramie and North Platte Rivers. Beaver pelts were nearly gone, and buffalo hides were anticipated to be the next substantially demanded hide.

1838: Trail of Tears. Fifteen thousand members of the Cherokee nation were pressured to give up their land east of the Mississippi River. The military forced the Cherokee to march to present-day Oklahoma, and along the way they were subjected to hunger, disease, and exhaustion. Over four thousand died.

1845: Smallpox outbreak throughout the northern plains.

1849: The United States purchased Fort Laramie from the American Fur Company and assigned troops to the fort.

1849–1850: Outbreaks of white-man diseases such as smallpox, cholera, and measles hit the Indian tribes. Cholera was especially prolific. The Brulés and Oglalas fled north from the southern plains in an attempt to avoid the diseases. They went to a former campsite on the White River in Dakota Territory. Soon every villager was dead inside their tipis, which still stood in the wind. The cholera epidemic killed nearly half of the Cheyenne and was nearly as destructive to the Lakota. In 1850, the smallpox epidemic killed hundreds of additional plains Indians. The Indians believed the white-man diseases were a wicked spell placed upon their people, and they wanted revenge.

1851: Fort Laramie Treaty of 1851. The white man invited all tribes of the western plains to meet with the purpose of agreeing on a plan that would allow them to live in harmony. Between eight thousand and thirteen thousand natives attended the Fort Laramie Council. The eighteen-day council resulted in the first Fort Laramie treaty, which was signed by some tribes. The treaty identified the territory reserved for the tribes and also allowed the safe passage of whites through the territory on the Oregon Trail in exchange for payments to the tribes. The tribes who signed the treaty remained good on their word for three years and did not battle the thousands of settlers who flowed through their land. They also did not fight amongst themselves. However, the United States broke the treaty when it did not make the promised payments of "$50,000 a year for ten years, or maybe five more, not for more than fifty years."

1851: Whites settled in the area now known as Minnesota. Two treaties were negotiated, Traverse des Sioux Treaty and Mendota Treaty. The white leaders purchased the woods and prairie from the Lakota. They gave the Lakota three million dollars over fifty years and told the Lakota they would give them land on agencies. Some of the agency land was fertile, but some was very poor. Many of the Lakota did not know the poor quality of the land before they signed the treaty. The Lakota claimed that they were cheated by the white man because they did not understand the words in the treaty. The payments were made, but much of the money went to traders and mixed bloods.

1854: Approximately four thousand Brulé and Oglala Lakota lived in villages near Fort Laramie, in accordance with the terms of the Treaty of 1851. A group of Mormons were traveling along the Oregon Trail, and one of their injured cows lagged behind the wagon train. A visiting Miniconjou followed the cow and killed it, bringing the meat home to the starving village. Conquering Bear, the chief of the Brulé camp, was concerned and rode to Fort Laramie, offering to pay ten dollars for the cow. The Mormon settler was also at the camp and demanded twenty-five dollars for the cow, which Conquering Bear did not pay. A small detachment of soldiers, led by the inexperienced and arrogant Lieutenant Grattan, went to the large encampment to arrest the warrior who had killed the Mormon settler's cow. Conquering Bear refused to deliver High Forehead to the fort, but he offered a horse to repay the party for the lost cow. As tensions rose, partly due to the drunk translator who insulted the Lakota, a soldier shot and killed Conquering Bear as Grattan turned to walk away from the group. The Brulé Lakota returned fire and killed the thirty-one-man party. This "Grattan Massacre"—as the press called it—is considered the first battle of the Great Sioux War.

1855: Colonel William Harney and 1,310 soldiers were sent from Fort Leavenworth to retaliate against those who killed Grattan and his men. He surrounded the camp of Little Thunder, who claimed no responsibility for the Grattan incident. Colonel Harney and his men massacred the entire Brulé village before even one warrior was able to defend himself. One hundred thirty six Indians were killed, and the soldiers mutilated the bodies of the women and children. Colonel Harney was nicknamed "Squaw Killer Harney" by red and white alike. Spotted Tail was injured in this fight. Colonel Harney told the village that Spotted Tail and two other warriors were to surrender or he would come back in six months. Spotted Tail reported to Harney within a few weeks. The Brulé were willing to give up their freedom, and possibly their lives, to protect their people from another attack. The Indian men were dressed in war clothes and sang death songs as they approached the soldiers. The soldiers did not kill the warriors, but took them to Fort Leavenworth and eventually released them.

1857: The Lakota held a council and agreed that if the white man attacked again, then the Lakota would fight.

Spring 1858: Indian representatives traveled to the US capital because traders were not giving out the promised annuity payments. The desperate Sioux signed two more treaties to sell more land. In the end, the United States paid nearly nothing, and the Sioux Nation lost one million acres. The US leaders created policies that instructed the Lakota to farm, which was nearly impossible since the soil was poor and the Lakota no longer had enough land to feed their people in their traditional ways of hunting and fishing.

March 1861: Dakota Territory was established. To the white man, this annulled the 1851 Fort Laramie Treaty.

April 1861: The American Civil War began.

1862: The Homestead Act allowed the white man to flood in from the east.

1862: Santee survivors were driven west, starting the Sioux Uprising.

December 26, 1862: Thirty-eight Indians were executed in Mankato, Minnesota, for supposed crimes during the Sioux Uprising.

1862–1863: The Great Winter of 1862–1863 was one of starvation for the Indians. They tried to farm, as they had promised, yet the crop failed and left them hungry. The natives were promised annuities and goods in June 1863, but the white man lied again.

The natives felt the white man was trying to starve the natives because the food was locked up in white-man buildings. The prairie braves could not watch their children cry for food any longer. They stormed the buildings and took the food by force. More food was promised by the white man. It never came. Hunger demoralized the Indians, and when the white man brought devil water (that is, alcohol), their thinking was clouded. A few braves killed the first settlers and started the war.

1863: President Abraham Lincoln delivered the Emancipation Proclamation.

1864: The Bozeman Trail, which accommodated gold seekers, was opened into Montana. The Indians called it the "Road of Thieves" because it cut straight through Indian buffalo hunting grounds and broke the Fort Laramie Treaty promises. The Oglala, Brulé, Cheyenne, and Arapaho had been pushed too far and declared war along the South Platte River. They attacked and plundered white settlers, burning ranches and stage stations. They attacked wagon trains, burned railroad stations, destroyed telegraph poles, and stole cattle and horses. The Hunkpapa, led by Sitting Bull, raided the whites from the Powder River to the Missouri.

November 29, 1864: Massacre at Sand Creek. Colonel Chivington led a troop of soldiers and volunteers to a peaceful Indian camp in Colorado whose chief was Black Kettle. The military told the Indians in the camp that they would be safe if they camped there. Black Kettle flew the American flag and a white flag. The troops massacred between one hundred fifty-two and two hundred Indian women and children, in addition to twenty-eight men.

They scalped and mutilated the Indian bodies, wearing chopped-off body parts as ornaments on their hats and saddles. The massacre led to more talk of revenge and less talk of peace.

April 9, 1865: The Civil War ended when Lee surrendered to Grant at Appomattox.

April 14, 1865: President Lincoln was assassinated. Andrew Jackson became president.

July 1865: Powder River Campaign. Brigadier General Patrick Conner invaded the Powder River Basin with three columns of troops, totaling one thousand troopers and two hundred fifty Pawnee scouts. They had one order from General Conner, to "attack and kill every male Indian over twelve years of age." He built a fort on the Powder River to protect wagon trains on their way to the Montana gold rush. Nelson Cole, with an additional fourteen hundred troopers, was to meet Conner as he moved north.

July 24–26, 1865: Battle of Platte Bridge. The Lakota and Cheyenne attacked the post and killed all members of a platoon that had been sent out to protect a wagon train. They also killed the wagon train drivers and escorts.

August 1865: Battle of Tongue River. General Conner's column killed over fifty Arapahoe villagers and destroyed their winter food supply, tents, and clothing.

September 1865: One of the plains greatest warriors, a Cheyenne named Woqini (Roman Nose), led hundreds of Cheyenne warriors into a fight against worn-out and starving army mounts.

They continued to harass the starving soldiers who were trying to return to Fort Laramie. The Cheyenne attacked in revenge for the Sand Creek Massacre but did not overtake the soldiers because they had limited weapons.

October 1865: The Southern Cheyenne signed a treaty giving their land to the United States.

October 1865: General Connor returned to Fort Laramie and left troops at a fort at Crazy Woman Creek and Powder River. Red Cloud isolated the fort, and the soldiers were forced to survive all winter without supplies. Many died of malnutrition, scurvy, and pneumonia. Colonel Carrington's company finally rescued them on June 28, 1866.

Late fall 1865: Nine treaties were signed with the Indians. None of the chiefs signed the treaties.

April 1866: Congress overrode President Johnson's veto of the Civil Rights Bill, which gave equal rights to all US-born citizens excluding Indians.

Late spring 1866. The Red Cloud War. Chief Red Cloud, Spotted Tail, Standing Elk, and Dull Knife came to Fort Laramie, intending to negotiate a Powder River Basin treaty. Meanwhile, Colonel Carrington marched with hundreds of infantry up the Bozeman trail to establish forts. This began the Red Cloud War, which gave Crazy Horse great battle skills. In a council meeting just before the war, Chief Little Crow told the braves that they were little children drinking white-man devil water. He told them they were little herds of buffalo where great herds once stood. He warned them that the white men were locusts of the prairie and were as thick in the sky as a snowstorm. He foresaw that if they killed one or two or ten white men, then ten times the number of white men would come kill them. The younger braves convinced Chief Little Crow to lead their fight anyway. His pride was great, and he did not want to appear timid like the other elders who were against an uprising. As a result, the uprising took place, without guilt, because the white leaders were starving the natives. The Indians killed hundreds of the white men, while only a few dozen brave warriors were lost. The white man lost the war and closed the Bozeman Trail in 1868.

June 13, 1866: The Fourteenth Amendment to the US Constitution gave blacks the right to citizenship.

July 13, 1866: Colonel Carrington began building Fort Kearney. The Cheyenne were angry because the land was in the middle of their prime hunting ground. However, the colonel's forces were strong. Strategically, the Cheyenne spent the summer harassing the troops while forming stronger alliances with other plains Indians.

November 1866: Colonel Carrington received reinforcement from Captain William J. Fetterman and his troopers.

Early December 1866: Crazy Horse and other Lakota warriors lured soldiers out of their fort, killing several officers and wounding others.

December 21, 1866: Fetterman Massacre/Battle of the Hundred Slain. Two thousand warriors, including Red Cloud and twenty-two-year-old Crazy Horse, waited while selected decoy warriors lured troops into their trap. Eighty-one soldiers were killed. Indian casualties were high because the military outgunned them with their new Springfield and Spencer repeating rifles. Fetterman claimed earlier that he could wipe out the entire Sioux Nation with one company of men. The bodies left at the Fetterman Massacre were mutilated in a similar fashion to those left at the Sand Creek Massacre.

Summer 1867: Crazy Horse, Sitting Bull, and Red Cloud attended the grand council of six thousand tribes at Bear Butte. They pledged to fight all encroachment by the whites.

1868: Sioux Treaty of 1868/Treaty of Fort Laramie (1868). A group of Lakota tribal leaders signed the Fort Laramie Treaty of 1868. The army agreed to close all forts along the Bozeman Trail. The treaty created the Great Sioux Reservation, although the Lakota did not give up their hunting grounds. The Lakota were also given the Black Hills. In exchange, the Indians agreed to "civilize themselves" and give up their nomadic lifestyle in exchange for government rations and a land of their own, which was a large portion of what is now western South Dakota. Other leaders refused to sign the treaty because they did not want to give up their nomadic lifestyle and freedom. Sitting Bull and Crazy Horse refused the proposed system and did not sign the treaty, so they were under no obligation to follow the treaty restrictions, which made them heroes among young warriors who were oppressed on the reservations.

1868: General George Custer gains the reputation as a successful Indian fighter by leading his troops at the Washita Massacre, where Black Kettle was killed. This was his first significant Indian War battle.

1870: The Massacre on the Marias. US soldiers massacred 173 Blackfeet men, women, and children on the Marias River in Montana as retribution for the actions of a small group of Blackfeet men who killed Malcolm Clarke and wounded his son.

1872: White men started trespassing into the Black Hills, in search of gold.

1873: Custer and the Seventh Cavalry move to the northern plains to protect surveyors for the Northern Pacific Railroad. Custer has a chance encounter with Crazy Horse, resulting in Custer's second and third battles, of four total, during the Indian Wars.

1873: A US financial panic turned into a depression that lasted until 1877. Grasshopper plagues swept the plains, where the grasshoppers piled two feet deep in places. A yellow fever epidemic also struck.

1874: General George Armstrong Custer led one thousand mounted soldiers on an expedition into the Black Hills, which was a direct violation of the Fort Laramie Treaty of 1868 because the land had been designated for the Lakota. General Alfred Terry drew up written orders for Custer to explore the Black Hills for natural resources and for a logical location for a fort. On the expedition, gold was indeed discovered by geologists in the party, and word spread quickly. Settlers rushed into the Black Hills, an act that was strictly forbidden by the Fort Laramie Treaty.

Winter 1874–1875: The winter was extremely cold on the plains, with heavy snow and temperatures reaching below negative forty-five degrees. Touch the Clouds moved to Red Cloud Agency and did not stay long because he found the life unfulfilling. He fled back to the Powder River area and rejoined Crazy Horse and the Indians hostile to the white man.

1875: The Lakota flowed into the agencies, and the number of hostiles had shrunk from ten thousand to three thousand.

Spring 1875: Hundreds of white prospectors were scattered throughout the Black Hills. A few miners were removed by the army, but when no legal action was taken, word circulated, and more prospectors flooded in, knowing there was no punishment for doing so. Red Cloud and Spotted Tail complained to Washington officials.

September 1875: The US government tried to purchase the Black Hills from the Lakota for five million dollars, but the amount was refused. The Treaty of 1868 stated that three-fourths of all Lakota men must sign any future agreements regarding the sale of land. White-man commissioners knew they would not gain enough signatures, and during the meeting on the prairie, the Indians rode in war paint and threatened the commissioners. Finally, the commission offered to pay the Indians four hundred thousand dollars a year for mining rights or six million dollars, in a lump sum, for the Black Hills. The twenty chiefs refused, and the meeting ended.

November 3, 1875: President Grant held a top cabinet meeting, whose members agreed that the "hostiles" should be forced onto reservations because the Black Hills needed to be developed. General Sheridan attended.

December 1875: John Q. Smith, the commissioner of Indian affairs, ordered all Sioux to report to their respective reservations by January 31, 1876. He labeled those who did not comply as "hostile." The demand was impractical even for peaceful Lakota because they took cover from harsh winters in protected areas of the Black Hills. To report to a reservation on a treeless prairie in the middle of winter would surely have caused their demise. Many villages did not learn of the ultimatum until after the deadline.

January 31, 1876: Most Lakota did not report to their agency, and the next day the secretary of the interior, Zachariah Chandler, handed the matter over to the War Department.

February 1876: The tide of compliant agency dwellers ceased, and the majority of Indians moved back to the hostile camp. By May 1876, the agencies lost had lost fifty percent of their population as the Indians returned to roaming as hostiles. While the government labeled them as noncompliant, they were not supplying food to the agencies, which caused the remaining agency dwellers to starve and to be desperate to leave the agencies for the possibility of hunting near the Yellowstone River.

1876: General John Gibbon and 450 men moved out of Fort Ellis, near what is now Bozeman, Montana.

February 1876: Sitting Bull organized the final gathering of Indians on the northern plains. He sent out runners to the agencies to spread the word of the grand Sun Dance, real buffalo hunts, and a community of union. Sitting Bull passed on the word of how they would make a good fight against the soldiers and many would count coup. He invited the Cheyenne to join in the festivities and fighting. The Indians knew of the threat and banded together for safety.

March 1876: General Philip Sheridan ordered four columns of several thousand troops, both cavalry and infantry, to seek out any hostile Lakota and force them back to the Great Sioux Reservation.

March 1876: Fifteen thousand whites lived in the Black Hills.

March 1876: Brigadier General George Crook, with Colonel Joseph Reynolds, attacked a Cheyenne village situated on the Powder River. He claimed the village was led by Crazy Horse and destroyed the entire village. Temperatures dipped to under twenty degrees below zero, and the survivors fled to the camp of Crazy Horse. Crazy Horse did not have enough supplies for the group, so he led them to Sitting Bull, who provided shelter.

May 1876: Brigadier General George Crook left with one thousand men from Fort Fetterman, located in central Wyoming.

May 17, 1876: Brigadier General Alfred H. Terry and General George Custer left with 879 men from Fort Abraham Lincoln near Bismarck, North Dakota. The lack of communication between the officers was a known weakness that limited coordinated attacks on villages. Further, the Lakota frequently moved, which complicated strategies for uniting forces.

June 1876: In early June, the united Indians moved their camp to the Little Bighorn Valley. When the grass became thin, they moved to the Rosebud Valley, where they held a Sun Dance, during which Sitting Bull had the vision of defeating the white men.

June 17, 1876: Battle of Rosebud. Crazy Horse and his warriors attacked General Crook. Twelve soldiers, and between twelve and twenty warriors, were killed. Crook retreated south, up the Tongue River, which prevented his positioning his troops to assist the armies of Crook, Terry, and Gibbon.

June 21, 1876: Terry held a council of war meeting with Gibbon and Custer on the steamboat *Far West,* located at the mouth of the Rosebud. Terry and Gibbon estimated that they would have to fight one thousand warriors, while Custer estimated fifteen hundred. The meeting focused on not letting the villagers scatter when the soldiers approached. Custer left with fourteen days of rations and orders to complete the campaign as he determined, under whatever unforeseen circumstances.

June 25, 1876: The Battle of the Little Bighorn. General George Armstrong Custer led 210 men into a battle where all under his command were killed. Reno's command lost 53 men, for a total of 263 army casualties. The Teton (Hunkpapa, Blackfoot, Oglala, Brulé, Two Kettle, Sans Arc, and Miniconjou) and the Northern Cheyenne were gathered when Custer and his men attacked. The Indians suffered about sixty warrior casualties, and about eight women and children were killed. Gibbon's column was half a day behind schedule.

June 26, 1876: The battle continued in the morning. The Indians broke camp and departed. They stopped that night for a few hours and did not set up lodges; they continued to travel upstream through the Little Bighorn Valley.

June 27, 1876: The Indians stopped traveling around 2 p.m. below the mouth of Lodge Grass Creek at the base of the Bighorn Mountains. Finally, they celebrated.

June 27, 1876: The Seventh US Infantry and Second Cavalry came upon the battlefield, only to find bodies rotting in the heat; maggots already feasted on the gaping wounds of swelling bodies. Blackened, scalped, and decapitated bodies were strung out in the field. Blowflies also rested and laid eggs on the openings of the bodies, whether from cut-off body parts or battle wounds made by gunshots, arrows, or blunt trauma. Gibbon rescued Reno, Benteen, and the Seventh Cavalry survivors.

June 28, 1876: With only two shovels available, the bodies were placed in shallow graves, or covered with dirt or branches. General George Custer was said to have been buried the deepest, at only twelve inches. The soldiers found gravely wounded cavalry horses; Comanche became the only survivor.

Two skin funeral lodges held dead warriors and chiefs. The military men stole the dead warriors' and chiefs' robes, clothing, war bonnets, beaded shirts, moccasins, saddles, and Indian artifacts.

Made in the USA
San Bernardino, CA
24 June 2016